D1017131

FIRE AND ICE

Also by Dana Stabenow

The Kate Shugak Series

A Cold Day for Murder
A Fatal Thaw
Dead in the Water
A Cold-Blooded Business
Play with Fire
Blood Will Tell
Killing Grounds

The Star Svensdotter Series

Second Star
A Handful of Stars
Red Planet Run

DANA STABENOW

◆ ◆ ◆ ◆ ◆ ◆ ◆ ◆ ◆ ◆ ◆

FIRE AND ICE

◆ ◆ ◆ ◆ ◆ ◆ ◆ ◆ ◆ ◆ ◆

A LIAM CAMPBELL MYSTERY

A DUTTON BOOK

DUTTON
Published by the Penguin Group
Penguin Putnam Inc., 375 Hudson Street, New York, New York 10014, U.S.A.
Penguin Books Ltd, 27 Wrights Lane, London W8 5TZ, England
Penguin Books Australia Ltd, Ringwood, Victoria, Australia
Penguin Books Canada Ltd, 10 Alcorn Avenue, Toronto, Ontario, Canada M4V 3B2
Penguin Books (N.Z.) Ltd, 182–190 Wairau Road, Auckland 10, New Zealand

Penguin Books Ltd, Registered Offices:
Harmondsworth, Middlesex, England

First published by Dutton, an imprint of Dutton NAL, a member of Penguin Putnam Inc.

First Printing, October, 1998
10 9 8 7 6 5 4 3 2 1

Copyright © Dana Stabenow, 1998
All rights reserved

 REGISTERED TRADEMARK — MARCA REGISTRADA

LIBRARY OF CONGRESS CATALOGING-IN-PUBLICATION DATA:

Stabenow, Dana.
    Fire and ice : a Liam Campbell mystery / Dana Stabenow.
        p.   cm.
    ISBN 0-525-94438-9 (alk. paper)
    I. Title.
    PS3569.T1249F57   1998
813'.54—dc21   98-14581
                                                                                          CIP

Printed in the United States of America
Set in Cochin
Designed by Leonard Telesca

PUBLISHER'S NOTE
This is a work of fiction. Names, characters, places, and incidents either are the products of the author's imagination or are used fictitiously, and any resemblance to actual persons, living or dead, events, or locales is entirely coincidental.

Without limiting the rights under copyright reserved above, no part of this publication may be reproduced, stored in or introduced into a retrieval system, or transmitted, in any form, or by any means (electronic, mechanical, photocopying, recording, or otherwise), without the prior written permission of both the copyright owner and the above publisher of this book.

This book is printed on acid-free paper.

for my aunt
Patricia Perry Carlson
Liam looks a little like Mel Gibson
just for her

My thanks again to my father, Don Stabenow,
always my first and most important resource,
and who has certainly never ever been quoted verbatim
in any of my books, goodness me, no,

and to Pati, for the drunk shaman,

and to Sifu Marshall V. Clymer,
for his years of skill and kindness,

and to John Evans of the Dillingham Police Department
and Dyanne Inglima Brown of the Alaska State Troopers.
They can be the cops on my beat any day.

ONE

Liam boarded first and watched the rest of the passengers troop down the aisle. It was a full load, a disparate group that he had already typed and cross-matched with their potential for future crime.

There was the Alaskan Old Fart, short, dark, a grin one part mean to two parts pure evil, who had poacher written all over him. There was the tall man with a shock of white hair and his green-eyed daughter, who would both of them have helped the Old Fart skin out whatever he took whenever he took it, but only so much as they could use in a winter. There was the Moccasin Man, tall, loping, clad in fatigues and beaded buckskin moccasins with matching belt pouch that Liam instantly pegged for growing wholesale quantities of marijuana in his back bedroom, and the Hell's Angel, Moccasin Man's sidekick, barrel-shaped beer belly, black leather boots with a shine on them to match the one reflected by his shaved, bullet-shaped scalp with a meth lab in his spare room. The Flirt, on the other hand, should have been arrested for incitement to riot the second after she'd stepped out in public that morning: she wore a red silk shirt with no bra beneath it and a long skirt that accentuated the deliberate sway of her very nice ass. Moccasin Man had demonstrated an immediate and obvious admiration for that sway, and had been granted the privilege of escorting the Flirt to her seat.

The rest of the manifest wasn't as interesting. There was the Bush couple, a nondescript husband and wife who looked like card-carrying members of the proletariat who took their seats and melted into the bulkhead. They were followed by a family of five, white father, Yupik mother, and three small children, one still nursing, a tall, spare, grizzled man who had looked long and hard at Liam and who had almost spoken to him in the terminal but then appeared to think better of it, a plump woman who just missed being grandmotherly by two streaks of ice blue eye shadow and a slash of maroon lipstick, and the airline's station manager for King Salmon, who curled up in the front-right-hand seat and promptly went to sleep, snoring loudly enough to be heard over the engines.

Liam envied him deeply. He himself was occupied with holding the fourteen-seat Fairchild Metroliner up in the air by the edge of his seat as they rose smoothly over Knik Arm and banked south down Cook Inlet. It was half past three o'clock on the afternoon of May 1. Breakup was late, temperatures still dropping to or below freezing at nights, stubborn ice ruts refusing to melt from the roads, snow clinging obstinately to the Chugach Mountains. It wasn't the only reason Liam was glad to be leaving Anchorage behind, but it would do, and it was almost enough for him to forget that he was ten thousand feet up in the air.

Almost.

Within minutes they were out of the low-lying clouds clustered over the Anchorage bowl, and mountains Denali and Foraker loomed up on the right. Foraker looked like a square, stolid Norman keep, and Denali like a home for gods. Susitna and Spurr were beneath them, the Sleeping Lady undisturbed beneath her lingering white winter blanket, Spurr worn down to three or four lesser peaks by an average of one eruption per decade. Redoubt, a once perfect cone blown to a shark's tooth, barely registered through the window before the plane banked right and southwest. Liam swallowed hard.

Now it was the Alaska Range, an entire horizon filled with sharp, unfriendly peaks, and no place that he could see to land safely. But there was for a miracle little turbulence, and the smooth ride and the drone of the engines eventually dulled him into an unexpected, uneasy doze, where his subconscious, that sly, slick bastard, was lurking, loitering with intent, just waiting to raise his viperous head and hiss a reminder that Liam had yet to call his soul his own. A jumbled mass of images fast-forwarded in front of him: laughing, loving Jenny with the light brown hair, his father's implacable eyes, Charlie's gap-toothed grin. Alfred and Rose, faces dull with grief and despair. That old black Ford sedan stuck on the Denali Highway, the bodies huddled together in the backseat for a warmth that failed them in the end. The disappointment and determination on John Barton's face. Dyson groveling on his knees, begging for his life.

She was there, too, of course, the brown-eyed, blond-haired witch. Once again she turned and walked away, down the street, around a corner, and out of his life, and once again the grief of parting jerked him up in his seat with a jolt, heart pounding, palms sweaty, the loss as sharply felt as if he had suffered it yesterday. They were descending, and the clouds had closed back in and brought turbulence with them. Liam looked out the window, where a thin line of frost was forming on the leading edge of the wing, and he welcomed the distraction the terror of the sight brought him.

He watched the line of frost attentively, until they came out of the clouds at seven thousand feet and it vanished and the Nushagak River and Bristol Bay came into view. To Liam it looked like the approach to heaven, an image enhanced by the golden rim of sunshine shining through the gap between the clouds and the vast expanse of gray water that took up the whole southern horizon.

Ten minutes later they were on the ground, at the end of a paved runway six thousand feet in length; plenty long enough for 737s loaded with herring roe and salmon, the reason for the city of Newenham's existence, the raison d'être of Bristol Bay, and, at least indirectly, the cause of Liam's new posting.

Congratulations, he thought. You're a trooper. Again. He'd removed his sergeant's insignia from his uniform before he'd left Glenallen, and had it cleaned twice to fade the marks where it had been. With luck, no one would know. His uniform was packed in a bag stored in the hold. All the pictures on the news had been of him in his uniform; he wanted to avoid recognition for as long as possible.

The Metroliner turned off onto the taxiway. In a voice that carried to the back of the cabin, the pilot said, "What the hell!" and they screeched to a halt, the engines roaring a protest. Everyone was thrown forward against their seat belts, and some who had unbuckled too soon found their faces right against the backs of the seats in front of them. By the time Liam got his heart restarted, the pilot had shut down both engines and the copilot had the door open and the steps let down. Liam unbuckled his belt with shaky hands and was on the ground right behind him.

The Newenham airport was ten miles south of Newenham proper, forty miles short of Chinook Air Force Base. It was of recent construction, not five years old, and replaced the previous airstrip, which, if it had held true to old-time Bush construction, would have run either parallel to or right down Main Street, where people could step out their front doors and onto a plane. Nowadays they built Bush airstrips ten to fifty miles away from the town, forcing everyone to buy cars to get back and forth.

A series of prefabricated corrugated steel buildings of various sizes marched unevenly down one side of the runway, opposite a wide gravel area dotted with tie-downs. A third of the tie-downs were occupied by small planes of every age and make, some big, some small, most with two wings and a propeller, some with four wings, some with two propellers, some with wings made of fabric stretched over aluminum tubing, some built of aluminum from the inside out. Most of them looked neat and ready to fly and some looked like they would drop right out of the sky, providing they got up into the air in the first place.

They all looked alike to Liam. They were planes. He didn't need to know any more, thank you.

The buildings consisted of a terminal and hangars, offices for air taxis and a Standard Oil office with a tank farm looming up in back of it, and a couple of aviation parts stores and a tiny little log house that would have looked like a cache without the stilts that bore a sign proclaiming it YE OLDE GIFTE SHOPPE.

Small planes buzzed overhead on takeoff and landing. There was another small plane pulled around in front of the Standard Oil pumps, a red one with a pair of wings that looked larger than its fuselage and white identification letters down the side ending in 78 ZULU. Liam's heart gave an involuntary thump, and then his eyes dropped to the ground in front of the aircraft.

"Oh my God!" the near-miss grandmother said from the top of the Metroliner's stairs.

A body lay on the ground, a bright red circle spreading rapidly from beneath its head, or where its head used to be. The propeller of the little plane was stained the same bright red.

TWO

For a moment, no one could move, except for the square-jawed young copilot as he heaved up his breakfast. The people on the ground, the people in the plane, the people staring in horrified fascination out of the terminal's windows all stood in frozen silence.

There was a woman kneeling in front of the body, her back to the runway. Dressed in worn jeans and denim jacket, the only clue to her femininity was the fat braid of golden brown hair that lay along her spine, strands escaping to curl madly all around her head. Liam found himself behind her without any conscious recollection of moving. It took him three tries to say anything, and when he could speak his voice seemed to come from very far away. " Wy." She refused to look around, but a visible shudder ran over her body, and he was close enough to see the sudden prickling of the skin on the back of her neck. Her head came up like a deer on the scent of danger. "Who is he?"

She didn't turn, but then she didn't have to. Wyanet Chouinard was a brown-eyed blonde, thirty-one years old, five feet five inches tall, with full breasts, a small waist, and lush, full hips that looked better in denim than any figure had a right to. Her voice came out low and husky, but that could have been stress and shock. From what was lying on the ground in front of her, or from what was looming up in back of her? Both, Liam hoped, with a sudden ferocity unknown to him until that moment. It surprised him, and with the surprise came a hot rush of sheer pleasure. He hoped he threatened her. He wanted to strangle her.

He pulled himself together. First, the job. "It's Liam, Wy."

"I know who it is," she said without moving.

"Who is he?" he repeated.

"Bob." A long, shuddering sigh. One hand reached out as if to touch the still shoulder closest to her, dropped. "Bob DeCreft."

The deceased was male, taller than average with well-defined shoulders and large, scarred hands. He'd dressed that morning in faded Levi's and a blue plaid Pendleton shirt with both elbows threadbare. He had a black leather knife sheath fastened to his belt, the flap still snapped, and Sorels, the ubiquitous Alaskan Bush boots, on his feet. The hard rubber heels were close to being worn flat. Liam forced himself to look, but it was impossible to see the dead man's features or the color of his hair. The plane's propeller had done a thorough job.

He looked up at it. Both blades stained dark red. A faint cry came from near the plane, and Liam turned his head to see the Flirt being enfolded in Moccasin Man's comforting and by now distinctly proprietary embrace. He looked back at the crowd, beginning to come to life, muttering and shifting. A breeze had come up off the river, and people were starting to get cold but didn't feel quite right about leaving. Either that, or were too curious to go. Liam understood both reasons.

He slipped easily into investigatory mode. "Did anyone see what happened?"

No one said anything. A few people looked at another man standing to one side, a thin man of medium height in his mid-thirties with dishwater blond hair and a pallid face. He was chewing something steadily, cheek muscles moving without pause, like a cow chewing a cud. "Who are you, sir?"

The man opened his mouth and almost spit out a large wad of pink gum. His face turned the same color. He sucked the gum back in and said, "Uh, Gary Gruber. I'm the manager."

"Of what?"

"Oh. Uh, of the airport?"

It didn't sound as if Gruber were all that certain just what he was managing, but then sudden, violent, proximate death had a way of casting everything in one's life into question. Liam waited with that outward attention and patience cultivated by an Alaska state trooper, at the same time completely and over-whelmingly conscious of the woman standing at his side.

After a moment Gruber, apprehensive and flustered, contin-ued. "I make sure the planes are parked in the right spaces, advise about the scheduling, watch for theft, sub for ATC and weather and the fueler when they go on break." His voice trailed off.

"Did you see the accident?"

Gruber shook his head violently, chewing hard at his gum, jaw moving like a piston. "No. No no no. I was in the terminal. I only came out when I heard people shouting. And then I saw —" His voice failed him again.

Liam raised his voice. "Did anyone else see what happened?"

No one had, or weren't saying if they had. "Does anyone know how it could have happened?"

Wy said, "He must have primed the prop by hand."

"What?" Liam still couldn't look at her directly. He looked at Gruber instead.

Gruber swallowed again, Adam's apple bobbing in the open throat of his shirt. "I guess she means Bob must have pulled the prop through by hand."

Liam looked again at the prop. At his height it was nearly eye-level. Despite the rays of the early evening sun peering through the break in the clouds, a light rain was falling. The blood on the tips was beginning to run, coalescing into fat red drops that fell with audible plops to the mangled flesh of the man beneath. "Huh?"

"You reach up, grab a blade, and rotate the prop a couple of times," Wy said.

"Oh, you mean like —"

Gruber choked on his wad of gum, and Wy said, "Don't do that!"

She grabbed his half-raised hand. Her touch seared right through the surface of his skin. She let go, a brief flush of color in her cheeks. "Sorry," she said gruffly. "I haven't checked her out since I got back and found Bob. Whatever was wrong with her still is."

"Oh." Liam, feeling suddenly warm, unzipped his jacket and turned his face up to catch a little of the cooling drizzle on his overheated skin. "Why would he do that? What did you call it, 'pull the prop through by hand'? I take it that isn't standard procedure." He looked at Gruber because he wasn't sure what his face would show if he looked at Wy.

"No." Gruber looked at the pilot standing silently next to the trooper. Liam waited. "He was an old-timer," she said finally.

"An old-timer? What's that got to do with anything?"

She looked up, and slowly Liam turned to meet her eyes, which were as bleak as her voice. "A lot of the old-time pilots are used to the old round engines, which had a habit of leaking oil into the cylinders. Pilots would pull their props through to make sure no leaky oil had caused a hydraulic lock. If they didn't pull it through, they could blow a jug."

"Blow a what?"

"A jug. A cylinder."

"Oh," he said.

She gave a faint shrug. "I pull the prop through in the wintertime myself, just to see if it's moving freely."

"It's never done this to you," Liam observed, and knew a momentary spear of terror. Goddamn flying anyway, it'd kill you in the air or on the ground, made no difference.

She shook her head. "I always check the magneto twice. Always. Sometimes three times." Her brow creased. "But so does Bob. I don't understand this."

"The magneto?"

"The switch connected to the p-lead. Controls power to the ignition."

Liam thought about it. "So if it's off, the prop shouldn't do this."

"No."

"Show me."

She hesitated. Her hand came out in a futile gesture.

"Don't," he said, understanding.

Her hand dropped, her shoulders slumping.

"Mr. Gruber?" Liam had to say the airport manager's name twice before the man could tear his eyes from the body. "Why don't you get a tarp or something to cover him up?"

Gruber shifted from one foot to the other. "Uh, listen, no offense, but who are you, anyway?"

Liam glanced down involuntarily at his clothes. He was dressed much as Wy was—jeans, sneakers, plaid flannel shirt beneath a windbreaker. "Sorry. I'm a state trooper, just transferred to the Newenham post. Liam Campbell. My uniform's packed." He hooked a thumb over his shoulder at the Fairchild Metroliner, one prop shut down now, the other still whirring. He fished out his badge.

Gruber's jaw hung open in mid-chew, the wad of gum gleaming pinkly between his teeth, pale eyes staring from the badge to Liam and back again.

"That tarp, Mr. Gruber?" Liam said.

Gruber flushed, nodded once, and went off, shifting the gum from one cheek to the other, the cheek muscles working like pistons again.

The two halves of the small red and white plane's left-side door were folded open, the top portion fastened to the wing with a quick-release latch, the bottom half left to hang. The cockpit of the plane was, to put it kindly, utilitarian. The seats were little more than plastic stretched over a metal frame, the interior was without the usual fabric covering, and the dash was held together in places with duct tape. She'd seen better days.

Wy saw his look. "She flies," she said.

Liam let that pass. "Where's the ignition?"

Liam had spent his life in a concentrated effort to learn as little about flying as he possibly could, which was a neat trick given his profession and where he practiced it. There were roads in Alaska: one between Homer and Anchorage, two between Anchorage and Fairbanks with a spur to Valdez, and one between Fairbanks and Outside. You needed to go somewhere there wasn't a road, you flew. Troopers needed to go everywhere, so troopers flew, some in their own planes, some that they contracted. Liam contracted.

Wy had been his pilot, and 78 Zulu had been her plane, back in the days when there was a lot less duct tape and a lot more spit and polish about her. It was because of 78 Zulu that Liam could recognize a Piper Super Cub when he saw one. It was the only plane he could recognize, outside of a 747, and that only because of the bump on its nose.

They stood shoulder to shoulder, staring at the inside of the little plane. He looked at Wy from the corner of his eye. To anyone else, to anyone who didn't know her as well as he did, as intimately as he had, she would have looked calm, controlled, perhaps a little pale, understandable in the circumstances. But he knew what to look for, always had, and he relished the pulse thudding rapidly at the base of her throat, at the way her gaze avoided his.

She pointed beneath a row of gauges that meant nothing to Liam, and he saw a knob with four settings: Right, Left, Both, Off. It was set at Off. He stared at it in puzzled silence for a moment. "Where's the On?"

"What?"

"If there's an Off, there ought to be an On."

Seemed simple enough to Liam, but Wy shook her head. "Magnetos are little generators, their own power source. There are two of them, and they're always on. This isn't really an on-off switch, like a"—she cast about for a comparison to something he might understand—"like a light switch. It's a kill switch. Either their power is available to the engine, one or the other or both of them, or it isn't."

"And according to this switch, power from this one wasn't when Mr. . . ."

"DeCreft."

"When Mr. DeCreft pulled the prop through."

"No. But it must have been, or—" She stopped, and added, almost against her will, "I don't get it."

"Get what?"

"This." She waved a hand, inclusive of the deceased, the Super Cub, the dash. "Bob was even more careful than I am. He never would have pulled the prop through with the mag on."

Liam regarded the knob in frowning silence. "How old was DeCreft?"

"Sixty-five."

"Sixty-five?" He raised an eyebrow and looked at her, something it was getting easier to do.

"Sixty-five going on thirty," she said. "He passed his flight physical every year, including this one."

Liam let that pass, too. The Cub contained two green headphones with voice-activated microphones attached, one hanging from a hook over each seat, and two expensive-looking handheld radios sitting on the backseat, as if carelessly tossed there on the way out of the plane. He looked back at the dash, stooping to examine the switch more closely. "Hey. What's this?"

"What?" She peered around him and reached between him and the doorjamb to slap his hand as it stretched toward the dash. "Don't touch anything."

Again his skin burned where it had grazed hers. Their bodies had been forced very close together in the open doorway of the little plane. He took a deep breath and said, pointing from a safe distance, "What's that wire?"

"What wire?"

"That wire coming from out of the bottom of the dash."

"What?" All self-consciousness gone, she elbowed him aside and bent down, breast against the forward seat, nose inches from the bottom of the dash. Her braid slid forward to fall between the seat and the right-side door, and he resisted an impulse to pull it back. "What the hell?" She reached out, and it was his turn to reach over her and slap her hand aside, leaning against her back as he did so. She jumped. So did he. His voice was gruff. "What is it? What's wrong?"

There was a brief silence, just long enough for him to imagine everything she wasn't saying. "The p-lead's off."

"The p-lead?" He wasn't thinking all that clearly, and it took him a moment to follow. "Oh, yeah. The wire connected to the ignition, I mean the mag switch." He did look at her then, eyes all cop. "You mean it's not connected to the switch?" he said sharply.

She nodded dumbly.

"So the switch was . . ."

"It was on," she said. She jerked her chin toward the front of the plane. "It was on when Bob thought it was off. When he pulled the prop through."

There was a stir in back of them, and a bluff voice calling out, "What the hell's going on here? Get the hell outta the way, Gruber, let me see." Heavy feet slapped to a halt against the pavement, followed by a long, drawn-out, "Jeeeesus H. Key-riiiiiist."

Liam turned. Gary Gruber had returned with a blue plastic tarp. He was holding up one end for the perusal of an Alaska state trooper in full-dress blue and gold glory, a square red face beneath the badge pinned to the center of the black fur cap, earflaps tied neatly together over the crown, bushy black eyebrows over deep-set dark eyes. He wore sergeant's stripes.

The new arrival took in the body, the silent crowd, Liam and the pilot standing next to the Cub. His eyes, their look of surprise fading into the professional assessment of the practicing policeman, narrowed on Liam's face. "Well, well, well. Liam Campbell, isn't it? Sergeant Liam Campbell?" he added, emphasizing the first word.

Face wiped clean of all expression, Liam replied in a neutral voice, "Trooper Campbell now, Sergeant. Roger Corcoran, isn't it?" He held a hand out. "I believe I'm relieving you."

"You're out of uniform, trooper," Corcoran said.

Wy looked from the trooper to Liam and back again, a frown puckering between her brows. Gary Gruber let the tarp fall and stepped out of range to join the crowd, which was following along with a curiosity they didn't bother to hide. Liam nodded at the Metroliner, still sitting where it had slid to a halt fifty feet away. "Just got in. Haven't had time to change." He kept his hand out.

Waiting just long enough for his hesitation to become obvious, Corcoran took Liam's hand in the briefest of grasps and immediately released it. "How's Glenallen these days? Arresting any drunk drivers up there lately?"

Next to him Liam heard Wy draw in a sharp breath. "Like always," he said, his voice steady.

There was a tiny pause. Then Corcoran, evidently abandoning the effort of trying to get a rise out of Liam, nodded at the body lying in front of the plane, the rain keeping the blood a rich and vivid red. "Walk into the prop?"

"Maybe. Maybe not."

Corcoran's brows rose. "Oh?"

Liam jerked his head, and Corcoran came over to stand next to them. Dropping his voice, Liam said, "The p-lead was disconnected."

"What the hell's a p-lead?" Corcoran was no pilot, either.

Liam let Wy explain.

The tufted brows disappeared into the fur edge of the hat. "Really. Excuse me." They stepped aside, and Corcoran bent over the seat to examine the dash, poking at the wire with one gloved finger.

They waited. The crowd shifted and muttered, and began to drift away. "Hold on a minute," Liam said, and began collecting names and phone numbers, although to a man and woman they protested they had seen, heard, and said no evil. Moccasin Man pulled up in a gunmetal gray Isuzu Rodeo with PITBUL on the license plate and a tiny Stars and Stripes flying from the antenna. Could have been worse, Liam thought, could have been the Stars and Bars. The Hell's Angel and the Flirt climbed in and the Rodeo pulled out with an ostentatious screech of rubber on pavement, just as Liam was approaching with pad and pencil. The airline crew began loading luggage into the Metroliner. A small plane took off down the strip, another taxied up to the fuel pumps. The pilot got out and stood for a moment, watching, before he fetched the hose and began fueling his plane. Business as usual.

Liam walked over to Wy. "What were you doing up?" She looked blank and he said impatiently, "What work? What job were you on? Who were you flying for?"

"Oh. Spotting. We'd been spotting." She looked up and caught his expression. "For herring. Bob was my observer."

Liam felt a chill run down his spine. Spotting—using a small plane to find schools for the fishing boats in the water below—was like playing Russian roulette, only with five bullets in the gun instead of one. Kind of like glacier flying in and out of

Denali, he thought, and she used to do that, too. "Still living dangerously, are you, Wy?" he said tightly, every muscle under control, every cell in his body humming with what might have been rage.

Wy didn't answer him. Corcoran looked around, one speculative eyebrow raised as he took in the strained expressions on both their faces. "You two know each other?"

Liam was silent. Wy took her cue from him.

"Well, well, well," Corcoran said, a sly smile spreading across his face. "I think I'm kind of sorry to be leaving after all. Things might finally be getting interesting in this shithole of a town."

"Sergeant?" The copilot tapped Corcoran on the shoulder. He was still pale and he kept his gaze rigidly averted from the body on the ground. "We're leaving."

"Okay. I'll be right there."

"What?" Liam said.

"Trooper, you relieve me," Corcoran said, giving his hat an unnecessary adjustment. "I'm outta here."

"Bullshit," Liam said, forgetting their comparative ranks. "We haven't had any kind of a handover, I don't know anything about this posting, who the local cops are . . . You haven't even shown me where the office is!"

"It's not that big a town, Campbell. You'll manage." Corcoran's grin was a taut stretch of skin, bare of humor or good feeling. "And if you don't, it's not my problem. My time is up, and I am history. Got me a posting to Eagle River, which is close enough to Anchorage to suit me just fine. Got me three girls lined up already, one in Wasilla, one in Spenard, and one in Girdwood, far enough apart not to find out about each other and close enough together for an easy commute between beds." Corcoran winked and touched his fingers to the brim of his hat. "So long, Ms. Chouinard. It's been real." He reached out and gave her a chuck under her chin before she could move out of the way. "Should have been nicer to me. I could have stuck around to help you out of this."

Liam gave Wy a sharp look, but her expression gave nothing away.

Corcoran turned and began walking toward the plane, and

Liam was abruptly recalled to his situation. "Wait a minute," he said, "wait just a goddamn minute! What about this mess?"

"Like I said," Corcoran called over his shoulder. "Your problem. Airport's outside the city limits, so this baby's all yours. Depends on whether the p-lead fell off on its own or got yanked off with intent. I'd look into that if I were you." He stooped to pick up his bags without missing a step and followed the copilot, pausing long enough at the top of the Metroliner's stairs to give a cheery wave. "Good luck, Campbell!" He added something else that might have been, "You're going to need it," but the wind had picked up by then and Liam couldn't be sure.

THREE

"Liam," Wy said in an urgent undertone.

He watched the Metroliner line up on final as if his life depended on its pilot's perfect takeoff. "What?"

"I have to fly. It's how I make my living. Herring seasons don't last that long. Fish and Game could announce an opener at any moment. I've got to get back in the air. Can I take my plane up?"

He was looking at the plane in question, the red and white paint job, the faded red fabric of the wings, the worn white call letters down the side. If he looked hard enough, he was sure he would find a scratch in the right-side door that he himself had put there while loading a cooler with Pete Petersham's severed head inside into the plane. Two years and a lifetime ago. Seven-eight Zulu. The lines of the little plane were almost as familiar to him as the laugh lines at the corners of its pilot's eyes. "No," he said. "You can't take her up. Not yet."

A variety of expressions crossed her face: anger, frustration . . . fear. Why fear? A cold knot grew at the pit of his stomach. "Wy, where were you when this happened?"

The anger was back with a vengeance, then. "Oh, so I sabotaged my own plane to kill a guy I'm not going to be able to spot without, just so I won't make my loan payment and my insurance payment and my tax payment, not to mention attorney fees for—" She bit the rest of her words off with an effort.

He waited patiently. Better than most, she knew the drill.

After a moment she said curtly, "I was getting us lunch at Bill's."

"Who's Bill?"

"Bill's Bar and Grill. It's a bar and a restaurant in town. There isn't one out here at the airport." She walked over to her truck and wrenched open the door, producing a grease-stained brown paper shopping bag. Making an elaborate show of it, she opened it and displayed the burgers and fries inside, both wrapped in foil and exuding a heavenly aroma.

Liam's stomach growled. Glancing at his watch, he saw that it was almost six o'clock. He'd had a McDonald's sausage biscuit for breakfast and an apple for lunch, but then he hadn't been hungry lately. He was now. He couldn't remember the last time he'd been so hungry. Yes he could—the last time he'd been really hungry he'd been sitting down to dinner across from the brown-eyed blonde glaring at him now.

Well. No point in letting the food go to waste, especially if it tasted anywhere near as good as it smelled. He reached for one of the burgers, unwrapped the foil, and bit in. It was lukewarm but juicy and had just the right ratio of onion to meat. The fries were good, too; real potatoes, heavy on the salt and greasier than the bilge of a boat.

Wy looked startled, and then, fleetingly, amused.

There were one or two exclamations of disapproval from the remainder of the crowd, as if there was something intrinsically profane in ingesting nourishment in the presence of the dead, but after some hesitation, a little muttering, and a few pointed glances at the mound beneath the blue tarp, they began to drift away, to their homes and kitchens. It was dinnertime, after all.

Liam took another bite of burger and motioned to Gary Gruber, still hovering indecisively around the periphery. Liam couldn't decide if Gruber had remained because the death had happened on his watch on property for which he was responsible, or out of a perverse fascination with the act itself. From his expression, half appalled, half inquisitive, it was probably a combination of both. "Have you called an ambulance?" A thought struck him and Liam swallowed a mouthful of burger. "Newenham does have an ambulance, don't they?"

Gruber nodded. "Yes. I called the dispatcher and she said she'd find him and send him on."

"Only one?"

Gruber nodded, watching with fascination as Liam munched steadily through burger and fries and washed everything down with the large Coke Wy produced from the truck's cab. It was a fountain Coke, and a good one. Liam was going to have to cultivate this Bill guy.

"Gary?" Wy said. "I need another spotter." None of them looked at what was left of her last one, which might not have been the best incentive for accepting her offer of employment. "Can you take a day? I pay the standard percentage."

"I told you, Wy," Liam said, "you can't take this plane up. Not right now. It may be a crime scene."

"I've got another plane," she informed him, and couldn't hide her pleasure at his surprise. "It's a 180, so it won't be as good for spotting as the Cub is, but it'll do." She saw his expression and said, urgency back, "I've got to get in the air, Liam. The whole fleet's out now, waiting on an announcement from Fish and Game to put their nets in the water. The herring season only lasts until they catch the quota, and I'm spotting for the high boat in the bay. And Cecil Wolfe didn't get to be high boat with his spotter on the ground," she added with feeling.

"No shit," Gruber said with equal feeling.

"All right," Liam said. "You can fly, but first let's take another look at that p-lead." He would have waited for the forensics team to show up and dust everything for prints, but since this wasn't *NYPD Blue* there would probably be an awfully long wait.

The two of them crowded into the open door of the Cub. "Can you unhook it or unscrew it or something?" Liam said.

"You aren't afraid I'm going to destroy evidence that might convict me of murder?" Wy said sarcastically.

Liam gave her a steady, unsmiling look. "All right," she muttered, and reached beneath the dash. A moment's fumbling, and two pieces of thin plastic-coated wire were resting in the palm of Liam's hand.

"It's been cut," Wy said, staring.

It was true. Normal wear and tear would not have produced the neatly severed ends of the little wire.

"Somebody must have reached up under the control panel and pulled down the lead and nipped it with a pair of wire cutters, and then shoved it back up again," Wy said. The tightness was back in her voice.

Liam allowed his free hand to give her shoulder a quick, reassuring squeeze. For a moment, for a brief, halcyon moment, he felt her relax into his touch. In the next second, she had tensed and pulled away.

He would have gone after her this time, even with Gruber watching, even if the crowd had still been there, even if somebody had been selling tickets, but a construction orange Chevy Suburban V-8 Turbo Diesel roared up to skid to a halt five feet from the Cub. The door opened and the grizzled old frowner from the Anchorage flight yelled, "You the new trooper?"

"Bad news travels fast," Wy muttered.

Liam shot her an unfriendly look and said to the man, "Yes, sir. What can I do for you?"

"Some drunk's shooting up Bill's," the man said. "Get in."

Liam, out of uniform and unarmed, said, "What about the local police?"

"We just lost two officers to the goddamned troopers," the man said, "two more went fishing, and we've got two left to do a six-man job. The one on duty right now is on the other side of town trying to keep Nick Pauk from killing Johnny Wassillie, and the wife of the other one flat won't wake him up from the first good sleep he's had in a week. You coming or not?"

Liam looked at Wy. He looked at the body lying on the ground in front of the Super Cub, which had no useful advice to offer. He looked at Gruber. "You stay here, watch the plane and the body, see that no one interferes with them. All right?"

Gruber, pausing in the act of jamming a fresh wad of bubble gum into his mouth, said blankly, "What?"

"Nobody touches that plane until I get back. When the ambulance shows up, tell the paramedic he can load the body but to wait here for me."

"What?"

"I'm deputizing you for the duration. Nobody else touches anything." Liam looked over at Wy. "Nobody. Got that?"

She looked up at that, and said with a trace of defiance, "I'll stay, too."

"I thought you had to get in the air."

"You just co-opted my spotter," she said, jerking her chin at Gruber. "And the Cub is my plane. I don't want anyone messing with her, either."

Good, Liam thought. Should the subject arise later, for whatever reason, Gruber could testify that Wy had gone nowhere near the Cub while Liam was gone.

"Goddammit, get the lead out!" the grizzled man said testily.

"One minute." Liam buttoned the severed p-lead into an inside pocket and went to the terminal to find his bag. Another police officer would have carried his weapon on board, but Liam was always afraid it might accidentally discharge in the cabin and blow up the plane. He located his bag—the rest of his stuff was being shipped—strapped on his regulation Smith & Wesson automatic, and went back outside to find that the old man had pulled up to the door. Liam climbed into the passenger seat and the old man slammed the Suburban into first and they pulled forward with a jerk. Liam slapped a hand on the dash to brace himself against the man's careless shifting, not improved by the many and deep potholes on the road between the airport and town. It was a jolting, bouncing ride. "They ever grade this road?" he said above the noise.

The man grunted. "Every week." He thrust out a ham-sized right hand. "Jim Earl. I'm the mayor of Newenham."

"Oh." Liam took Earl's hand. Hizzoner had a firm, callused grip. "Liam Campbell."

"I know. Thought that was you when I saw you in the Anchorage airport. We heard you were coming."

"Oh," Liam repeated, and wondered what else they had heard. A crater the size of Copernicus loomed up in front of them. Jim Earl drove right through it. When he came down off the ceiling Liam wedged himself into the corner as firmly as he could, one hand gripping the back of the seat and the other pressing against the glove compartment. "What's the situation with the local cop? Should we maybe detour over there first, see if he needs backup?"

"Shit no." Earl spit out the window, fortunately rolled down. In retaliation, a large blast of wet, cold air flooded the cab. "The way I hear it, Amy Pauk thought Nick was safe out fighting for his share of herring, so she invited Johnny Wassillie over for the morning. Johnny and Amy got this thing going," Earl added parenthetically. "They think nobody knows about it." He snorted again. It seemed to be his favorite expression. "Fine, fine, most of us could give a shit who's screwing who, and I'm all for a quiet life anyway. Only trouble is Nick's boat broke down and he had to limp back into the harbor early. Goes home to grab some grub, catches Nick and Amy in the sack, goes for his rifle, starts a little ventilating. Dumb bastard." The mayor shook his head. "It's too early in the day for that shit."

Liam checked his watch. It was just coming up on six-thirty. As casually as he could, he said, "So it's a hostage situation? Are there any children involved? What kind of gun does Pauk have? Did he shoot his wife? Did he shoot Mr., uh, Mr.—"

"Wassillie, Johnny Wassillie, and hell yes, he shot him. Only winged him, though." Jim Earl seemed regretful to report this. He tapped the scanner hanging beneath the dash. "On the way over to get you, I heard Roger Raymo report in to the dispatcher. That'd be our day shift officer, the one we got left," Earl added with some bitterness. "He said he'd managed to disarm Nick before he got around to shooting Amy." Earl grinned. "Scared her, though, I bet." He thought about it. "Maybe. Amy's pretty scary herself, when she's of a mind to it."

Liam's hand slid from the holster, and he let out a long, slow breath. "Okay," he said, he hoped mildly. He hadn't been on the ground for—he checked his watch—three hours, and already there had been two and possibly three attempts at murder.

Maybe four, once he got his hands on Wy.

"No, we're headed for Bill's," Earl said with grim satisfaction. "Local watering hole, open from six a.m. until midnight, two a.m. on Fridays and Saturdays. Best burgers in town." He shot Liam a sardonic look. "Only burgers in town."

"Uh-huh," Liam said, dragging his attention back to the situation at hand. "You said there'd been shooting?"

Jim Earl snorted. "No shit, Sherlock."

Liam waited. "So, who got shot?"

"Not who, what."

"I beg your pardon?"

The Suburban bottomed out over another pothole. Liam winced at the resulting tortured scrape of metal. Jim Earl didn't seem to notice. "Teddy Engebretsen's boat broke down just about the time the gun went off for herring. He and Nick limped back into the harbor together; Nick went home to see if he could bag hisself a Wassillie, Teddy went on up to Bill's to drown his sorrows. Reasonable response," Earl added parenthetically. "Hell of a thing to miss out on, herring. Enough money in one set for the boat payment and the insurance payment and a new engine and a trip to Seattle. If you make the right one in the right place."

Liam made a small noise that could have meant assent. He knew even less about herring fishing than he did about aviation, although in the case of the former it was distance and inexperience, not terror and intent that kept him ignorant.

"So, Teddy gets a little liquored up." Earl paused. "Well, okay, maybe a lot liquored up, and he takes exception to what's on the jukebox." A small shudder seemed to ripple up Jim Earl's spine. "Bill keeps a thirty-ought-six behind the bar in case of trouble. Teddy grabbed it and shot out the jukebox. Right in the middle of 'Margaritaville.' Dumb bastard." He shook his head. "Poor, dumb bastard." He spit out the window again and added, "Poor dumb dead bastard is what he's going to be if we don't get there in time."

They were in town now, a confused mass of buildings built on a series of small rolling hills that reminded Liam of sand dunes in shape and size, sand dunes covered with a thick encrustation of pine and spruce and alder and willow and birch. The town's buildings varied in construction from prefabricated corrugated metal to rickety two-story wooden plank to split log, lining the sides of a labyrinthine arrangement of streets. Paved streets, both Liam and Jim Earl's truck were glad to notice. They passed two grocery stores, one with its corrugated metal siding painted an electric blue and a small front porch that was crowded with a group of teenage boys.

As the Suburban passed the store, the group of boys spilled down the steps and into the street. Jim Earl leaned on the horn. The boys looked around, mimed astonishment at this appearance of a wheeled vehicle in the middle of the road, and one by one and as slowly as was humanly possible drifted to the curb.

One boy in particular, shorter and younger than the others, was even more obvious than the rest. He wore jeans that bagged out down to his knees and a baseball cap on backward. He stooped to fuss with a cuff, which although rolled three times, was still dragging the ground, and barely twitched when Jim Earl's horn gave another impatient blast. He took his time straightening up, adjusted his cap, and gave Jim Earl a sideways glance that bordered on insolence. He was short and stocky, with straight black hair and the classic high cheekbones, tilted eyes, and golden skin of the upriver Yupik. "Goddammit, kid, move outta the goddamn way!" the mayor bellowed out the window, and hit the horn again.

The other boys had retreated to the porch and were whistling and hooting and catcalling. The boy looked from them to the truck and back again, held a brief, internal debate, and then with an almost imperceptible shrug moved ever so slowly to one side of the street. "About goddamn time," Jim Earl bellowed again, and trod on the accelerator.

Liam twisted his head to watch the boy swagger up the steps to the porch, where he was greeted like a conquering hero, with a lot of back- and hand-slapping, shoulder-shaking, and fist feints to the jaw. The boy turned suddenly and caught Liam's eye. He smiled, slowly, arrogant satisfaction sitting on his young face like war paint, and then the Suburban went around a corner and the boy was lost from view.

The potholes had given way to pavement, but the streets were a warren of sudden rises and dogleg curves. Jim Earl swooped down one such rise and around one of the doglegs, whipped past a large group of buildings on a wooden dock that could have been a cannery or the local fuel dock or the SeaLand warehouse — they were going too fast for Liam to be sure — and pulled up with a jerk at a sprawling, one-story building that featured a shallow-peaked tin roof and green vinyl siding. It sat in the middle of a large parking lot, about three-quarters filled.

The sight did not fill Liam with joy, who had visions of all the vehicle owners being held hostage at gunpoint. "Mayor—" he began.

"Call me Jim Earl," the mayor said, turning off the ignition without bothering to throw out the clutch. The Suburban lurched and gurgled. "Everybody does." With a protesting diesely rattle, the engine died.

"Hold on a minute," Liam said, raising a hand. "You're saying there's a man in there with a gun, right? How many other people are in there? Is he holding them hostage? What kind of gun does he—"

Jim Earl snorted again, spit again, and slammed open the driver's side door. "Shit, Liam, Teddy don't got no gun. Bill done took it away from him."

"What?" Liam got out and slammed shut his own door. "Then what the hell am I doing here?" Ten miles from what might be a real murder scene, and farther than that in space and time from Wy. Suddenly he was furious. "Now, look, Jim Earl"—it was difficult to separate those two names—"I just set foot in Newenham, and I know, because you've told me, that your local force is shorthanded, but I've got some real work to do out at your airport, and—"

Mayor Jim Earl snorted, spat, and swore all in the same breath. "Shit, boy, I didn't haul your ass all the way in from the airport to take Teddy into custody." The tall, grizzled man walked around the hood of the car and poked Liam in the chest with a bony finger. "You're here to save his ass. You don't understand: Teddy shot the jukebox in the middle of 'Margaritaville.' He'll be lucky to get out of there alive." He grinned for the first time, displaying a set of large, improbably white teeth. "I wouldn't care but he's my son-in-law, and I don't want the raising of his kids. Hellions, every one of them. You might be arresting me for murder my own self, should I be fool enough to take on that job."

And with that he vaulted the faded gray wooden steps and disappeared inside the building with the sign on it that said in unprepossessing black block letters, BILL'S BAR AND GRILL.

From the top of a nearby streetlight, an enormous raven surveyed the situation with a sardonic eye and croaked at the mayor's receding back. When Liam looked around to meet the black bird's steady gaze, the raven clicked at him, a series of throaty cackles that sounded somehow mocking.

It was the last sound Liam heard before he went in the door of the bar, from which he promptly came staggering out backward, falling down the stairs and landing with a thump on the pavement, fanny-first. "What the hell?" He looked up just in time to see a tangle of bodies roll down the steps and right over the top of him, to hit hard against the already bruised bumper of the construction orange Suburban. The tangle resolved itself into three people, two men and one woman. One of the men had a rifle and the second man and the woman dove on top of him and the resulting scuffle looked like something out of a Tom and Jerry cartoon.

He fumbled to his feet, brushed off the seat of his jeans, and tried out his trooper voice. "Now, just hold it right there!"

The scuffle paused, looked him over, saw a tall man with an authoritative frown but nothing much else to recommend they obey him, and resumed the scramble. The man with the gun managed to get his finger on the trigger and the gun fired, *bang!* The bullet glanced off the windshield of the Suburban but there were already so many cracks in it Liam couldn't really tell if it had left a mark.

Enough was enough. He waded into the fray and grabbed someone by the scruff of the neck and someone else by the seat of the pants. "Hey!" a voice said indignantly, and he looked down to see that he had the woman by the seat of the pants.

"Sorry," he said without apology, dropped her and the unarmed man, and grabbed for the rifle, which went off again just before his hand closed around the barrel. The bullet sang past his ears and clipped the branch the raven was sitting on. The bird rose up in the air with an affronted squawk and a tremendous flapping of wings to hover over the shooter and unload a large helping of bird shit down his cheek and the front of his shirt. He squawked again, a somehow menacing sound that promised more of the same should he be disturbed a second time, and went back to the spruce tree to land on a branch a little higher up the trunk.

"Eyaaaagh!" said the shooter, and the woman, glaring at him, snapped, "Serves you goddamn right, you nearsighted little bastard! If you'd just buy some glasses maybe once in a while you could hit what you aimed at!" She hauled him to his feet by the collar and hustled him up the steps.

"Wait a minute—" Liam said, standing still with the rifle in one hand.

The second man followed the first two up the steps.

Liam stared at the door. "What the hell?"

From his new branch, the raven croaked at him. "Who asked you?" Liam retorted.

He climbed the steps again, keeping to one side this time. The door opened inward, and he hooked a cautious eye around the edge.

Inside, it was a bar like any fifty other Alaskan bars he'd been in, from Kenai to Ketchikan, Dutch Harbor to Nome, Barrow to Anchorage. He stood in the doorway, allowing his eyes to adjust to the dim light. A bar ran down the left side of the room; booths and the jukebox lined the right side. There was a stage the size of an end table against the back wall with an even smaller, imitation parquet dance floor in front of it. The rest of the floor was covered with tables and chairs. There was a window into the kitchen through the back wall, and the air was filled with the tantalizing odor of a deep fat fryer on overdrive. The floor was gritty beneath his feet, and the rafters were unfinished timber festooned with caribou racks, lead line, cork line, green fishnets, and various animal pelts. Neon beer signs glowed from every available inch of wall space. There were two windows overlooking the parking lot, grimed with years of condensed fat. More signs blinked on and off in them.

Something was missing. It took a moment for Liam to realize what it was. There wasn't any television. No thirty-two-inch screen blaring out the latest Madison Avenue seductions into overspending your income on like-a-rock pickups, after which tall black men would chase after balls of assorted shapes and sizes, unless it was short white men whacking the hell out of a puck, when they weren't whacking the hell out of each other. Sports made no sense to Liam. The only form of exercise he considered worth pursuing was undertaken horizontally. "Push-ups?" Wy had asked oh so innocently when he had propounded this theory to her. "Bench-pressing? Oh, I know, wrestling," and she had tumbled him back onto the bed and demonstrated various holds.

The memory, flashing in from nowhere, halted him in his tracks. He came back to himself and, flushing slightly, looked around for Teddy, whose ass he was there to save.

It wasn't only that there was no television and that the jukebox wasn't playing—the bar was quiet. Too quiet, especially for a bar in the Bush at the beginning of the fishing season. The booths and tables were full, the bar was lined with patrons, and there should have been talk, laughter, more than a few feminine shrieks of delight or dismay, and at the very least two men arguing blearily over who corked who during last summer's salmon season.

But it was quiet instead, with a quality of silence Liam might have expected to find at a drumhead court-martial. There were maybe thirty people present, most of them standing in a semicircle a respectful distance from the action without being so foolish as to put themselves out of range of hearing every word. Liam cast a quick eye over the group. It was a varied bunch, about two-thirds male, white, Native, mixed race, and what appeared to be a couple of heavy equipment salesmen from South Korea who looked delighted with fortune's putting an event in their path that had previously only been granted them via John Wayne movies. There was an ethereal young blonde with a bar towel wrapped around her waist, one hand on her hip, who was tapping an impatient foot as if to indicate she was ready to get back to generating tips now, thanks. Their shoulders stooped and hands crabbed from a lifetime of picking fish, three or four old fishermen in white canvas caps worn a dull gray watched everything out of bright, avid eyes. In a back booth one man had his head pillowed in his arms and was sleeping through it all. A barfly with glassy eyes and a lot of miles on her hung affectionately on the arm of the man Liam recognized from the altercation outside, a stocky young man with a merry grin that displayed irresistible twin dimples. "Come on, Mac honey," the barfly said in a slurred voice. "Les go back to my place, hmm?"

Mac honey was sober enough to catch the barfly's hand as it slid to his crotch, and to get while the getting was still good. "Sorry, Marcie," he said, draining his beer and setting the empty bottle on the bar. "I've got a party to go to, and a girl-friend to keep happy."

He threaded his way through the throng, nodding politely as he passed in front of Liam, and the sound of the door closing behind him was magnified by the hush surrounding the main event. The only noise came from a man Liam recognized as the Old Fart from the plane that afternoon. He was standing in front of the jukebox, whose clear plastic lid was marred with a neat round hole surrounded by a starburst array of cracks. The lid was back, and the Old Fart was tinkering with the insides. He looked around once when Liam came in, said "Huh!" in a loud voice, and selected a larger screwdriver before returning to his work.

Liam looked further for the source of quiet. It wasn't hard to find. It hadn't taken them long, once they got him inside; the man who had been separated from the rifle was seated in a chair and immobilized with enough bright yellow polypropylene line to restrain King Kong. He was maybe thirty years old, five-eight, thickset, with matted brown hair and terrified brown eyes that stared at Liam over the bar rag that had been used to gag him.

Teddy Engebretsen might be drunk, but he wasn't so drunk he didn't know his life was in grave danger.

Standing opposite him was a woman, a woman who towered over Teddy in presence if not in height. The same woman who had rolled over the top of Liam outside, she was about five feet two inches tall and plump as a pigeon, her body a cascading series of rich curves; cheek, chin, breast, belly, hip, thigh, calf, a model for Rubens clad in clean, faded jeans and a gray T-shirt cinched in with a wide leather belt. Zaftig, they called it, Liam remembered from somewhere, as in making a man's palms itch.

All attention in the room was focused on these two. No one seemed to be moving; no one, with the exception of the Alaskan Old Fart, seemed to be breathing. Liam, mindful of his training, gave his gun belt an authoritative hitch and said in his calmest, deepest voice, "What seems to be the trouble here?"

The woman turned to look at him, and Liam registered three things immediately. Her eyes were the blue of glacier ice and thickly lashed, her well-filled T-shirt had a picture of a beribboned mask with the words "New Orleans Jazz Fest" written beneath it, and she had one of the firmest jaws he'd ever seen. She spoke, moved, and acted with a vigor that belied the lines on her face and the color of her hair, a thick silver swath combed straight back from her face that fell to a neatly trimmed line just above her shoulders.

"Who in the hell are you?" she demanded. "Give me that."

She made as if to snatch the rifle from him. He moved it away and she said irritably, "Oh, don't bother, you damn fool, I'm the magistrate for this district."

He looked at her for a long moment, and then sought out Jim Earl's face in the crowd. Jim Earl gave a confirming nod.

"Uh-huh," Liam said, but he kept hold of the rifle. "State Trooper Liam Campbell, ma'am."

"And don't call me ma'am," she snapped. "Makes me feel like I'm a hundred years old."

"Close enough!" the man at the jukebox said without turning around.

"Oh shut up, you old fart," the woman said. Again she reached for the rifle, and this time Liam let her take it. "The name's Billington, Linda Billington. You can call me Bill; everybody does." She shifted the rifle to extend a hand. Her grip was dry and firm—one pump, up and down, and withdrawn. She looked him over critically. "Liam Campbell, is it? We heard you were coming. They get that mess cleaned up at Denali?"

Liam thought "mess" was an inadequate way of referring to the screwup that had cost five lives and his job. "Yes," he said briefly.

Bright eyes examined him shrewdly. "Buck stopped on your desk, I hear."

"Yes. Look, what—"

"Didn't help they were a family of Natives, and you and the other two troopers involved were as white as you can get without bleach."

"No." He could feel the eyes of many trained upon him. This was even worse than he had expected. "What seems to—"

"You'll have a lot to prove here, Liam," she said. "But it's a good town. Pretty fair-minded bunch of people. They'll judge you, all right, but they'll judge you on what you do here, not what you did before you came here."

"Yes, ma'am," Liam said woodenly.

"Bill, dammit. I don't want to be called ma'am until I'm at least a hundred."

"Won't be long now!" the Old Fart bellowed.

"Oh shut up," Bill said without heat. "In the meantime, Liam, this here is Teddy Engebretsen, who's got nothing better to do on a fine spring day such as this than to come in and shoot up my bar with my own rifle." She glared at the miscreant, who whimpered behind his bar rag gag. "And then when we think he's all calmed down, he has the gall to go for it a second time!" Teddy whimpered again. "I'm just figuring on what to do with him."

"Uh-huh," Liam said, because for the life of him he couldn't think what else to say. He shuffled his feet and cleared his throat. He was, after all, the first officer on the scene. It was up to him to establish his sense of authority. He buried his resentment at the woman's blabbering of his private affairs—as private as they get when they've been on the front page of the *Anchorage Daily News* for a week straight—to most of the population of Newenham. "Well, Ms. Billington—"

"Who's that?" she demanded. "I told you to call me Bill. That's my name. Liam," she added pointedly.

So much for establishing his sense of authority. "Okay, Bill," he said, trying an ingratiating smile. She didn't visibly soften, but then the smile hadn't been all that sincere, and he persevered, ever mindful of the clock ticking in the background on the crime scene—if it was one—at the airport, and even more conscious of the burning if irrational need to get back to Wy before she vanished on him again. "What exactly happened here?"

"Teddy shot up the place," she replied promptly. "He come in here all liquored up, then got more so—my fault for not cutting him off sooner. He takes exception to what's on the jukebox, which isn't any of his goddamn business and he can go down to the Seaside and listen to punk rock music and like it from now on." She glared again at the miscreant, who seemed to shrink inside his clothes.

"And?" Liam prompted.

Her face darkened. "I got to him before he got more than one off, but that one hit my jukebox. Right in the middle of 'Margaritaville.' " She looked back at Liam. "Nobody does that to Jimmy Buffett. Not in my bar. Nobody."

"Uh-huh," Liam said. Bill's priorities seemed a little skewed to him, given the number of people in the room who could have been shot instead, herself included. "And we are doing—what, now?"

"I was deciding on that when the cavalry barreled in the door," she said with a sardonic look. "By the way, where is your uniform, trooper?"

Bill was an officer of the court, and as such his coconspirator in upholding the letter as well as the spirit of the law in this section of the Alaskan Bush. Liam reminded himself of this, and took care to keep his tone civil. "In my luggage. I just got off the plane," he added, sounding to his own ears a little aggrieved.

"Uh-huh," she mimicked him, and smiled suddenly. He stared, dazzled. It was like the sun coming out on a bare and wintry day. Her face was strong of brow, nose, and jaw and her skin was lined at the corners of eyes and mouth, but there was no mistaking the warm humor, the manifest charm, and the undeniable sex appeal.

"Watch it, boy," someone growled, and Liam turned to see the Old Fart glaring at him. "She's taken." He pointed with the screwdriver. "And so are you."

Liam blinked. A ripple of laughter went around the room, defusing some of the tension. He shook himself. The Old Fart must have picked up on Wy at the airport. It seemed unlikely, given that the Old Fart must have adjourned to Bill's early on, but then if any part of what Liam had been feeling had showed on his face, he had probably been lit up like one of the neon signs on the wall behind him. It was an uncomfortable thought for a deeply private man, and he turned back to Bill. "What were you intending to do with Mr. Engebretsen, Bill?"

They both regarded the bound man for a moment. The bar watched and waited in silence. "Well," Bill said finally, "I was thinking about supergluing his shooting hand to one cheek of his ass and his other hand around a beer bottle."

Liam stared. She appeared to be absolutely serious. He opened his mouth, and she said, "He drinks too much, does Teddy. I'm not totally unfeeling—the bottle of beer will be a full one, but after it's gone, that's it."

"I like it," the Old Fart said, and grinned evilly when Teddy's eyes bulged over the edge of the gag.

"Or we could just shoot him," she said, and raised the .30-06 to work the action. She gave a satisfied nod. "Plenty of ammunition. 'Course at this distance I really only need one."

The crowd, as a unit, took one step back.

Not just a court-martial, Liam thought, but an execution as well. He admired Bill's efficiency. He started to say something soothing, only to be beaten to it by Jim Earl. "Now, Bill—"

"Put a lid on it, Jim Earl," Bill said. "You been letting this boy run wild since he starting courting your daughter in high school." She bent a severe look upon the mayor. "Why you let him court her is something we won't get into right now." The mayor's face went red, and he began to splutter. Ignoring him, Bill continued, "Fact is, somebody's got to shake some sense into Teddy, and it looks like I've been elected. Besides," she added inexorably, in what was becoming a litany, "he came into my saloon, and he shot up my jukebox, and he shot it up when

Jimmy was singing, and he shot it up when Jimmy was singing 'Margaritaville.' Nobody does that in my bar. And nobody ever, ever does that to Jimmy."

"Uh," Liam said.

"Yes, Liam?" Bill said, looking at him with a bland smile.

Liam made what felt even to himself like a feeble attempt to gain control of the situation. "Surely there has to be a local ordinance against the shooting of a firearm within the city limits."

Bill raised her brows. "I'm sure there must be. And your point is?"

"Well, I—" Liam was beginning to sweat, although not as freely as Teddy Engebretsen. It didn't help that the rest of the people in the bar were fully alive to his dilemma and thoroughly enjoying it. Liam felt like the star attraction in a three-ring circus. He looked back at Bill, and for the first time noticed the twinkle lurking at the back of her eyes. He stared at her, and the twinkle grew.

"There, that oughta do it." The lid on the jukebox came down with a solid thud and the Old Fart dropped a quarter into the machine and punched in a selection. Nothing happened. The twinkle in Bill's eyes vanished, and Teddy looked even more terrified, if that was possible. "Come on, you son of a bitch," the Old Fart said, and squared off to give the jukebox a quick kick in the side. The machine hiccuped once and came alive with the sound of steel drums and a harmonica collaborating on a Caribbean rhythm that inspired one couple into an impromptu jitterbug. Jimmy was back.

Tension visibly eased. The Old Fart packed up the toolbox and lugged it to the bar, where he let it drop with a resounding crash. He looked impatiently around for Bill. "Well, come on, woman, don't just stand there, get me a beer!"

Bill grumbled but did as she was told, absentmindedly handing off the rifle to Liam as she passed. The Old Fart looked at him. "Get your butt up here, too, boy—I'll buy you a drink. Bill, pour him some o' that Glenmorangie—you know, that stuff bottled by the only ten honest men on the Isle of Skye, or some such."

Bill snapped her fingers and pointed at the Old Fart. "*That* was why you made me buy this stuff."

The Old Fart shrugged. "What can I say? I'm good."

Liam found himself standing at the bar. If he'd had time to think about it he might have wondered how he got there, especially with what was waiting for him at the airport, but for the moment he didn't seem to have much choice in the matter. It all seemed somewhat dreamlike, anyway—the body at the airport, the reappearance of Wy in his life when he had thought her lost to him forever, a practicing vigilante who moonlighted as the local magistrate, and now, a soon-to-be-drunken jukebox repairman. He was wrong—this wasn't a three-ring circus, it was an alternate plane of existence.

The Old Fart was a foot shorter than the trooper, which he rectified by hoisting himself up on a stool. He turned to Liam and stuck out a hand. "Moses Alakuyak, shaman."

His beer and Liam's single malt arrived. Moses held out his bottle of beer and Liam clinked his glass against it. "To women," Moses said. "Not all of them leave, you know."

"I beg your pardon?" Liam said.

Moses drained his bottle in one long, continuous swallow. "Barkeep! Do it again! Not that it matters," he said, turning back to Liam. "Pretty soon there'll be nothing left of this goddamn planet but a garbage dump and a grave."

Ten years of practicing law enforcement with the Alaska State Troopers was an excellent way to hone one's survival skills. Liam murmured something that could have been agreement, and sipped cautiously at his glass, but it was the real thing all right: Glenmorangie single malt scotch. He swirled the liquid around in his glass and inhaled with reverence.

"People think survival of the fittest is all right for animals but not for people," Moses explained expansively. "We're not culling the human herd the way we oughta. We're saving the weakest: the ones with AIDS, the folks in Africa who can't figure out how to feed themselves, them Serbs who can't stop shooting at their neighbors. We're gonna rescue 'em all, and wipe out the human race doing it." The old man snorted, a comprehensive sound issuing forth from his snubbed nose. "By God," he said, voice rising, "we're living in the best of times right now, because it sure as hell ain't gonna get any better."

The scotch slid down Liam's throat like melted butter. He set the glass down. "Thanks for the drink, Moses," he said, and paused. "Wait a minute. How did you know I drink single malt scotch?"

"I know a lot of things about you," Moses said, knocking back his second beer and waving for a third. Bill brought it, and set it down gently in front of him. There was none of the condemnation in her expression Liam had seen there for Teddy Engebretsen. Of course, Moses had fixed the jukebox and returned Jimmy Buffett to his natural setting, a bar, so Bill was no doubt inclined to look kindly upon him.

Bill stretched out a hand and cupped Moses' cheek. "Going to be one of those nights, huh?" she said in the softest tone Liam had yet to hear her use.

"Don't worry about it," Moses said gruffly, but he didn't turn away when she leaned over the bar and kissed him. It wasn't the kiss of a friend, either; it went on for a while, and Moses hooked a hand around the back of Bill's head and cooperated with enthusiasm, to the vocal approval of the bar's other customers.

Bill pulled back and gave Moses a sweet smile. "Later, lover."

He caught at her hand before she could move down the bar, and kissed it. "Later."

There was a wealth of promise in both word and kiss. Liam was trying to read the fine print of the labels on the line of bottles on the opposite wall when Moses dug an elbow into his side. "Okay to look now, trooper." The Old Fart grinned up at him, and now that he was looking for it, Liam could see the Alakuyak in him, in the barely perceptible slant of his eyes, the high, flat cheekbones, the snubbed nose. Come to think of it, his height should have been a dead giveaway—most Yupik men ranged between four-eight and five-five. But his skin was olive, not golden, his hair a grizzled brown, not the sleek black cap found in the villages, and his eyes were a startling gray, a gray so light they had almost no color at all. They were looking at Liam now, clear, cool, assessing, and Liam could not

shake the uncomfortable feeling that they could see right
through him.

Moses didn't help when he said, "Yeah, I know a lot of things,
about everything, but right now I want to know why you're
keeping a girl as fine as Wyanet Chouinard waiting on you."

The accusation took Liam aback, and he fumbled around for
an acceptable answer. "Well, I—everything's happened so fast,
I didn't know—the mayor came and—"

"I don't mean this bullshit." An all-inclusive wave of one
impatient hand took in Teddy Engebretsen, still bound and
gagged. "Why didn't you come after her?"

Liam felt disembodied. "I'm married," he heard someone say.

"Like hell you are." Moses stared at him, not without sympathy. "That's no kind of way to live, boy."

"It's my life," Liam said, and the anger came back again,
anger at himself, at Wy, at Jenny, at fate.

Moses regarded him impatiently. "Ain't never going to be a
good time to make the break, boy. Your situation, painful
though it is, aggravating though it is, is familiar to you. You've
become comfortable in it. You don't want to make a mess, cre-
ate fuss and inconvenience. Tell you something." The shaman, if
that was what he was, snorted a laugh. "Tell you a lot of things,
because I know a lot of things, but right now listen to this."
Moses drained his fourth beer, and pointed to it for emphasis.
"Life isn't neat. Know why? Because it's run by imperfect people who make messes, who then have to go around cleaning up
after themselves." Moses gave Liam a severe once-over. "You're
not much of a cleaner-upper, are you, boy?"

Liam could feel the heat rising up beneath his skin. All he
could think of to say was "You don't talk like someone raised in
Bush Alaska. Where did you go to school?"

"Hah!" Moses said, triumphant. "I can't talk like this because
I was raised in a village, is that it? You got a lot to learn, boy,
and I'm just the one to teach you. Stick around." He drained his
glass with a satisfied smack of his lips, followed by a resonant
and contented burp. "But not tonight. Bill! Hit me again!"

"In a minute." Bill took Liam's glass, drained it, and used the
thick end to rap the bar, twice, sharp, quick raps, bringing

everyone to momentary attention. She bent a severe eye on Teddy Engebretsen, still bound and gagged. He quailed. "Teddy Engebretsen, in my capacity as magistrate of the state of Alaska, I charge you with being drunk and disorderly in public, discharging a firearm within the city limits, and just generally being a pain in the ass. I find you guilty of same. Court's adjourned." She thumped the bar with the glass twice again. "He's all yours, trooper. Legally, anyway."

"What am I supposed to do with him?" Liam said.

Now it was Bill's turn to regard him with impatience. "Toss him in the hoosegow. What the hell kind of trooper are you?"

A magistrate for the state of Alaska didn't need a law degree, didn't need much more than a high school diploma or its equivalent and some standing in his or her community. Official arrest procedures called for the swearing out of a warrant, a reading of rights, an arraignment, a grand jury, a trial, a conviction—all those nitpicky little due-process things required by the Constitution of the United States and affirmed by the Bill of Rights, not to mention two hundred and twenty years of Supreme Court case law. Belief in those things made Liam the kind of trooper he was, but they didn't seem to count for much here and now. "Where exactly is the, er, hoosegow?" he said meekly.

"At the cop shop. Jim Earl'll show you."

"How long do I leave him there?"

"Long as I say so," Bill said.

"Oh."

Moses grinned at him.

It could be worse, Liam thought. At least Newenham's magistrate had taken the Sixth Amendment to heart, if no other. Teddy Engebretsen's trial had been speedy, and it sure as hell had been public.

A dimension beyond sight and sound, he thought, going down the stairs and out to the construction orange Suburban. A dimension known as the Twilight Zone.

FOUR

Teddy Engebretsen was freed from bondage and deposited safely, if a bit tearfully, in one of the six cells available at the local jail. The dispatcher, a leathery middle-aged woman with a harassed look on her face, tossed Jim Earl the keys while talking nonstop through her headset, something about a joust between two dueling snow machiners on the Icky road. The Icky road? It was the first week of May, and Liam hadn't seen any snow on the ground either from the air or Jim Earl's truck. He decided not to inquire if the Icky road was municipal, state, or federal. Some things it was better he should not know.

Afterward, Jim Earl dropped Liam at his office, where the trooper discovered the door unlocked and the keys in the ignition of the white Chevy Blazer with the Alaska State Troopers seal on the door. Mindful of the scene still waiting at the airport, Liam did little more than toss his bag behind the desk and lock the office door before climbing into the Blazer. The engine turned over on the first try, and he didn't get lost more than two or three times on his way back to the airport.

He arrived at the same time as the ambulance, and made a resolve then and there never to be shot in the line of duty during his posting to Newenham. He checked his watch. It was eight-thirty. Unbelievably, it was only three hours since his plane had touched down. Surely too much had happened to fit into that small a space.

He raised the watch to his ear. The ticking should have reassured him that time was passing with its usual, inexorable forward motion, but it didn't.

Wy was still there, sitting in the cab of her truck. It was drizzling. An older man, unshaven and wearing salt-stained clothes, was talking to her through the open driver's-side door. Wy caught sight of Liam over the man's shoulder as he pulled up next to her. By the time Liam had gotten out the older man was walking away, a pronounced limp in his gait. "Who was that?" Liam said.

She shrugged. "Just another fisherman. Wanted to know what happened."

She couldn't quite meet his eyes, and he regarded her for a speculative moment.

Gary Gruber was still there, too, shivering beneath the eaves of the terminal and gnawing at what might have been a candy bar. People came and went, planes taxied to and fro, and barely a glance was spared for the mound beneath the blue tarp, which seemed to have shrunk since Liam last saw it. It looked very lonely lying next to the little red and white Super Cub, which looked more than a little forlorn itself.

The ambulance was under the command of a single emergency medical technician, a slim, intense young man who introduced himself as Joe Gould. He knelt to inspect DeCreft's body. "Not much to be done here," he observed. "Okay to take the body to the morgue?"

"We've got a morgue?" Liam said.

"We've even got a hospital," Gould said with a cool smile.

"Hold on a second," Liam said, and went to search the Blazer for an evidence kit. It was in a case behind the backseat, and, typically, Corcoran had left no film in the camera inside and no spare rolls in the case. Liam found a yellow legal pad and a pencil he had to sharpen with a pocketknife, and with the evenly spaced halogen floodlights around the airport casting long, faint shadows in the dim light drew a rough sketch of the scene, pacing out the distances between terminal, plane, and body before helping Gould zip DeCreft into a body bag and load it into the ambulance. "Have we got a pathologist, too?" Liam asked Gould.

"Not forensic," Gould said, "but cause of death is obvious, and time of death was witnessed, so—"

"It was?" Liam said. "Who by?"

Gould had thin, self-sacrificial features that would not have looked out of place beneath a tonsure, belied by a pair of satanic eyebrows and a sly smile. "Somebody was yelling about it on the radio. The dispatcher picked it up, and passed it on to me."

"When was this?"

"Right about the time it happened, I guess. Ask the dispatcher."

"And you rushed right on over to help out," Liam observed.

The EMT slammed the doors of the ambulance and paused to give Liam a level, considering stare. "Guy walked into a propeller," Gould said. "The initial report from the scene, as conveyed to me by the dispatcher, indicated that the victim was dead before he hit the ground." He had been leaning on the ambulance. He straightened now. "I was delivering a breech baby in Icky at the time." He went around the ambulance, climbed into the cab, and drove off.

"Icky?" Liam said to the air. As in the Icky road?

Nobody answered him, so he fetched a flashlight and a garbage bag from the Blazer and went to inventory the contents of the Super Cub.

There were a handful of candy wrappers, two maps of Bristol Bay, five small green glass balls Liam recognized as Japanese fishing floats, a walrus tusk broken off near the root, a survival kit, two firestarter logs, two parkas, two pairs of boots, a liter-sized plastic Pepsi bottle half full of yellow liquid, a clam gun, a bucket, three mismatched gloves, and three handheld radios, which to Liam seemed a bit redundant. He put everything into the garbage bag and tied the neck into a firm overhand knot, then set it to one side on the tarmac.

He stuck his head back inside the airplane to make sure he hadn't missed anything. He reexamined the control panel. To his deliberately uneducated eye, it sported the usual array of dials, knobs, bells, and whistles. He pointed. "What's that?"

Next to him he felt Wy start, and smiled grimly to himself.

Good. She should know by now that he was still as acutely aware of her presence as she was of his, that he could have told her the instant she stepped from the truck, that he had known to the inch how close she was standing next to him now.

"It's a radio," Wy said.

"I can see that much," Liam said. "Why is it bolted to the bottom of the control panel instead of being built in like the other one"—he pointed—"and why does it look so much newer?"

He turned to look down at her, and again surprised that look of fear on her face. It vanished, but he had seen it, it had been real, and he knew a cold feeling in the pit of his stomach.

"It's a special radio. I installed it at the request of the skipper who heads up the consortium I spot herring for."

"What's so special about it?"

"It's scrambled. So if anybody stumbles across our channel, and I'm telling the skipper where I spotted a big ball of herring, nobody else can understand what I'm saying."

"I see. I suppose there's a descrambler on the skipper's end."

"Yes."

Liam pointed at the garbage bag that held the Cub's inventory. "Then why these other three radios?"

"Backups."

Again, she couldn't quite meet his eyes. Liam waited, but she didn't volunteer any further information. He looked at Gruber, who had materialized on the other side of the strut and who was engaged in wiping his runny nose on the sleeve of his brown jacket, jaws champing again at a wad of bubble gum. He blew a bubble that broke with a splat against his nose, and he slurped it back into his mouth.

"Want me to take that?" Wy said from Liam's other side, and he turned to see her indicating the garbage bag.

"No problem," he said, "I've got it."

He walked over to deposit the bag in the passenger seat of the Blazer, and as an afterthought locked the doors. It was evidence of a sort, after all, although he didn't have a clue yet as to just what it was evidence of, other than a serious sweet tooth and bad housekeeping. Back at the plane, he said to Wy, "Can you lock this thing up?"

"She should move it out of here," Gruber said. "It's kind of in the way."

"Have you got a tie-down?" Liam said. Wy nodded at the apron. "Okay, let's do it."

Wy walked around him to the tail of the plane, picked it up, and began towing the Cub toward the section of the apron she had indicated. Liam and Gruber caught up to help, but the little plane was so light it wasn't really necessary.

Wy's tie-down was some distance down the commercial side of the Newenham strip, off the main taxiway and behind three rows of other small planes. The tiny square of tarmac was at the very edge of the pavement, with a building the size and shape of an outhouse placed on the gravel directly behind it. Looking around, Liam saw other little houses lining the strip like so many miniature garages. Wy's was painted powder blue, and Wy towed the Cub to the tie-down in front of it.

The tie-down itself consisted of two small hoops of bent metal rod set into the pavement. A length of manila line, black electrician's tape sealing the ends, was fastened to each hoop by an eye sealed with more electrician's tape. Liam threaded one length of line to the matching fastening on the right strut, Wy elbowing Gruber aside to do the other.

Liam ducked out from beneath the wing. "At least I can do that much," he said, and smiled at her.

She almost smiled back, and he rejoiced silently. This time he wouldn't back down, he wouldn't walk away. Not this time.

She gestured at the prop. "Can I wipe that down?"

Liam turned. The rain had pretty much washed the prop clean. "You sure it's okay?"

"I disconnected the mags."

"I thought I told you not to mess with it while I was gone," he said in a long-suffering voice. He looked at Gruber. "I thought I told you to keep everyone away from it."

Gruber shifted his gum. "Well, yeah, but, you know. I mean, it's her plane."

Liam suppressed a sigh. "So, can I clean the prop?" Wy said.

"Sure," Liam said. "You can steam-clean the interior if you want. Doesn't much matter now." He hung back, Gary Gruber a silent ghost at his elbow, watching as she fetched a rag from the powder blue shack and carefully cleaned the propeller blades. "Wy?"

She stiffened. "What?"

"What and where is Icky?"

He could almost see the tension leaving her body. "It's what the locals call Ik'ikika. It's a village about forty miles north, on the shore of One Lake."

"You can drive there?"

She nodded. "It's a dirt road, but it's passable. Mostly."

Thinking of the roads he had traveled in Newenham made him think that this was a matter of opinion.

"I've got to get home," she said, and turned abruptly to walk back to her truck.

"Me, too," Gruber said, and made a vague gesture with one hand. "Anything you need, officer."

"Yeah, thanks," Liam said, eye on Wy's retreating back. "If you could come into the office tomorrow, we'll type out your statement and you can sign it."

By the time he caught up with Wy, she was almost to her truck. He caught her elbow. "What's your rush?"

She pulled away. "I have to get home. I'm late already."

Gruber passed them like a gray ghost and vanished into the terminal. A moment later all the halogen lamps but one went out, a door slammed, and they heard the sound of a vehicle starting and fading into the distance.

"Don't you need to call your boss?"

"I already did. Fish and Game never did call an opener. Lucky for me."

Liam gave her a sharp look. "How? I thought you didn't leave the airport."

"I used one of the handhelds in the plane."

He found relief in a small eruption of temper, all the sweeter because he'd been sitting on it for three hours. "Goddammit, Wy, I told you not to go anywhere near that damn plane!"

She glared at him. "We both went, Gary and me both, when I explained to him what I needed to do. I had to disconnect the mags anyway."

He was skeptical, and sounded it. "You can reach the Bay from one of those handhelds here on the ground?"

"I called the processor in the harbor," she said, looking suddenly weary, as if all the fight had gone out of her. "They relayed the message."

"Who is he? Your fishing boss?"

"Cecil Wolfe. He owns the *Sea Wolfe*. With an *e*."

"Tell me you're kidding."

She shook her head, the trace of a very faint smile lighting her face. It was as rapidly gone, and she turned again to the truck.

"Wy, wait." Again he caught her arm.

"What, Liam?" she said, and this time the weariness was in her voice. "What more do you want?"

"This," he said, goaded, and reached for her.

Her lips were soft and cool, her face and hair damp from the rain. At first she braced her arms against his hold, murmuring a protest, and in the next instant she was clinging fiercely, returning kiss for kiss, caress for caress.

An exultant thrill raced up his spine when he realized she was just as hungry, just as needy as he was. Her skin . . . he'd never been able to get enough of that smooth, warm skin. He bit the pulse at the base of her throat. She opened her legs and slid her hands down over his ass, arching up to rub against him. Her head fell back and a purr rippled out, a sound that seemed to trigger the animal in both of them. They stumbled against her truck, parked just outside the circle of pale illumination cast by the light mounted on the terminal wall. It was the only light, the low-lying rain clouds blocking the setting sun. The deep-throated rumble of a pickup could be heard, but it stopped before it got too close. The last plane had taken off an hour before, and the airport was shut down for what remained of the night. The twilight of an Arctic spring evening closed in around them, and all sense of time and place was lost.

He shoved a rough hand beneath her shirt; her legs came up to wrap around his hips. Somehow she fumbled the door open and they fell onto the bench seat. Liam hit his elbow on the dash, Wy her head on the steering wheel, and neither of them noticed. "Hurry," she whispered frantically, "hurry, hurry, hurry." He felt her hands at his fly and reached for her zipper, opening it and stripping her of jeans, underwear, shoes, and socks in one sweep. The smell of her was so strong and so tantalizing that he would have buried his face in it if she hadn't pulled him up by his hair. He reached for her braid and freed it, burying his face in the resulting curls with an inarticulate murmur. He had never forgotten her smell, intrinsic to her, rich, spicy, infinitely arousing.

Her legs encircled him again and she wrapped a hand around his cock and he almost came then and there. "No! Don't you dare!" She guided him to her and he almost came again when he felt how wet she was. He hung over her, drenched with sweat, trembling with need, waiting, and she dug her nails into the base of his spine and arched up. With one thrust he buried himself inside her, and it was all he remembered, all he had dreamed of, all he had ever wanted. Thirty-one months of wanting and not having had built to this, and he couldn't wait, not one minute, not one second more. "I'm sorry, Wy," he muttered, "I'm sorry," and he thrust, once, twice, three times and that was all it took, it boiled up out of him in a scalding flood and into her, and dimly he felt her nails dig deeper into his back, her legs tighten around his ass, her back arch so powerfully it raised them both off the seat, heard her voice cry out his name, and knew with a dim rush of pride and pleasure that she had come with him, that he had not been cast up on the beach alone.

It was a long, long journey back, and when he made it, he became slowly aware of the separate sensations of the now slack embrace of her legs, the rise and fall of her breast beneath his, the tickle of her breath against his ear, the seep of fluid out of her and over him. He wanted to reach down and rub that fluid into her skin, marking her with the smell and taste and touch of him. The need to put his brand on her became too powerful to resist, and he turned his head to nuzzle beneath the hair on her neck. He bit her, at first softly, and then harder, knowing a fierce and proprietary joy at once again being able to stake a claim. He had Wyanet Chouinard in his arms again, and never had his world seemed so rich with promise. He wanted to shout for joy. He wanted to weep with relief. He wanted to shake his fist to the sky and curse God for taking her away. He wanted to get down on his knees and thank Him for bringing her back. He wanted nothing more and nothing less than to lie in this woman's arms for the rest of his life.

It wasn't long before he noticed that these feelings of joy unconfined might not be returned. She was trembling, and when he raised his head he saw tears sliding fast and hot down her face. "What?" he said with quick dismay. "Don't," he said, when she tried to shove him off. "Wy, don't."

"Please," she said, and he had no defense against that. His legs offered no guarantee they were going to hold him up, but he managed, staggering a little. He got his jeans back on all right, though it took his shaking hands two tries to get his fly fastened.

She put herself to rights more swiftly, and was in the cab of the truck once more, reaching to close the door. He smacked his palm against the edge just in time. "Don't do this, Wy. Don't walk away from this. Not again. I don't think I can live through it a second time."

In that moment he would have gone down on his knees, and something in his voice told her so. Her hand slid from the keys. Her head drooped forward, to rest against the steering wheel. Her hair, that glorious mane, fell forward to hide her face, and her voice was so muffled he had to strain to hear. "I can't do this, Liam."

"Yes you can," he said, terrified now. "You have to. I need you. I need you, Wy." His voice deepened. "And you need me, too. Hell," he said, with a gesture that included the bench seat, "you may even need me more."

She was silent for a moment, before raising her head and brushing the hair back from her face so she could look at him. In the single floodlight of the terminal building, her face looked bloodless. "It's been almost three years —"

"It's been nothing. It was yesterday." He took a deep breath, fighting for control, fighting for his life now. "It was this morning, goddammit."

She was silent again. He waited. At last she said, her voice low, "Liam, my life has changed. I have—"

"What? What have you got that you can't fit me in around, us in around? What?"

She met his anger with her own, and it was kind of a relief to be fighting again. "I didn't lay down and die when I left, Liam. I moved on, and along the way, I acquired—" She hesitated, and then said firmly, "I acquired some new obligations."

"Obligations? What the hell does that mean?" he demanded, and then added cruelly, "If what just happened in the cab of this truck means anything, it sure as hell doesn't mean another man." She shook her head, and he grabbed her arm. "You were with me every step of the way. You haven't been with anyone else either, have you?" She didn't answer, and he gave her a rough shake. "Have you!"

She slid out of the cab and gave him enough of a shove so that he fell back a step. "No I haven't! So what! It doesn't mean I'm ready to fall at your feet!"

"I didn't ask you to fall at my feet! Share my home, yes! Sleep in my bed, yes! Live with me for the rest of my life, yes!"

She drew herself up to her full height and looked him straight in the eye. "How's Jennifer?"

The breath caught in his throat. When he could speak he said, with difficulty, "Low blow, Wy."

She knew it was, too. Conflicting emotions chased themselves across her face, and it was an obvious struggle before she could settle on sympathy. "I'm so sorry, Liam. When I heard, I almost—but there was nothing I could say that would help then, either." She swallowed hard. "Your boy, Charlie. I know how much you loved him."

"Yes." Liam leaned up against the truck and closed his eyes. Rain fell on his face, cool, clean, oddly comforting. Charlie had loved the rain, laughing out loud as his little wobbly baby legs, unsteady but determined, would stamp through puddles, his tiny baby's grasp hanging on to Liam's for support. Those first few horrible weeks after Charlie's death, Liam had run from the pain of such memories. Now, he welcomed them. For eighteen precious months, Charlie had been a part of him, and beyond that, a part of his life's blood, his promise of immortality.

His hostage to fortune.

No, he wouldn't trade his memories for anything in the world. Not even for the love of the woman standing next to him now.

She swiped at her face with an impatient hand, mixing rain and more tears. "Do you ever think about fate, Liam?"

"Fate?" he said.

"Yes, fate. I give you back to your son, and then fate takes him away. It's almost . . ."

"What?"

"It's almost like punishment," she whispered.

He turned his head to look at her. "No, Wy. Been there, done that. We didn't kill Charlie. A guy name of Rick Dyson got drunk, climbed in his car, and ran a stop sign at seventy miles an hour. He killed them. We didn't."

Another pause. "How is she, Liam?"

It was his turn for the fight to drain out of him, and he slumped back against the truck. "The same. Day in, day out. Nothing ever changes. She just lies there."

"Did you—how often did—"

"All the time. I drove down to Anchorage every Friday to spend the weekend with her. I read to her. She never was much for reading, but I kept thinking, she's going to hear my voice, she's going to hear me calling to her, she's going to wake up. It's happened before, to other people, why not Jenny?" All the old familiar frustration and guilt and rage welled up inside him and he balled his hand up into a fist and struck the side of the truck, once, twice, three times, hard enough to hurt his hand. "No. Nothing has changed."

"How could you let them—" She stopped, and bit her lip.

"How could I let them transfer me here? I didn't have much choice, Wy. Barton was pretty clear; it was take the posting in Newenham or take a hike." He wiped a hand across his face and it came away wet, mostly from the rain. "I didn't have much left but the job, Wy. I took the transfer. I'll get back as often as I can."

Her voice was a ghost of sound. "I'm sorry, Liam. I'm so sorry."

"So am I."

"Do you ever sometimes wonder . . ."

He looked at her. "If she won't come back because she knew about us?"

It had been like that from the start, the instantaneous communication, the link between them, one beginning a sentence only to have the other finish it. "Yes," she whispered.

"She didn't know," he said strongly, willing himself to believe it. "She didn't know; she never knew. We were always careful. No one knew."

A stifled sob made him turn. A tear slid down her cheek. "It's the worst thing I've ever done in my life," she whispered. "Sleeping with you when I knew you were married."

He couldn't answer, because he knew she was right. And besides, it was the worst thing he'd ever done, too. He thought of Jenny, laughing, loving Jenny with the light brown hair. She had deserved better.

"I have to go," she said. "It's so late, there's—I have to—" She couldn't or wouldn't finish the thought.

Again, he caught the pickup's door before it could close. "You have to come down tomorrow, and make out a statement."

She stared at him, uncomprehending. "What?"

"You were Bob DeCreft's pilot, Wy. He was your spotter. You would have all the opportunity in the world to sabotage your own plane. Shit, you're probably my prime suspect."

Her voice distant, she said, "You think I killed him, then?"

He wanted to slap the stony expression right off her face. "No," he said through his teeth, "no, I don't think you killed him. I don't think you've got it in you to kill anyone. But I still have to find out who did, and you're an eyewitness to some of his last moments alive."

Her face relaxed. "All right. I'll come down in the morning."

"You don't have to fly?" he said, in belated concern.

"I don't know. I won't know until I check the schedule, see what Fish and Game has decided." She reached again for the ignition.

"We're not done, Wy," he warned her.

She stared out the windshield, delicate profile silhouetted against the merciless rays of the halogen light. "I know," she said finally.

It was enough for now. He closed her door. She turned the keys, the engine rolled over, and she drove away.

Liam, light-headed with a mixture of emotions he could neither separate nor quantify, was in the Blazer with his hand on the shift when he realized he had no place to sleep. Oh well, it wouldn't be the first time he'd slept in an office chair. Of course, first he'd have to find the post again before the sun came up.

Sighing, he started the Blazer and put it into gear. As he started along the tarmac, tires hissing through the returning rain, a figure detached itself from the shadow of the terminal and moved down the runway toward the small plane tie-downs. Liam let up on the gas, watching. It was a hulking figure, ogrelike in shape and size, but that could have been the magnifying effect of the dim light. It was moving stealthily, ducking from shadow to shadow, working its way steadily forward.

Liam gave the Blazer enough gas to keep moving, drove around the terminal out of sight and sound of the figure, parked, and hotfooted it to the other side. The figure had vanished into the gloom. Liam walked forward, threading his way between parked planes, ears pricked, eyes roving from side to side. The planes all looked alike to him so he tried not to look at them, tried instead to register what was out of place in his peripheral vision.

He heard a sound like the ripping of fabric. He stopped, the better to hear it. It stopped, too. He waited. There it was again, and he walked toward it. It stopped again, and he stopped again. Footsteps then; careful, quiet footsteps, soles slapping gently against pavement, then crunching against gravel, then pavement again, then a repeat of the ripping sound.

It was coming from very near to where Wy's Cub was parked. Liam moved forward to crouch behind a plane on wheel-floats. He peered around the rudder.

He recognized the little red and white plane as 78 Zulu, but now it looked like the wing closest to him had been through a

Cuisinart. Their fabric coverings had been shredded, so that the Dacron hung in thin, ragged strips, exposing the steel tubes beneath. On the far side, a large figure worked at the second wing with what looked like a crowbar, shredding it as well.

As an act of malicious, wanton waste it was enough to take Liam's breath away. It brought him involuntarily to his feet, his head smartly smacking into his hiding place's fuselage with a clang that reverberated down his spine and for a hundred feet in every direction.

All sounds from the Cub stopped.

His scalp had caught some sharp edge. Warm fluid seeped down the side of his face and into his left eye. "Ouch!" He clapped one hand to his head and the other to his holster. "Dammit! Hey! State trooper! Knock that shit off right now!"

The big figure, caught with his crowbar raised over his head, froze in place. And I picked tonight to forget the goddamn flashlight, Liam thought as he stepped unsteadily into the open. "Just hold it right there, mister. Just—shit! Halt, goddammit!"

The figure, moving with alarming speed for something of its bulk, had turned to run. Liam ran after him. "State trooper, I say again; stop or I will shoot!" Which would have been a neat trick with his gun still holstered. Liam unsnapped the cover as he ran, the rain in his face, running into wingtips, tripping over tie-down lines and tie-downs and just generally blundering around like a drunken elephant.

He thudded full tilt around the tail of a plane so yellow it nearly glowed in the dark and caught the merest glimpse of a tall dark monster looming up on his left before the sky fell on him with a thump that caved in the left side of his face. He had a brief flash of jumbled images that included the monster stooping over him, an upraised arm, the claw end of a crowbar; and then things got really weird—the beat of wings, feathered this time, sharp talons and a razor beak, a challenging, inhuman scream answered by a very human shriek of pain, as the menacing hulk looming over Liam was enveloped in darkness.

The rain woke him, a few minutes or a few hours later, beating against his face, soaking his clothes, and forming puddles around his body. He opened his eyes, and found himself staring up at the underside of the yellow plane's right wing. A wind had come up and was driving the rain sideways, causing it to tippety-tap against the aluminum side of the plane.

So far as he could tell, he was alone in the airplane parking lot.

Or not. There was a kind of scraping sound overhead that he first mistook for more rain, but a movement caught his eye and he looked up again, squinting against the rain, to see the head of a raven peering over the side of the wing, its black head gleaming wetly. It looked irritated. It sounded it, too, when it croaked at Liam.

Liam blinked back. The raven gave a sour-sounding caw and launched itself into the air. A second later, it had vanished, black shape into rainy night.

Head wounds were tricky things, he knew. They bled worse than any other injury, and anyone suffering a head injury was entitled to a hallucination or two.

It was either that or he'd wound up in the middle of a science fiction remake of *The Maltese Falcon.*

The thought surprised him into a laugh, which made his head ache but also propelled him to his feet. He had to lean up against the plane until the wave of dizziness had passed.

He should go the hospital, he thought, have himself checked out.

He should report this incident to the Newenham police.

He should call Wy, tell her about her plane.

Instead he staggered back to the Blazer, fell in, and drove himself to his office, by a miracle finding it on the first try. It looked like the end of the rainbow that night, the one dry place in Newenham he had a key to.

Bad news keeps.

And besides, it had been a very, very long day.

FIVE

There was a thump at the door. Liam, asleep in the office chair with his feet up on the desk, started awake. The chair rolled back and Liam slid off the seat and crashed to the floor. "Ouch! Goddammit!" His head gave a tremendous throb and then settled into a steady ache just above his left ear. He raised an investigatory hand. The wound was swollen, but less so than when he had come in last night. The cut on the crown of his head was better, too; still tender but crusted over.

He shoved the chair away from him and it went, casters protesting creakily. He rose almost as creakily to his feet, rubbing at the small of his back. He stretched, popping his joints, and gave a mighty yawn, in the middle of which someone thumped on the door again, the same bone-jarring thump Liam recognized as his original alarm clock.

Without waiting for an invitation, the door swung back on its hinges. In the door stood a man it took Liam a few befuddled moments to recognize. It was the Alaskan Old Fart, the drunken shaman, Moses Alakuyak. The shaman stared at him, hands on his hips.

"Well?" Liam said testily. He wasn't a morning person.

"Well," Moses said, emphasizing the word with awful sarcasm, "get your ass out here. It's late—we've got work to do." And he vanished.

Liam blinked once, then felt around for his watch. The little red numbers blinked back at him—6:00 A.M. His teeth were furry, he'd had maybe five hours' worth of uneasy sleep perched on his makeshift office chair bed, and he needed to pee.

"Get out here, dammit!" Moses' voice barked. Liam considered his alternatives, and then braved the shaman's displeasure by relieving his most pressing problem in the bathroom.

He examined himself in the mirror. His hair covered most of the damage. He splashed cold water on his face, drank about a quart of it straight from the faucet, noticing a faintly sulfuric taste, and filled up the bowl to sluice the blood out of his hair. There was a roll of paper towels on the back of the toilet; he used those to dry off.

"Goddammit," the shaman bellowed, "get your goddamn butt out here before I lose my goddamn temper!"

He could always arrest Moses for disturbing the peace, Liam thought hopefully. And then bethought himself of Bill's burgers. Given the obvious relationship between Bill and Moses, it would behoove him to stay on Moses' good side. Or at least that's what Liam told himself. He took a deep breath and stepped out on the porch.

The Newenham troopers' post was one small building consisting of an outer office, an inner office, a lavatory, and two holding cells. The right side of the building was surrounded by a paved parking lot enclosed by a ten-foot-high chain-link fence. Current occupants included a rusted-out white International pickup, a brand-new Cadillac Seville, and a dump truck. Liam hadn't had time yet to look at the files and see why they had been confiscated.

He could probably make a fairly accurate guess as to why the truck and the Caddy were there (DWI for the one, drugs for the other) but the dump truck had him stumped. What could you do with a dump truck that was criminal? Haul toxic wastes, maybe, but that would be a federal offense. Wouldn't it? He made a mental note to look up the relevant statutes.

The Newenham post sat on a side road a few blocks from downtown, a stand of white spruce crowding up against it, brushing the corrugated steel roof with long green branches. The road was paved, and there were five parking spaces in front of the building, what looked like a warehouse on one side, and a vacant lot on the other. Beyond the vacant lot was the city dock, and beyond the dock the mouth of the Nushagak River and the entrance to Bristol Bay.

Something was wrong. It took a minute for Liam, balancing uncertainly on the top step, to realize what it was. "Hey," he said. "It's not raining."

Liam was a tall man, six foot three inches, and where he stood his hair nearly brushed the eave of the building. From directly overhead he heard a loud croak, followed by a rapid clicking and another croak. He looked up and recoiled to find himself nose to beak with a raven—sleek, fat, with utterly black feathers that shone in the morning sun with an iridescent luster. He was either the same raven Liam had seen outside the bar the day before, or its twin. He was perched at the very edge of the roof, talons curled around it, peering down at Liam with a bright, intelligent, speculative gaze that knew far more about the human race than any member of a winged species had a right to.

"Wait a minute," Liam said. There had been a raven, hadn't there? The night before? He reached up and touched his wound, or wounds. The hell with it—he must have been more out of it than he'd thought. And after two cracks on the head a man was entitled to a few delusions.

That thought, too, had an uncomfortable echo.

"Well, come on," Moses bellowed, "quit lollygagging around; get your ass down here."

Liam looked from the raven to the shaman, standing in the exact center of one of the empty parking spaces in front of the post. In the distance a truck engine turned over, the generator on a boat kicked in, a small plane took off, a seagull screamed. But right here, right now, it was still and silent—no traffic on the street, no voices. Just the shaman, the raven, and Liam.

Giving the raven a wary look—that beak looked sharp—Liam descended the steps. "What's going on, Moses?"

Moses ignored him. He was dressed in a frogged jacket with a mandarin collar and pants whose hems were secured with cloth ties a little above his ankles. Jacket and pants were made of black cotton; his shoes were black canvas slip-ons with flat roped soles. His expression was serious, even solemn, and his eyes were not, so far as Liam could tell, even a little bit bloodshot.

"Get over here," Moses ordered.

Not only was Liam not a morning person, he hadn't had any coffee yet, but despite this he found himself complying, standing an arm's reach away from the old man, facing the same direction. Moses fixed him with a bright, knowing gaze that reminded Liam uncannily of the raven's. "Put your feet a shoulder width apart, toes turned out. Feel the connection of the earth to your heel, to the ball beneath your big toe, and the ball beneath your little toe." Looking up, he caught Liam gazing at him, brow furrowed, and said impatiently, "Well, come on. It's called a Modified Horse Stance. Bend your knees, get into it."

Not sure why, Liam obeyed. The old man bent over to push Liam's right toe a little in, his left toe a little out, and both knees into a deeper bend. "I want to see a plumb line from your knees to your toes. All right. Now, picture the crown of your head held up by a string. Let your whole spine hang from that string. Fix your feet to the ground, heel, toe, and toe; hang your spine from the sky. Root from below, suspend from above."

The old man walked around Liam twice, examining the trooper's stance with a critical eye. "All right, I suppose that's about as good as we can expect for the first time." Liam began to straighten up, and Moses said, "Where do you think you're going?"

Dutifully Liam sank back down, and over the next half hour Moses began to teach him the rudiments of the first two movements of what the old man finally deigned to tell him was tai chi ch'uan, an ancient Chinese physical discipline based on a form of martial arts known as soft boxing. Those first two movements were called Commencement and Ward Off Left, and consisted of shifting weight from one leg to another, the turning of the torso, and the forming and unforming of the hands and arms into a ball, all beneath the sardonic supervision of the raven, who occasionally added a click of reinforcement to one of Moses' brusque commands from the low branch of a white spruce. The spruce was, evidently, a better spot from which to oversee than the roof of the post.

The Alaska State Troopers require their officers to be physically fit, and Liam was. He could run two miles barely breaking a sweat, he could pull himself over a six-foot fence and hit the ground running, and at the end of the obstacle course he could pull out his weapon, put the barrel in the cardboard circle, and hit what he aimed at without touching the sides of the circle. He ate right most of the time, he worked out, he didn't indulge in too much of anything. Except perhaps Glenmorangie, but that wasn't overindulgence, that was the stuff of life. Even at the bottom of the pit, after Wy's farewell, Charlie's death, Jenny's coma, the debacle at Denali, his demotion, when the future looked as bleak as an Arctic landscape and hope that things would ever get better was long lost to him, he had regulated his health and his fitness. Sometimes it was all he had left to hang on to.

So, if he wasn't precisely hale and hearty, which implied a certain optimism of outlook, he was capable of vigorous exertion in the fulfillment of his duties. It was a matter of common sense, as well as pride. No cop wants to lose a footrace to a bad guy, and he or she definitely has no wish to be forced into going back to the cop shop and admitting to it.

This was a different kind of activity. This required control, focus, discipline, and the kind of dedicated concentration Liam had hitherto given only to the pursuit of criminals and the opposite sex.

And, while it didn't completely cure it, it made his headache recede somewhere to the back of his mind, turning the pain into something he could deal with or ignore, as he wished.

At the end of an hour, Moses grunted a grudging satisfaction with Liam's progress and ordered a by now profusely perspiring Liam back into the modified horse stance. "Stay," he commanded, and Liam stayed while the old man changed into jeans and flannel shirt.

"Er, you want to use the john in the office?" Liam said, thighs trembling, sweat running down his spine.

"What for?" Moses said, with what appeared to be genuine

surprise. He packed his tai chi uniform into his truck, a red Nissan long bed with a white canopy on the back, both colors nearly obscured by a thick layer of mud. He walked around Liam one more time, muttering a disapproving comment here, giving a nudge there, standing back finally with a dubious nod. "Best that can be hoped for, I guess. All right. I'm going for coffee."

He climbed into his truck and drove off.

Liam continued to stand there. Five minutes passed. Ten. His shins began to hurt. Fifteen, and his thighs began to vibrate like the wings on a mosquito. Liam could practically hear them humming. After twenty minutes the raven gave a nasty cackle and flapped off toward the river, probably for breakfast, the lucky bastard.

A truck came down the road and stopped somewhere behind Liam. A door slammed, steps approached, the heavenly smell of coffee teased his nostrils. "He's not coming back, Liam," Wy's voice said.

Liam stayed in position. "What do you mean? He said he was going for coffee."

"He didn't say he was bringing any back, did he?" she said. "I ran into him at the espresso stand in NC. He told me he'd been giving you your first tai chi lesson, and I knew what that meant." A cup, a grande by the size of it, appeared in front of his face like an apparition. "He does this to all his beginning students. Come on, come out of it. Stand up, if you can. Slowly."

Liam came up out of it, slowly, and on trembling legs tottered over to the steps, there to subside into a weak pile. He accepted the cup of coffee and sipped it gratefully, savoring the first swallow with closed eyes. "Hey," he said, opening them and smiling at Wy, "you remembered. I like a little coffee with my cream. Good coffee, too. I was worried if I'd find any here."

"Oh yeah," Wy said. "Alaska is getting to be as bad as Seattle—you can't walk a quarter of a block without bumping into an espresso stand."

Liam stared at her for a moment and said finally, "I fail to see the problem there, Wy." She laughed, and he knew a warm feeling around his heart. He could still make her laugh.

She seemed relaxed this morning, in a determined kind of way. Dressed in tennis shoes, jeans, and a green and gold University of Alaska hockey sweatshirt, her dark blond hair picking up highlights from the rising sun, she was willing to meet his eyes, if fleetingly, and was capable of casual small talk, if somewhat constrained and never anything verging on substantial. By merely existing on the planet she tempted him in a thousand different ways, but this morning she was excruciatingly careful, doing nothing overt to provoke. He followed her lead, content for the moment to tuck away the memory of their hasty coupling the night before. He would not forget it, though, and knew she wouldn't, either. The reckoning on their relationship, whatever it was and wherever it was going, had only been postponed.

His transfer had come through so hastily that he knew very little of Newenham or Bristol Bay beyond what everyone knew—fish, fish, and more fish—and he had yet to sift through whatever information Corcoran might or might not have left behind. He asked Wy for a rundown now, he admitted to himself, as much to hear the sound of her voice as to gain information on his new posting. His new home, it turned out, had a population of two thousand in the winter, five thousand in the summer, state and federal government providing most of the year-round jobs. It was the headquarters for three national parks, one state park, four game preserves, a dozen wildlife refuges, and a federal petroleum reserve that had yet to be tested. The population of the town itself ran about three-fourths white, one-fourth Native, mostly Yupik, with some Inupiaq transplants from up north, some Aleut transplants from down south, and one lone Tlingit family that got sidetracked during a move from Sitka to Nome back in the fifties, homesteaded a hundred and sixty acres twenty miles up the Icky road, and never left. "It makes for a lively time during the quarterly meetings of the local Native association," Wy said.

Newenham was the largest city in southwest Alaska, and the staging area for the biggest salmon fishing fleet in the world. "Wait till you see, Liam," she said, shaking her head. "In a couple of months you'll be able to walk across Bristol Bay without getting your feet wet, there will be so many boats on it."

He was satisfied to listen, happy just to savor her presence, but duty called, and reluctantly, he answered. "Let's get your statement down while you're here."

"All right," she said equably, and followed him inside.

She talked, he typed, once he figured out how to turn the post's computer on. There were another few blasphemous moments while he figured out how to turn the printer on, too, after which minor victory of man over machine he fed the form in, hit the print button, and had her sign the result.

"That wasn't so painful," she said, handing back his pen.

"No." He knew something that was going to be, though. He filed the form, stalling for time.

She noticed. "What's up? Is there something wrong, Liam?"

He sat back in his chair, raising a hand to smooth his hair, touching gently the lump over his left ear. "Yeah, there is. I'm sorry as hell to have to tell you this, Wy, but something happened after you left last night."

She stared at him, puzzled. "At the airport? What do you mean, something happened? Oh."

Something sure had, but it wasn't what either of them were thinking of. He watched the rich color run up beneath her skin, and images of the moments in the front seat of her truck caused his own inevitable response. He had a man dead, probably murdered, and all he could think of was the next time he'd get Wy in bed. So much for duty.

"Yes, something happened." He drained his cup and rose to his feet. His headache was only a remembered throb, easily ignored, and he knew a moment of gratitude to the Alaskan Old Fart. Might be something to this tai chi stuff. "Let's take a ride out to the airport."

The damage looked far worse in the full light of day.

The little plane's wings were shredded, long tails of stiff red fabric fluttering in the slight breeze coming off the bay. The steel tubing beneath was clearly visible. She looked all the more pitiful sitting between 68 Kilo, the faded but neat Cessna 180 on her left, and the Super Cub with the brand-new teal and green paint job on her right, which planes Liam was able to identify because their manufacturers had been thoughtful enough to stencil make and model on the side in nice black letters.

Wy was out of the Blazer before it had come to a complete stop. Liam followed more slowly. When he caught up, she was running her hands over the frame, partly in a search for further damage, and partly, he thought, in a soothing, healing motion, as unthinking as it was useless. He looked once at Wy's face, and then away again.

It was early enough that the damage had yet to attract a crowd. He was glad, for her sake.

She stood back finally, face set, hands hanging at her sides.

"I'm sorry, Wy," Liam said. "I tried to stop him."

Her head snapped around. "You caught the son of a bitch?"

"I tried," he said, and sighed, one hand going to his head. "He brained me with a crowbar and took off."

"What?" A hasty step had her peering up into his face. "Are you all right?" Her hand followed his to his head. "Liam! There's a big bump there!"

"I noticed." Gently, he removed her hand. "It's okay—he didn't hit me hard enough to break the skin, and it doesn't feel like anything's broken." His smile was crooked. "Believe it or not, I think the tai chi helped a little. It hardly hurts at all now."

Her hand dropped slowly to her side. "Good. I'm glad. I'd hate to think that you got hurt protecting—" She looked again at the Cub, and whatever she had been going to say died.

"How much to fix it?" he said.

She closed her eyes and shook her head. "Five grand, average. Maybe more, maybe as much as seventy-five hundred."

"For both?"

She almost smiled at his naïveté. "Each."

"Jesus." He took a deep breath, let it out. "So, ten thousand dollars. How long will the plane be out of commission?"

She shrugged. "The work will take a week a wing. Maybe more." She looked around as if just waking up from a bad dream, only to find the bad dream reality. "Are any of the other planes—"

"No, Wy," Liam said, sadly but firmly. "No. This wasn't random. This wasn't a bunch of vandalizing brats out to see how much havoc they could wreak in one night. I saw him sneaking around and I followed him. He headed straight for your plane. This was directed at you, and only at you. And now you're grounded for, what, a minimum of two weeks? I don't know much about it, but I know the herring fishing season is short." He raised an eyebrow.

She nodded numbly. "Days. Hours. Minutes even, sometimes."

"I thought so. Since this is the plane you spot in, the damage pretty much puts you out of the running for this herring season, doesn't it?" She nodded again. "So, who doesn't want you spotting, Wy?"

"You mean—?" He raised an inquiring eyebrow, and she said forcefully, "No, Liam. No. No way."

"No?" He gave her a long, thoughtful look. "How much herring did you help catch last year?"

"It doesn't matter," she flared. "I can't think of a pilot in the world who would do this to another pilot. Besides, if they were after me, why didn't they go after my 180, too, just to be on the safe side." She indicated the blue and white plane sitting next to the Cub, wings intact.

"Maybe because I got here before they could," he said, and added, "Doesn't have to be only the wings they went after. I'd have your mechanic check it out, stem to stern or whatever you call it on a plane, before you go up in her again."

"No," she said, but she had weakened.

"It doesn't have to be another pilot who did it, either," he said inexorably. "Could be a fisherman, and in that case he might not know about your other plane, he may only have seen you up in the Cub. He may only have her tail number. Did you spot last year from the 180? The last opener?"

She was shaking her head back and forth. "No, Liam. No way."

"Uh-huh," he said, unconvinced. He thought about it, and added, "Well then, who else have you pissed off lately?" She said nothing, staring at the Cub with a dumb misery that struck to his heart. "Wy, dammit!" He grabbed her by the shoulders and shook her once, roughly. "Don't you get it? Maybe it was only bad timing that that prop caught Bob DeCreft upside the head. Maybe it was meant to catch you."

She shivered beneath his hands, and with a slight shock he knew he had not been the first to realize this. "Wy, dammit! What have you been up to? I can't help you if you lie to me, or hold back! Tell me what's going on!"

She opened her mouth to reply, maybe even with the truth, which was why it was especially annoying when the mayor's orange Suburban raced around a corner and swooped to a screeching halt. Jim Earl stuck his head out the window. "Get in the truck, trooper—somebody's been shooting up the post office!"

"This is getting to be a habit, Jim Earl," Liam said, letting Wy go reluctantly. "The post office inside the city limits?"

"Of course! What of it?"

"So you should call the local police."

"I did, goddammit! They ain't none of them available. Roger Raymo's tracking down Bernie Brayton, who some damn fool in Eagle River let loose of before his sentence was up, and Cliff Berg's wife flat won't wake him up! Come on!"

Liam, in what he considered to be the voice of sweet reason, said, "So why don't you wake him up?"

"Because the last time I tried she met me at the door with a loaded twelve-gauge is why. Now will you goddammit get a move on!"

Liam paused, one hand on the door of the Blazer, and looked at Wy. "Can you grab a ride back to your truck?"

She nodded.

"Okay." Still, he hesitated, while Jim Earl rolled his eyes and muttered beneath his breath. "I'll see you later."

She was silent for a moment, thinking over the implied question in his words. At last she said, "All right."

"I'll call. We have phones here, don't we?"

She recovered enough to make a face. "Of course we have phones here, Liam. We've even got cable."

"Just like downtown," he said. He let go of the door and walked back to her, ignoring Jim Earl's impatient snort. "I'll catch the bastard who did this, Wy. I promise." He put a hand beneath her chin and forced her to meet his eyes. "If you'll help me."

"You're still outta uniform, trooper," the mayor said disapprovingly through his open window.

"You're right, Mr. Mayor, I am," Liam agreed cheerfully. He climbed into the Blazer. "Lead the way," he called out the window, and waved to Wy as he drove off. In the rearview mirror, he watched Wy's figure grow smaller and smaller, standing forlornly next to the tattered remnants of her Super Cub.

The post office was a one-story building out of the same mold as every other post office in the Alaskan Bush: a shallow, corrugated metal roof, a sloping ramp leading up to the front door, the Alaska and American flags flying out front (the Alaska flag flying a little higher than the American), banks and alcoves of keyed boxes with metal doors, and a small room at one end with a counter dividing it. There were six or seven people inside. One of them greeted the mayor with relief. "Jim Earl! Dammit, when do I get to mail my package!"

It was the grandmotherly type from yesterday's flight. Today her eye shadow was forest green and her lipstick cranberry red. Her brassy blond hair was piled into a beehive and she was tapping very long, very pink fingernails against a fearsomely taped cardboard box sitting on a high table opposite the counter.

"Now, Ruby, you just hold your horses," the mayor ordered. "We've had a shooting, and we need to clear that up before we open the post office for business again."

Ruby grumbled. "I thought neither snow nor sleet nor dark of night stayed the mailman from his appointed rounds."

"That oath doesn't say anything about bullets, now, does it?" Jim Earl demanded. Ruby subsided, but not graciously.

Jim Earl led Liam through a door behind the counter. The room was an office, containing a desk, two chairs for visitors, and a row of filing cabinets. There were two people already in the room. The one window looked out on the work space of the post office, and Liam peered through it with interest.

The innards of the post office consisted of one large, continuous room full of conveyor belts and gray plastic carts overflowing with piles of white envelopes. A man in a post office uniform shirt loaded a pile of green duffel bags into one of the carts. At one counter a woman sat, running envelopes from another cart through a machine that looked like it was canceling their stamps. A second woman stood at another counter behind the side of the post office boxes the public never sees, throwing mail into the boxes so rapidly that her hands were a blur. Ruby would have felt reassured if she'd seen that it indeed appeared to be business as usual, come rain, snow, sleet, or bullets.

The rear wall had garage doors, and one of them was open to reveal the maw of a freight igloo sitting on a trailer hitched to a semi, into which the man in the post office uniform shirt, now operating a forklift, hoisted a pallet with packages strapped to it. The sun shone so brightly through the gap formed between the igloo's end and the garage door that man, forklift, and pallet seemed to vanish into outer darkness once they had rumbled across the knobby steel runners laid from building to vehicle.

The most interesting thing about the window Liam was looking through was the bullet hole in it. Two of them, in fact, neat holes that had left equally neat starbursts behind in the thick glass pane. He bent to look more closely. "Thirty-caliber, I'd guess," he said, straightening.

"Well now," Jim Earl said, "you don't have to sound so awful goddamn cheerful about it, do you?"

Developing a habit where you showed up after all the shooting was done was definitely something to cheer about, in Liam's opinion, but he kept it to himself.

"This here's the postmaster," Jim Earl said, indicating the man behind the desk. "Name's Richard Gilbert." He failed to identify the woman standing off to the side.

Richard Gilbert was a thin, short man wearing a white uniform shirt, a pair of dark blue uniform pants, and thick-soled black loafers. There was a not very bloody crease across his upper left arm, and his long, narrow face was contorted with rage.

"Mr. Gilbert," Liam said. "I'm Sergeant—I'm Trooper Liam Campbell. Do you know who shot you?"

"Of course he knows who shot him, you damn fool," Jim Earl barked.

Liam looked at Jim Earl, and back at the postmaster. "Might this person have a name?"

"Of course he's got a name—everybody's got a name," Jim Earl said.

Still patient, Liam said, "And this name might be?"

"Oh," Jim Earl said. "That'd be Kelly McCormick."

The mayor looked at Liam expectantly. To the postmaster Liam said, "Mr. Gilbert, did you see Mr. McCormick shooting at you?"

"Of course he did!" Jim Earl's bark was back. "Shot at him right through that loading door there."

Liam looked at the loading door blocked by the igloo on the trailer backed up to it. The man in postal uniform was piloting another palletful of mail on board. "Was the van there at the time?"

For once, Jim Earl seemed stumped. He looked at the postmaster for reference. The woman behind Gilbert, wearing a white uniform shirt and blue pants identical to Gilbert's, was now uttering little cries of solace as she tried ineffectually to sponge the wound with a polka dot scarf that looked as if it had recently been tied around her hair. The postmaster slapped her hands away. "Knock it off, Rebecca, you're only making it worse."

"Mr. Gilbert," Liam said, producing a pad and pencil. For some reason a pad and pencil always helped to focus people's attention, and this time was no exception. Gilbert fended off Rebecca once more and she retreated obediently back into a corner. He straightened in his chair and looked at Liam through thick-rimmed, thick-lensed glasses. "Mr. Gilbert," Liam repeated, "could you please tell me exactly what happened here this morning?"

Then an odd thing occurred. Like crumpled cotton under the heat of an iron, the rage smoothed out of the postmaster's face. Gilbert stiffened his spine and folded his hands on the desk before him, and when he spoke his voice was calm and his words were measured, studied, almost pontifical. The effect was somewhat ruined by the voice itself; it was thin and high-pitched, erring occasionally to a raspy squeak. "How do you do, officer," he said formally. "This is Rebecca."

The woman, short, stubby, and dark-haired, made a sort of curtsy in Liam's direction and offered him a timid smile. "Ma'am," Liam said, and inclined his head in lieu of touching the brim of his hat, which was back in his bag at the office. He'd responded to three calls in twenty-four hours, and not one of them in uniform. He was liable to be fined for it if his boss ever found out.

"Precisely what is it that you wish to know, officer?" the postmaster said.

Equally formal, in trooper mode at least endlessly patient, Liam repeated, "Could you please tell me exactly what happened here this morning?"

The postmaster frowned at his folded hands, formed them into a steeple, and looked to the ceiling for guidance. Next to Liam the mayor shifted, and the trooper said quickly, "Jim Earl, do me a favor? Call dispatch and see if there have been any other incidents of shooting this morning? Be a good idea to see if this guy's been practicing on more than one target." Jim Earl made a move toward the phone on the desk, and Liam said even more quickly, "Mr. Gilbert, is there a phone in the other office the mayor can use while we talk in here?"

The woman in the corner positively leapt forward to be of assistance, and with reluctance Jim Earl followed her from the room, casting a doubtful look over his shoulder on his way out the door. Liam closed it firmly behind him and turned once again to the postmaster, who had lowered his gaze from the ceiling and was regarding Liam over the tips of his steepled fingers, the thick lenses of his glasses enlarging his eyes to the point that they seemed to be protruding from his head. Exactly like a goldfish in a bowl, Liam thought.

"Now then, Mr. Gilbert, please tell me exactly what happened this morning."

"Certainly, officer," Gilbert replied. "I was sitting right here, at my desk. I had—"

"What time was this?"

"Oh. A few minutes after eight—we'd just opened. I was settling down to work on some of the month-end reports when I heard shouting out in the shop." He gestured behind him. "I turned to look and I saw Greg—that's Greg on the forklift—running away. I stood up, and I saw Kelly McCormick in the open doorway of the freight bay."

"The semi with the freight igloos in it wasn't backed up there at that time?"

"Almost. You see, Greg had been backing it in, in preparation for loading it. The plane leaves—"

"So Greg must have jumped down from the cab when he saw Kelly McCormick."

Gilbert didn't look as if he was accustomed to being interrupted. "Yes."

"And he ran because—?"

The postmaster's lips thinned. "He ran because he saw that son—because Mr. McCormick was carrying a rifle."

Liam looked out into the freight bay. It faced directly east. The door of the building was larger than the back of the igloo, and the morning sun poured in through the open space and formed a blinding frame of light. "You say you saw Mr. McCormick."

"Yes. Standing in the door of the freight bay."

"And he was holding a rifle."

"Yes."

"What kind of a rifle?"

Gilbert smiled. "I'm afraid I don't know, officer; I'm not all that familiar with firearms."

I bet you're the only red-blooded Alaskan male within a thousand miles who can say that, Liam thought. "How was he dressed?"

"Who?"

"The man who shot at you. Did you see what he was wearing?"

"What does that matter?" Gilbert said, a trace of impatience in his voice. "I know who he is, I know where he lives; it's not like you have to put out an APB or anything."

"Indulge me," Liam said, and smiled his politest smile.

Something in that smile made the postmaster suddenly cautious. "Well, I don't know exactly, I was kind of busy diving for cover at the time," he said, and tried a smile of his own. "He was wearing clothes," he tried again, smiling more widely. Liam waited, the picture of polite attention, pencil poised. The postmaster cast about for inspiration. "Well, I don't know, I guess a kind of checked shirt and jeans?"

Liam made a noncommittal noise and wrote "checked shirt and jeans" on his notepad. He looked up. "Could we call—what was his name, Greg?—could we call Greg in here, please?"

"Why, I hardly think that's necessary, I've—"

Liam gave him the smile again. "If you don't mind." The smile told the postmaster that the trooper didn't care if he did, and sullenly Gilbert turned in his chair and knocked on the window. He pointed at Greg, backing the forklift out of the trailer, and made a crooking motion with his finger. One of the women trotted over to tap Greg on the shoulder, and a moment later he was in the office.

"Greg Nielsen, this is Officer . . . Officer . . ."

"State Trooper Liam Campbell," Liam said. "Mr. Nielsen, I understand you were a witness to this morning's shooting."

Greg Nielsen was a fair-haired, pink-cheeked, amiable young giant who, Liam estimated after a few minutes of conversation, was smart enough to run a forklift and no more. He agreed with the postmaster that the post office had barely begun its business day when Kelly McCormick had arrived. "Kelly and I shoot a little pool down at the Seaside," he confided, "and I could tell he was already half in the bag." He shook his head and gave an admiring smile. "That Kelly—when he goes on a tear, he don't wait for the bars to open."

"So he was on a tear?"

Greg grinned. "Looked like to me. Waving that big bastard of a gun around, and cussing to beat the band."

"Rifle or handgun?"

"Oh, handgun," Greg said without hesitation. "He had it stuffed down the pocket of his Carhartt's. I remember especially because them overalls, they were just covered in grease, looked like he'd been up all night changing out the impeller on his drifter again. I swear, that Kelly, he has more bad luck with—"

Liam very carefully did not look at Gilbert, who was sitting extremely still behind his desk and, if Liam was any judge, doing his damndest not to glare through his thick-lensed glasses at his happily oblivious employee. "Mr. Nielsen, do you know why Mr. McCormick was so upset with the post office that he had to come shoot it up?"

Mr. Nielsen became suddenly wary. His eyes slid in what he obviously thought was an inconspicuous manner to his boss, and then away. "Well, I—I don't—well, heck, officer, Kelly's just a good old boy who tends to get liquored up and go on a tear once in a while. He don't make a regular thing of it. Much." He managed a sickly smile. "And, heck, everybody's mad at the post office at one time or another. I figure our number just came up on Kelly's list."

Not a bad recovery, Liam thought with dispassionate approval. He turned to the postmaster. "Mr. Gilbert, you said you knew where—"

There was a piercing shriek from the next room, loud and anguished enough to cause all three men to start. It was followed by a shrill wailing sound. Beneath it Liam heard the muffled tones of Jim Earl trying to soothe someone.

Two pairs of footsteps approached the office door, which opened to reveal the woman who had been fluttering around the postmaster's wound sobbing into her hands. She was supported by an extremely uncomfortable mayor, who patted at her shoulder ineffectually while repeating, "There, there now, Rebecca. Come on, girl, buck up." He looked at the postmaster. "I'm sorry as hell about this, Richard. Rebecca and I got to talking about the hooraw at the airport yesterday. I thought everybody already knew."

He guided the sobbing woman into a chair and, having discharged his duty, stood back with an air of palpable relief. "I didn't know you folks were that close to poor old Bob. I wouldn't have said, if I'd known." He cast an uneasy look at Rebecca, who was bent over, her face buried in her arms. "I'm just sorry as hell," he repeated.

"That will be all, Greg," the postmaster said, rising to his feet, and Greg shot out of the room as if he'd been fired out of a cannon. To Jim Earl and Liam the postmaster said, "Would you excuse us, please?"

Jim Earl fell all over himself making for the nearest available exit. Liam hesitated.

"Kindly permit me to deal with my family in my own way, officer," the postmaster said.

"Family?" Liam said.

His lips a thin line, Richard Gilbert said, "Rebecca is my wife."

Liam looked at the woman in the chair, who was now rocking back and forth slightly, shrill wail dropped to little moans that came out of her every time she touched the back of the chair. "Of course, Mr. Gilbert," he said. He paused, one hand on the doorknob. "I'm sorry for your loss."

The door closed on the sight on its pneumatic hinge, but before it did, Liam heard Gilbert's voice. "Oh for heaven's sake, Rebecca. Stop making a spectacle of yourself."

Not as grief-stricken as his wife, and not the most loving and comforting spouse, either, Liam thought.

The door closed softly behind him, cutting Rebecca's soft keening off as if someone had thrown a switch.

SIX

Seen in sunlight, the town of Newenham rambled across twenty-five square miles of rolling hills, all of which looked alike, with one important difference: they were either on the river, or off it. The roads ranged from the two-lane gravel monstrosity that connected the town with the airport to the narrow streets of downtown that were more patch than pavement to half-lane game trails that ended abruptly at plywood and tar-paper cabins built on the bluff of the river, said bluff usually crumbling beneath them.

That morning Liam made three wrong turns, one that ended on a shaky dock built of oiled piling and worm-eaten planks jutting over the river, one that ended in a minisubdivision of six two-story houses on a perfect circle, all with identical blue vinyl siding, green asphalt shingles, and rooster weather vanes, and a third that would have taken him twenty-five miles south to the small air force base at the end of the road. Fortunately, there was a sign halfway there announcing that he was fifteen miles away from joining up. His father would have loved that.

He turned around and headed grimly back to town, throwing himself on the mercy of the first person he saw, a plump woman driving a Ford Aerostar with five children and a load of groceries in back. She was willing to help but a little distracted. Liam thanked her, drove around a corner, and was flagged down by a man waving vigorously from a parking lot. He remembered it vaguely from Jim Earl's quick and dirty drive-by the day before as the parking lot of one of the local grocery stores. The punks on the porch had vanished, with the exception of the one at present being held firmly in the grip of the man waving Liam down.

Liam muttered something beneath his breath and brought the Blazer to a stop. Through the open window he said, "Was there something I could help you with, sir?"

"There sure as hell is," the man said hotly. "I'm the manager over to NC, and this little brat's buddies know I won't let them into the store, so they been sending him in to steal for them instead." He shook the kid again. "This time by God I caught him at it, I caught him with the goods in his hand!" He brandished two packs of Camels triumphantly, and shook the kid a third time.

Liam put the Blazer into park and stepped out. "First of all, sir, it's not a good idea to be shaking the kid like that."

"If I let him go, he'll just run off," the man said indignantly.

"Let's chance it," Liam said, and with reluctance the man let the kid go.

The kid was quick, but Liam was quicker—he caught him before he'd gone two steps. "Slow down there, son, you're not going anywhere." He settled one large hand on the nape of the kid's neck and left it there. The body beneath it vibrated with tension and resentment. He wouldn't look up, presenting Liam with a view of a head of thick black hair that was shiny and clean, although it looked as if it hadn't been brushed in a week. Liam turned back to the store manager. "Now then, what's the story, Mr. . . ."

"Gunderson, Dewayne Gunderson, trooper," Gunderson said, seizing Liam's hand and pumping it up and down. "You are the trooper, aren't you?" He gave Liam's blue shirt and jeans a dubious glance.

"Yes, I'm the trooper," Liam said, compelled to add, "I just got here yesterday—I haven't unpacked my uniform yet."

Mr. Gunderson waved his hand, too taken up with his own concerns to worry about a little thing like a trooper's being out of uniform. Lucky for him he didn't work for John Barton. "Where do I sign?"

Liam blinked. "Sign what?"

"A complaint!" Gunderson said. "I want to prosecute the thieving little bastard! You don't know what monthly inventory's been like since—"

The kid had gone very still beneath Liam's hand. "Mr. Gunderson," Liam said, trying to stem the flow, without much success.

"Cigarettes, candy, double-A batteries by the twelve-pack—packages of T-bone steaks, for crissake! It's a wonder they didn't wheel in a hand truck and start hauling stuff out by the case! I oughta—"

"Mr. Gunderson!"

The tirade halted.

"Mr. Gunderson, do you have concrete evidence of anything else being stolen by this young man—what is your name, son?"

The kid didn't answer. "I'll tell you his name, it's Tim Gosuk, and we oughta ship the little bastard back to his village before he robs the whole goddamn town dry!"

The kid raised his head and said something in a guttural language that sounded less than complimentary. Gunderson reddened and raised his hand.

"That'll do, Mr. Gunderson," Liam said sternly. "Do you know who Mr. Gosuk's parents are?"

Gunderson sneered. "He doesn't have any parents. He lives with that woman pilot over to the airport."

The boy's head snapped up. "She's not just some 'woman pilot'—she owns her own air taxi," he said in a shaky but determined voice. "And she's my mother."

Something in the angle of his cheekbones gave him away to Liam: he was the boy on the street from the day before, the swaggerer with a penchant for holding up traffic. "What's your mother's name, Tim?"

"Wyanet Chouinard," the boy said, meeting his eyes defiantly.

Liam was silent for a moment, staring down into the boy's face. "Yeah," he said at last, on a long, drawn-out sigh of realization and resignation. "Of course it is."

Liam sat in the chair behind his desk, hands linked behind his head, and contemplated the boy seated opposite him.

Tim Gosuk returned the trooper's stare with an underlying

nervousness he tried hard to cloak beneath a layer of defiant bravado. "Well? Aren't you going to fingerprint me or something?"

"Or something," Liam agreed peacefully. He eyed a red mark on the boy's left cheek. "Did Mr. Gunderson hit you, Tim?"

The boy ducked his head, disdaining an answer.

Liam left the subject for now, resolving to have a word with Dewayne Gunderson at his earliest opportunity. "Tell me about yourself, Tim."

"What?" The boy stared at him, puzzled. "What do you want to know?" A look of wariness settled down over his features, and he glanced at the door. "What's going on here? I want you to call my mother."

"In a minute," Liam agreed, still peacefully. "But first we're going to get to know each other a little better."

The boy was on his feet and the defiance was back at full throttle. "I don't want to get to know you at all! I know the law—I'm underage, you have to call my mother!"

"You're right," Liam said, nodding. "I have to call your mother if you're underage. Probably your friends told you that to get you to steal for them. All over sixteen, are they? What are you, twelve? They probably told you you wouldn't pull time, you weren't old enough yet. Right?"

"You have to call my mother," the boy repeated, but his voice was now more sullen than defiant.

Liam unlinked his hands and placed them flat on the desk. His eyes bored into the boy's. "Sit down," he said.

His words were flat, unemotional, and so imbued with menace that the boy dropped back into his chair without a word. Great, Liam thought, something else I've always wanted: the ability to cow little kids into submission. "How old are you?"

The boy fiddled with the arms of his chair. "Twelve," he muttered without looking up.

"How long have you lived with Wy—with your mother?"

The boy shrugged. "I dunno. Two years, I guess."

"Where did you live before that?"

"Ualik," the boy said.

"Ualik," Liam echoed. "Where's that?"

The boy nodded vaguely. "Up the river a ways."

As soon as he could, Liam was going to have to settle down to a map of his new posting and locate all the towns and villages that came under his jurisdiction. "Who did you live with in Ualik?"

There was a short silence. The boy's face paled, and he seemed to shrink in his chair. His words barely audible, he said, "With my mom."

Liam's brows knit. "With Wy?"

The boy shook his head. "No. With my real mom."

Liam was going to ask more questions, but something about the hard line of unhappiness around the boy's mouth stayed his words. "Okay, Tim, look," he began.

The door burst open and Wyanet Chouinard came through it like a whirlwind. "Where's my kid, Liam, you son of a bitch! Where is he?"

"He's right here," Liam said mildly, at about the same time Wy spotted Tim.

Wy took one step forward and yanked the boy to his feet. "Are you all right? That damn Gunderson is telling everybody he had you arrested and put in jail! What the hell is going on?"

Tim kept his face down and didn't answer. Wy's fierce gaze transferred to Liam. "Well?"

Liam met her eyes calmly. "Mr. Gunderson down at the NC Market says he caught Tim here shoplifting. Says it's a habitual thing. Says Tim steals for his gang."

"Gang?" Wy said incredulously. "Tim doesn't belong to any gang! There aren't any gangs in Newenham, for crissake!" The other shoe dropped. "Stealing?" she said. She looked at Tim. "You were caught stealing from the store? Tim! Is it true?"

A dark red flush crept up the boy's cheek.

"Oh, Tim," Wy said, her voice breaking. "After all we've been through, after — Tim, you know what's at stake here." She caught his chin in one hand and forced him to meet her eyes. "You know better than I do," she said. "You can't put it at risk like this." Her voice almost a wail, she repeated, "You can't."

Tim blinked rapidly. In a very small, very gruff voice he said, "I'm sorry, Wy."

Wy closed her eyes and let her head touch his, lightly, briefly.

Liam waited, watching. The intensity of the connection between woman and boy was palpable. It was obvious that both of them considered Tim to be a permanent part of Wy Chouinard's life. In which case, he was now a permanent part of Liam Campbell's life as well. Liam wondered if Gunderson would accept restitution in return for dropping charges.

She let the boy go, took a deep breath, and sat down. "What did he steal?"

"A couple of packs of Camels," Liam said. "This time."

"Cigarettes?" Wy's voice went up a notch, and she turned to look at Tim. "You're smoking, too?" Tim hunched an impatient shoulder.

"Mr. Gunderson seems to think hanging, drawing, and quartering would be too good for him," Liam said.

"Oh hell, that Dewayne is a—" Wy remembered who else was listening and bit back the words. "He made you arrest Tim, is that it?"

Liam said wryly, "Wy, Alaska state troopers don't spend a lot of time apprehending people for shoplifting. Mr. Gunderson caught Tim stealing and was in the act of hauling him down to the local police station when I drove by in the trooper vehicle. He waved me down." He paused. "Mr. Gunderson says it isn't the first time Tim has stolen from his store."

Wy looked to Tim for confirmation. Tim stared steadily at his feet, dark color creeping up his neck.

"Mr. Gunderson seems to think that there is a gang of boys that gets Tim to steal for them, essentials like cigarettes and candy and batteries."

"Tim?" Wy said.

Tim raised his face, pale again but determined. "I won't rat them out. That's like the lowest. I won't."

"Besides," Liam added helpfully, "they'd beat the shit out of you if you did."

The boy flashed him a startled look.

"Is this Joey and Jerry Atooksuk?" Wy said. "Tim, I've told you to stay away from them."

"They force you in, Tim?" Liam said, man to man.

Tim's head snapped up. So did Wy's. "What do you mean,

force?" she said, bristling. "Tim, did they hurt you? Did those boys threaten you or —"

"Wy," Liam said.

She stopped, looking at him. "Mr. Gunderson got his property back, undamaged. He's mad now, and he wants to throw the book at your boy, but if we give him a while to cool off I think he'll come around. He's probably not going to want to see Tim in his store for a while. If ever," Liam added, watching the boy, and was rewarded when a brief flash of intense relief flooded the young face. "Let me talk to him. In the meantime, take Tim back to school. Or no, it's Saturday, isn't it. Home, then."

"Fine," Wy said promptly, and the grip she fastened on the boy's arm had more the look of military police than maternal concern about it. But then Wy hadn't been a mother long, Liam reflected as the door closed behind them.

It swung open again almost immediately. "Liam? Thanks. Thanks a lot. You don't know what this means; you don't know what —"

"I'm going to know, though, aren't I, Wy?" Liam said.

He threw the question down between them like a gauntlet, and left it lying there for her to pick up or not, as she chose.

Five minutes later the door opened and Gary Gruber stuck his head in. "Trooper Campbell?" He sidled inside and stood hesitantly in the still-open doorway, jaw champing at a bubble gum cud.

"Mr. Gruber, come on in." Liam waved the thin man to a chair. "Thanks for coming down."

Gary Gruber perched himself gingerly at the very edge of his seat. "You said you wanted a statement."

"Yeah, wait a minute while I get the computer fired up. Took me ten minutes to find the On button this morning. Computers. Sheesh." He grinned at Gruber. "I'm getting acclimatized to the twentieth century just in time for the twenty-first."

Gruber returned a weak smile and shifted the omnipresent pink wad from one cheek to the other. Could have been worse, Liam thought, could have been chewing tobacco. "I don't know what I can add to what I told you yesterday. It's like I said, I didn't really see much of anything."

"Tell me what you did see, then," Liam said as the screen filled with the proper form.

He'd been in his office, Gruber told him, when he heard a scream from the lobby in the front of the building. He'd rushed to see what was going on, and there was Bob DeCreft, stretched out in front of 78 Zulu.

"Not a pretty sight," Liam said sympathetically.

A slight shudder passed over Gary Gruber's thin frame, and he swallowed spasmodically. "No," he agreed, shifting his gum again.

"In fact, not much to tell you it was Bob DeCreft," Liam observed. "Tell me, how did you know it was him?"

Gruber stopped in mid-chew. "What?"

"Well, I was there, too, and there wasn't much left of his face. How did you know that the man lying on the ground in front of that Cub was Bob DeCreft?"

Gruber floundered for a moment. "Well, I—well, I just assumed it was him."

"Why?" Liam asked in an interested voice.

"Well, I—well, I—" Gruber had a flash of inspiration. "Everybody knew he was spotting for Wy. Who else could it have been? Nobody's gonna go messing around with somebody else's plane, not without their permission. Good way to get shot, out here," he added, gaining confidence. "Had to be Bob, since it wasn't Wy."

"And since it was 78 Zulu," Liam prompted.

"Well, yeah."

"So 78 Zulu is known as belonging to Wy Chouinard."

"Well, sure. She's in and out the airport all the time. Everybody knows Wy."

Liam printed out Gruber's statement; Gruber signed it and sidled out in the same vaguely furtive manner with which he had entered.

Liam rifled through the various statements he'd taken at the airport the day before. Nobody saw nobody doing nothing, he reflected sadly. At a conservative estimate, culled from Gruber's statement, at the time of Bill DeCreft's death there had been at least ten small planes in the act of landing or taking off, one DC-3 freighter off-loading a hold full of lumber, a 737 on a short final, and three small craft inbound. There were fourteen people in the terminal waiting to board the Metroliner Liam had flown in on, another thirty waiting either to pick up the inbound passengers on the Metroliner or to board the 737, and who knew how many mechanics and fuelers and wand wavers and baggage men and support personnel standing around with their fingers up their noses, not to mention whoever ran Ye Olde Gifte Shoppe.

And nobody saw nothing. He sighed.

He called the hospital. The doctor he reached there sounded impatient and irritable. "Cause of death? For Christ's sake, officer. The man walked into the rotating propeller of a small plane. What do you want, an exact description of what that does to the human head?"

Liam said no, thank you very much all the same, and set the phone down gently in its receiver. He called the bank, forgetting it was Saturday, and had to track down his quarry at home. Fortunately the banker was hooked into her database by computer. "Gosh," she said in thrilled accents, "we've never had a depositer murdered before!"

Liam thanked her and hung up, and looked at the amount he'd written down on the yellow pad. Two thousand one hundred and seventy-three dollars and sixty-eight cents. The bank held no outstanding notes in Bob DeCreft's name. There had been no recent withdrawals of any substantial size, just the usual bill payments for heat, light, gas, groceries.

He turned on his computer, called up the modem, and tapped out a sequence that got him into the Department of Motor Vehicles. Bob DeCreft had had one vehicle registered in his name, a 1981 Ford four-wheel-drive pickup. No lien holder was listed, and he'd been up to date on his tags. No emissions test necessary, since he'd lived in the Bush.

The Division of Revenue listed one airplane in Bob DeCreft's name, a Piper Super Cub the state had valued at $35,000. DeCreft was current on the personal property taxes for the

Cub, too. He'd had the usual collection of king salmon tags, duck hunting stamps, and moose hunting permits. He'd had his permanent fund dividend check direct-deposited to his bank account every October, and he'd been deemed eligible to receive the dividend every year since the first one was issued in 1981.

Liam disconnected the modem and got up from the computer. It was more than time to change into his uniform, but when he unpacked it, it was so hopelessly crumpled that it was unwearable. He rummaged around for a phone book and searched for a dry cleaner. There wasn't one listed in the entire town of Newenham.

"Well, hell." He closed the book and sat back to run his newest acquaintances through his mind. He knew firsthand Wy didn't own an iron. If you couldn't wash and wear it Wy didn't buy it. Moses seemed an unlikely candidate, about as unlikely as Bill. Maybe Jim Earl. He consulted the phone book again, and dialed the number for Newenham, City of. "An iron?" Jim Earl bellowed. "Jesus Christ, son, what in the ever-loving hell would I want with one of them things?" Liam thanked him and set the phone down in its receiver as gently as before. He looked at the uniform shirt and pants draped across the chair. He didn't even have a shower he could steam them in.

Which reminded him—he didn't have a place to live, either.

He found a copy of the *Newenham News* on the table holding up the coffeepot, not too far out of date, and turned to the real estate section. There was exactly one house for sale, none for rent, and no apartments for rent listed.

Looked like another night in the chair.

Since he couldn't yet don his uniform, and since the prospects for house-hunting looked slim, the only fallback was work.

He called up the report summaries on the computer and scrolled through the past month. As was usual in police work, the same names kept popping up over and over—a lot of Gumlickpuks, Macks, and Haines. In the past two weeks there were nineteen citations for herring fishing during a closed period, seven for fishing with unmarked gear, and one for sportfishing in a closed creek. These reports were signed by a Trooper C.

Taylor, from which Liam deduced Trooper Taylor was his opposite number on the Fish and Wildlife Protection side of the Alaska Department of Public Safety. On his side, Corcoran had charged one man with felony third-degree assault, one man with felony second-degree burglary, and one man with importation of alcohol to a local option area, otherwise known as bootlegging, always a problem in dry Bush communities. One man had been charged with third-degree criminal mischief and resisting arrest, which must have given Corcoran a thrill. There was the usual assortment of domestic violence, disorderly conduct, and DWI charges, and one of second-degree sexual abuse of a minor.

Liam had never understood the necessity of varying the degrees of sexual abuse with which an alleged suspect could be charged in assaulting a minor. Either someone old enough to know better forced sexual attention on someone too young to resist, or they didn't. The law was you didn't screw babies, and so far as Liam was concerned babies were babies until they were of legal age. He made a mental note of the perp's name for follow-up.

He ran out of reports, turned off the computer, and fetched the garbage bag holding the inventory of 78 Zulu. Clearing his desk, he began laying items out in rows.

There were the wrappings from a strawberry Pop-Tart, a Snickers bar, and a package of M&M's. A tiny wad of paper turned out to be a mangled Bazooka bubble gum wrapper, and after a moment's thought Liam identified the white square of thin cardboard as being part of the packaging of a Reese's peanut butter cup. It appeared that junk food went hand in hand with herring spotting. Liam could relate; it went hand in hand with stakeouts, too.

There were the two maps of Bristol Bay, one old and generously patched with Scotch tape, one comparatively new. There were the six Japanese glass floats, the broken walrus tusk, the survival kit, the two firestarter logs, the two parkas, the two pairs of Sorels, the Pepsi bottle full of pee, the clam shovel, the empty bucket, the three gloves, and the two handheld radios.

He didn't know much about radios. Again, he had recourse

to the phone book, and was shortly dialing an 800 number for Sparky's Pilot Shop. He was mildly surprised and pleased when instead of being shunted into phone mail someone actually picked up.

"Sparky's Pilot Shop."

"Hi, this is Officer Liam Campbell of the Alaska State Troopers, calling from Newenham, Alaska. I'd like to talk to someone about radios."

"What kind of radios?"

Liam picked up one of the radios lying in front of him and examined it. "Battery-operated handheld radios. Uh, like walkie-talkies, you know?"

"What brand?"

"One says it's a King, the other says it's an Icom."

Amused, the voice said, "One moment, please."

Neither music nor Muzak was played at him while he waited, which made Liam think even better of Sparky's Pilot Shop.

Another voice, raspy and irascible, barked, "What?"

Liam went through his spiel.

"Whaddya wanta know?"

"Ah, um, well, first of all, do you know what kind of radios are used for herring spotting?"

"Scrambled marine VHF."

"Uh-huh. And I suppose the receiving radio would have a descrambler to translate incoming messages."

"You suppose correctly. What else you want, I'm busy."

Liam remembered the radio bolted to the dash. "Are spotters' radios usually handhelds?"

"No."

"Why would a spotter be carrying handhelds?"

"Backup for main radio breakdown, why do you think?"

"I wouldn't know, that's why I'm asking," Liam said. "How much do these radios sell for?"

"Six hundred apiece minimum for the good ones. What else?"

"Uh-huh," Liam said, dutifully scribbling this down. "Is there some way you can tell if you sold these particular radios, sir?"

"Gimme the serial numbers."

Liam did so.

"Gimme your phone number."

Liam complied.

"I'll get back to you."

Click.

For the third time Liam set the receiver down in its cradle. He looked down at the yellow legal pad. Six hundred apiece. Not chump change. And probably the one bolted to the dash, being bigger and fancier, would be even more pricey.

The yellow pad was the same one he'd written the Cub's inventory down on the day before, and he flipped idly back through the pages and read over the list, comparing it with the items on the desk.

He sat suddenly upright in his chair, went to the top of the list, and ticked off the items one by one, beginning to end, comparing the list with what was spread across his desk. He did it twice, because he didn't believe his eyes the first time.

When he was done he sat back in disbelief and gathering rage. "Son of a bitch," he said. "Son of a *bitch*."

SEVEN

It was almost one o'clock, and Bill's was riding out the lull between the draft beer crowd that came in for lunch and the evening party-hearty bunch. One man was asleep, head down in a front booth. Another man held a cold bottle of Rainier to the side of his face. His eyes were closed and he seemed to be praying. Four older women played Snerts at a corner table, slapping down cards and knocking back Coors Lights with equal enthusiasm.

Bill herself was taking the break as an opportunity for a little self-enrichment. "Did you know that the Ursuline Convent in New Orleans is the oldest building in North America?" she said to Liam.

"Uh, no, I didn't," Liam said.

"Of course, once the nuns built it up and made it nice the priests moved in and booted the nuns out," Bill said.

"Of course," Liam said obediently. The air was redolent of wonderful things deep-fried, and his stomach growled. Bill cocked an eyebrow. "Cheeseburger and fries do you?" She laughed at Liam's expression. "Pull up a stool," she said hospitably. She closed her book and went into the kitchen, and fifteen minutes later Liam was attacking a heaping plate. "Like to see a man enjoying his food," Bill said, gratified. Like any good hostess, she knew enough not to bother a hungry customer with conversation, and so retreated behind her book once more.

Liam mopped up the last of the salt on the plate with his last fry and let out a long, satisfied sigh. Taking this as a signal to resume their conversation where it had left off, Bill lowered her book and said, "Not bad, huh? Bet it's a while since you had a burger that dripped that much juice down your chin."

"You'd lose that bet," Liam said, swallowing. "I had one just as good yesterday." Bill bristled, and Liam held up one hand, palm out. "From here, Bill, takeout."

Still suspicious, Bill said, "Takeout? I don't do takeout."

"You don't?" Wy had told him she'd gotten the burgers at Bill's.

"Hell no. Too much trouble, and I hate those plastic containers—they take a million years to decompose, and we've fucked up the environment enough for one lifetime as it is. 'Course," she added, "you bring your own bag, I'll wrap your order up in tinfoil." She rubbed her chin and added meditatively, "Although I've been thinking about charging a fee for the tinfoil." She fixed him with a severe look. "Tinfoil ain't cheap."

Liam remembered the greasy brown paper shopping bag Wy had produced, and breathed again. If Wy was buying burgers at Bill's, she wasn't anywhere around when Bob DeCreft walked into the prop of the Cub. He wanted Wy's alibi to be ironclad, impenetrable, intact. More than that, he didn't want to think that she'd lied to him within minutes of seeing him for the first time in over two years.

Although everybody lied, he knew that. It was the first rule any cop learned on the job. And it would have been easy enough for Wy to cut the p-lead and leave Bob DeCreft to his fate. It was what someone had done, after all. Yes, Wy had had all the opportunity in the world, and since she did most of her own mechanical work, the means as well. And motive? No. He didn't, wouldn't, couldn't believe it. He said, "Bill, do you know Wy Chouinard?"

"Of course. Pilot. Nice gal. She's Moses'—" She paused. "She's one of Moses' students."

Liam wondered what she had been going to say. "Did she order a couple of burgers yesterday?"

She eyed him. "What is this, an interrogation? Yeah, she was in, ordered two cheeseburgers, two fries, two Cokes; she brought an NC shopping bag with her. We visited some over the bar while she waited. She told me there was still a chance Fish and Game was going to declare an opener so they were going back up, and I told her all about the Mystic Crewe of Barkis." She cocked an expectant eyebrow, but he didn't bite, and she sighed. "Anyway, that New Orleans sure is one hell of a party town. Christmas, Mardi Gras, Strawberry Festival, Jazz Fest. The Neville Brothers come from New Orleans, did you know that?"

"All I know about New Orleans is that in 1814 we took a little trip."

Bill wrinkled her nose. "Johnny Horton—good God. He ain't the Neville Brothers, I'll tell you that for nothing."

"Really?"

Bill's blue eyes narrowed. "You ever hear of the Neville Brothers?"

"No," Liam admitted.

Bill muttered something uncomplimentary under her breath and marched over to the jukebox, the very set of her shoulders indicating she was on a mission from Jelly Roll Morton his own self. A coin rolled into a slot and the sweet, sad strains of "Bird on a Wire" rolled out.

"Nice," Liam commented when the song was done.

Bill rolled her eyes and heaved an impatient sigh at his lack of enthusiasm. "Nice, the man says. Nice."

Liam liked classical music, its intricate melodies and rhythms, its careful crafting, its honest passion. Jenny had called him a throwback, displacing Beethoven for the B-52's on their stereo whenever he turned his back, and Wy—he pulled himself together. He hadn't come to Bill's for a walk down memory lane or a lesson in contemporary pop rock. He'd come for lunch and for information, in that order.

Short of a parish priest, who was bound to an inconvenient confidentiality by oath, a local bartender was more privy to more information on the native population than anyone else. Liam had cultivated bartenders in other towns, and had found them to be a source that never failed, and a much quicker route to the information he needed than going through more conventional channels. Not to mention the added advantage of Bill's position as magistrate. She'd know all the repeat offenders, would be able to fill him in where Corcoran hadn't. "Bill," he said, "what can you tell me about Bob DeCreft?"

"Bob DeCreft," she said. She sighed. "Poor old Bob." She gave Liam a sharp glance. Save for the man with his head pillowed in his arms in the front booth, the man with the Rainier bottle still pressed to his face, and the dulcet tones of Aaron Neville, they were alone in the bar. "You here to pump me for information, is that it, Liam?"

Liam smiled at her. "As much as I can get," he agreed. "That, and food—that's all I want you for."

She laughed, throwing her head back and displaying a set of teeth that were just saved from being perfect by overlapping incisors that made her look faintly vampirish.

Which, now that Liam thought about it, would explain that air of eternal youth.

"Bob DeCreft," she said, meditatively. "He moved here, oh, about five, no, six years ago now, I think it was."

"Why?"

She shrugged. "Why does anyone move to Newenham? Why did you? Starting over is a time-honored Bush Alaska tradition." Liam tried not to squirm beneath the penetrating look she shot him. "You're pissed at me, aren't you?" she said suddenly. "For blabbing your story out in the bar yesterday?"

Liam said nothing, examining the glass of Coke in his hand with an air of total absorption.

She pointed her finger at him. "Best thing I could do for you. No sense in trying to make a secret of things in the Alaskan Bush, Liam."

"Five people died on my watch," he found himself saying. "Never mind they shouldn't have been driving on the Denali Highway in February in the middle of a thirty-below cold spell with no survival gear and three little kids. Never mind they should have checked the level of antifreeze in their car before not doing any such thing. Two troopers under my command ignored two calls—not one but two—alerting our post reporting those folks missing. Maybe we could have got to them in time, maybe not. Fact is, we didn't, they died, and I was in charge." He looked Bill straight in the eye, unsmiling. "I'm about as white as you can get without bleach. So were the two troopers who missed the calls. The family that died was Athabascan, from Fort Yukon. You know how hard it is to get the villagers to trust us in the first place, Bill. How much harder is it going to be for me with the villagers around here, coming in under that kind of cloud?"

"Exactly why I told your story," she replied promptly. "You think the news didn't get here before you did? The Bush telegraph is better than smoke signals or jungle drums any day. It wouldn't have been long before everybody knew it. If you'd tried to hide it, there's some would have used it against you. Best to have it all out in the open."

Liam said nothing, and Bill heaved an impatient sigh. "Give them a chance, Liam. I meant what I said yesterday—you do your job right, that's what they'll judge you on."

"Even the villagers?"

"Especially the villagers," she retorted. "The Yupik have a strong sense of family, and an even stronger sense of community. The ones that aren't head down in a bottle, which is about half of them, are firm believers in law and order; in fact, they generally try to dispense it themselves through their village councils. When the councils fail, they'll call you in. They'll do everything they can to avoid it, but when the elders can't resolve the problem, or when the offense is just too much for the village to stomach, they'll call you in. You'll be their last hope, their last resort. They want to trust you. They want to believe that you'll do right by them."

"If you say so."

"I do say so," Bill said, "but I can tell that the only way you're going to be convinced is to see for yourself. You will. Anyway," she said, jumping back to the original subject in a way that he would come to recognize was characteristic of her conversation, "I could go outside and throw a rock and be guaran-damn-teed to hit somebody who got sick of their spouse, their marriage, their job, their home, or all of the above, and subsequently got on a plane going north and got off here, ready to start over."

She refilled Liam's Coke and drew one for herself. "Had three of 'em in the bar last night. One woman was living in Denver, Colorado, walked out on her air force husband with the clothes on her back and their daughter, and wound up sliming fish on a processor off Newenham. Now she's opening an espresso stand down to the docks. Another woman walked out on an abusive husband in Scottsdale, Arizona, and a week later was dispatching for the cop shop in Newenham."

"That'd be Molly?" Liam said, remembering the pudgy little woman, her brown hair flattened by the headset, talking nonstop into the mouthpiece, dispatching emergency services to those in need all over the town. She'd looked harried, true, but not the least bit victimized.

"That'd be Molly," she confirmed. "One guy had two businesses, three Mercedes, and four ulcers in Missouri, threw in his hand and came up; now he's a cop for the Newenham P.D."

Liam hazarded a guess. "Roger Raymo?"

She shook her head. "Cliff Berg."

"Oh yeah. He's got the wife with the shotgun."

Bill laughed, tossing her head back, her full silver mane shaking behind her shoulders. She looked even more zaftig close up, Liam thought.

He felt a presence next to him, and turned to look up at the man who had been holding the cold bottle to his face. This close, you could see why. There was an angry-looking weal down the side of his face, beginning on his forehead, continuing over his left eye, and ending in a torn left earlobe. The man himself was tall, six-six, Liam estimated, with the shoulders and forearms of a lumberjack. His face was heavy and bluntfeatured beneath close-cropped white-blond hair, and his eyes were a light blue so pale they seemed almost colorless. His grin was a cross between the Joker's and Yorick's, wide and mirthless. He threw down a five. "Thanks, Bill."

"You're welcome, Kirk." Bill was civil but not friendly. "You met the new trooper? Kirk Mulder, Trooper Liam Campbell."

"How do, Trooper Campbell."

"Mr. Mulder." Liam inclined his head, every nerve on alert. At some visceral level, he was aware of being in the presence of the enemy.

The colorless gaze looked him over. "Where's your uniform?"

Liam, in an unaccustomed moment of bravado, pulled his badge. "Figure this is all I need."

"Maybe so." This is all I need, his mocking gaze seemed to say.

Liam took the war into the enemy's camp. "Nasty scratch you got there."

The rictus grin flashed again. "Nothing a cold beer can't fix."

Bill handed over change, Kirk shoved it back. "That's fine, Bill. See you next time."

Bill and Liam watched the young giant saunter out. "I swear to God, I think Wolfe's got some place he breeds 'em up special for his crews." She nodded at the change. "He could have left the five on the table, or even on the bar. But no, he has to stand there and wait for me to make change, so he can make the magnanimous gesture, so I have to thank him for it. They're all like that, that bunch."

"Which bunch?"

"Cecil Wolfe's bunch," she said.

"Cecil Wolfe of the *Sea Wolfe?*"

She sneered. "Yeah, probably the only book he's ever read in his life." She nodded at the closing door. "That's his first mate, Kirk Mulder. Arrogant little bastard."

There was nothing little about Kirk Mulder, but then Liam didn't think the reference had been to Mulder's physical size.

And he worked for Cecil Wolfe. So did Wy, Liam thought.

The scratch on his face looked like it had been left by an animal. A cat, maybe? Mulder didn't look the type to have a cat around, or the type any self-respecting cat would stay around for long. A dog? Same thing. An eagle? Eagles didn't attack humans, or not in Liam's experience.

A raven? For a moment Liam was back beneath the wing of the 206, with the rain falling on his face and a big black bird peering down at him. He shook himself. Get a grip, Campbell.

Making another of her conversational leaps, Bill got back to

Liam's question. "I figure Bob DeCreft was no different than any of the rest of us. He came looking for a life with a little more freedom in it, a little more color, a little more adventure." She cocked an eyebrow at Liam. "It can still be had in the Alaska Bush, you know."

She swept both hands up over her long fall of gray hair, and Liam couldn't help noticing how the movement thrust her very nicely shaped breasts against her shirt. She noticed him noticing and flashed a flirtatious smile with no hint of encouragement in it. "Anyway, one year Bob flew in and bought himself a little house on the bluff."

"What year, exactly? Do you remember? Were you here then?"

She grinned at him. "Honey, I been here forever, and I'll be here when you've been and gone." She knitted her brows. "Let's see now, when would that have been? Five years ago? No, six—he showed up the same year that prick Cecil Wolfe did. Bob got a job spotting herring for him that day. Pissed off a lot of the local pilots—for a while, anyway, until they knew what Cecil was like. Then they figured they'd been saved by a higher power."

The buzz on Wy's employer was not encouraging. "Did DeCreft have another job? Other than herring spotting, I mean?"

"He had about twenty of them, like everybody else in the Bush. He fished some, he hunted, might maybe even have done a little prospecting up in the Wood Mountains. He did the finish work on the bar when I remodeled it last year." Her hand stroked the polished oak surface lovingly. "He was a good craftsman. And reliable. If he gave you a bid he stuck to it, and if he said he'd show up at eight, he was here and had the hammer in his hand at eight oh-one. Unlike some people I could name," she added with bitter emphasis.

"Did he have any enemies?"

She shook her head.

"Any friends?"

She shook her head again. "Not particularly. Bob kept himself pretty much to himself."

"Was he married?"

Bill shook her head. "Nope."

"Oh." Well, hell. If Bob DeCreft had been murdered, Liam needed to know a lot more about the man than this.

"Had a live-in, though," Bill said, and in her turn enjoyed the way the rangy, well-muscled body went on alert.

"He lived with a woman?"

Bill pursed her lips. "Best you go see for yourself." She leveled a threatening forefinger. "You go easy on Laura, you hear? She's had a lot to bear in her life, one way and another, and now this. She didn't take the news well. I won't have her harassed."

Liam drew himself erect. "Alaska state troopers are not in the habit of harassing witnesses."

Bill's features relaxed into an infuriating grin. "Now, don't get on your high horse, Liam Campbell. Go on, you're liable to miss her—she's due at work at five, and it's after two o'clock now."

She tried to shoo him out of the bar then, saying she had to make ready for the serious spenders of the evening. Her shooing woke her sleeping patron. He rubbed his face with rough hands, stretched until his bones cracked, and limped to the bar for a refill. The limp identified him; this was the older man Liam had seen talking to Wy at the airport the day before. "Hi," he said as the man leaned on the bar next to him.

The man stared at him blearily. "Hi. 'Nother beer, Bill?" He waved a generous hand at Liam. "And for my friend, too."

Bill's voice was gentle but firm. "I think you've had enough for today, Darrell."

Darrell drew himself upright, wavering a little on his feet. "Sennonse. It's the evening of the shank. We're getting started just here."

"It's after two o'clock in the afternoon," Bill said dryly, "and we're getting finished just here."

Darrell said craftily, "My leg's paining me something fierce, Bill."

"I know, Darrell. Why don't you go home and take a couple of aspirin?"

Darrell's face crumpled. "Ain't got no home. Mary threw me out."

"Never knew she had that much sense," Bill said beneath her breath, and in a louder voice said, "How about the officer gives you a ride down to your boat, then?"

Darrell squinted. "Officer? Don't see no officer around here."

Bill was about to introduce them when Liam said smoothly, "My name's Liam, Darrell. I've got a truck; how about I give you a ride down to the harbor?"

Darrell leaned across the bar. "You sure about that beer, Bill?"

"I'm sure, Darrell."

Darrell heaved a sigh. "Well, okay then. Might's well go hit the bunk, I guess."

Moses Alakuyak came in as they went out, and they paused on the doorstep. "How long'd you stand post after I left?" Moses asked.

"Too goddamn long," Liam said.

Moses grunted. "Not long enough to teach you respect for your teacher, obviously."

He went inside, not slamming the door behind him exactly, but certainly closing it firmly.

A croak sounded from the top of a tree, and Liam looked up to see the enormous raven looking down at him with a knowing black eye. He croaked again. "Oh shut up," Liam said.

"What'd I say?" Darrell asked in dismay.

Darrell more or less folded up on the Blazer's front seat. Liam went around the other side and got in, to find his passenger blinking at the upright shotgun locked against the dash between the front seats. "What the hell?" Darrell asked, looking around. "I'm in a police car?"

"It's okay, Darrell," Liam said soothingly. "I'm just giving you a ride."

"Yeah, just giving me a ride to the pokey!" Darrell clawed at the door.

"No, just giving you a ride down to your boat."

"Forget it, I can get home on my own," Darrell said, but he was unable to figure out the Blazer's door handle and gave up, whimpering a little.

"Darrell," Liam said.

Darrell cringed. "Don't you hit me. Don't you hit me, I ain't done nothing wrong."

"I'm sure you haven't," Liam said soothingly. "I'm not going to hit you."

Darrell plucked up some spirit from somewhere. "Like hell. I rode with the last guy to drive this rig. He always hit. Always."

Liam met Darrell's rheumy eyes and said with all the persuasion he could muster, "I'm not him, Darrell. I don't hit." With slow, nonthreatening movements, Liam started the car. "Now, which way to the boat harbor?"

"Boat harbor?" Darrell stared around vaguely. "That way, I guess." He pointed up the street.

Liam estimated that Darrell's directions took him a good ten minutes out of their way, but he was starting to make some sense of the series of deltaic hills that held up the town of Newenham and its snakelike road system, and they did pull up at last in front of the dock that led to the ramp down into the harbor. He went around and helped Darrell out. "Which one's your boat?"

Darrell shook off Liam's hand and stood up, wavering a little. "I can get there; I don't need any help."

Liam said diplomatically, "Of course you can, Darrell. I'd sure like to see your boat, though. I hear she's a pretty little thing."

"Not so little—she's thirty-two feet," Darrell said indignantly. "I'll show you."

It was an enormous harbor, the largest Liam had ever seen, featuring row upon row of boat slips attached to row upon row of floating docks. It was full, too, jam-packed from stem to stern and fore to aft, if that was the correct terminology, with boats of every shape and size, from hundred-foot processors docked near the mouth of the two enclosing rock arms of the harbor to open skiffs clustered closest to shore. Seagulls squawked overhead, and a harbor seal surfaced and blew near the edge of the ramp, hoping for scraps.

Liam followed Darrell out onto the dock and down the ramp,

and was ready with a steadying arm when Darrell tripped, lost his balance, and nearly pitched headfirst into the harbor. A passing fisherman, toting a cardboard box loaded with spindles of green mending twine, laughed and said, "I see Jacobson spent the morning up to Bill's again."

"Looks that way," Liam agreed.

The fisherman pointed. "The *Mary J.*'s down there—the gill-netter with the pink trim line." He grinned again. "His wife made him do it."

"And then she kicked me out," Darrell said mournfully, relapsing into melancholy.

"Thanks," Liam told the fisherman, and took Darrell by one arm. Together they made their way down the wooden slips to the gillnetter with the pink trim and the matching pink letters spelling out her name in fancy script. Liam helped him up over the gunnel and onto the deck. Darrell shoved the hatch back and tumbled down the stairs into the cabin. Liam followed him and muscled him into one of the two bunks tucked into the bow. The other bunk was already taken. The lump beneath the open sleeping bag never stirred. "You okay, Darrell?"

"Sure am," Darrell muttered. "Awfully early to be going to bed, though." He raised his head and said hopefully, "You sure you don't want a beer? There's a liquor store not a mile from the harbor."

"Never touch the stuff," Liam said. "I'm allergic."

"Allergic to beer?" Darrell said incredulously. "You poor bastard."

"Yeah," Liam said. He waited for Darrell to settle down before saying in an offhand voice, "How do you know Wyanet Chouinard, Darrell?"

"Who?" Darrell said fuzzily, already half asleep.

"Wyanet Chouinard. The pilot. I saw you talking to her at the airport yesterday."

"The pilot? Oh sure, Wy." Something, some instinct of self-preservation, shook Darrell from sleep. He sat up, banging his head on the bulkhead. "Ouch. Goddammit all, anyway."

The lump in the starboard bunk stirred and grunted.

"Oh shut up, Mac," Darrell told it. He rubbed his head and

said almost tearfully, "You'd think a man would get used to sitting up careful in a bunk he'd slept in off and on for ten years, now wouldn't you?"

"You'd think," Liam agreed. "How'd you come to be at the airport yesterday, Darrell?"

Darrell rubbed his head some more and avoided Liam's eyes. "Oh, I guess I heard about all the commotion when I got into port and wandered on up. Damn, my head hurts."

"You out fishing for herring yesterday, too?"

"Well, yeah, sure, wasn't everybody?"

"How'd you do?"

"Lousy, same as everybody—there wasn't no opener. Goddamn Fish and Game, they say the roe ain't ripe. My ass. Look, I'm tired, I want to go to sleep now." Darrell flopped back on the bunk and pulled the blanket up over his head.

Liam regarded his recumbent form. "Okay, Darrell," he said after a moment. "I'll see you around."

"Sure," came Darrell's muffled voice. "See you around. And thanks for the ride."

"No problem," Liam said cheerfully. He went forward and climbed the steps to the aft cabin. Sink, stove, table, chemical toilet, and bunks were in the forward cabin; the controls were in the aft cabin, including the steering wheel, what looked to Liam's inexperienced eye like a throttle, and a bunch of unidentified knobs and levers and gauges set into a control panel. There was a marine radio bolted above the panel; the receiver locked into a hook fastened to its side, with a small black plastic handheld radio lying next to it. A fathometer and a compass were bolted to the overhead. A lot of tattered charts were rolled and tucked into a rack that was also bolted to the overhead.

"Who the hell are you?" a voice said.

Liam turned to see a young man dressed the same as Darrell watching him suspiciously from the open hatch. "Liam Campbell," he said.

"What are you doing here?"

Liam examined the young man's face. "You must be Darrell Junior."

"It's Larry; Darrell's my dad. Who are you, and what are you doing on my boat?"

"I thought this was Darrell's boat."

The young man snorted. "Yeah: his, mine, and the bank's."

"I'm Liam Campbell. Your father was up at Bill's, needed a ride home." Liam jerked his head toward the forward cabin. "He's lying down."

"Shit. Is he drunk again?"

" I wouldn't say drunk," Liam said tactfully. "He's feeling no pain. He ought to sleep it off in a couple hours or so." He stuck his hands in his pockets and cocked his head. "You fish with your dad?"

"Yeah, I fish with him. What of it?"

"You go out with him yesterday?"

The young man looked suddenly wary. "Yes."

"Fishing herring?"

"Yes."

"How'd you do?"

"Lousy, like everybody," Larry said, echoing his father's words. "There weren't no fishing, since Fish and Game couldn't make up its mind to declare an opener. Guess they want to let all the goddamn fish spawn before we can get a crack at them." Larry came the rest of the way down the steps. "Why all the questions?"

Liam figured he'd taken things about as far as he could without revealing his identity and turning this into an official interview. He shook his head and smiled. "No reason. Just making conversation. Well, gotta go. Nice meeting you, Larry." He went past him and up the steps.

"Yeah, sure," Larry said, and added, almost reluctantly, "and thanks for giving Dad the ride."

Liam gave him a cheery wave. "No problem. Anytime." He stepped from boat to slip and walked away.

It wasn't until he was fifty feet down the float that he realized he was going in the wrong direction. He paused next to a dapper white thirty-six-footer with a swooshy red trim line that looked like the detailing on a hot rod, which rejoiced in the intoxicating name of *Yukon Jack*. He looked around, getting his bearings, and excused himself to a man with a coil of new line over one shoulder and a seven-pound Danforth dangling from one hand. "Could you point me toward the gangway?"

The man jerked his chin in the opposite direction. "Don't matter, though," he said, changing the anchor from one hand to the other. "There's another gangway up ahead. Just keep on straight; you'll see it on your right."

He thanked the fisherman and found the second gangway leading to the second dock. Made sense in a harbor this big to have two docks, Liam thought, but then he had to walk all the way back to where he'd parked the Blazer.

One way or another, he'd been lost since he got off the plane.

It was after three o'clock when he pulled up in front of the deceased Bob DeCreft's log house on the bluff. He stopped the engine and got out. It was very still but for the occasional inquiring chirp of a bird and the distant rumble of fast-moving water. Liam looked up and caught the steely blue flash of a tree swallow as it swooped and dived in the aerial hunt for mosquitoes, although it seemed far too early for either and the thicket of alder, birch, spruce, and willow appeared much too dense for such acrobatic maneuvers.

He turned to survey the yard. Newenham must be the banana belt of Alaska. There was no snow or ice left, and the sun glittered off the river and through the bare limbs of the trees like a benediction. It was most definitely spring.

He climbed the front steps and knocked on the door.

At first there was no answer. He looked around at the two cars parked next to his. One was a rusted-out mint green Ford pickup, an '81 Super Cab F250 short bed with four-wheel drive. It looked like it had been rode hard and put away wet more than once, or in other words in about as good a shape as any primary vehicle was in the Alaska Bush. The second car was a study in contrasts, a bright red Chevy S10 long bed with an extended cab, also with four-wheel drive, that was so new Liam was surprised to see it had tags.

Somebody had to be home. He turned to knock again.

He sensed rather than heard the movement from behind the

door, and cocked his head. There was a sound like a muffled cry, filled with pain. He raised a fist and hit the door three times. "Alaska state troopers, open up! Now!"

There was an exclamation, male this time, a curse perhaps, and then a scraping sound, as if someone had bumped into a piece of furniture and shoved it a couple of inches across the floor. Liam was in the act of raising his fist again when the door opened.

A man stood in the center of the living room, hands on his hips, surveying Liam with irritation. "Well?" he said. His voice was hard-edged and impatient, the set of his chin arrogant and too self-assured. He looked like a man accustomed to giving orders.

Liam had never been a man who liked taking them. "I'm looking for Laura Nanalook."

"And you are?"

"State Trooper Liam Campbell, Mr.—"

"Cecil Wolfe," the man said without hesitation. He didn't hold out his hand, making it manifestly obvious he felt it unnecessary to curry favor with the police by displaying even the rudiments of good manners.

Well, well, Liam thought. The prick himself.

Wolfe surveyed him. "You don't look much like a trooper. Where's your uniform?" He grinned, a wolfish grin, hard and hungry. "Your Smokey the Bear hat?"

Liam produced his shield. He offered no explanation for his lack of uniform.

Cecil examined the shield carefully, and handed it back with a grunt that was an offense in itself. He waited, arms folded.

Liam, like all good police officers, knew the value of an expectant silence, and did not rush to fill it, instead looking over the cabin.

The logs had been Sheetrocked inside, and taped, mudded, and painted a soft eggshell white by an expert hand. The floor was linoleum, a close match in color for the walls, and probably more practical for a Bush lifestyle of skinning out game and tanning hides than a carpet. There was a brown overstuffed couch and matching love seat and a cheap oak veneer coffee table. An entertainment center featuring a twenty-five-inch television and a library of videotapes dominated one wall. A gun rack with one rifle and one shotgun on it hung from a second, and several painfully amateurish gold pan oil paintings of caches and cabins in the snow beneath the Northern Lights were mounted on a third. One door led into a kitchen, another down a hallway.

A toilet flushed and water began to run into a sink, which explained where Laura Nanalook was. It might have been his imagination, but he thought Wolfe started a little at the sound. He covered it up by saying in a too hearty tone, "Women. Always primping."

Since Liam had scored a tactical victory by not speaking first, he could now ask pleasantly, "What are you doing here, Mr. Wolfe?"

Wolfe's eyes narrowed. "Bob DeCreft was one of my spotters. I came out to offer my condolences to his next of kin." He grinned his wolfish grin again. "Such as she is."

He was daring Liam to comment. Liam said, "And how has the herring season been for you this year, Mr. Wolfe?"

"When the fish hawks let me put my nets in the water, high boat," Wolfe said, adding, inevitably, "as usual."

"Of course," Liam said agreeably. "I hear tell that is often the case for you."

"You've heard of me then," Wolfe said.

"Of course," Liam repeated, still agreeably.

Wolfe preened. He was tall and well proportioned, but his neck was too thick for his collar, his arms too long for his sleeves. His features were strong and should have been pleasing to the eye, but a too heavy brow and an even heavier jaw threw them out of proportion, leaving the viewer with the impression of raw, crude, almost bestial strength, an impression strengthened by the wolfish grin. In repose the grin relaxed into a small, pink rosebud of a mouth startlingly at odds with the rest of his face. He wore button-front Levi's, almost new but washed enough times to fit snugly to his crotch. His blue shirt perfectly matched the blue of his eyes, and his fair, straight hair was fashionably cut in a style designed to downplay the thinning on top. He was cleanly shaven, his socks and Reeboks dazzlingly white. The package was well wrapped, but the wrapping wasn't bright or shiny enough to hide what was inside.

A brute, Liam decided. Crafty rather than smart, fearless, and as devious as the day was long. Everything about Wolfe was a little too well controlled, giving the impression that there was a great deal there to be controlled, as if it might go out of control without a strong enough hand on the reins.

Liam, falling back into his habit of assessing everyone by what crime they would be most likely to commit, decided that anyone who took that grin at its face value did so at his own peril. Wolfe was a predator out only for himself, who would flatten anyone in his way and wouldn't care who he hurt or what laws he violated in the process. He would have strong appetites, for money, for power, for toys.

The water stopped running in the bathroom, and the door opened. Both men looked around.

And for sex, Liam thought. Definitely a strong appetite for sex. Especially when faced with this kind of hors d'oeuvre.

She looked vaguely familiar to him, and then he had it. It was the impatient blonde in the bar from the day before. Her impact was much stronger and more visceral at closer quarters. She had hair like spun gold and skin like a velvet rose with just a hint of the dew on it. Her eyes were a dark velvety brown and widely set on killer cheekbones, her mouth red and full-lipped, her neck a long and graceful stem that flowed into graceful shoulders. Today she wore a white T-shirt whose soft knit fabric lovingly cupped the large, round breasts beneath, and did nothing to hinder the jutting nipples that crowned them, either. The T-shirt was tucked into a pair of chinos cinched in at the impossibly small waist with a woven leather belt. The long, lithe pair of legs that were made to lock around a man's waist and stay there for the rest of his natural life was just a bonus.

Liam made a heroic effort and managed to get his tongue back into his mouth. She didn't do anything to help, standing hipshot, chin down, one thumb hooked into her belt, staring at Liam with an up-from-under look designed to smelt steel.

When the steam dissipated a little, his professional instincts kicked in, and something in him went on alert.

Laura Nanalook was trembling. It was a fine, almost imperceptible shaking that he wouldn't have noticed, and didn't at first, until she had cause to lean slightly against the arm of the couch to steady her knees. He looked back at her face with a cop's eye. Her lower lip was slightly swollen beneath its coat of red paint. Her wrists had the beginnings of bruises around them.

He turned to look at Cecil Wolfe and caught the man in the act of giving her a warning stare, filled with menacing promise. Liam noticed something else that he hadn't noticed before, too: Wolfe's shirt had been a little too hastily tucked into his jeans — one corner of the hem was caught between a button and a hole of his fly.

He looked at the room again. The cushions on the couch had been pushed to the floor, and the slipcover of the couch wedged deeply down into one crack, as if the couch had seen some recent rough and hasty use.

Liam took a smooth step forward, inserting himself between the two of them, and smiled down at her. "Excuse me, ma'am, we haven't been introduced. I'm Liam Campbell, the new state trooper assigned to Newenham."

"Trooper?" Her head whipped up and a panicky look came into her eyes. "Why are you here? What do you want? I didn't call you."

"Well," Liam said, and shuffled his feet, giving her his best aw-shucks, apologetic look. "I'm investigating the death of Bob DeCreft."

The panicked look faded, and her shoulders slumped infinitesimally. "Oh."

"You're Laura Nanalook, is that right?"

"Yes."

She volunteered nothing further. This was worse than pulling teeth. Liam produced what had never failed him before, his trusty pad and pencil. "And you lived here with Bob DeCreft."

She eyed notebook and pencil without interest. "Yes."

"Just what is the problem here, officer?" Wolfe said. Liam looked around and found himself nose to nose with the other man. "Little Laura here and I are friends. I'd hate to think you thought she was in any way responsible for the awful accident which befell poor old Bob."

Wolfe was crowding him, physically and verbally. Liam regarded him thoughtfully without moving, and without answering. Wolfe was unaccustomed to this kind of response, and his look intensified into a glare.

With superb indifference, Liam turned back to Laura. "I'm sorry for your loss, Ms. Nanalook, and I'm very sorry to have to bother you at a time like this, but in cases of this kind, I'm afraid there are questions that must be asked."

"Cases of what kind?" Wolfe said.

Liam, careful to keep his voice as neutral as was humanly possible, said, "Mr. Wolfe, just what is your interest here?"

He regretted the words as soon as they were out. Wolfe looked at the blonde, and smiled, slowly, a predatory smile full of anticipation and arrogant assurance. She didn't flinch away from that look, but Liam did. He said, "I understand Mr. DeCreft was spotting herring for you, Mr. Wolfe."

Wolfe's smile faded. "What of it?"

"Had he worked for you before?"

Wolfe's eyes narrowed. "This was the second year. Him and that flying dyke of his. And he wasn't working for me, he was working for her."

It didn't take an Alaska state trooper with ten years of investigatory experience behind him or a prior relationship with Wy to deduce that Wolfe had come on to Wy and been summarily dismissed. In spite of the situation Liam had to bite back a smug smile. Ah, testosterone, he thought, and this time the inner smile was directed more toward himself. He said, "I was given to understand that he had worked for you before."

Wolfe was surprised. "And how would you know that?"

Liam shrugged, and waited.

"Yeah, he worked for me, spotted for me, one season about six years ago. So what?"

The woman moved away, navigating a large, careful circle

around both men, and subsided into a straight-backed chair pushed against one wall. She folded her arms, hugging herself, knees pressed tightly together.

Liam turned to find Wolfe looking at him with a speculative gleam in his eye. "When was the last time you spoke to Mr. DeCreft?" Liam said.

Wolfe gave a careless shrug that was a little too studied for Liam's taste. "I don't know, probably the last time they were in the air for me."

"When was the last time you saw him?"

"I don't really know," Wolfe said, still careless. He was watching Liam from beneath lowered brows, an intent, speculative gaze. "Might have been last year when I settled up with the two of them." He added condescendingly, "You see, officer, in herring fishing you don't ever have to see your spotters. They're up in the air, telling you where the fish are. You're on the water, going after the fish where they tell you."

"How do you settle up?" Liam was curious to know how Wy had been earning her living.

"What with the quotas nowadays, the seasons never last long. Chouinard usually met me at the dock. I'd show her the fish tickets"—some hidden joke amused Wolfe for a moment— "we'd add up the tonnage, multiply it by the going rate, figure her percentage, and then I'd write her a check."

"And she'd settle with Mr. DeCreft."

"That's how it works." Wolfe looked around and found his jacket, a leather bomber jacket with a fleece-lined collar that had never seen the inside of a Flying Fortress. "I'm off. Laura? Thanks for the—visit. I'll catch you later."

He emphasized the last words. Her head snapped up and he grinned at her. Her face went white.

With difficulty Liam remembered his sworn oath, and managed to refrain from taking out that grin, and the man along with it.

The door slammed shut behind Wolfe, leaving the little cabin vibrating in his wake.

Liam crossed the floor to kneel in front of Laura Nanalook. "Ms. Nanalook. Ms. Nanalook, are you all right?"

She raised her head again and smeared away a tear with the back of one hand. "Yes, of course. I'm fine." He regarded her steadily, and she added, "I'm just upset about Bob, is all."

"Uh-huh," Liam said, and waited. When she offered nothing further, he said, "What was your relationship to Bob DeCreft?"

Pausing in the act of pushing back her hair, she gave him a look that puzzled him with its sudden suspicion. "We lived here together."

"Uh-huh," Liam said, remembering the dead man's age. He wondered what attraction an older man might have had for such a young and beautiful woman. The cabin didn't show signs of affluence, and with her extraordinary looks Laura Nanalook could have sold herself to a much higher bidder.

Cecil Wolfe, for example.

"When was the last time you saw Mr. DeCreft, Ms. Nanalook?"

"Yesterday morning," she said steadily.

"About what time?"

"Late morning, around ten or so, I guess. He was headed out to the airport. Fish and Game said there might be an opener yesterday afternoon, and he and Wy were going up to do some scouting."

"Uh-huh," Liam said, making a note of the time. "Ms. Nanalook, I'm afraid there are some questions about Mr. DeCreft's death."

"What questions? He walked into a prop," she said. Her full, beautiful mouth tightened. "He walked into a goddamn prop, the stupid bastard." Tears formed in her eyes, and the anger was gone and as quickly replaced with grief. A mercurial temperament, difficult to live with. Or at least difficult for Liam to live with.

He refrained from telling her about the p-lead. A little pompously he said, "Alaska state law requires a thorough investigation of any accidental death." He folded up his notebook and stowed it. "So Mr. Wolfe just stopped by to offer his condolences?" He ended the sentence on a faintly interrogatory note.

She stared at him, brown eyes overflowing with tears.

"Yeah," she said, "that's it. He wanted to comfort me in my loss." She started to laugh then, and it was an ugly sound, high-pitched, hysterical, uncontrolled. She must have heard how it sounded to Liam, and fought a visible battle it was painful to watch to bring herself back under control. She did it, a piece at a time. She might be volatile, but she was strong.

"I'll get you some water," Liam said, and rose to his feet before she could protest.

He went into the kitchen, a small room with an oil stove, a table with four matched chairs, and cupboards all showing signs of being lovingly crafted by hand, and ran a glass of water. There was a box of Kleenex on the counter, and he snagged a handful of them, too.

On his way back into the living room he took the opportunity to peek into the other rooms. Two small bedrooms and a bathroom. Both bedrooms sported twin beds, one each, both neatly made up. The closet in one room was lined with Blazo boxes stacked on their sides and filled with jeans, shirts, shoes, shorts, T-shirts, and socks, everything neatly folded. The closet in the second room was a riot of color and fabric and there was nothing neat about it. This room had a dresser, too, plus a mirror festooned with necklaces and a large stand hung with dozens of pairs of earrings. The dresser looked handmade, and matched the headboard of the bed and the small nightstand next to it, all three smooth as silk and gleaming with polish.

When he got back into the living room, Laura Nanalook had her head back against the wall. Her eyes were closed.

"Here," Liam said.

She opened her eyes and blinked up at him. In her grief and confusion, she looked about ten years old. So long as he kept his eyes above her chin.

He held out the glass. "Some water for you," he said.

"Oh," she said, looking bewildered as he pressed the glass into her hand, but she drank obediently.

He took the glass back and set it down on an end table. On the table was a homemade picture frame made of light oak, as carefully crafted and polished as the furniture in the kitchen and the second bedroom. It held a picture of Laura Nanalook and an older man Liam realized must be Bob DeCreft. He picked it up.

Bob DeCreft was tall and broad-shouldered, with thick blond hair that had resisted aging along with the rest of him. His eyes were narrowed against the sun, so that Liam couldn't see what color they were. He had crow's-feet but no laugh lines, a broad brow, a firm-lipped mouth, a strong chin. His smile was tentative, and he had an arm around Laura's shoulders, resting somehow gingerly on them, as if he couldn't quite believe his luck. Between them Liam could see over the bank of the river and down into the river itself. Laura had her arms folded across her chest, standing hipshot, chin up, staring straight into the camera with an I-dare-you look in her eyes.

DeCreft reminded Liam of someone, but he couldn't remember who, so he put the picture down. He knew it would do no good, but he couldn't stop himself from saying, "You could press charges against Wolfe, Ms. Nanalook." He held out the Kleenex.

She blew her nose ferociously. "I've got to get to work—it's after four o'clock. Bill'll skin me if I'm late."

"You could press charges," he repeated. "I'm a witness, at least after the fact."

"He'd kill me," she whispered.

"No he wouldn't." Liam's voice rose slightly, as if volume alone could banish her demons. "I wouldn't let him."

"You don't know him," she said. "You couldn't stop him."

"I can take you to the hospital, where you can be examined, pictures taken, evidence gathered. And then I will arrest him. He won't be able to hurt you again."

She shook her head, slowly at first and then faster, her hair tumbling wildly around her face. He didn't make the mistake of offering any gesture of physical sympathy; he had interviewed rape victims before. "You don't know him," she repeated.

"By God," Liam said, realization breaking over him. "This isn't the first time, is it?"

"You don't know him," she said for the third time. She looked exhausted. "He'd kill me."

Liam tried his only remaining shot. "Ms. Nanalook, you know if you don't press charges against him, he'll come back."

A shudder ran over her. She wouldn't look up, glorious golden hair still hiding her face.

"I know." She squeezed the Kleenex into a tight little ball. "They always do."

Liam left the house in a simmering rage and slammed the door to the Blazer hard. It didn't relieve his feelings, and it didn't do the Blazer door any good.

Sighing, he started the engine and shifted into reverse. A white station wagon came barreling down the game trail that passed for a driveway to DeCreft's cabin and nearly rear-ended him. He stamped on the brakes, slapping his head into the headrest on the rebound.

The station wagon went around him, clipping a slender birch in the process, and slid to a halt in front of the cabin. Without wasting a glance on the Blazer, Rebecca Gilbert shot out of the driver's seat and ran through the front door of the house without knocking.

Liam stared at the house for a moment, but it didn't yield up any secrets. He sighed. So what else was new. He was a stranger in a strange land.

The white station wagon, a little Ford Escort, was idling in park. Liam got out to turn off the ignition and close the driver's side door, and then he went on his way.

EIGHT

The phone was ringing as he walked into the office. "About goddamn time," a voice barked at him.

Liam sat down. "Hello, John."

"Where the hell have you been? I've been calling all day. Don't you have someone to answer the friggin' phone down there?"

"Not in the office," Liam said. "I guess the dispatcher takes all the calls."

"Goddammit," Barton said, "how the hell am I supposed to practice goddamn law and order if I can't even talk to my goddamn officers?"

It was a rhetorical question, and Liam didn't bother trying to answer.

Barton went on. Barton always went on. "What's this I hear about you stepping off the plane into the middle of a murder?"

Liam sighed, leaned back to prop his feet on the desk, and rubbed his eyes. "Don't tell me, let me guess. Corcoran."

"Hell yes, Corcoran," Barton said, adding with awful sarcasm, "and a good thing, too, since my own officer on the scene can't be bothered to phone in a report."

"Lay off, John," Liam said. "I haven't been here two days, I got no handover from Corcoran, I don't know the territory or the locals, and already I've responded to two shootings and a possible murder. Not to mention which I don't have a place to sleep and I can't find anyone to press my uniform."

Barton was outraged. "You're out of *uniform*?"

Liam had to laugh, but under his breath and out of John Barton's hearing.

Lieutenant John Dillinger Barton was a twenty-five-year veteran of the Alaska State Troopers. An air force brat like Liam, his family had moved all over the world during his childhood, ending eventually at Elmendorf Air Force Base in Anchorage in 1957, when his father, under pressure from his mother, retired to sell and service Xerox copy machines. He attended Seattle University with the goal of joining the Jesuit brotherhood, elected a philosophy class in which a Washington state trooper came to lecture on the ethics of criminal justice, and on that day gave up the priesthood forever. Upon graduation he returned home to be promptly accepted into that year's trooper academy class. They'd done away with the height requirement by then, which was a good thing since he topped out at five feet four. Barton was gorillian of build, all of it muscle, and Churchillian of jaw, all of it stubborn, but for all that amazingly good at not trampling over the authority of village elders. He rose high and fast in the department.

He was now the outpost supervisor for Section E, which included Liam's previous post of Glenallen as well as his new one, Newenham. He was Liam's boss, and had been for seven years. He had spotted Liam's potential early on, had mentored his swift rise through the ranks, and had marked Liam as someone who would always make him look good. It was tacitly understood by both men that this would always be in a subordinate capacity, and if Liam had his own ideas about that he was smart enough to keep them to himself.

Barton had also orchestrated Liam's recent and rapid fall from grace, and his transfer to Newenham.

"So what have you been doing?" Barton said, voice rich with sarcasm.

Liam thought. "Well," he said, "I had my first tai chi lesson." He had to hold the phone away from his ear when Barton, predictably, erupted again. Liam waited patiently, smiling to himself. When he thought about it later, he was amazed that he still remembered how.

When he got a chance, he told Barton of the scene he had stepped into at the airport.

At the end of it Barton grunted. "Ninety people milling around and nobody sees a thing. Bullshit. What about the pilot?"

"Out getting lunch."

"Check the alibi?"

"Yes."

"Well, shit." Barton always preferred the easy answers, and on every case but this one so did Liam. "Who didn't like him?"

"No one, apparently, but then no one seemed to know him all that well. No wants or warrants, no record of him having been tanked for anything so much as a parking ticket. Good reputation with the local magistrate."

John interrupted him. "That Bill Billington?"

"Yeah. Why?"

"No reason." But Barton chuckled, a full, rich, knowledgeable sound.

Uh-huh, Liam thought, and said, "I called the bank, he had two thousand and change in a checking account, no big withdrawals recently. No mortgage on his house; I guess he paid cash. He owned a pickup and a Super Cub, both free and clear, too."

"I'll run a check on him from here, see if we come up with anything."

"Thanks."

Barton cleared his throat, and when he spoke again his voice was gruffer. "Thought you'd like to know. The wife and I visited with Jenny this weekend. Her folks were there, and they said to say hi when I talked to you."

"Tell them I'll call when I get a phone, and I'll be up when I can," Liam said, and couldn't stop himself from adding, "Any change?"

"No, Liam," Barton said steadily. "She's just sleeping, like she always does. Curled up on her side like a baby in a crib." Liam heard the creak of a chair shifting. "How are you and Wy getting along?"

Liam took the phone away from his ear again, this time to

stare at it incredulously. It refused to yield up any secrets on its own, and he put it back to his ear cautiously. "What did you say?"

Barton was impatient. "I said, Campbell, how are things between you and the girlfriend?"

Liam said slowly, "You knew about Wy and me?"

"Jesus Christ, Liam, this is the goddamn Alaskan Bush. Everybody knew about it."

"You son of a bitch," Liam said, perhaps not the most felicitous manner in which to address one's boss. "You knew she was here?"

"Yes, I did, you bullheaded bastard," Barton bellowed, "and, yes, I posted you to Newenham because of it!"

Liam was speechless.

Barton waited for a moment before continuing in a calmer voice. "Face it, Liam. You were one big, walking, talking open wound. Goddammit, we could practically track you by the fresh blood you left behind. Somebody had to do something."

"You could have told me" was all Liam could find to say. "You could have let me decide for myself what I wanted."

"Yeah, we could have," Barton said evenly, "if we wanted to wait another five years for you to make up your friggin' mind. I wasn't in the mood." Barton sighed. "Look, friend. You're in about the worst possible place there is for a man to be. You lost your son. I don't want to even think about what that could do to someone. You got a wife in a coma, with no hope of recovery." Barton was good with blunt. "It might take her years, but she's dying. You know it, I know it, her parents know it. We all know it. You looked like crawling in next to her and going with. I wasn't going to let that happen if I could help it. So I put you in the only place I could think of where there was someone who might do you some good."

"Did you think the demotion was going to help, too?"

"Aw shit," Barton said. "Answer me this, Liam. When you fuck up, who do you think gets it up the ass?"

"I didn't fuck up," Liam said distinctly.

"No, you didn't, but the people who worked for you did, and you weren't watching them."

Liam said nothing, and John Dillinger Barton got uncharac-
teristically defensive. "Don't talk to me about personal problems. You got them up the wazoo, agreed, in spades. But a cop
can't turn his job on and off like a switch. You knew that coming in. We all know it coming in." The chair creaked again. Barton was a fidgeter, constantly in motion—shifting in his chair,
shuffling the papers on his desk, doodling with his pencil, wax-
ing Machiavellian with his brain. "You done your box thing yet
on this DeCreft murder?"

"I don't know that it is murder."

"You said the wire was cut."

"It was."

"Think that happened accidentally?"

"Maybe. Maybe somebody was reaching under there trying
to cut something else."

"Yes," Barton said, "that's what I figure a pilot good enough
to spot herring is gonna do, go poking around underneath the
control panel of a plane he's gonna be flying in with a sharp pair
of nippers. Or letting some yo-yo mechanic do the same thing.
Uh-huh. Gotta hand it to you, Campbell, you got that situation
piped." He added, as an afterthought, "Who is the pilot, anyway?"

Liam was silent.

"No," Barton said. "Shit, no."

Liam sighed. "Yeah, John. It's Wy."

"Aw fuck," Barton said heavily. "Goddammit anyway." He
was silent for a moment. "She a suspect?"

"No," Liam said immediately.

Barton was silent again, his silence more eloquent than most
people's conversation. "Okay, you're there, I'm not. But I'm
running a report on her anyway; I'll get back to you. In the
meantime, you do the box thing, you hear?"

"All right, all right, I'll do the box thing," Liam said irritably,
but a smile tugged at the corners of his mouth.

"Good." Barton hung up.

The "box thing" was something Liam did early on in every
investigation in which he participated. Sometimes, redrawn
and relettered and blown up, it found its way into court as

Prosecution Exhibit A. It had been a while, but he thought he still remembered how. He took a deep breath and got a clean sheet of paper out of the printer. By fortune good or ill, in the middle drawer of the desk he found the writing implement of his choice, a Pentel Quicker Clicker, with spare leads and erasers. No hope for procrastination there, either, so he began.

The first square was drawn in the center of the page and labeled Bob DeCreft. He looked at it for a while, ruminating. A second square was added, with a dotted line connecting it to the first, and labeled Wyanet Chouinard. A third square connected to them both, labeled Cecil Wolfe.

A fourth square, Laura Nanalook. Another line connected Laura Nanalook with Cecil Wolfe.

He thought about that for a while, and to Laura's square added a lightly drawn fifth square, labeled Rebecca Gilbert, with a question mark after her name.

There. He sat back and surveyed the neat boxes and their straight little connecting lines, what he knew of Bob DeCreft's life reduced to connect-the-dots.

Bob DeCreft, sixty-five years old, a member in good standing of the community, according to Bill. A sixty-five-year-old man shacking up with a, what, twenty-year-old girl, a staggeringly beautiful twenty-year-old girl. Sex and money, those were the two main motivations for murder in Liam's experience, and one look around Bob DeCreft's house had told him DeCreft didn't live large.

Take sex, then. Maybe Laura Nanalook wanted out of the relationship with DeCreft and sabotaged the plane herself. She had said she'd been working when DeCreft was killed. He'd have to confirm that with Bill.

Maybe she had a lover, and he cut the wire.

Maybe someone else wanted the girl, and so killed DeCreft to get him out of the way? Somebody, say, like Wolfe?

Liam contemplated that possibility with satisfaction, and traced the line around Wolfe's box until it stood out in bold relief from the others. It was not going to hurt his feelings at all if he had to arrest Cecil Wolfe for murder. He only hoped Wolfe would resist arrest.

Although, much as he hated to admit it, it was more Wolfe's style to rape Laura Nanalook occasionally behind Bob DeCreft's back, so he could enjoy that knowledge when he met Bob DeCreft face-to-face. He would need DeCreft alive to do that, and to spot herring for him.

He needed to find out who Wy's mechanic was. If she was doing her own A&Ps, she still had to have a certified mechanic to sign off on them. Probably somebody local, because Wy was a smart woman who'd know it would pay to keep her business local.

One thing was certain: the killer had to be someone who knew something about aviation. Not much, Liam realized ruefully, because if Wy could explain magnetos to him and make him understand how they functioned in five minutes, anyone could.

Knowing how a thing worked gave you the power to make it not work. A little knowledge is a dangerous thing.

And then there was Rebecca Gilbert. Liam had seen her twice now, once at the post office this morning and once this afternoon. In all, he'd seen about three different women inside the same body: the hovering helpmate, the hysterical mourner, and—what? What had she been doing, roaring up to DeCreft's place that way, slamming inside without so much as a knock at the door? If she and her husband—who had seemed less than distraught at the news of DeCreft's death—if she and her husband had been friends of Bob DeCreft, then they might have been friends of Laura Nanalook as well. Or maybe the two women were friends. They weren't much of an age, but then it wasn't all that big a town, and there probably wasn't that much choice. Although, given the disparity in age between Nanalook and DeCreft, the couple must have come in for some disapproval on the part of the community. Not to mention jealousy. The entire below-thirty male population of Newenham had probably gone into mourning when Laura and Bob took up housekeeping, and for all Liam knew Bob DeCreft was the over-sixty female's dream man.

If he could get Rebecca Gilbert away from her husband for five minutes, he might learn something of interest.

He reached up to touch the lump beneath his hair, shrunken and less tender now. He looked back at the box marked Cecil Wolfe and thought of Kirk Mulder, Wolfe's first mate, then traced the dotted line back to Wy. He added another box and labeled it Jacobson, the gimpy fisherman Liam had seen at the airport talking to Wy, the same gimpy drunk he had hauled down to his boat, as lightly penciled as Rebecca Gilbert's square and with another question mark beside it.

He thought back to his conversation with Barton, to Barton's visit with his wife. Jenny, laughing, loving Jenny of the light brown hair, in the poet's words that had become a family joke. Jenny, who loved the Beatles and the Beach Boys and the Boston Bruins, who never read a book that wasn't assigned in class, who was the first person in Glenallen to buy a VCR so she could tape *All My Children* every day, and who talked back to the television while she was watching as if the characters were in the room with her. He'd bought her season tickets to the University of Alaska Anchorage Sea Wolves hockey games, and she had responded with such fervent gratitude that he'd had a hint, that first winter they were together, of what they'd been missing. Jenny, whom he knew too late had always been more like a sister to him than a wife.

"I didn't know, Jenny," he said out loud, for the thousandth time. "I didn't know that what we had wasn't the best that there was. We settled, you and I. I didn't know, until Wy, what was possible." He waited stoically for the wave of sorrow and guilt to pull him under. It came, as it always did, swamping him with grief and remorse. His hands curled into fists and he shut his eyes against the familiar tears. "Goddammit!" he yelled. "God-damn you for leaving me like this, so I can't even ask for your forgiveness!"

As always, thoughts of Jenny brought thoughts of Charlie, too, and again he held his son in his arms. He remembered best reading him to sleep, those evenings when he made it off duty early enough to catch Charlie still awake. He read to him, *Good Night, Gorilla* and *Paper Bag Princess* and *The Velveteen Rabbit* and *The Wind in the Willows*, and every now and then from *Bushcop* by Joe Rychetnik, just so the kid would know the kind of business his father was in. He knew Charlie couldn't understand the words yet, but he wanted him to grow up hearing them anyway.

Charlie would fall asleep in his arms, lulled by the sound of his father's deep voice, in the process his body temperature seeming to rise ten degrees and his body weight to increase ten pounds. Liam would put him to bed and hang over the edge of the crib, watching his little chest rise and fall. For the first few months he'd been terrified at how quietly Charlie slept, and had on more than one occasion gone into the boy's room in the middle of the night, just to make sure his small miracle was still breathing.

With a jerk that brought him up out of his chair, Liam came back into himself again and battled for control. Bit by bit, it did come back, leaving him drained and spent.

He checked his watch. Seven o'clock. The sun was streaming in the window, long glissading columns of incandescent light. Somewhere nearby was the one person who could offer him comfort, and maybe even make him dinner. He went out to look for her, leaving his memories littered on the floor of the post.

He stopped by Bill's for directions, if she could be persuaded to give them, and found Moses perched on what Liam was coming to consider his usual stool. The shaman greeted the trooper with his usual respectful welcome, "Ah yes, here comes the man without a clue!" He drained his beer, wiped his mouth on the sleeve of his shirt, and added, "Root from below, suspend from above. It won't give you everything, but it'll give you something." He fixed Liam with a piercing if somewhat bleary eye. "Let her go. She's on her own journey; you're only slowing her down by hanging on to her with your grief and your guilt."

With ponderous dignity he descended to the floor and made for the men's room. He didn't miss a step when he flipped off Cecil Wolfe, who was presiding over a boothful of boisterous young men. Cecil threw back his head and roared with laughter, which sound brought Moses to an instant halt.

Moses looked straight at Cecil Wolfe, his voice clear, his

words sober and distinct and audible to everyone within earshot. "You will pay," Moses said.

Cecil was startled for a moment, but only for a moment. He laughed again, slapping Kirk Mulder on the back. "Of course I'll pay—I always pay for my crew, that's why they stick with me!"

Mulder laughed with him, and the rest of the men in the booth joined in, a hearty, forced sound. They couldn't keep it up forever, and Moses waited patiently. When the conditions were right, he spoke again. His voice was dispassionate, matter-of-fact. He wasn't making a threat or sounding an alarm. He was simply reporting the truth, without bias, without prejudice, really without much feeling of any kind. "Wolfe, you're an asshole and don't deserve warning. Nevertheless, it is true. You will pay."

Wolfe's expression indicated that few people called him an asshole to his face and got away with it. Liam made as if to step forward.

"No," Bill said, putting out a restraining hand. "Moses will handle it. He always does."

Wolfe eyed Moses for a fulminating moment. Moses stared back, unblinking, unafraid. Everyone waited.

Wolfe broke the silence with another of his bellowing laughs. "Ah hell, Moses, you're too little to slug and too drunk to know what you're saying. Come on, boys, I'll buy us another round. And," he added with a broad wink at Moses, "just so you don't break your streak as a soothsayer, Moses, I will pay. Barkeep! Another round for the table! Hell, another round for the house!"

"See?" Bill said. She turned to ring the brass ship's bell fixed to the wall, and the resulting clang brought whoops of joy from every corner.

"Yes, but he didn't handle it, Wolfe did," Liam said.

Bill smiled. "Did he?" She began setting up glasses and uncapping bottles.

Laura Nanalook came up to the bar carrying a tray loaded with empty bottles and glasses. She looked up and caught Liam's eye. "Oh." A flush swept up over her face. "Hello."

Bill filled another glass, topped it off with an onion, and nodded toward Wolfe's table. "Serve Cecil's table first—he's buying."

If Liam hadn't been watching so closely, he would have missed the expression of revulsion that swept fleetingly over Laura's angel face. It was as rapidly gone, and she loaded her tray with professional efficiency and took it to the booth. Wolfe, sitting on the outside, laid a hand on her hip. It was a brief gesture, but it was heavily suggestive of both knowledge and possession, and it was not lost on the other men sitting with him. Laura Nanalook was private property, off-limits to the rabble. The rabble saw, and understood. They'd wait. They'd been thrown scraps before after Wolfe had taken the edge off his appetite.

Gary Gruber sat at one end of the bar, a besotted look on his face as his eyes followed Laura Nanalook about her business. She moved through the crowd with grace and efficiency, dispensing drinks from her tray with a wide, mirthless smile flashing on and off as if controlled by a switch. Gary Gruber wasn't the only one; Moccasin Man and the Hell's Angel were watching her from a corner booth. Liam wondered where the Flirt was, and as if in answer to his thought, she came in the door, dressed now in cutoffs and a T-shirt cut up to there. She spotted Moccasin Man, noted who he was watching, slid into his lap, wrapped an arm around his neck, and kissed him, long and hard. Moccasin Man lost interest in Laura Nanalook, especially when the Flirt wriggled around in his lap like a cat making a place to curl up for the duration.

The Hell's Angel watched laconically, until another man stopped by the booth. They spoke briefly, and something changed hands, followed by something else. The Hell's Angel gave a casual look around the room. His eyes met Liam's. Even more casually he turned back to the table and said something to Moccasin Man, whose hands stopped moving. The Flirt pouted in protest. Moccasin Man held her still, and with an elaborate show of nonchalance looked around the bar, eyes coming to rest finally on Liam's face. Liam didn't move. A hand slid up to cup one of the Flirt's full breasts, and the Flirt gave a voluptuous wriggle and pressed against him for just a moment before moving the hand back down to her waist with a playful slap and a promising glance from beneath her lashes. Over her head

Moccasin Man smiled at Liam, revealing a mouthful of small white pointed teeth.

Liam didn't smile back.

"I don't know why Tiffany bothers owning a house with a bedroom in it," Bill said disapprovingly at Liam's elbow. "What'll it be, whiskey or beer?"

"Tiffany?" Liam said. "That's the Flirt's name, Tiffany?"

"The what?"

"The woman sitting in Moccasin Man's lap."

"Who?"

He jerked his head in the direction of the booth.

"Oh, you mean Evan. Yeah, that's Tiffany Saunders. How do you know her?"

"We flew in on the same plane, along with Moccasin Man and the Hell's Angel."

"Hell's—oh. Oscar. Right." A slow smile spread across Bill's face. "I guess he does look sort of like a Hell's Angel."

Laura returned to the bar, reloaded her tray with a wooden expression, and departed again.

"Never mind her for now—you can't help someone who won't accept it," Moses said at his elbow, causing Liam to start. "Bill! I need another beer! What!"

This to a young man and woman standing a few feet away. The young man looked a little disdainful, the young woman painfully respectful. Both were Yupik in appearance: short, stocky, golden of skin, raven of hair, brown eyes tilted upward in the fashion of their Asian ancestors. "Uncle," she said, bowing her head.

She nudged the young man. "Uncle," he repeated. He didn't bow his head.

"What?" Moses said, climbing back on his stool.

The young woman screwed up her courage. "We will marry next week. We want your blessing."

"No you don't," Moses snapped, and gulped at the beer Bill brought him. "You want to know if you'll live happily ever after. You shoulda asked me that before you went and popped the question, now shouldn't you, Amelia?" He drained his glass and fixed her with a steely stare. He spoke two words, and two words only, in what Liam assumed was Yupik.

The young woman's face turned dead white and her body swayed as if receiving a blow.

Moses turned his back on them. The young man muttered something beneath his breath, grabbed her arm, and hustled her out of the bar.

Liam watched the door shut behind them, and turned to Moses. "What did you say to her?"

Moses was staring at his hands. They were powerful hands: brown, seamed, with large knuckles and thick, well-kept fingernails. "I told her his father's name," he said, and the sorrow and foreboding in his voice stopped Liam in his tracks.

Confused, Liam said, "She didn't know it before?"

"Oh yeah, she knew it," Moses said glumly. "She just didn't *know* it."

Bill came down the bar. "You okay?"

Moses dredged up a smile. "I will be." The smile turned lecherous. "I know I will be later."

She allowed herself to be sidetracked, and leaned across the bar for a kiss. Again, Liam was awed and a little embarrassed by the display of passion, the obvious appetite, the frank lust.

Moses pulled back and saw the look on Liam's face. "What, you think people over sixty can't have sex or what? Just because you ain't been getting any lately don't mean it's over for the rest of us! Now get the hell out of here! She's waiting on you, God knows why."

"Who is?"

"Who is—don't get cute with me, you dumb bastard, I'm your sifu. Her house is out on the bluff. Go south on Main, turn left on the river road, go three miles, and turn right just after the pavement ends." Moses turned away, and then turned back. "And if you have the strength of will to haul your sorry ass out of a bed with Wy Chouinard in it, stand post for at least twenty minutes tonight." He leveled a finger at Liam, the same finger he had leveled at Wolfe. "You don't use it, you lose it."

The glint in his eye told Liam that Moses wasn't referring solely to tai chi.

NINE

The Blazer was the property of the state and as such should only have been driven on official business, but since Liam didn't have a car yet, along with an apartment or an iron, he decided to risk the wrath of observant citizens and drive it anyway.

Like DeCreft's, Wy's house was on the river bluff. The road in was, again, almost but not quite lost in a tangle of brush and trees. When he had bumped his way to the end of it, he found a surprisingly neat clapboard cottage painted white, with a detached garage and shop, also painted white. Both buildings were old but well kept.

Wy's truck was in the garage. Good. There was a battered white Isuzu pickup parked behind it. Wy had visitors. Not so good. He climbed the steps to the door and raised his hand to knock. The door opened before he could.

"Liam!" Wy said brightly.

There were two people standing behind her in the act of shrugging into their jackets. A tall man with white hair, and a stocky woman with intent green eyes. He recognized them at once from the plane: the other Alaskan Old Fart, with Daughter.

"I don't think you've met Dan and Jo, have you?" Wy said, still in the bright, artificial voice. "Daniel Dunaway, Joan Dunaway, this is Liam Campbell. Liam, this is Daniel and his daughter, Jo. Dan is a friend of my parents. Jo and I went to high school and college together."

"How do you do?" Liam said, holding out his hand.

After a moment of hesitation, Daniel Dunaway took it. His grip was dry, callused, and hard. When Liam turned to Jo, she had her arms folded across her chest and was staring at him out of narrowed eyes. Liam thought better of holding out his hand to her.

Daniel settled one big hand on Wy's shoulder. "It was great seeing you, girl. I'll call your folks when we get back, let them know you're all right."

"Thanks, Dan."

Jo broke off staring at Liam long enough to give Wy a fierce hug. "Anything you need, you call, you hear? And I'm coming out over Labor Day for a week or ten days, okay?"

"Okay."

Daniel Dunaway put one large hand on Wy's shoulder and bent a forbidding stare on Liam. "Wy's one of the family."

"Yes, sir," Liam said.

"She's like blood to us. To me."

"Yes, sir."

The older man gave a curt nod. "So long as you know."

His daughter was a hair less subtle. As she brushed by him on her way out, she said in a low voice, "You hurt her again and you're toast, asshole."

"Yes, ma'am," Liam said. It seemed the most politic response.

The Dunaways climbed into the rental, waved good-bye, and were off.

"Friends of yours?" Liam said neutrally.

"The best," Wy agreed. "Come on in."

"What do they do?" Liam said, following her inside.

"Daniel's retired, sort of. Used to be a heavy-duty mechanic; he's got an IBEW pension. Nowadays he amuses himself with hunting, fishing, and some wheeling and dealing around the Bay. He's got a piece of property out at the airport—he's trying to sell it to one of the local fishermen."

"And his daughter?"

"Jo's a reporter for the *Daily News*. She just came along for the ride, and for the chance to visit with me."

Liam got his first good look at her, and blinked. Wy was wearing an apron. At least he thought that was what it was—

he'd never seen her wearing one before. If he wasn't mistaken, there was lace around the hem.

"I'm just cooking dinner. Would you like some? I tried to get Dan and Jo to stay but they had to catch a plane."

He opened his mouth and his stomach growled, loud enough to be heard over the strains of Constance Demby floating in from elsewhere in the house. Constance Demby was one of his favorite composers, and he had given a CD of hers to Wy. If he wasn't mistaken, the particular cut playing just now was "Oceans Without Shores."

"Well," Wy said, bright and chipper, "I guess you're hungry." She gave a hostessy little laugh that sounded so unlike her he almost asked what was wrong.

Instead, he followed her through to the kitchen. It was a large room that took up the whole south side of the house. The south-facing wall was almost all window. A door opened out onto a large deck that faced the mouth of the Nushagak River where it flowed into Bristol Bay.

The broad expanse of grayish brown water, more than a mile across, moved steadily, powerfully, inexorably south between low bluffs thickly encrusted with trees and brush. Here, the current had swept a stand of spruce trees growing too close to the edge for comfort out to sea. There, it had carved out a back-water and lined a sand beach in a perfect crescent shape with a tidy row of driftwood bleached white by water and time. Far-ther down, where freshwater met salt, a dozen little estuaries nourished tall stands of marsh grass and dozens of species of wildfowl, from the elegant Canada geese to widgeons with calls like rubber duck squeeze toys to the long-legged, long-billed lesser yellowlegs. An immature eagle, as yet uncertain of the newfound power of his great wings, landed for a breather in a nesting area and was instantly dive-bombed by a flock of furi-ous seagulls. A male merganser, red of neck and of temper, chased off a rival for the affections of the female merganser at his side. A large salmon jumped free of the current and smacked back into the water again with a large, loud splash that echoed clearly up to the top of the bluff and through the open windows of the house perched there.

The sun was still well up above the southwestern horizon, pouring an unceasing flow of golden light over them all. That same sunlight gilded the interior of Wy's house, and Liam tore his eyes away from the incredible view and took stock of his more immediate surroundings. There was a dining room table big enough to seat eight on the left and the kitchen on the right, the two separated by a counter and pass-through. Wy pulled out a stool and he sat down and accepted the glass she handed to him. One sip, and he knew the buttery-smooth slide of twenty-year-old Glenmorangie, which retailed for something like eighty bucks a bottle in Anchorage. God knew how much the stuff cost in the Bush, and Wy didn't drink hard liquor. He picked up the bottle and looked at the label. It was about two-thirds full, the same as the bottle at Bill's. Had she bought it from Bill to serve especially to him? That was how Moses had known what he drank, he realized with a rush of something like relief. There. He always appreciated a nice, rational explanation for the oddities of life.

A little voice whispered that the explanation might not be quite that easy in the long run, but he banished it at once and took another sip. "Nice," he said, putting down the glass. He didn't want anything about this night to be clouded in his memory. "How did you know I was coming?"

She was stirring something in a boiling pot. "What? Oh. Bill called. Said you were on your way."

"Where's Tim?"

Her face darkened. "In his room." She managed a smile. "He'd better be studying for his civics exam, or I won't just ground him until the next century, I'll ground him for life."

Liam studied the golden brown liquid in his glass. "We've got some catching up to do."

He felt rather than saw her pause. "Yes," she said, her voice a little breathless but determined enough for all that. "Yes, we do."

"You first," they said together. Their eyes met and they both broke into laughter. It was nervous laughter, but nevertheless it sounded good to Liam. It must have to Wy, too, because when the phone rang she said, "Shoot!"

"Let the machine pick up," Liam suggested. Phone and machine were sitting on the kitchen counter.

She hesitated, hand hovering. "No," she said, and gave him a rueful smile. "Might be work." She picked up the receiver. "Hello? Oh." Her face changed. "Just a minute." She held the receiver to her chest. "Liam, I'm sorry. This is kind of personal. Would you mind?"

He did, big time, but it wouldn't do to say so, or at least not yet.

He wandered into the living room, listening to the sound of her voice as he inspected the furnishings.

"Harry, I sent you a copy of the police report, and a copy of the statement made by the doctor who examined him when I brought him home with me. Plus Mrs. Kapotak's statement. You know what he's been through. He can't go back there. He won't go back there, and even if he would I wouldn't let him."

The living room was smaller than the kitchen and dining room. One small window looked out on a stand of birch and alder. There was a blue denim couch and two armchairs, shabby but comfortable. The beige carpet was worn but scrupulously clean. A do-it-yourself bookshelf stood against one wall, filled to overflowing with paperbacks, some history, some mystery, some both, and an eclectic mixture of nonfiction: *The Home Book of Taxidermy. The 1998 Federal Aviation Regulations and Aeronautical Information Manual. The Gun Digest* and *The Shooter's Bible, The Handbook of Knots and Splices, The Field Guide to Edible Wild Plants, Bears of the World*, a Yupik-English dictionary.

Liam pulled this last out and thumbed through it. "Ik'ikika" was defined as an exclamation meaning "so much" or "so many" or "so big." So much or so many or so big what? Liam wondered. Probably salmon, he decided, and replaced the dictionary on the shelf. Every other word of Native Alaskan he'd ever run across—Athabascan, Eyak, or Yupik—seemed to relate to salmon in some way. If it was Inupiaq now, he'd figure maybe it would modify snow. He'd heard the Inupiaq had fifty different words for snow.

An entertainment center held a small television and a component stereo system. The videotape collection was not genre-specific, either, including as it did *The Little Mermaid, How to Steal a Million, Casablanca, Ruthless People, The Hospital, Little Shop of Horrors,* and *Aliens.* The CDs ranged from the Beach Boys to the Indigo Girls. He felt a pang at the knowledge that Jenny and Wy had had something in common.

There were four CDs by the Neville Brothers and a dozen by Jimmy Buffett. Wy must have been hanging out at Bill's and been converted. There was the CD by Constance Demby, another by Louis Gottschalk, other albums he recognized as gifts from him. He was surprised she hadn't tossed them, and glad.

He himself hadn't been able to throw away anything she had given him, not the copies of her favorite books, not the picture of the moose triplets she'd taken during a charter into Denali, not even the Don Henley tape she'd made for him, which like to melt his eardrums the first and only time he'd played it.

Wy's voice sharpened. "Harry, what judge in his right mind is going to send a twelve-year-old boy back to his mother after what she did to him?"

There was a neat stack of magazines on the coffee table. Liam riffled through them and found a catalogue for Sparky's Pilot Shop. He thumbed through it. Everything you ever needed if you drove a plane. Sparky's F7C, a flight computer that would plot your course, file your flight plan, chart your location, predict your destination, divine your arrival time, and sugar your coffee, all for $69.95. There were videotapes: *The Wonderful World of Floats, The Art of Formation Flying, Taming the Taildragger.* There were Sic-Sacs for sale, just what they sounded like, and Little Johns, also just what they sounded like. There was a Mile High Pin (specify gold or silver) that Liam couldn't figure out. What was so special about getting to 5,280 feet in an airplane? Ten thousand jets did it every day.

Wy said, "What the hell am I paying you for? You're supposed to be Tim's advocate, Harry." A pause. "Then *be* his advocate!"

Liam wandered not so casually down the hall, walking softly. The boy's door was open a crack, and the boy himself was lying on his bed, Walkman earphones clamped to his head, textbook open in front of him. Even from the hallway Liam could here the faint staticky sound of rap music coming from the headset. The boy didn't look up.

A whole generation of Americans was going to grow up deaf, Liam thought. Sony had a lot to answer for.

He padded on to the next room, Wy's. It was small and neat—a single bed with a down comforter, a closet, a chest of drawers. Unlike Laura Nanalook's, the top of Wy's dresser was neatly arranged. She had a small embroidered box she had brought back from Greece the summer her parents took her there, which held all of her jewelry—a dozen pairs of earrings, the strand of pearls her mother had given her when she graduated from high school, the gold nugget watch her father had given her on the same day.

He opened a few drawers. The second held a purse, a couple of scarves, gloves, and three nightshirts. He found what he was looking for buried beneath the nightshirts.

But it wasn't the discovery he made, or even the unconscious fears it confirmed that gave him pause; it was what it came wrapped in that held him rooted in place, immobile, speechless with shock. One trembling hand smoothed the vibrant blue spill of silk, the rich fabric catching on the roughness of his skin, and he had a sudden and unbearably clear recollection of the time and place when he had seen it last. He forgot who he was and the shame that had become invested in that man, he forgot the disgrace that had caused his reduction in rank and his posting to Newenham, he forgot even the bloody, lifeless sprawl that had been Bob DeCreft. He looked at the length of blue silk and was instantly transported back in time to those few halcyon days in Anchorage, so long ago and so far away.

It was the first week of September again, two, going on three years before, an Indian summer of warm, golden days and crisp, clear nights. Liam had driven to Tok, where Wy had picked him up in a plane she'd borrowed from another pilot (they had always been discreet to the point of paranoia), and they had flown into Anchorage, landing at the Lake Hood strip. The alder and birch and cottonwood were a continuous, rippling golden mass, the sky a bright, deep blue, and the peaks of the Chugach Mountains wore only the faintest layer of termination dust, winter as promise instead of threat.

They had four days. They biked the Coastal Trail, shopped along Merrill Field for parts for Wy's Cub (including a set of tundra tires whose possibilities Liam found perfectly appalling), bought Liam a new pistol (a Smith & Wesson 457 that kicked like a horse and cost more), stocked up for the winter at all the used bookstores, held hands through a movie, had gyoza at Yamato Ya and four-cheese pizza at L'Aroma and pasta alla arrabiata and too much red wine at Villa Nova.

They had four nights. They came home every evening to the Copper Whale Inn on the corner of Fifth and L to spend long hours in the enameled brass bed, loving and sleeping and waking to love again. Their host, a friendly, chatty young man, thought they were newlyweds and left them to themselves. They would have been grateful, if they'd noticed.

There were discoveries. They both loved raspberries, playground swings, the American Southwest, the sound track from the movie *The Last of the Mohicans*. Flying terrified him; it was her profession. He'd quit smoking, but walked slowly through the smoking section of a restaurant inhaling deeply for his nicotine fix. "In lieu of a bowling alley," he told her, grinning. She wore contact lenses she had to remove for twelve continuous hours once a week, and after he got over the mild shock he decided he kind of liked her in glasses. He listened to classical music, she sang backup for the Ronettes, and they wrangled over the radio settings in their rented Ford. She wanted the tipsy clams at Simon and Seafort's, and when there were no reservations available he asked the hostess, "Well, then, do you maybe have something left over from lunch?"

They read to each other from Steinbeck's *Sweet Thursday*, and they talked, nonstop, an unceasing flow of communication on every level that amazed them with its ease and empathy. "I didn't know," she said one night. "I didn't know I could talk to a man about everything, about work and poetry, about music and the movies, about society and sex."

Oh yes, the sex. They came together the first time like thunder, ardent, urgent, demanding, and it was so easy and so effortless and so incredibly satisfying that they both lay stunned in the aftermath.

Later, when there was time for play, she bound his wrists with a long blue silk scarf and he, the man always and forever in control, astounded himself by lying back and loving it. He made her come and come again, with his hands, his cock, his tongue, and she was amazed at her response and, she confessed, her head hidden in his shoulder, a little alarmed at her loss of control. He rolled to his back and said, "Feel free," and she startled them both by slithering down his torso and taking him in her mouth, until he was as mindless as she had been. "Jesus, woman," he said the fourth night, "is this the way it is with everyone? Have we been missing out?"

"No, Liam," she said, a little sadly. "It's the trusting."

He craned his head to look down at her. "What? What do you mean?"

She looked up to meet his eyes, and repeated, "It's the trusting." She blushed slightly. "Like the other night with the scarf. You trusted me not to hurt you. I trusted you not to be shocked, or offended."

After she was asleep he lay wakeful, turning her words over in his mind. He had put their attraction down to chemistry, plain and simple. He'd felt it before—not this strongly, true, but there had been times in his life when he had come together with a woman with whom he had absolutely nothing in common but sexual attraction. Why should this be any different?

But it was, and he knew it.

Later, he roused to find himself alone in the bed, and sat up to see Wy in one of the chairs in the bay window that overlooked Knik Arm. Moonglow silvered her hair, cupped her breast, gilded a smooth hip. He heard a soft, muffled sound and realized she was crying. "Wy?" he said, getting out of bed and dropping to his knees next to her. "What's wrong, sweetheart?"

She wouldn't look at him. "I'm going home tomorrow."

"What? But—Wy, we've got a week. Is something wrong, did somebody call?"

She shook her head.

"Then why? We planned this for three months. I want my week."

She looked up. "Liam, I have to go. And you have to let me."

He made as if to touch her, stopped himself when she warded him off, one hand upraised. "I always knew we had to go back. I always knew I had to let you go. But we agreed on a week." He was beginning to be angry. "I want my seven days."

She swiped at her tears with the back of a hand. "I can't do this. I don't do this," she said, angry in her turn. "I don't know how I got here. You are married," she said, and repeated it a second time as if to remind them both, as if both of them needed reminding. "You are married. You're a father."

What could he say? It was true. "Don't leave. Please don't leave. You promised me seven days. I want those seven days. Then we know if it's real. Then I can make some decisions."

"No you can't," she whispered.

"Wy—"

She shook her head fiercely, and he stopped. When she spoke again, her voice was so low and so filled with pain that he could barely hear it. "I can't do this. I can't live like this, live with it. I can't live with what we're doing, what we might do. And I hate all this sneaking around. It makes me feel cheap." After a moment, she added, "It makes us cheap."

"But—"

"No! Liam, don't." She held out her hands, and he put his own into them, the despair welling up like a black tide. "You have responsibilities. You can't turn your back on them. You shouldn't try."

"But—"

"No, Liam. You know I'm right." She paused, and he was silent. Her attempt at a smile was shaky. "You see? You know I'm right. I'm flying home tomorrow. Alone. You can take an air taxi."

He traced the back of her hand with his thumb. "All right," he said at last. "Call me in a couple of days. Or I'll call you."

She shook her head. "You know you can't." She took a deep breath, let it out, and continued in a steady voice, "And I won't be there long. I've found another job."

"What?" The panic was sharp and immediate. "Where?" She shook her head. "I'm leaving on Wednesday."

"Wy," he said, drawing her name out. "No. Don't do this."

She put gentle fingers over his mouth. "We'll both be better off if we don't see each other after tomorrow." Again, she tried to smile. "It's not our time, Liam. Maybe in the next life."

She took him back to bed then, and they made love in a fury of pain and loss and despair, and when he woke the next morning she was curled in a ball against his chest, her shoulders shaking, her face wet against his skin.

She refused to let him drive her to Lake Hood, saying her good-byes at the car. She looked down at their clasped hands. "I've gotten used to this hand," she whispered. "This hand in mine. Your skin against mine. Warm. Strong. Holding me."

He couldn't speak. It took him three tries to get in the car, until finally she gave him a gentle push. "Go on. Go on, now. Your son is waiting."

Chin up, shoulders back, eyes blinded by tears, she walked steadily down to the intersection of Fifth and L. She did not look back. He knew, because he watched her in the rearview mirror, her hair a dark blond tumble against the blue silk scarf wrapped round her neck, until the light turned green and the car behind him gave an impatient honk. He stepped on the gas and started through the intersection.

When he looked up again, she was gone.

"Harry, dammit, I know it's not in the job description but try for a little friggin' compassion, would you!"

Wy's voice, angry, impatient, and just a little frightened, brought him back into the present with a jerk. He looked down to discover that he'd wound the scarf around his wrists, straining the delicate fabric between them. With an effort, he freed himself and replaced everything as it had been. He closed the drawer again and, still moving softly, went back out into the living room.

There was a framed poster on one wall with the title INTER-NATIONAL SPACE YEAR 1992 running across the bottom. It had a couple of galleons sailing rough seas out of the bottom-left-hand corner of the frame and into space in the upper-right-hand corner of the frame, with ringed planets and gas giants and moons and comets interspersed with blueprint drawings of spacecraft.

Wy was a big follower of the space program. She wanted someday to go to Florida to watch the shuttle take off, and stay to watch it land, and in between to live at Spaceport. "Did you ever think of becoming an astronaut?" he'd asked her, and she had replied, with a twisted smile, "My parents wanted me to become a teacher. So I became a teacher."

He'd wanted to ask her how she had made the jump from teacher to pilot, but the memory was so obviously painful that he left it for another time.

In those days they were easily distracted. That other time never came, and soon afterward she left.

This time, he thought, staring at the poster, this time he would know it all.

Wy voice's became edgy and defensive. "I said you'll get it, and you will. I keep my word, Harry. And I pay my debts."

Footsteps came down the hall. Liam looked around to see Tim Gosuk standing in the doorway.

"Hey," Liam said.

Tim's expression was aloof, giving nothing away. "Hey."

They regarded each other in silence for a moment. Everything Liam knew about kids could have been written on the head of a pin. On the other hand, he'd been a trooper for over ten years and knew more about human nature than most shrinks. He was also older and tougher and probably smarter than the boy, which would help. "Finish studying for your civics exam?"

Tim looked toward the kitchen and back at Liam. He was still dressed in urban punk: bagged-out jeans, oversized plaid shirt, and backward baseball cap. At least he didn't have a do rag. "Yeah," Tim said finally. "What's it to you?"

His voice was curt but not necessarily challenging. Liam shrugged. "Just making conversation." He wasn't going to force himself on the boy, but he was equally determined not to be shut out. "What other subjects you studying this year? What grade are you in, anyway?"

"Eighth."

"Really?" Liam said, adding mendaciously, "I thought you were older. So?"

"So what?"

"So what else are you studying? English, history, what else?" It was the boy's turn to shrug. "English, history, what else."

"Math?"

Tim made a face, the first natural expression Liam had seen there. Aha, a breakthrough. "Algebra."

"Yuck."

The boy made a noise somewhere between a snort and a grunt. "It's not so bad. Mrs. Davenport is a good teacher. It's hard, but she makes it fun."

"I was lousy at math," Liam observed. "Never got all that business about *x*s and *y*s straight in my head. Geometry was better; I liked fooling with the volume of all the figures." He grinned. "And I liked Mary Kallenberg, who sat next to me in geometry class and helped me find the area of the three different kinds of triangles. Can't for the life of me remember what they're called now."

"There aren't three, there are six," Tim said promptly. "Right, isosceles, equilateral, obtuse, acute, and scalene," and he actually smiled.

"Yikes. You're scaring me." Liam smiled back. "Not much call in the trooper business to figure out the area of a right triangle."

"You don't use it, you lose it," Tim said, his words an uncanny echo of Moses'. "Mrs. Davenport says that a lot. She loads us up on the homework like you wouldn't believe."

Inwardly Liam marveled at the way the boy's face had metamorphosed from sullen, wary, potential juvenile delinquent to animated, intelligent teenager. In this persona, it was easy to see why Wy had taken him on.

The smell of something wonderful wafted in from the kitchen, and their stomachs growled in unison. Both males were surprised into laughter. Mutual laughter, once enjoyed, is a hard thing to step back from. "Maybe if we go into the kitchen and squawk like seagulls she'll feed us," Liam said.

"Works for me."

They walked into the kitchen in time to hear Wy say into the phone, "Oh, like this phone call didn't cost me a hundred and fifty bucks! Look, Harry, I'll get you the goddamn money just as soon as I get paid myself! Okay?"

She slammed down the receiver and turned to see Liam and Tim standing in the doorway watching her. "Oh hello," she said, bright smile newly polished and back in place. "Ready for some dinner?"

When Liam looked at Tim, he saw the sullen look had descended again like a cloud.

The Constance Demby CD ended. Bon Jovi's *Keeping the Faith* blared out in its place. In spite of himself Liam winced, and they both saw it. Even Tim laughed, and it eased the tension.

"Feed *me*," Liam said, and they both recognized the line from *Little Shop of Horrors* and laughed some more. It got them to the table in something approaching amity, and Wy served up a kind of pork sparerib stew with pea pods in a delicious sauce. When Liam asked what went into the sauce, all Wy would say is, "Secret Filipino ingredient," and it wasn't till he helped clear the table and saw the empty can of Campbell's cream of mushroom soup in the garbage that he realized what it was.

"When did you learn to cook?" he asked her as she ran the sink full of hot water and soap.

"My college roommate's dad was Filipino, and a chef. I went home with her a couple of times, and Freddy would cook for us." She closed her eyes in remembered ecstasy. "Adobo, sweet and sour spareribs, long rice, bagoong. Anybody who likes to eat should have a Freddy Quijance in their life, just once."

Tim had vanished back into his room, and the sound of a thumping bass could be heard in the distance. It made Liam cringe, but it wasn't as bad as some of the car stereos he had heard driving by his house in Glenallen, so he held his peace. Wasn't his house, anyway.

Yet.

Which reminded him. "That couch of yours fold out, Wy?" he said, stirring half-and-half into his coffee. She'd even remembered that, he thought with a secret smile.

She looked up. "Why?"

"I haven't had time to look for a place."

"Where did you sleep last night?"

"In the desk chair in the troopers' office."

"Oh. Ugh." She hesitated. He waited, enjoying the play of emotion across her face. "No," she said finally.

"No, it doesn't fold out, or no, I can't sleep on it?"

"Both."

"Why not?"

"Tim," she said.

"I'm not asking to share your bed," he pointed out.

Yet.

She shook her head. "No, Liam," she said firmly. "I'm sorry, but you'll have to find another place to sleep. There's a hotel across from city hall. I know the night clerk; I could give her a call."

He wasn't going to push it, not until he was more sure of his ground. "That's okay, I'll figure something out." But that didn't mean he wasn't going to do his level best to change the situation. He reached for her hand. Her fingers curled naturally around his. Encouraged, he raised them to his lips. Her skin was warm, and he felt her pulse skip a beat. He looked up and smiled at her as he turned his mouth into her palm and nuzzled it.

"Liam." Her voice was unsteady.

He touched his tongue to the center of her palm, tracing the lines he found there. The mound at the base of her thumb was plump and tantalizing. He bit it, gently, and heard her breath catch.

"Liam!" Her free hand flashed up around his neck and pulled his face to hers. She nipped at his lower lip, ran her tongue over his teeth. He found himself on his feet, reaching out to drag her across the counter.

"Don't mind me," a voice said, and they looked up to find Tim standing in the doorway, the line of his mouth set and vulnerable.

"Tim!" Wy said, and then didn't seem to be able to think of anything else to say. She pulled free of Liam and slid to her feet.

There was nothing she could do to hide the brightness of her eyes or the flush in her cheeks.

Liam didn't say anything, meeting the challenge in Tim's eyes with calm recognition and, he hoped, no answering challenge. He needed badly to rearrange the fit of his jeans, but considered it diplomatic to refrain for the moment.

"I just wanted a Coke," Tim said, and walked around Wy to the refrigerator.

By the time he was back in his room, Liam's heartbeat had slowed down to something approaching normality. Wy smoothed back her hair with a trembling hand. Liam's was a little steadier when he reached for his mug, but not much. "This is a nice house. I looked in the paper; I didn't see much for sale or for rent. How did you luck into here?"

Watching him warily, as if she was determined to thwart any effort he made to pick up where they had left off, she said, "It came with the business."

"The air taxi?"

She nodded. "The owner wanted to retire, and he put the business up for sale. One plane, a Cessna 180, the two tie-downs, a lease on a hangar, this house, and the goodwill. That, plus the Cub, is what there is of the Nushagak Air Taxi Service."

"How did you hear that it was up for sale?"

"Bob DeCreft told me."

"You knew him before?"

She nodded again. "You know how it is with Bush pilots. If you don't know them, you've heard of them."

"Which was it with the two of you?" He saw her look and sighed. "Come on, Wy. You've been close enough to the business to know how it works. I have to ask."

She held his gaze for a moment, and then looked away. "Yeah, I know how it works." She sipped at her coffee, put down the mug, and looked at him squarely. "I've known Bob DeCreft since I was a kid."

Liam did not greet this news with overt joy. He didn't want her to be so well acquainted with the victim of what might have been murder.

"You know I come from Newenham originally, more or less," she said, raising her eyebrows. He nodded. "Well, Bob was a Bush pilot, and he flew in and out of Bristol Bay on a lot of different charters, some government-related, some ANCSA-related, some both. He knew my parents, and he'd spend the night." She paused. "One day he was supposed to fly the local Native association board into Togiak or somewhere, only the weather was socked in there. So he took me up instead." She smiled, her eyes looking over his shoulder at a fond memory. "He had a Skywagon in those days, with dual controls. He let me fly her. I was hooked. From that day on, I didn't want to do anything but fly."

"How old were you?"

"Sixteen."

"But you went to college."

She shrugged, the glow fading. "It was what my parents wanted. I figured I'd do what they wanted, and then I'd do what I wanted."

"How did they take it?"

Her smile was wry. "They didn't like it much, but they got over it. They helped me buy the air taxi."

"Must have cost a bundle."

She nodded. "Pretty much. I'm in hock up to my eyebrows. It was worth it, though."

To get away from me? The question hung between them, unsaid, but she flushed a rich red in spite of it. "I didn't mean that."

He didn't say anything, and in an obvious attempt to shift the focus, she said, "And you? What have you been up to?"

Her interest was as false as her question. "Come on, Wy, you knew I was coming. Didn't you? That's why you weren't surprised when I got off the plane."

Her eyes slid away. She didn't reply. He sighed. "Yeah, well, after the mess up at Denali, Barton transferred me here."

"I didn't hear much about that, I . . ." "I on purpose didn't listen," he thought she was going to say. Instead she said, "I would have thought you would want to stay in Glenallen, no matter what, and then . . ." Her voice trailed off.

"And then I could see Jenny every weekend," he agreed evenly. "It wasn't up to me. John transferred me after my demotion came through, and that was that." He could have added that Barton had transferred him to Newenham because Wy was there, because their relationship had not been the secret romance they had always been confident of, but he didn't.

Her voice was low, and she wasn't looking at him. "How is she?"

"The same."

"How often are you going to get back to see her?"

"At least once a month." He studied the coffee in his mug. "We took her off the respirator."

He heard the sharp intake of her breath. "I didn't know that."

"She's fed through a tube, Wy," he said. He stated it as a fact, not a horror or a tragedy. He'd had too much time to become accustomed to his wife's physical and mental state; it no longer held any terror or disgust for him. "She wears diapers. She's home with her parents, and they've got money, so she's got twenty-four-hour care." He closed his eyes. "Do you know how long Karen Ann Quinlan lasted after they disconnected her life support?"

Her voice was infinitely gentle, infinitely sorrowful. "No."

"Nine years." He opened his eyes and tried for a smile. From her wince, he knew that he hadn't quite made it. "Nine years and change."

"Liam, I am so sorry. So very sorry."

"Yeah. Me too." He rose to his feet and took his mug over to stand in front of the window, staring unseeingly out at the vast expanse of river, roiling and tumbling and gray with glacial silt, driving forcefully for the Bay and points south. Soon it would be filled with salmon, king and silver and sockeye and humpy and dog, all driving just as purposefully upstream, fighting the current to return home to the stream in which they were spawned, there to spawn in their turn and die.

"It's different here," he said. "Hard to get used to not having mountains to bang your nose against."

"I know. The Wood Mountains start at Icky, though. It's only forty miles up the road. The blink of an eye if you fly."

"The blink of an eye," he echoed. "You know something, Wy? It constantly amazes me just how fast a life can turn to shit. I was the golden boy: straight As straight through school, graduated college magna cum laude, I was first in my class at the Academy, I made sergeant before any of my classmates and before a lot of prior graduates, John Barton handpicked me to lead the Petersham task force, which got me headlines all the way Outside, I was headed straight up the ladder and I knew it and so did everyone else. To top everything off, just the icing on the cake, I married me a rich, beautiful, loving wife. Nothing could stop me, nothing could touch me, I had the world by the tail."

He turned to look at Wy. "And then, in the blink of an eye, I didn't."

She stared at him, stricken.

"They busted me down to trooper," he said. "Just before they transferred me here."

She said slowly, "That's what you meant yesterday, when Corcoran called you sergeant and you said no, just trooper."

"Yes."

"What happened, Liam?"

He shook his head. "Doesn't matter. Buck stopped on my desk. Barton was right to do it." He gave her a twisted grin. "So here I am, in Newenham, a trooper again, starting all over at the bottom of the ladder. My wife is in a coma four hundred miles away, and the woman I love —"

"Don't, Liam."

"The woman I love," he repeated firmly, "is up to her eyebrows in a murder." He laughed, because there wasn't anything else to do, except maybe get drunk. "Just when you thought it was safe to come back to life."

He walked back to the counter and sat across from her. "How did you come by the boy?"

She thought about that for a minute, as if she were deciding how much it was safe to tell him. He held on to his temper, and waited. "It was my first week here," she said finally, looking toward the back of the house and dropping her voice instinctively. "I flew into Ualik with the mail that morning. Jeff—Jeff Webster, he's the guy who sold the business to me—Jeff rode shotgun with me for a month before he'd let me loose in his plane on his routes. Anyway, Jeff walked me through the procedure, getting all the right signatures from the postmaster, that kind of thing, and then he went off to say good-bye to a friend of his. I went back to the airstrip to repack the plane."

She looked at him. "Have you ever been to Ualik?" Liam shook his head. "Ever been to any of the western Bush villages?"

Liam shook his head again. "I've been pretty much an urban cowboy all my professional life." He paused, and added, "Or as urban as it gets in Alaska."

She nodded. "I didn't think so. It's different out here, Liam. It's different in Ualik."

"Different how?"

"Well, for starters it's a Yupik village, about six hundred people, and for the most part good people. But, like most Bush villages, the worm in its apple is booze."

"They're not dry, then?"

"They've been dry," Wy said grimly, "and they've been damp, and they've been wet, sometimes all three at once. Right now they're wet again."

"Let me guess," Liam said. "The local liquor store owner petitioned for a vote when all the families were at fish camp last August."

"The August before."

"Figures." He shook his head. "God, you'd think every village in this state would look at Barrow and see what happened there when they went dry. The first month—the *first* month, Wy—there was something like an eighty percent drop in alcohol-related instances of child abuse, wife beating, and assault."

"Booze is the worm in the Bush apple," she repeated.

"Including Ualik," he said, nudging her back to the subject.

"Including Ualik," she agreed. "So I went back to the plane to repack it and wait for Jeff. You know how airstrips are practically the main streets of a lot of the older villages?" He nodded. "It's like that in Ualik, a lot of houses lined up along one side of the strip, and the town kind of meanders down to the Ualik River from there. I was walking down the strip past one of the houses. I heard this kind of whimper. I thought it was an animal. It wasn't. It was Tim."

Her face flushed with remembered fury. "He was curled up in a ball underneath the porch of his mother's house. Both of his forearms were fractured, both eyes were swollen shut, one of his front teeth was dangling by a piece of flesh, his nose had been broken, there were patches of hair missing from his scalp." She closed her eyes and shook her head. "I got him out from under the porch and strapped him into the plane, and I went looking for Jeff. Jeff told me not to get involved, that it was a village matter, and took me to find the vipso."

A VPSO was a village police and safety officer, a local citizen trained by the state troopers to deal with minor infractions and call in the troopers when necessary. It was a great idea, especially given the fierce independence of most village councils, but often did not work out so well in practice. "You find him?" Liam said.

"Oh yeah, we found him," Wy said wearily. "He was home, mending nets. Give him credit—he came and looked at the boy and agreed we should fly him into the hospital here. Then we all trooped over to the house where I found the boy. He lived with his mother, and a guy she called his uncle, although later the vipso said he was no such thing." She shuddered. "The place was a pigsty, Liam. I mean it even smelled bad—kind of sour, like someone had barfed in every room and no one had ever bothered to clean it up. They were both drunk. The 'uncle' still had blood on his knuckles. The vipso wouldn't arrest him."

"Probably his brother, or his brother-in-law."

"Probably. All I knew at the time was that the mom came roaring out of the house and down to the plane and tried to jerk the boy out of it. He was all but unconscious by then, but he woke up all right when she started yanking on one of his broken arms. He started screaming, and then his grandmother showed up."

"His mom's mom?"

She nodded. "She's great; her name is Sarah. She's this little old lady who weighs in at about eighty pounds, all of it tiger. She grabbed Tim's mom by the hair and hauled her down the strip while we loaded him back into the plane and took off."

"I'm guessing that'd be Mrs. Kapotak," Liam said.

Surprised, she said, "Why, yes, how did you—oh."

"I was listening from the living room," he admitted without shame. She might as well know from the get-go that he refused to be kept out of anything.

"I see." She was silent for a moment. "Well, we brought him back here. He was in the hospital for three weeks. Turned out he had a lot of old scars, and DFYS got involved, and when it came time for him to come out of the hospital they looked around for somewhere for him to stay." She shrugged. "I'd flown him out, I'd been visiting him. I felt, I don't know, responsible for him in a way. And Sarah, she visited when she could coerce Bob into flying her over. We got to know each other, and she suggested I keep him. She said she would have taken him, but she'd already tried that once. Lasted a week before her daughter missed her punching bag and came looking for him."

"I would have thought she'd want him in a Native home."

She looked at him. "I'm a quarter Yupik, Liam."

He looked at her, noticing again the high, flat cheekbones, the slight golden cast to her skin, the almost imperceptible tilt to her eyes. As with Moses, if you didn't look for it you'd never see it. He shook his head. "I keep forgetting. Of course you are."

"Tim's half," she said. "His father was some pilot that blew through Ualik twelve years ago." She looked at him squarely. "It can be tough, very tough to be a mixed-blood in the villages. The elders, a lot of them are okay with it, but the next generation is all for tribal rights and sovereignty and purity of the species, or whatever they call it. They can make it very, very hard on someone who's part white."

There was a ring of certainty in her voice that Liam hadn't heard before. "I know you were adopted from one of the villages, Wy," he said. "Where were you adopted from?"

She smiled. "Not from Ualik, Liam. But close enough in spirit as to make no never mind." She sighed. "Well, anyway, the long and short of it is, I brought Tim home with me." She waved a hand at the house. "I have the room—it came with the business. I have the stability DFYS wants in foster parents." She smiled. "And I like him, and for some mysterious reason, when he's not playing the role of Teenagerus horribilus he will admit I'm fairly tolerable my own self." She met Liam's eyes. "And after you, after us, I was lonely, and I was drifting, and I needed a reason to get up in the morning."

"And Tim was it," Liam said.

"And Tim is it," she said firmly. "Understand one thing, Liam. Tim is with me for good. He is my son now. I've started adoption proceedings."

If she'd expected him to run screaming into the night, Liam thought, she'd picked the wrong guy. "Okay," he said equably. "If he's yours, he's mine, too."

"Liam," she said warningly.

"What?"

She took a deep breath. "Look, I admit, the attraction is still there. But you are still married to Jenny. I'm sorry, God I'm sorry, for her, and for you, but you can't divorce her, you simply can't." She straightened in her chair. "I'm actually glad that you've raised this—this situation, so we can talk it through. I'm adopting a child, Liam. The authorities are going to look very carefully at my private life. So far in Newenham, and for all they know for my whole life, I am squeaky clean."

So long as they didn't talk to John Barton. Liam smiled at her. "There hasn't been anyone since me, has there?"

"Liam!" she said, exasperated. "That's not the point, and you know it."

Their conversation was interrupted by the phone. "Don't answer it," Liam said, but Wy fairly snatched up the receiver. "What? No lie? Great! Okay, will do."

She hung up the phone and stepped around the counter to where a marine radio sat. She switched it on and turned to Channel 15. A voice came on, a male voice, dry, academic, reading from something. "I repeat, this is the Alaska Department of Fish and Game announcing a possible herring opener in the Newenham district for both seine and drift net at noon tomorrow, May fifth. Tune in to this channel tomorrow at ten a.m. for confirmation. Over and out."

Wy looked up, eyes bright. "Yes!"

"I thought you just had a herring opener," Liam said.

"We didn't make the quota," she said, grinning. "Fish and Game's giving us another shot at it." And then her smile faded. "Oh. That's right. I don't know if I'm fired or not. I haven't talked to Cecil yet."

As if on cue, the phone rang. Wy lifted the receiver. "Yes? Oh, hello, Cecil. Yes, I heard it. Yes, of course. Well, there is the 180—no, sure, I can get hold of another Cub, not a problem."

Oh really, Liam thought.

"Yes, of course I can find another spotter." She climbed up on a stool and swung one leg over the other, wiggling her foot. "I am still waiting on last period's check, Cecil. Yeah, I know it's only been a couple of days, and I know it won't be much, but I flew for you, I earned it, and I want it now. Um-hmmm. Sure. Fine. Okay, I'll be in the air at six. Right after I pick up the check at the cannery office. You can leave it there in an envelope for me, okay?" Wolfe's growl was audible even to Liam, and a satisfied smile spread across Wy's face. "You going out tonight? Okay, drop the gas at the usual spot on the beach, one up, two down, gas pump on the upright barrel. Okay? Okay." She hung up, jumped down from her stool, and pumped her hand once. Her face was exultant. "Yes!"

"What other Cub?" Liam said.

"What? Oh. There's an Anchorage dentist who parks his Cub next to mine. I keep an eye on it for him, service it when he calls to let me know he's coming down to hunt caribou or whatever."

"Does he know you're taking it up to spot herring?"

"Shit!" she said, elation fading from her face. "Where the hell am I going to find me a spotter between now and tomorrow morning?"

"Wy," Liam said carefully, "you once told me that herring spotting was the surest way to get yourself killed short of jumping off a cliff."

She shrugged this off, tapping one fingernail against the counter, eyes narrowed on some distant object.

"Wy, they had a herring opener in Prince William Sound two weeks ago," Liam said, voice rising. "One plane ran into another's float. He crashed, and it totaled the plane and killed him and his spotter."

"Uh-huh," Wy said.

"Wy," Liam said, rising to his feet and giving her the benefit of full volume, "last summer a couple of spotters had a midair in Kachemak Bay! What makes you think it won't happen to you?"

She blinked at him, drawn out of her absorption by his vehemence. When she spoke, her voice was low, reasonable, and utterly infuriating. "Liam, I own a flying business. People pay me to fly. I fly passengers, I fly freight, I fly supplies into hunting and fishing lodges and mining camps. I fly archaeologists out to old burial grounds and villagers out to fish camps and federal marine biologists out to count walrus. I even fly state troopers out to crime scenes," she added pointedly. "And when somebody like Cecil Wolfe, who has been high boat on the Bay for the last four years, when Cecil Wolfe calls and offers me a fifteen percent share—fifteen percent of three boats, Liam—then I fly for him." She stared at him challengingly, hands on her hips.

"Jesus, Wy, I'll loan you the money. I've got over a year's worth of back pay in the bank; you can have it, every dime."

"Who said I needed money?" she demanded hotly, and flung up a hand before he could answer. "Oh that's right, I forgot you eavesdropped your way into that little tidbit of information. Look, Liam, I'm spotting herring for Cecil Wolfe because he needs a spotter and that is part of what I do for a living. Is that clear?"

"Very clear," Liam said.

"Fine," she said. "Now where the hell am I going to find me a spotter?"

"Beats the hell out of me," Liam said, hoping she wouldn't find one in time.

"I'll go up with you, Wy."

Both adults turned to see Tim standing in the doorway. An empty Coke can dangled from one hand.

"Like hell you will," Liam said before he thought.

Wy glared at Liam. "Back off, this is my business." She turned to Tim. "Like hell you will."

"Why not?" Tim said. "I've been herring fishing before, on one of my uncle's boats. I haven't seen herring from the air, but I've spotted them balling up from the crow's nest. I know what to look for."

"Wy," Liam said. "You can't."

"Why can't she?" Tim said. "She needs a spotter. I've spotted before. What, you gonna spot for her instead?"

Liam stared into the boy's defiant, challenging eyes. "Yes," he heard himself say. "Yes, I am."

TEN

The ring of the phone woke him the next morning. He groaned and rolled out of the sleeping bag Wy had lent him and onto the cold, hard, not entirely clean office floor. The phone rang again, insistent. He reached up with one hand and fumbled around until he found the receiver. "Hello?" Shivering, he slid back inside the plaid lining and tried to generate a little body heat. "Oh. Hello, John."

"There's no easy way to put this, Liam," John said, wasting no time on politesse. "Wy needs money, and she needs it bad. She's running a tab with everyone—Chevron, NC, she took out a second mortgage on her business, which payments have been late a time or two. No wonder she decided to spot herring."

Liam was wide awake now. He said, "Did you find out why?"

"She's up to her ears in a court case, has been for a year. She's trying to adopt a kid. Did you know that?"

"I've met him."

"Jesus, Liam, did you know the kid's mother accused Wy of kidnapping?"

Liam sat up, sleeping bag falling away. "No, I didn't know that."

"She filed a complaint about nine months ago."

"What?" Liam tried to sort this out. "Only nine months ago? I don't get it. Wy's had him for two years."

With awful irony, Barton said, "Apparently it took that long for Mom to notice the kid was gone."

"Shit," Liam muttered.

"My sentiments exactly."

Liam ran rough hands through his hair. "How did you get all this stuff so quick? I figured it'd take you a couple of days at least. At least until Monday, when the state courts opened back up for business anyway."

"Deb—you remember Deb, my very own personal ferret— she called in a favor at TRW. Right away she picked up on all the checks Wy was writing to an attorney. She went over to the courthouse yesterday afternoon with a buddy of hers, who just happens to be one of the clerks of the court, and they dug up the case. The tapes had just been transcribed, and I spent last night reading them." John snorted. "Hamilton—Theodore Hamilton, you remember him, he presided over the Murdy murder trial—anyway, Hamilton seemed to actually have a clue, that day anyway, so he didn't give the kid back. But the bleeding heart bastard gave the mom a chance to dry out and straighten up her act." Barton snorted contemptuously. "So now Wy is suing for the severance of parental rights and full custody. It's costing her. It's costing her a bundle. And she's not doing real well at keeping up."

"I'll bet." Liam remembered the phone call from the night before. "Who's her attorney?"

"Abood. Harold Abood."

Harold. Harry. As in, *Look, Harry, I'll get you the goddamn money just as soon as I get paid myself.*

"Liam?" Barton said.

"What?"

Barton sighed, once, a deep, heavy, unhappy sigh. Blunt as he was, John Dillinger Barton took no pleasure in being the bearer of bad news. "The only person Wy doesn't owe is her mechanic. She's been paying his bills regularly every month."

"What's his name?"

"Fred Barnes, as in Fred's Fly-in and Fix-it Shop. He's in Newenham, close to the airport from the address."

There was a perfunctory knock on the door. It opened, and Wy stuck her head in. "It's six o'clock; come on, we've got to get in the air."

"Who's that?" Barton demanded.

"My pilot," Liam said. "Didn't I mention, John? I'm going herring spotting today."

He got to his feet, clad only in boxer shorts, and saw Wy's expression. He grinned at her. She reddened. "I'll wait for you outside," she said, and closed the door a little harder than necessary to make the latch catch.

Barton was sputtering into his ear. "Herring spotting? Are you out of your goddamn mind? You've got work to do—you don't have any goddamn time to go gallivanting off on some goddamn herring spotting excursion! Besides, you're liable to get yourself goddamn killed! Crazy goddamn bastard!"

Patiently, Liam waited for Barton to run out of steam, at least momentarily. "John, I don't have a clue as to what DeCreft was doing immediately prior to his death. I don't know anything about the herring fishing business or what spotting is like, except for what I read in the papers. If there were another trooper here, more knowledgeable about the lifestyle, I'd—why isn't there another trooper here?" he said in sudden realization. "In a town this size, there ought to be at least one other trooper, and a sergeant as well. What's going on? Why am I here all by myself?" Silence on the other end of the line. "John?"

Barton sighed. "Okay, look, I'll tell you, but this is strictly confidential. Did you ever stop to wonder why Corcoran would want to transfer out of a Bush post that pays seven steps above basic and into an urban post that pays only basic?"

"I haven't had time to wonder about anything except where I'm going to sleep from night to night," Liam said slowly. "Why?"

"Like I said, this is strictly on the QT. I wouldn't be telling you but for the fact that you might run into some of the fallout. He really fucked up an investigation down there. There was a local pharmacist who was trading drugs for sexual favors from teenage boys. Corcoran busted the guy, forgot to Mirandize him, and then roughed him up in sight of the perp's family and friends."

Liam remembered Darrell, and his fear of getting in the trooper's vehicle. Corcoran seemed to have made a habit of beating on the local populace. He grimaced inwardly. The job was hard enough without having to reinstill the trust in your office that your predecessor had so comprehensively abused. "How rough?"

"The guy wound up in the hospital." He paused. "And when he could, he walked."

"Jesus."

"Yeah. The community was not happy with Corcoran, or with us for posting him there. Corcoran pulled some other stunts, too, but that was the last one. That's why he's gone and you're there."

"Why am I here alone?" Liam thought about the size of the judicial district he would be responsible for, the villages scattered from Newenham to Newhalen, from Togiak to Ualik, from Kilbuck to Kaskank, and recoiled at the thought of how many hours in the air he'd be logging to do his job. "Why was Corcoran?"

There was another pause, followed by another sigh. "Corcoran got the last trooper assigned to his command pregnant. She resigned. We haven't been able to fill her place yet—no one wanted to work with Corcoran, seven-step-increase notwithstanding. It'll be different now."

"Yeah, I'll bet they'll just be lining up around the block to come work with me," Liam said, "the guy who was relieved of command and busted down for falling asleep on the job while a Native family of five froze to death in Denali Park. Did you ever think of that, John?"

"Ah, quit your bitching, you're employed, aren't you?"

Liam swore beneath his breath. "Look, John, I've got to go."

"Herring spotting?"

"Yep," Liam said, repressing a shudder.

There was a brief pause. "But you're afraid of flying!" Barton said at last, as close to pleading as John Dillinger Barton ever got.

"Don't remind me. And quit your own bitching—you're the one who posted me here." He hung up. Not many people had hung up on John Barton and lived to tell the tale. Liam hoped he would be in the minority of survivors.

He reached for his pants. He'd taken a spit bath the night

before in the post's one bathroom, so he didn't actively smell, and at least he had clean clothes, although he would run out of them soon if he didn't find him a place to stay with a washer and dryer in it.

He paused, considering. He could ask Wy to wash his clothes for him.

Of course, he could just cut his own throat and be done with it that much quicker, too.

He grabbed for the baseball cap with the AST patch on it that along with his weapon were still the only two outward indications of his profession—the hot water faucet in the sink in the bathroom hadn't generated enough steam to smooth the wrinkles out of his uniform—and opened the door.

And came face-to-face with Moses Alakuyak. He and Wy were standing post next to each other. "Oh shit," Liam said, but he said it to himself.

"Get your butt down here, boy," Moses barked.

A harsh croak seconded the command, and Liam looked up to see the big raven regarding him mockingly from what seemed to be his personal branch. He was so big the branch of the spruce tree curved downward at a severe angle—possibly even an acute angle, Liam thought, remembering Tim from the night before—and the big black bird bobbed up and down like a puppet on a string, if a puppet could ever look that completely self-willed.

"Look, Moses, I—"

Moses' voice was like the crack of a whip. "Get your butt down here."

Liam looked at Wy, who rolled her eyes but didn't move out of her modified horse stance. He bowed to the inevitable, and went to take his place on Moses' other side.

They worked together for twenty minutes, standing post, working on the previous day's two movements, commencement and ward off left and adding a third, right push upward. It was hard work, and Liam kissed last night's spit bath good-bye. At least he was going to be cooped up in the same small space with a woman who was working as hard as he was. With luck, they'd cancel each other out.

At the end of the exercise Moses signified grudging

approval, although he did say, cocking a knowing eye at each of them, "You didn't practice last night, either of you."

They both looked undeniably guilty. He shook a finger at them. "Practice! Practice, practice, practice!" He made a fist of his right hand, enclosed it in his left palm, and bowed once. Liam awkwardly, Wy with grace and assurance, followed suit.

"I'm outta here," Moses decided, and walked to his truck. He paused, one hand on the cab, one on the door, one foot on the step, and yelled, "Keep the goddamn beach on your left, Chouinard! You got that?"

"I got it, Moses," she said.

"And you, trooper, you stay awake!" He slid into the truck, slammed the door, started the engine, ground the gears into first, and jerked off down the road.

"Let's go," Wy said.

They strapped into the borrowed blue and white Cub, Wy up front on the stick, Liam seated directly behind her in the plane's only other seat, his knees bumping against the back of her seat and his shoulders nearly brushing both sides of the interior. There was glass from his seat forward on both sides, meeting at the windshield, and a glass skylight overhead. Liam didn't like the skylight; it was cut into the roof where he felt there ought to have been a ridgepole connecting the wings, a ridgepole of tempered steel or maybe titanium. Something stronger than glass, anyway.

"Okay," Wy said, twisting her neck to look at him, "you understand what your job is?"

Liam could feel the panic rising up from his belly, and beat it back with grim determination. "Yes."

She wriggled the stick between her knees, and the stick between Liam's knees waggled in response. "Keep your hands off this."

"Not a problem," Liam said fervently. "I'm not touching nothing nohow never."

"Good." There was no amusement in her voice. Wy was all business this morning. "All right, put on your muffs."

Liam reached for the green headphones hooked over a piece

of bare airframe and put them on. "The mike is voice-activated," she said, her words reaching him clearly. Her braid hung over the back of her seat, and he resisted the urge to give it a tug. "Purse your lips, adjust the mike so it just touches them, and give me a test count."

"One, two, three, four, five, four, three, two, one," he said obediently.

"Push the mike a little closer and repeat," she said. He did so. "Good," she said. "When you want my attention, what do you do?"

He poked her shoulder. "Good, or slap my head, or kick the seat, or whatever you need to do. When you need me to look at something immediately, what do you do?"

He pointed, his arm extended over her seat and shoulder so that she could see his hand and pointing finger. "Good. Okay, you'll be able to talk to me, and I'll be able to talk to you over the mike. You'll be able to listen to me talking to the boats, but you won't be able to talk to them yourself. Understand?"

"Got it."

"Okay then, let's get this puppy in the air."

He knew her hands were moving on the controls but he couldn't see what she was doing, and was glad of it. The prop turned over, once, twice, three times, and caught, turning into a blur through the forward window, pulling the Cub's nose down. All Cubs were taildraggers, which only meant that the third gear was attached to the rear of the fuselage so that on the ground the little plane sat back on her tail, and not so coincidentally was why neither Wy nor Liam could see over the control panel. This necessitated a crossing back and forth of the taxiway, kind of like a sailboat tacks back and forth across the wind, so that Wy could watch where they were going out of the side windows. Liam didn't like that, either.

Over the headphones he heard Wy talking to traffic control, seeking permission for taxi and takeoff. It was granted, and the Cub snaked out onto the taxiway between a DC-3 freighter headed for Togiak and a Fish and Game Cessna 206 with a long-distance tank fixed to its belly that gave it a distinctly fecund appearance.

They trundled down to the end of the runway, waited for an

Alaska Airlines 737 to land, and followed the DC-3 into the air. As always, Liam clutched when he felt the reluctant earth let go of their wheels. The good news was that, once in the air, the tail came up and he could see over Wy's head out the windshield. He rummaged around for his water bottle, drank deeply, and didn't feel much better, the water sloshing around in his stomach like a sea working up to a storm. There was an airsickness bag in the pocket of Wy's seat back. He devoutly hoped he would not have to make use of it.

The Cub's engine was loud and rattled the fillings in his teeth. The seat cushion was thin and the aluminum frame beneath hard on back and behind. At least Liam, sweating with a steady frisson of fear, had the comfort of knowing that the slow-flying Piper Super Cub was the quintessential Bush plane, and that if they did run into trouble Wy had a good chance of putting them down safely almost anywhere.

He wouldn't have gotten in the plane at all if Wy hadn't been on the stick. She was a natural pilot: good, steady hands, an encyclopedic knowledge of the limits of her aircraft, twenty-ten vision, and an uncanny instinct for weather. He remembered one day she was supposed to fly him out to Nizina. When she met him at the airstrip she had a frown on her face. She pointed into the southwest. He'd looked, and hadn't seen anything but a light haze lying low on the horizon. He'd told her so, and she'd shook her head. "I don't like the look of it," she had told him. They hadn't flown that day, and that night a storm blew into the interior from the Gulf of Alaska that toppled trees and blew off roofs—and wrecked planes—from Cape Yakataga to Copper Center.

He comforted himself that he was in the best possible plane in the best possible hands and nerved himself to look around.

He hated to admit it, but the view was superb. There are few places to look at more beautiful that the coast of Alaska, and few places better to look at it from than the window of a small plane. To the south, Bristol Bay rolled out like a plush green carpet, sunlight caught like gold dust in the nap. To the north was the immense body of the mainland, what the Aleuts used to call *alyeska*, or greatland, to distinguish it from the Aleutian

Islands. Coastal lowlands rose slowly into mountain ranges, the ranges marching irregularly up the interior like soldiers shouldering angular blue-white packs. One range ran into another with barely a river or a lake or a valley between, the Wood River Mountains, the Ahklun Mountains, the Eek Mountains, the Kilbuck and Taylor and Kuskokwim Mountains. Soldiers wasn't a bad simile, he thought. The mountains were the last line of defense against the encroachment of settlement. They would be a harsh trial, as well, sorting out in swift order the quick and the dead.

Below them the Nushagak Peninsula curved southeast, and to the west he could glimpse the enormity of the Bering Sea beyond. It was a breathtaking sight, and he could tell Wy knew it by the smile in her voice. "Enough mountains for you, Liam?"

For one halcyon moment he forgot that his ass was hanging out a thousand feet up in the air and laughed for the sheer joy of it. "I guess so, after all," he admitted.

A few minutes later she spoke again. "Okay, we're here."

He tore his eyes from the distant mountains and looked down, catching his breath sharply when she put the Cub into a shallow descent, banking right in a wide, gentle circle.

"They call it Riggins Bay," Wy said. "I heard after the surveyor that worked this coast. You know, this coast wasn't charted even in the Coastal Pilot, not in any well-defined way, until the late seventies."

"And they fished it anyway?"

"They fished it anyway. They've been fishing it since before the turn of the century. For a long time they fished it in sailboats."

"Sailboats? You mean like with no engines?"

"Yeah, they weren't allowed to fish motorized vessels in Bristol Bay until 1951."

Riggins Bay was one of the many lesser bays that formed the coastline of Bristol Bay, but it was big enough for Liam. It had a curving beach that looked at least twenty miles long to Liam's less than experienced eye, the inner arc of which faced southeast. Each end sported prominent rocky towers and shoals, and the incoming tide was caught in the act of covering up a nice collection of boulders covered in dark green seaweed that waved gently in the ebb and flow of the water.

And the bay was simply boiling with boats. "Jesus, Wy! How many boats are down there?"

He immediately regretted asking, because Wy banked left to get a good look at the armada. "I'd say about two hundred, right around the same amount we had at the last opener. Not everybody who has a permit fishes it, you know."

Liam didn't know, and if he understood her implication, it meant that there could be even more boats out there than there already were, but for the life of him he wouldn't have known where to put them all.

"Some of them are rerigged gillnetters, some of them are purse seiners," she told him.

"Where are ours?"

"I'm looking." They flew around for a few moments, always turning left, Liam noticed. "Look for an orange buoy in the crow's nest."

Liam looked. "They've all got orange buoys in their crow's nests, Wy."

She sighed, heavily enough to be heard over the headphones. "You know, this would be such a great business, if it weren't for the fishermen."

She pulled out of the pattern and proceeded toward the beach. "We were about a hundred miles south of here day before yesterday," she told him over the earphones.

"Why not go back there?"

"Because the herring have moved since then, up the coast. We're following them."

"Why do they move up?"

"They're looking for kelp to spawn on," she said, and nodded out the window at the enormous beds of kelp, one after another, that lined the coast offshore. "The egg sacs adhere to the kelp, and hang on until hatching."

"The roe is what sells the herring, right?"

"Yes."

"Why not just wait for the herring to spawn and harvest the kelp then?"

"Some do. Others go for the fish, by purse seine or gillnet. It's a matter of what the Japanese buyers want more, plain roe or on kelp, and a matter of quotas—each method has a quota in tons. Fish and Game projected this year's biomass at a hundred twenty-five thousand tons, about seven percent below last year's."

Liam knew nothing about herring, but he knew just enough about salmon, Alaska's leading industry before the discovery of oil at Prudhoe Bay, to ask, "How much of that can you catch?"

"All the fleet, all together? Twenty-five thousand."

"Tons?"

"Tons."

Liam did some quick figuring. "Fifty thousand pounds. Doesn't seem like very much."

"I'd agree with you." She tossed him a quick, tight grin over one shoulder. "If we weren't getting fourteen hundred a ton."

"Fourteen hundred?" Liam's voice scaled up in disbelief. "Dollars? Fourteen hundred dollars per ton?" She nodded, and the dark blond braid bobbed with emphasis. "Jesus H. Christ on a crutch," he said, stunned.

"Best price we've ever had," she agreed. "We usually average around a thousand a ton, but I guess the Japanese are hungry for roe this spring."

Liam tried to do some more figuring, but too many zeros kept coming up on the ends of all the numbers. "How much in an average catch?"

"There is no average catch. You get what you can."

"Well, okay, how much do you want to catch?"

"All of it," she replied promptly. He heard a faint chuckle over the muffs. "But I'd settle for, oh, I don't know, two hundred tons." Suddenly wistful, she added, "Two hundred tons would be one hell of a haul."

"Two hundred for one boat?"

"Yes."

Liam blinked. Two hundred tons at $1,400 a ton was $280,000. "And you're spotting for how many boats?"

"Three."

"And you get fifteen percent of each boat's catch?"

"Yup."

Liam's heart sank. Fifteen percent of $280,000 was $42,000. For that kind of money, Wy could buy herself a dozen kids, and a judge to give them to her.

Especially if she didn't have to share it.

"Uh, Wy?"

"What?"

"How much do I get for riding back here?"

Wy's voice was mocking, reminding him irresistibly of the tone that big bastard of a raven used whenever he was in Liam's vicinity. "Why, Liam, and here I thought you were suffering through this all for love of me. Hold on to your tonsils."

"What? Hey!"

They banked hard right and descended in a series of tight spirals that had Liam bracing both arms against the sides of the plane and praying for a quick, merciful end.

When he ventured to open his eyes again they were flying low and slow along the inner curve of the long beach, and Wy was cursing softly over his phones. "What's the matter?" he said, panicking again. "What's wrong?"

"This would be such a great business if it weren't for the goddamn fishermen," she said bitterly. "Look at that, I told that son of a bitch two barrels down and one barrel up with the gas pump on the standing barrel. Look down there—can you see any barrels standing up?"

Liam swallowed his gorge and leaned over to look out the window. The ground seemed to be moving by awfully fast to him, but he saw a dozen dumps of 55-gallon drums, from one to five barrels each. None of the barrels was standing upright.

"Well, hell," Wy said, and pulled the Cub around in a large left-hand circle and set it down neatly at the edge of the receding tide, about five minutes ahead of another Piper, a Tripacer this time, coming in right behind her. There were already three other planes on the beach ahead of them.

It wasn't the first beach landing Liam had made, but he had enough trouble with Anchorage International and two miles of paved tarmac stretching out in front of him; a slanted gravel beach was considerably harder on the nerves. Wy taxied to the nearest pile of drums and cut the engine. The Cub shuddered and the prop went from Liam's blurred lifeline to full stop. Wy folded the door out of the way and deplaned. "Come on, Campbell, let's top off the tanks."

"We haven't been in the air much over an hour," he said, climbing out gladly enough.

"With herring you top them off every chance you get," she informed him. "And the dentist didn't put a long-range tank on his plane." There was a pump and a wrench on the gravel next to the barrels. "Come on, help me roll this down." He joined her and they rolled one of the barrels to beneath the right wing and stood it on end. She went to work on the cap with the wrench.

"So," he said, feeding one end of the hose into the drum, "when do we know if or when we can go fishing?"

"Fish and Game said there might be an opening last night, not that there would be for sure. They'll be out here themselves already"—she nodded at the bay—"either on a boat or in a plane. Probably in a plane."

"Maybe the 206 taking off after us."

She nodded. "Maybe. Probably yesterday they got one of the fishermen to sample the herring, see if it's ripe."

"They trust what the fisherman tells them?" Liam said skeptically.

She gave him a tolerant look. "Why would he lie? He can't sell them green."

"Oh. Sure, that makes sense."

Wy fetched a stepladder from the back of the Cub and stood it beneath the wing.

She climbed the ladder, opened the tank, and fed the other hose in. "Pump," she said.

He pumped. The sun was up and playing hide-and-seek with the cumulus clouds scudding across the sky before a brisk wind. There was a light chop across the bay but nothing serious. From here the boats scattered across the water looked less like an armada and more like the residents of a small boat harbor, a forest of masts and booms on the horizon. "How do they test them?"

"What?"

"How do they test the herring?"

"Oh. They come up on a ball of them and dipnet some out. They break the fish open to look at the roe. When they're ripe, or just about to spawn, the eggs turn a little yellow."

"Yum," Liam said.

"Hey," she said, draining the last of the aviation gas out of the hose before closing the tank back up, "we don't have to eat 'em." She gave the cap a last twist, and grinned down at him. "We just have to help catch 'em and sell 'em."

He couldn't help grinning back. She stood at the top of the ladder, her face and form outlined against the blue sky, wisps escaping her braid to curl around her face, all the hidden lights in her dark blond hair glinting in the sun, her brown eyes alive with mischief. She looked so desirable to him that he knew a sudden wish to pull her off that ladder and tumble her onto the beach. His flesh rose at the very thought. Down, boy, he said to himself, and made a production out of removing the gas pump and closing up the drum. "So most of the herring goes to Japan?"

"Pretty much all of it." He heard her folding up the stepladder and replacing it in the back of the plane. "The Japanese like their seafood, bless them, and they consider herring roe to be a special delicacy."

"Hence the fourteen hundred dollars a ton."

"This year anyway," she said. "Last year it was only a thousand."

"Only," Liam muttered.

"Hey!"

They both turned to see a large man with a red face plowing toward them through the gravel. "What the hell do you think you're doing!"

"Gassing up our plane," Wy said mildly. "What's it to you?"

"That's my gas you're using!"

Wy looked from him to the fuel dump to the dozen other identical fuel dumps within eyesight along the beach. "How can you tell?"

"I told my guys to drop three barrels right about here, and a gas pump and a ladder with them!" The man seemed incapable of lowering his voice. The guy towered over her—towered over Liam, for that matter—and outweighed the two of them combined by at least fifty pounds. He had fists the size of rump roasts and shoulders like cinder blocks. He looked like the Incredible Hulk, and Liam didn't want to make him mad.

Neither did Wy. "Sorry," she said with an ingratiating smile, "we thought this was our dump. We told our guy to put ours here, too. And I brought our ladder with me." She pointed. "There's another three barrels right up the beach, with a ladder lying next to them."

The big man turned to look. "Shit, that must be another half a mile up!" He turned and glared at her. "This would be a hell of a business if it weren't for the goddamn fishermen, wouldn't it?"

"A hell of a business," Wy agreed, and he plowed off to yet another Super Cub that looked far too small to hold him, climbed in, and sprayed gravel all over them as he taxied down the beach.

"He's going to dig himself in if he's not careful," Wy said, observing the maneuver dispassionately. "Yup. Come on."

The big man was out of the little plane and cursing it with all his might when they arrived. Wy went to one strut, nodded Liam to the tail, and waited politely for the other pilot to finish relieving his feelings and take the other strut. He did, eventually, and they bulled the little craft up the beach to the next fuel dump. It was only a few hundred feet farther, but the sand and gravel were loose and when they were done Liam wanted a real shower and wanted it now.

He had to settle for a couple of sticks of beef jerky and a Hershey bar. "First class all the way," he said wryly. He washed down the jerky with bottled water. "So, is this pretty much the way the day went with Bob DeCreft?"

Her head snapped around and she gave him a sharp look. "Pretty much," she said cautiously. "The first warning announcement by Fish and Game came at ten a.m., the second at noon, the third at two. By then, the fuel dump was dry and Bob and I flew straight back to Newenham."

"Uh-huh. And Bob did pretty much what I'm doing, sat in the backseat watching for planes?"

"Pretty much."

"How long were you up?"

"Including stops to refuel? Maybe eight, ten hours."

"So, no herring caught that day. That's why they're opening today?"

"Why they're maybe opening today," she corrected him. "We did get a short opener three days ago in Togiak. April twenty-ninth, the earliest herring season has ever been. Didn't come anywhere near the quota, though, which is why we get another shot at it."

"When is herring season usually?"

"Another two weeks or so. Middle of May, sometimes later."

"Why is it so early this year?"

"They're saying El Niño—you know, that warm current of water in the equatorial Pacific that sometimes moves too far north and west and throws everybody's weather out of kilter?"

"No snow in Anchorage? Floods in North Dakota?"

She nodded. "That's it. It's affecting more than just the weather. They caught a marlin in Puget Sound, tuna off Kodiak Island."

"Herring in Bristol Bay two weeks before time."

She smiled, clearly pleased with her exceptional pupil.

"You know, last night when I was looking out your window I saw a king jump in the river. It occurs to me it's early for king salmon, too."

"Way too early."

"Wy, did Bob say or do anything out of the ordinary that day? Did he have a fight with anyone on the ground?" Liam hooked a thumb over his shoulder at the big man refueling his Cub. "Duke it out with a pilot over a misplaced fuel dump, maybe?" She shook her head. "Okay, did he get into an argument with anyone on the radio?"

"No. Remember, the spotter can't talk to the boats, only to the pilot."

"So did he get into a fight with you?"

Her hesitation was infinitesimal, and he would have missed it if he hadn't been watching her so closely. "No."

He gave a long stretch. She watched him like a mouse waiting for the cat to pounce. "So it was just a normal day in the air?"

"As normal as it gets during herring spotting. Speaking of spotting." She checked her watch, and this time there was no mistaking the relief in her words. "Two hours to the announcement, or so we hope. We'd better back get in the air."

"Why do we have to go up so soon?"

"We need to do some scouting," she said, and waved him forward. "Find out where those little silver bastards hang when they're making babies. Come on, come on, let's move like we got a purpose."

ELEVEN

So they moved like they had a purpose. The Cub raised up off the beach smoothly and without incident, Liam helping in his usual fashion by clutching the edge of his seat. They headed south down the coast for about thirty minutes before making a one-eighty and retracing their steps. Fifteen minutes later she pointed out the left side. "Look," she said. Even over the headphones her voice sounded tense with excitement.

"For what?" he said, forcing himself to look out.

"Herring."

"What do they look like?"

"Big dark patches in the water. If you see some, poke and point."

"Okay."

All Liam saw was an endless expanse of green with a shoreline that looked too far away, a couple of boats cruising through, their wakes zigzagging with apparent aimlessness, and three other small planes at one, three, and eight o'clock, flyspecks on a light blue horizon. Then there was a glint of something in the distance, at about ten o'clock. He focused on that spot, and saw it again. "Hey?"

"Poke and point," she said, and he poked her in the shoulder and pointed past her left eye.

"Attaboy," she said. "Let's take a look." She made a slow left bank that from a distance would have looked as aimless as the course of the boats below. Ten minutes later they were drawing a perfect circle in the sky, as if they hadn't a care in the world. It was herring, all right, a dark patch with occasional flashes of silver as the fish hit the surface.

"Too small to bother Wolfe with," Wy said. "He's high boat; he's not interested in less than the offspring of an entire species."

"You don't like him," Liam said, looking at the back of her head, which didn't reveal much.

"Nope," she said.

"Then why work for him?"

"Because he's high boat," she said, in a tone that made him feel a fool for asking. "I'd work for the devil himself if he'd been high boat for herring for four years running."

"Fourteen hundred dollars a ton," Liam said.

"We can only hope," Wy said.

They found two other schools—Wy called them skeins—both too small to bother with. One already had a couple of boats sitting on it, waiting for the go-ahead to drop their nets. The second was being scouted by another plane, a Cessna 172 on floats. Liam knew that because they got close enough for him to read the manufacturer's lettering along the side.

"Knock that crap off, Miller," Wy ordered, and it took Liam a moment to realize she was talking to the pilot of the other plane. The 172 waggled its wings and banked hard left rudder. It was a little above and a little ahead of the Cub, and Liam had an excellent view of the bottom of its floats through the skylight in the roof of the Cub as it roared overhead. "Sweet Jesus," he muttered, forgetting his mike was hot.

"Get used to it," Wy said. "And don't forget, when you see a plane out of the pattern, don't be shy about pointing it out. Yell; slap me if that's what it takes to get my attention. Got it?"

"Got it," Liam said, clenching his teeth as the Cub pulled what felt like ten *g*s as Wy circled to head back down the coast.

"Good."

"Tell me again about the pattern."

"There's really only two rules. One is, always circle to your left. Two is, always keep the beach on our left."

"Explain it to me again."

With saintlike patience, Wy explained it to him again. "If we're all circling left, we're all circling left. Minimizes the chance of collision with somebody circling right. As we circle, we come up on and cross the shoreline. As we cross the shoreline, if we keep the beach on our left, it keeps us in the circle and going the same direction."

Liam realized and appreciated her patience, but he needed the repetition. The rules were safety rules. The safer Liam felt, the less distracted he would be, and the less distracted, the more observant. Observant in particular of planes that didn't circle to the left and didn't keep the beach always on their left.

At ten the radio crackled into life, and the same lifeless voice heard the night before came on. "This is the Alaska Department of Fish and Game. There will be an announcement concerning a herring opener in the Nushagak District for both drift and seine at twelve noon, May 2, on this frequency. I repeat, this is the Alaska Department of—"

"The Alaska Department of Hurry Up and Wait," Wy finished for him. "Okay, that's it, the point of no return. Time to head back to the beach and gas up." She stood the Cub on one wing, Liam grabbed for his stomach, and they headed back the way they had come. Below passed boats too numerous to count, two and three and four and five at a time, each group guided by its own spotter. Wy shook her head and said disapprovingly, "Five boats is too many for one plane to spot for. So is four. Three is about right. Two would be better."

"Why?"

"Because you've already got too much to do. You've got to fly the plane, look out for other planes, spot the herring, track the herring, and advise your boats. Advising three boats where to put their nets is plenty. Advising five, something else suffers."

They set down on the beach without incident, although the tide was considerably higher, and the available landing strip, to Liam's terrified eye, considerably narrower as a result. Someone had been at their fuel dump while they were gone; the first barrel was empty. The other two hadn't been tapped, and Wy took the discovery philosophically. "Probably whoever took it will let me know and reimburse me."

"How do you know?" Liam looked up and down the beach again. "It doesn't look like any of the dumps are marked. How does anyone know which gas is his? If you're taking somebody else's gas, or he's taking some of yours, how do you know?"

She shrugged, getting the stepladder out again. "Happens every year. The dumps aren't well marked; we're all using the same gas; everybody's in a hurry. After the season closes, the pilot will put the word out that he took some gas he thought was his and turned out not to be, and who can he pay back?"

Liam thought about it, working the pump arm, listening to gas slosh through the hose. "I'm not going to get this, am I," he said finally.

She tossed him a cheerful grin. "Nope. But don't worry about it, I've never been shot at for thieving." The grin flashed again. "Not yet, anyway." She topped off the wing tank and closed it up. She paused, up on the ladder. "What's that?"

"What's what?" He looked up from closing the drum and saw her pointing at the edge of the beach where it began to slope down. There was a thick stand of tall ryegrass bending gently in the breeze.

She scampered down the ladder and hared up the beach. "Wow, look at that!"

He came panting up behind to find her burrowing into the soil with both hands. "Wy, what is it?"

"Help me dig!"

He saw a round shape emerging, and fell back with an explosive sigh. "Jesus, I thought it was a dead body at least."

"Come on, help me dig!"

He resigned himself, and helped her dig.

It was a glass float, one of thousands and over the years probably millions that had broken loose from Japanese fishing nets and floated across the Pacific Ocean to wash ashore on Alaska's coast. The usual find was four inches in diameter. This one, a clear green unbroken sphere with tiny bubbles of air caught inside the shell, was over eighteen inches across.

"Score!" Wy said, sitting back on her heels and beaming.

Liam remembered the glass floats from the Cub's inventory.

He sat back and brushed the dirt from his hands. "Beachcombing's part of herring spotting, I take it."

"Beachcombing is a part of everything," Wy said severely, getting to her feet. "You never know what you're going to find—a glass float, a walrus tusk, an eagle feather. A case of Spam."

"A case of Spam?"

She nodded. "I found one last year, washed up on shore south of here. The box was falling apart but the cans were okay. We're still eating them." She held the float up by its netting, admiring it. "I bet I could get a hundred bucks for this."

"You sell them?"

"Five bucks for the little ones, seven-fifty if they've still got their nets. And on up, depending on what kind of shape they're in and if they've still got their netting on." She grinned. "I get a lot of tourists my way, Liam. They don't call themselves that, of course, they are fishermen and hunters and hikers and like that, but they're tourists all the same, from Outside and overseas and all over the world. Most of them have never seen something like this. I've got a basketful of them in my shack at the airport."

"The door of which you oh so casually leave open while you're loading the plane."

"Every little bit helps," she said cheerfully. She placed the float in back of Liam's seat, wrapping it in her sleeping bag. "A good omen," she said, regarding it with satisfaction. "It's going to be a good day for us."

Liam thought of what was in store for him and shuddered, but maintained a diplomatic silence. Wy knew he didn't like flying, but pride had kept him from showing her how much, and he was damned if he was going to confess now. Instead he said, "You have dimples."

She blinked up at him. "I beg your pardon?"

"You have dimples," he said. He framed her face with his dirty hands. "One here"—he kissed it—"and one here." He kissed it, too, and drew back to smile at her. "Never saw them before."

He watched with a secret smile as it took her two tries to

fumble out the Ziploc bags full of sliced dry salami and Tilla-
mook extra sharp cheese. They ate a quick lunch, washing it
down with bottled water and following it with another Hershey
bar. Ten minutes later they were back in the air. By this time
Liam was inured to it, or so he told himself. Maybe he was
going to get over his fear of flying after all. Maybe, just maybe
he was going to learn how to climb on board a plane without
breaking into a sweat of fear.

They cruised down the coast for forty-five minutes, seeing
various groups of boats staking out various likely-looking
balls of herring. The radio crackled into life. "Wy, you up
there?"

"I'm up here, Cecil."

"You seeing anything?"

"Nothing worth mentioning."

"Get the goddamn lead out," Wolfe ordered. "We're an hour
away from the announcement."

"Where are you?"

"You can spot me easy—I've got an orange buoy in the
crow's nest."

Wy muttered something.

"What was that?"

"Could you be a little more specific, Cecil? Like what land-
mass is off your bow?"

There was a silence ripe with things unspoken. Liam imag-
ined Cecil rending the air blue with imprecations about uppity
bitches who had no business mouthing off to their employers.
Either that or Wolfe didn't know where he was.

"Dutch Girl Island," Wolfe said finally. "About ten miles
north."

"Roger that," Wy said. She goosed the Cub and fifteen minutes later they were circling three boats off a round island that
rose straight up out of the sea to a flattish, rounded peak. Two
rocky ridges jutted out of the sea to the east and west, forming
a vague similarity to a Dutch girl's winged cap, at low tide and
from a distance. Life clutched tenaciously to the steep sides in
the form of thick grass and brush and a swarm of slender black
seabirds. "What are they?" Liam said.

Wy looked through her binoculars. "Murres, I think." She let the lenses wander. "Well, well," she said with an undertone of excitement that made Liam sit up. "What have we here?"

She put the Cub in a slow, wide circle, and Liam looked out the window through his binoculars.

About five miles off the southwest side of the island he saw a silver-gray layer just beneath the green surface that seemed to go on forever, in every direction.

"Is that them?" Liam said in disbelief. He'd never seen so many fish in one place in his life.

"Oh my," Wy breathed. "Oh my my. And aren't they balling up nicely."

"That means they're about to spawn?"

"That's what that means," Wy said. She sounded tense and absorbed, and Liam shut up and let her concentrate. His eyes roved the sky for other traffic. So far, nothing.

Wy didn't dare complete more than one circle for fear that someone else, another spotter or a crew member of one of the hundreds of boats in the area, would see her and guess what they had found. She rolled out and headed straight for Wolfe's three-boat flotilla. When she got there she dropped down to fifty feet off the deck and folded up the left-hand window. Even with earphones clamped to his head the rush of air and the roar of the engine was deafening. Liam wanted to pray but he was so scared he forgot how, and he'd stopped believing in God a long time ago anyway.

Wolfe had come out of the cabin on his flying bridge and stared upward. The expression on his face was clearly visible, and the words on his lips easily read. "What the fuck do you think you're doing, Chouinard?" Next to him stood the immediately recognizable bulk of Kirk Mulder.

Wy leaned her head out the window and yelled, "Follow me!" She circled the boats once for emphasis and headed back to the ball of fish.

Liam managed to reswallow his heart and said, "Why didn't you just call him on the radio?"

"I was scared somebody might be listening in."

"I thought all the radios were scrambled."

"They are."

Not the trusting type, Wyanet Chouinard.

"Please, please, please," Liam heard her mutter over the earphones, "please, please, please don't let anyone beat us to it, please, please, please. You watching for traffic, Campbell?"

He hadn't been, and jerked his eyes guiltily to the skies. There were six or seven specks on the horizon, but nothing nearby. "All clear. So far so good."

"Good." Five minutes more and Wy said, "There's the little sonsabitches!" Again, she didn't dare sit on them for fear of calling attention and made a wide sweep around Dutch Girl Island instead, trying to look as if she hadn't found anything and was still searching. "What time is it?"

Liam checked his watch. "Eleven forty-eight."

"Okay."

Liam, caught between Wy's tension and his own fear, knew a compulsion to talk, about anything. "How big is that boat of Wolfe's?"

"Fifty-six feet," Wy said.

"How much you figure it cost?"

"The hull price was seven hundred thousand. With electronics, total price comes close to a million. Or so he likes to brag in the bars."

Liam whistled. "I can't even imagine what payments on a boat like that would be."

Wy snorted. "Try insurance."

"Yikes."

"Yeah. You can make a lot of money fishing, but you've got to spend a lot first."

They made another deceptively unhurried turn. There was a plane growing larger on the northern horizon. Liam poked Wy and pointed. "I know, I saw him. That's Miller Gorman, the guy in the 172 on floats who tried to sideswipe us earlier. He's spotted us, all right. But here comes the cavalry."

She banked the plane and Liam caught a glimpse of three boats approaching, all of them on the step with full white wakes. "The other two boats are a lot smaller."

"Thirty-two feet each," Wy agreed. "They're rerigged gillnetters. Most herring boats are. Wolfe's an exception. He does well enough to be an exception. Boat one, you read me?"

Wolfe's voice, unmistakable in its arrogant assurance, replied, "Read you five by, flygirl. I see them."

"I figure three hundred tons."

Wolfe's laugh was cut off by static, but his words came through loud and clear. "Try four."

"Four hundred tons?" Liam said. "Four hundred tons? As in fourteen hundred dollars per ton?" He tried to work it out in his head but again the number of zeroes defeated him.

"As in fifteen percent of fourteen hundred times four hundred tons," Wy said, her voice rich with satisfaction. Beneath it, because he was listening for it, Liam could hear the undercurrent of heartfelt relief. "Now all we've got to do is make sure we get most of 'em."

The tension and excitement were manifest in the set of her shoulders as she put the plane into a sweeping left circle, as they passed over it with the southwestern side of Dutch Girl Island always on their left. Other boats were arriving. Liam poked and pointed. "Yeah," Wy said, "there are always skippers watching what Cecil's doing. They know he's not going to get his nets wet unless—"

A new voice came on the air. "This is the Alaska Department of Fish and Game, announcing an opening for herring fishing in the Riggins Bay District. This opening will last for twenty minutes, beginning at twelve o'clock today. Five minutes to the opening."

"Twenty minutes!" Liam yelped. "We're doing all this for twenty lousy minutes' worth of fishing?"

Her sigh was audible in the earphones even over the noise of the engine. "Liam, one year the whole season was twenty minutes. We're just lucky we didn't pull our quota three days ago, that we've got another shot at it."

"Four minutes to the opening," the disembodied voice intoned.

"Shit," Liam said, and poked and pointed at a big blue and white plane approaching from the sea.

"Yeah, Fish and Game's 206," Wy said. "Don't worry, they'll stand off. They're just here to keep us honest."

"How do they do that?" Liam said, watching the float plane with his own service's insignia on the side climb to a higher altitude. The Fish and Wildlife Protection officers were state troopers, too. They went through the same training he did, but enforced the fish and game laws throughout the state, or tried to. Liam didn't envy them that task; he'd rather disarm an axe murderer before trying to relieve a rabid sport fisherman of his illegally caught king salmon, any day.

"They've got cameras with clocks in them bolted to the fuselage, and they're aiming them at the boats below. They'll know if we put our nets in the water one second before we should, or keep them there one second longer than we should."

"What happens if we do either of those things?"

"Then Cecil could probably kiss his million-dollar boat goodbye."

"They'd confiscate it?"

"You bet your ass. And, more important, we wouldn't get paid."

"Three minutes to the opening."

"Cecil," Wy said, "stay on course for another minute. Alex, stand to and prepare to drop your skiff where you are. Mike, you've got company, coming up hard astern."

Liam saw two more boats approaching. The second of the smaller boats in Wolfe's miniflotilla broke off from the steadily increasing ball of herring and put itself in the way of the oncoming boats. Liam poked and pointed. "Goddammit," Wy swore as the Cessna 172 insinuated itself into their circle. "It's okay, we got 'em, we got 'em." Barely audible over the headphones, Liam heard her say, "Please let us have them, please let us have them."

"Two minutes to the opening."

The two new boats broke ranks, one circling around Wolfe's second gillnetter, or Mike, which Liam supposed was the skipper's name. "Mike, stay on the first boat," Wy ordered. "Cecil, you've got company."

The big boat was on the other side of the ball of herring. It looked twice as large and three times as powerful as the little gillnetter heading over to challenge it. Wolfe's voice was elaborately casual. "What company? Oh, you mean that little itty-bitty skiff over there? I can hardly make him out, the little peckerhead's so tiny."

"Cecil—"

"One minute to the opening."

Cecil—by now Liam, too, was calling the boats by the names of their skippers—made a course correction and found itself directly in the path of the oncoming vessel. "Goddammit, Cecil, you're on his portside, he has right-of-way!"

"Is that a fact?" Wolfe sounded mildly surprised.

Twenty minutes was going to be just long enough for a fisherman on his toes to scoop up as many herring as he could. "With a ball of herring this bunched together," Wy said, her voice taut with excitement and anticipation and, yes, unabashed greed, "we're going to beat the hell out of them!"

Liam took this to mean that they were going to catch a lot of fish, as long as they could beat the other fishermen to them, and as long as—"Watch out!" he yelled, slapping the side of Wy's head as the 172 nearly brushed their wing with a float—as long as they survived the experiment.

"Miller, watch your goddamn six!" Wy roared.

"Ten seconds to the opening," the expressionless voice droned. "Eight seconds, seven seconds, six seconds, five, four, three, two, one, open; the herring season for the Riggins Bay District is open."

Suddenly Liam was too busy to be scared.

Wy's voice, excited but controlled, sounded continually in his ears. "All boats, drop your skiffs, *now*! Cecil, hard left rudder, hard left rudder!"

"Wy, watch it, traffic, blue plane with floats ten o'clock descending!"

"Alex, steady as you go, you got 'em, you got 'em!"

"Wy, watch out, you're coming up too fast on that red plane, back off, back off, back off!"

"Mike, come left, come left, come left, don't let him get around you!"

"Wy, Cub at two o'clock, go left, go left, your other left, dammit!"

Suddenly it seemed that the sky was filled with planes and the water with boats. Liam didn't have time to wonder where they'd all come from; all he could do was point and poke and prod and slap and kick and yell, all as Wy watched the water and directed the boats.

A hundred feet beneath the tight circle Wy had locked the Cub into, the fishing boats launched their skiffs. These weren't dories with little 40-horsepower Evinrudes, but powerboats with 250- to 300-horsepower outboards that were on the step practically before their hulls hit the water.

The way it worked was this. One end of the purse seine was fastened to the skiff, the other end to the boat. The idea was for the skiff to make a large circle around as many herring as possible and head back for the mother boat, which would then draw the bottom of the seine together, making a bag of the net. From there, they would use the boom to lift the net into the boat, or brail the fish into the hold one large scoop at a time, or deliver the fish to a waiting tender—Liam caught distant glimpses of three larger boats hanging around the perimeter of the action, but they weren't about to run into him so he ignored them. "Watch it, that green plane—son of a bitch!"

The green plane's pilot misjudged his altitude and the 172's speed and his gear glanced off the left wing of the 172 as it was coming up from behind. The 172's wing dipped sharply waterward, started to spin, and recovered, pulling up and banking right, out of the circle.

Something wet running into his eyes blinded him for a moment. Liam wiped it away and discovered that sweat was pouring down his forehead in rivulets. In front of him Wy was oblivious, all her attention trained on the water below. "Yes! Okay, Cecil, close it up, close it up, close it up!"

The expressionless voice came over the headphones. "Ten minutes remaining in the opening; I say again, ten minutes remaining in the Riggins Bay herring opener."

"Mike, you've got ten minutes to lose that jerk and set your net! Alex, hard right rudder, you got nothing but net if you close it up now! Cecil, you still got company off your stern, watch out he doesn't foul your seine!"

One of the two poaching gillnetters was still being fended off by Mike's boat, every zig of the gillnetter being met by a zag from Mike's. The boat tagging Cecil had dropped his skiff and was preparing to make a run for the fish.

Liam saw water boil up from Wolfe's stern, and the big seiner surged forward and ran right over the top of the other boat's skiff. The man in it dove over the side at the last possible moment, the prop of the big seiner passing over the exact spot he'd been standing not three seconds before.

"Jesus Christ," Liam said in disbelief.

"Nine minutes to closing; I say again, nine minutes to closing."

"Watch the sky, Campbell!" Wy snapped. "Close it up, Cecil, close it up, you've got nine minutes!"

There were six or seven planes—or maybe twenty; Liam was never really sure—in the same tight circle, buzzing around the fishing scene like angry wasps, the 172 recovering enough to rejoin the group. It seemed as if every time he looked up he saw a pair of floats through the skylight. Every time he looked right, another plane filled up the window, someone in the backseat slapping the back of his pilot's head. There was never a moment when it seemed to him that they were not in imminent danger of a midair collision. Here a pair of floats passed so closely by he could see water dripping from the rudders; there the face of another observer was so near he could see the strain and fear on it as plainly as he could feel his own. The sharp blur of a propeller reminded him of what had happened to the last person to fly observer for Wy, not a comforting thought. Liam's poking and slapping became less tentative. Yelling and cursing seemed natural; in the space of twenty minutes, Liam was learning a whole new vocabulary.

There was as much or more chaos on the water below, where twenty-five boats battled for sea room and herring, with more competitors arriving every moment. In between his constant scanning of the sky and the equally constant poking and prodding of Wy he caught glimpses of a continual game of bump-and-run, of the gillnetter's swamped but not sunken skiff, of a bulging purse seine black with fish—he hoped theirs, but for the life of him he couldn't tell one boat from another—of a gillnetter with its prop fouled in its own seine, of another adrift with a dead engine, of a third—Liam blinked. If his eyes did not deceive him, there were three men on the deck beating the hell out of each other.

The man who had dived off the swamped skiff had bobbed up to the surface and one of his crewmates on the gillnetter ran a boat hook out for him to grab on to and hauled him on board. From the brief glimpse Liam caught of him, he didn't appear to be bleeding. Bleeding or not, Liam had personally witnessed a third-degree assault, a class C felony at least. They came around again in their circle and Liam caught a glimpse of the big seiner getting its catch on board—lowering the boat considerably in the water—then running its net out again.

The dispassionate, disembodied voice came over the air once more. "Five minutes remaining in the opener; I say again, five minutes remaining."

Liam went back to watching the sky. Either everyone had slowed down or in the short space granted to him he had adjusted to the pace of the job. He felt like someone had switched him from 45 to 33 1/3. Everything took on a dreamy, slow-motion quality. There was plenty of time to spot traffic, forever to notify Wy, an eternity for her to find them safe passage. The loud jumble of excited voices over the earphone receded, and all he could hear was the sound of his own words, concise, deliberate, heavy with importance.

Slap. "Cessna on floats at ten."

Poke. "We're sneaking up on the red plane again; fall back, fall back, fall back."

Nudge. "Watch out, there comes that 172 again."

Point. "Trooper plane at two, trooper plane at two."

"One minute remaining in the opener; I say again, one minute remaining."

The Cub's circles seemed to tighten, and Liam's entire focus narrowed to five square miles of sea and air. Planes, boats, fish seemed to blur together; he heard his own voice speaking, saw his own hands moving, felt his own eyes roving back and forth, looking, watching, waiting.

"—ten seconds to closing, eight seconds, seven seconds, six seconds, five, four, three, two, one . . . The herring opener for seiners for the Riggins Bay District is now closed; I say again, the herring opener for seiners for the Riggins Bay District is now closed."

Wy immediately straightened out the Cub, heading it away from the scene on a southwest course. "What's it look like, Cecil?" There was no immediate answer, and she banked right and made a relaxed sweep north to look over the situation from what Wy considered a safe distance and from what Liam, returning slowly and reluctantly to real time and space, did not. He squinted at the sky as if he'd never seen it before. It had never seemed so blue. "Is it really over?"

Wy was busy going into a tight circle and didn't answer.

Directly below, one of the big processors had come alongside Cecil's fifty-two-footer. There was a widemouthed hose stuck into the bulging seine net, busily vacuuming up the herring penned there and sucking it into its own hold. The hose was transferred to Corseiner's hold, where it sucked up everything there, too. Alex was next in line with a catch a third the size of Wolfe's. Mike's catch looked smallest of all, but then he'd been busy for much of the opener fending off the encroaching gill-netter, which Liam privately thought was a little greedy of him—surely in a ball that size there was more than enough herring to go around. He knew better than to voice this thought in present company, however.

The other boats, the ones that had not fouled themselves in their own nets or had their sides stove in by someone else or whose engines had not failed them at the crucial moment—or whose crews had not mutinied—had done well, if not as well as the first three boats on the scene. Everybody had fish in their nets, including one tardy soul who failed to close up his purse in time. Over the radio for all the fleet to hear, he was commanded by the Fish and Wildlife officer in the air above to open his seine and let the fish go. It was one of the larger of the lesser catches, and it took a minute for the skipper to bring himself to do it.

"I say again," the Fish and Wildlife officer's voice said sharply, "F/V *Bonnie Doon*, you have exceeded the time allowed to fish; open up your seine."

The *Bonnie Doon* opened up her seine, and the teeming mass of herring boiled out into open water.

"Ouch," Wy said. "There goes about forty-five grand, swimming away. Cecil, quit sitting on your thumb and tell me how we did!" There was no answer, and she cursed. "Hang on, Liam."

"Wy," Liam said apprehensively. "What are you doing?"

"Just hang on."

"Wy!"

She waited for an opening and when it came, dived toward the big seiner, pulling up again at what Liam felt was the last possible moment. He was so terrified he couldn't catch his breath, let alone scream. "Cecil, goddammit, what have we got?"

It was with real gratitude that Liam heard the radio crackle into life. "Hold your goddamn horses, flygirl. We're busy."

"Well, get the lead out, I want to know if I get new wings for my Cub!"

The other planes were standing off, no doubt conversing impatiently with their own skippers. Wy flew a lazy eight pattern over the fishing ground and back around Dutch Girl Island for about ten minutes before Cecil came on again, while Liam indulged himself in fantasies of her slow and painful death, preferably at his hands. "Hold on to your drawers, flygirl. Looks like we got about a hundred sixty tons between the three of us, maybe a little less."

"What's the percentage?"

Liam could hear the grin in Wolfe's voice. "The Japs say it's looking good—about fifteen."

Wy's whoop was exuberant and deafening. The stick between Liam's knees came back hard and the Cub went into a steep climb. "You buckled up, Liam?"

"Wy? Wy, what the hell are you doing! *Wy!* WY! Goddammitohshitohshitohshiiiiiiiiit!"

She took them up to 2,500 feet, and they were cruising at 125 miles per hour with all the air room in the world between them and the next plane over when she put the Cub into a shallow dive, building up speed until they hit 140 miles per hour. She pulled back on the stick and pushed in the throttle and whooped again as they sailed around in a picture-perfect loop.

They regained level flight at precisely 142 miles per hour at 2,010 feet. "There," Wy said, and turned to grin at Liam. "We done good, Campbell. Goddamn, but we done good!"

Liam spoke between clenched teeth and meant every word. "I am going to *kill* you, Chouinard."

She laughed, the sound full of triumph. "Let's fuel up and head for home, stud! We are rich!"

TWELVE

Back in Newenham, Liam unfolded himself carefully from the little Cub and stood erect to blink in the sunlight. He felt strangely light-headed, elated, possibly even erring on the side of euphoric. He'd spotted herring and survived. You are feeling your immortality, he thought, and grinned involuntarily.

"What?" Wy said, pausing in the act of tying down the plane.

"I'm just feeling my immortality," he said.

She stared at him. "What?"

He waved a hand. "Never mind. Where's the Fish and Game tie-down?"

Her gaze sharpened. "Why?"

He shrugged. "She's a fellow officer. Figured I should introduce myself."

"Oh. Okay. That way." She pointed. "That's their office, that little blue building between the Era hangar and Ye Olde Gift Shoppe."

The Fish and Wildlife Protection officer was unloading her cameras. Liam tapped her on the shoulder and stuck out a hand. "Hi, I'm Liam Campbell."

She straightened and squinted at him. "Right, the new trooper, my opposite number. Charlene Taylor. I heard you were out there with us."

"You did? How? I didn't know I was going myself until last night."

She grinned. "Never underestimate the power and scope of

the Bush telegraph." She raised a quizzical eyebrow. "I thought that was my job."

"It is," he said, fervently enough to make her laugh. "It's all yours. I ain't doing that again never nohow not ever."

"I don't blame you," she said with a twinkle. "It does get a little hairy during herring."

She was about fifty, a stocky brunette with laugh lines radiating from the corners of her eyes and mouth. She didn't look even the least little bit wound up, whereas Liam's legs were still shaking from the effects of the loop and he could feel the strain and stress of the past hours humming through the very marrow of his bones. Adding insult to injury, her uniform shirt wasn't even sweated through, the brown fabric holding its neat creases and sporting the requisite number of badges and patches and nameplates and insignia. Liam formed a silent resolve to have the blue shirt of his branch of their mutual service pressed and on before another day passed, if he had to force someone to get out their iron and ironing board at gunpoint.

"What were you doing up there, anyway?" Taylor said, bending back over the camera.

"Partly a favor to a friend, partly an ongoing murder investigation on Bob DeCreft."

She stood erect again, startled. "Bob DeCreft? I hadn't heard that was murder, I thought he just walked into his own prop."

"Does that happen a lot?"

"I wouldn't say a lot," the fish hawk said thoughtfully. "It happens. Not very often, but it does happen, even with old-timers who know better. Especially during breakup, when everyone's working twenty-six hours out of the twenty-four to get ready for fishing season. What makes you think it was murder?"

"His p-lead was cut."

She stared at him, shocked. "What?"

"His p-lead was cut," Liam repeated. "And cut while the power was on, so that when DeCreft switched it off the power was still connected when he walked the prop through. It killed him."

She thought this over, frowning. "You sure it was cut? You sure it wasn't just frayed?"

Liam shook his head. "It was cut."

"Well, hell," she said, and shook her head. "Who would want to kill poor old Bob DeCreft?"

"Did you know him?"

She bent back over the camera. "As well as anyone did around here, I guess. He hunted and fished, so we had some conversation over moose and caribou and salmon seasons, like that. I never had cause to haul him in, although I expect he did his share of poaching."

"What makes you say so?"

She shrugged, her back to him. "Most of the old guys out in the Bush pretty much figure that their right to fish and hunt when and where they please was grandfathered in with statehood."

Liam had to smile. He couldn't see Moses Alakuyak waiting for a clock to tick down to put his net in the water, if he was up a creek and that creek was filled with fish. Of course as an Alaska Native Moses had subsistence rights, so long as he didn't abuse them by selling the fish he caught commercially, which he probably did the first chance he got.

"I did run into old Bob up a river off the Nushagak one time," Taylor said reflectively. "Years ago, that was." She popped a roll of film out of the camera and replaced it with another.

"What, was he poaching?"

She shook her head and stood upright, rubbing the small of her back. "No. Not that time, anyway." She cocked an eyebrow at Liam and grinned. "He had a girl with him."

"A girl? Oh, the little blonde? Laura Nanalook?"

"Oh, you know about her?"

"We've met," Liam said.

She gave him a sympathetic look. "Yeah, that's right, you would have. One reason I've always been glad to stay on my side of the service, I don't ever have to tell anybody their people are dead. Anyway, it wasn't Laura."

"It wasn't?"

"No."

"Who was it?"

"I don't know." She grinned again. "He was awful anxious to

get rid of me, old Bob was, and I thought for sure he had a bunch of king fillets in his cooler he didn't want me to see. King season not being open for another day," she added. "But it wasn't fish he was hiding, it was a woman."

"Who was it?"

"I don't know. I only saw her from a distance. We were on the sandbar and she was on the bank. Guess she'd waded across to tinkle or something, or maybe he'd waded back across for a beer."

"What did she look like?"

"Like I said, I didn't get all that good a look. She was short, kinda thick through the middle, dark hair." She looked at him. "One thing I know for sure."

"What's that?"

"She was somebody's wife."

"Why do you say that?"

Taylor spread her hands. "Why hide otherwise?"

Why indeed? Liam pointed at the film. "You got everything that went down out there?"

"Pretty much. Something always slips through, but I think I got everything I need. Why?"

Liam thought it over. He didn't want to mess up Wy's paycheck, but he knew a powerful wish to see Cecil Wolfe get a little of his own back again. "I saw an awful lot of boats running into each other out there."

"Yeah?"

She wasn't going to help him any. Liam said doggedly, "Some of it looked deliberate."

"That a fact," she said placidly. She saw his look and gave a snort of laughter. "Let me tell you a story, Liam. Last year during herring, season was on time instead of early like this year so it was, oh, second week of May, I guess, we had an opener down in Togiak. There was a collision between a couple of boats which involved the sinking of one of the boats' skiffs. The guy who lost the skiff filed a complaint, and Corcoran—you know Corcoran?" Liam nodded. By the very absence of emotion in her voice he could tell what Fish and Wildlife Protection Trooper Taylor thought of Public Safety Trooper Corcoran.

"Corcoran arrested the other skipper for assault. It came to trial last November. Guess what the verdict was." She paused expectantly.

He thought for a moment. "Who testified?"

"Oh, the whole kit and caboodle—both skippers, the deckhands on both boats, the guys on the skiffs, both spotters, and me. We all told the same story, with slight differences of opinion on whether the ramming was deliberate." She waited.

"Where was the trial?"

Her smile was approving. "Right here in Newenham."

"Acquittal," he said.

"You got it. Just like the last six cases where anyone could be bothered to bring charges. Probably one out of every two jurors from a panel generated from this judicial district is thinking, There but for the grace of God go I. So we get acquittals, now and then a hung jury. Sometimes," she said reflectively, "sometimes, in my more cynical moments, I think they've got it worked out beforehand, before they ever go into deliberation. But that's only in my more cynical moments. Most of the time I'm a regular Pollyanna when I look at our judicial system. Innocent until proven guilty, I always say."

"And everybody out there today qualifies."

"That's right," she said cheerfully. "You just have to understand, being found not guilty in Newenham of any fishing-related crime is not exactly the same thing as being innocent."

Liam had to laugh.

She grinned, satisfied. "And if there is one thing our local state attorney hates worse than an acquittal, it's a hung jury. Both are a waste of the judge's time, both cost the state money, and both get him grief from his boss in Juneau. Makes him hard to live with."

Liam raised an eyebrow. "How would you know?"

The grin widened. "He's my husband." She pulled a small grip from the back of the Cessna and closed the door firmly. "No one will be filing charges anytime soon for anything that happened out on the water today, Liam. That's just the way it is."

Liam got the feeling she was telling him this particular story for a reason. He took her implied advice and his leave.

It didn't matter all that much. Moses was right—sooner or later Cecil Wolfe would get his. His very arrogance would cause him to cross the line again and again, until one day he did it when all the lights were on and everyone was looking.

On that day, Liam would be watching, too.

He could wait.

But could Laura Nanalook?

Wy had taxied the borrowed Cub back to its tie-down and was busy removing all traces of its most recent trip from the interior. Liam stood watching her for a moment. "You didn't ask the dentist if you could borrow his Cub, did you?"

She started and froze for a moment. "Dammit, Liam, don't sneak up on a person like that." She gave the floor of the plane a final brush with a whisk broom and folded up the door. "And I do, too, have his permission to take her up."

From her airy tone of voice, Liam guessed, "Once in a while? Like maybe once a year? Say for a test flight just before he comes down to kill caribou?"

In that same tone of airy unconcern, Wy said, "He pretty much leaves that up to me."

"Uh-huh," Liam said. "You enter today in the log?"

Wy drew herself up to her full height and looked him straight in the eye. "Of course I did."

"Uh-huh," Liam said. He could have asked to read the log, but was unwilling to do anything so extremely foolish. About all he could hope for was that he wasn't mentioned by name. She began walking toward her own tie-down and he fell into step beside her. "You never did tell me, how much do I get paid for today's jaunt?"

As if in answer to his question, a bright red four-wheel-drive Chevy S10 long bed drew up with a flourish. Cecil Wolfe got out from one side, Kirk Mulder from the other.

Wolfe looked over her head. "Trooper Campbell."

Mulder nodded, his skeletal grin flashing out to blight the landscape.

"You made good time into port," Liam said. "I figured for another hour out at least."

Wolfe waved an expansive hand. "I've got a pilot boat on the payroll, comes out to pick me and Kirk up when we get done delivering. I let the crew bring her the rest of the way in."

Of course.

Wolfe slung a careless arm around Wy and pulled her next to him, grinning down at her. Liam noticed the stiffening of her shoulders, but he also noticed that she didn't pull away. "Hear you were up in the air with my flygirl."

"I was," Liam admitted.

"Well, by God you must be our lucky charm, because we beat hell outta the little sonsabitches today!" He lifted Wy up off her feet, wrapped both arms around her in a bear hug, and kissed her, taking a long time over it. Wy dangled limply, about as responsive as a sack of potatoes, the only thing that saved Wolfe from instant and total annihilation. Liam hung on to his temper and his patience, and eventually Wolfe dumped Wy back on her feet. Liam, watching her face, recognized the moment when she realized she couldn't spit and drag a sleeve across her mouth. Wolfe saw it, too, grinned his hard, feral grin, and chucked her beneath the chin, much as Corcoran had just before he'd boarded the Metroliner. "We done good, flygirl. We done real good."

"How good?" Wy demanded.

Wolfe pulled a spiral notebook from a pocket. "Mike got twelve, Alex got thirty-six, and I got a hundred and ten. Add 'em all up, you get—"

"One hundred fifty-eight tons," Liam said, and in spite of himself felt a little light-headed.

"The percentage stay at fifteen?" Wy said.

Wolfe nodded.

"What is this percentage business?" Liam said, remembering Wy asking Wolfe that question while they were still in the air.

"The percentage of total weight in roe," Wolfe replied. "Ten percent is considered excellent."

"And we got fifteen," Wy said, a slow smile breaking across her face. "How much did we get a ton?"

Wolfe's grin widened. "Top dollar."

"How much is top dollar?" Wy demanded.

"The most we've ever got," Wolfe replied, enjoying himself. In someone less arrogant, it might have been called teasing. In Wolfe, it was a demonstration of power on the schoolyard level: *I know something you don't know, I know something you don't know.*

"How much is 'the most we've ever got'?" Wy demanded.

"Eighteen hundred."

"Eighteen hundred a ton?" Wy's voice scaled up. "We actually got eighteen hundred dollars a ton?"

"Eighteen hundred a ton," Wolfe confirmed. "Here's your copy of the fish ticket."

Liam moved to stare over Wy's shoulder at the sheet of paper Wolfe handed her. He also had the check from the processor with him, which Wolfe flourished like the banner of a conquering hero. So many decimal places made Liam dizzy.

"This oughta pay for fixing up that plane of yours, Chouinard," Wolfe said. "Fearsome, what a crowbar can do to the fabric on a wing."

"How did you know they used a crowbar?" Liam said. "In fact, how did you know Wy's plane had been trashed?"

Wolfe gave a practiced shrug. "Hell, trooper, it was all over Newenham five minutes later, just like all the rest of the news."

"I didn't tell anyone about the crowbar," Liam said. "The only other person who knew about the crowbar besides me was the guy using it." He looked at Mulder. Mulder looked stolidly back.

He knew for sure, now, and Mulder knew he knew, and so did Wolfe. But he couldn't prove it, and they knew that, too. Wolfe gave Wy a sly nudge. "Anyway, lucky for you we did so good today."

"Luck had nothing to do with it," Wy said, lost to anything but the numbers on the fish ticket.

"Yeah, you earned your keep," Wolfe said, grin widening. "Well, I'm going to go deposit this check, clean up, and get the book work out of the way," Wolfe said, "and then I'm buying at Bill's. I'll be handing out paychecks there."

"See you then," Wy said.

Wolfe's grin widened even farther. "I just bet I will."

Master and man climbed into the Chevy and drove off. Liam liked nothing about Wolfe—not his cocky arrogance, not his cool assumption of intimacy with Wy, not his relationship, if you could call it that, with Laura Nanalook, and most especially not his air of knowing something Liam didn't. He didn't like Mulder, either, but that was personal, and would be settled personally, at a time and place of Liam's choosing. Alaskan fishing seasons were long, and so were the summer days. As with Wolfe, time was on Liam's side.

John Barton would not have approved, but then John Barton had not been coldcocked with a crowbar on a rainy airfield in the middle of the first night of his posting. In law enforcement, your reputation was even more important than your badge and your gun, and Liam had no intention of beginning his career in Newenham with the word getting around that he could be whacked with impunity. And if he read Wolfe right, word would get around.

He looked over at Wy, who was staring again at the fish ticket. Wy felt his stare and looked up. A tear slid down her cheek. She didn't notice. "You can't know what this means."

Liam remembered John Barton's call that morning. "I can guess." He gestured in the direction of the Cub. "Especially now."

She held the fish ticket up. "Ten percent of this is yours, don't forget." He started to say something, and she waved his words aside. "You earned it. You watched the sky and you didn't throw up down the back of my neck. Believe me, that's not bad for a first-time observer."

"Ten percent?" Liam said.

She smiled. It was a pale imitation of the real thing. "Ten percent. I've got to go—I want to clean up, too. See you later."

She walked off, no spring to her step, and for the first time since he had landed in Newenham no consciousness of their relationship coloring her demeanor, either. She wasn't thinking of him or of her or of them, she was thinking about her bank balance. Given what he knew of her situation, and the tattered wings of the plane parked a row up, he could hardly blame her.

She had mistaken his response. He had not been over-whelmed by his percentage; he had in fact been dismayed by it. Four thousand two hundred sixty-six dollars. That would have been Bob DeCreft's share, had he lived to earn it.

Say for argument's sake a lawyer billed at $100 an hour. It was more than that nowadays, but $100 was easy to divide into $4,266. Forty-two hours. Liam wondered how many attorney-hours the standard adoption case averaged.

He'd investigated murders committed for the loose change in a man's jeans. Four thousand two hundred sixty-six dollars was a lot more than pocket change.

There were public showers at the harbormaster's. Liam got in at the tail end of a long line and ran out of hot water halfway through. It was after seven before he got back to the post, and when he did, he found Jim Earl pacing up and down the office in an obvious snit. "Where the hell have you been?" hizzoner barked. "I been trying to track you down all day."

"Working on the DeCreft murder case," Liam replied, which was the truth, if not all the truth. He could have added, Not that I'm accountable to anyone except my boss for my actions, but he didn't.

That slowed Jim Earl up a bit, and Liam realized why with his next words. "Oh. Jesus, I forgot. Poor old Bob." By now, everyone Liam had spoken to had called DeCreft "poor old Bob." He hadn't been that poor or that old. Liam wondered what it had been about the man that made people pity him in retrospect. Other than his sudden and violent death.

Jim Earl rallied to his cause. "I wanted to talk to you about Kelly McCormick."

"Who?" Liam said, caught off guard.

Jim Earl glared. "Kelly McCormick, the guy who shot up the post office."

"Oh. Of course. I knew who you meant, the name just slipped my mind for a moment. Press of business and all."

It was a weak defense, and both men knew it. "You even talked to him?"

"Jim Earl," Liam said, a trifle impatiently, "I've been on the ground here in Newenham for"—he checked his watch—"not quite three days. I walked into the middle of a murder and two shootings, and I haven't had time to find someone to press my uniform, much less a place to stay. No, I haven't talked to Kelly McCormick. I've asked around about him. I haven't found out much, and I haven't found him."

With awful sarcasm, Jim Earl inquired, "Did you think of looking for him on his boat? Or at his girlfriend's?"

"I didn't know he had a boat. Or a girlfriend."

"Of course he's got a girlfriend," Jim Earl snapped. "Every girl in this town is looking for a way out of it from the time she reaches puberty on, and the fastest way to get out of it is to waggle their tail feathers in front of some young rooster with a boat and a permit."

"And Kelly McCormick qualifies?"

"You bet your ass he does," Jim Earl said. "In fact the only good thing I can find to say about that boy is that when he's sober, he's one hell of a worker. He catches himself one hell of a lot of salmon. 'Course he immediately drinks it all right down, so that don't mean one hell of a lot."

"What's his boat's name?"

"Hell, I don't know. He called it after some kinda booze or other, the *Wild Turkey* or the *Sloe Gin*, something like that."

Liam sighed. "Who's his girlfriend?"

Jim Earl eyed him. "Oh, so I'm supposed to do your work for you, is that it? Listen, boy, I don't expect one hell of a lot out of the Alaska State Troopers, considering the last three to occupy your spot."

The last three? Liam thought. So far he'd only heard about two. Was John holding out on him? What other horror in the Newenham trooper post's past was he responsible for living down?

"Well, hell, all that's past praying for, and at least you can't get knocked up." Jim Earl fixed him with a steely eye. "You can do your job, however, and I expect you to, and one part of your job is to find and arrest the man who fired on our postmaster. The Reverend Gilbert is a fine, good, upstanding, moral man, who never—"

"Reverend?" Liam said.

Jim Earl was momentarily thrown off his stride. "Oh. Ah. Well. Yes. Our postmaster is also the minister of one of our local churches." He brushed this aside brusquely. "But we're getting off track. Yes, one of our young women has set her sights on Kelly McCormick, and yes, he's keeping company with her."

"Does this young woman have a name?"

"Of course she has a name. Oh. Candy. Candy Choknok."

"Where does she live?"

"With her parents, of course."

"Fine," Liam said patiently, "and they live where?"

"Mile 5 on the Lake Road, you can't miss it. The local Native association has a subdivision going in there; Carl Choknok's the chairman of the board, he got the first house. First house on the right as you turn right, big blue mother."

There was still plenty of light for a drive out the Lake Road, also known as the Icky road. Not to mention which, it was always good for a trooper stationed in the Bush to curry favor with whatever local authorities there were. Liam combed his hair and then immediately ruined the effect by pulling on the gimme cap with the state trooper insignia on the crown. The lump on his head had almost vanished, and the band of the cap settled over it comfortably.

It took him longer to find the Lake Road than it did to drive to the Choknoks' house. The road was a high, level pile of gravel packed firm and flat, with no potholes to speak of and wide turns you could take a bulldozer around in perfect confidence that you would not sideswipe any oncoming traffic. Liam got to the five-mile marker in less than ten minutes. On the right side of the road was a large sign proclaiming, THE ANGAYUK NATIVE ASSOCIATION PRESENTS THE ANIPA SUBDIVISION: AFFORDABLE HOMES FOR NATIVE SHAREHOLDERS. A HUD PROGRAM.

That portion of the Lake Road that continued on beyond the sign deteriorated significantly; from where he sat Liam could see washboarding, soft shoulders, and a dozen potholes of a size to compete with the ones on the road from the airport. He turned off it with gratitude.

The first house on the right was big and it was certainly blue, an electric blue that looked as if it might glow in the dark. It was all blue, too—the porch and the steps that led up to it, the window frames, the door, the eaves. The only thing that wasn't blue was the roof, and that was because it was neatly shingled with black asphalt tiles. Liam got the feeling that if it had been at all possible, they would have been blue, too.

As he got out, a raven backwinged to a landing in a nearby tree and was scolded by a squirrel who had thought that it was his spruce. They yelled at each other while Liam went up and knocked on the door of the blue house. A young woman answered. She was short, stocky, and dark-haired, with a round face, clear skin, and intelligent dark eyes. She looked first at the badge on his cap and then at his face. "Hello."

He doffed his cap. "Hello, ma'am. I am State Trooper Liam Campbell. I'm looking for Candy Choknok."

"I'm Candy Choknok," she said.

Someone called from inside the house. "Candy? Who is it?"

"It's all right, Dad, it's for me. We can talk on the porch," she said, stepping outside and closing the door behind her.

"All right," Liam said. They leaned back against opposite sides of the railing and regarded each other in unsmiling silence. "Nice house."

She unbent a trifle. "Thank you."

He tried to break the ice, and gestured at the sign. "I'm new in Newenham, Ms. Choknok. Is 'anipa' Yupik for something?"

"Owl," she said.

"Owl," Liam said. "You get a lot of owls hereabouts?"

"A few." She regarded him steadily and without expression.

"I haven't seen any owls myself, at least not yet." The raven clicked at them from the tree. "On the other hand, I have been seeing a whole hell of a lot of ravens."

"Yes."

"Mmm." Enough small talk. "I'm really looking for Kelly McCormick, Ms. Choknok. I need to talk to him about an investigation I am conducting. I have reason to believe that you might know where he is."

"I might," she agreed. She was very much in control of herself and in command of the situation—a self-possessed young woman, with a natural dignity and a solid presence. "I imagine you want to talk to him about the shooting at the post office yesterday morning."

In Liam's professional experience, very few people were as forthcoming as Ms. Choknok without having an agenda of their own to put into motion. "I might," he agreed cautiously, and pulled out his notebook.

"Kelly's an idiot," she said in a tone of dispassionate observation, "and he is especially idiotic when he has been drinking."

"And had he been drinking yesterday morning?"

"I'd say he'd been drinking pretty much all night," she said coolly. "He started out at Bill's, as I understand it, and then continued on at Tasha's."

"Tasha's?"

"It was a party at a friend's house. Tatiana Anayuk." She spelled it for him and gave him the friend's phone number. "He had been drinking before I got there, and when I left, he still was."

"About what time was that?"

"A little after eleven. My curfew is midnight, and Tasha lives on the bluff south of town. I didn't want to be late. My parents worry."

"I see," Liam said, making a note. "Ms. Choknok, do you have any idea why Mr. McCormick would take it into his head to shoot up the post office?"

For the first time she hesitated, glancing back at the house. "Like I said, he'd been drinking. And when Kelly's been drinking, pretty much anything goes."

There was something she was not telling him, but that was all she was prepared to say at the moment, and by the stubborn set of her very firm chin he knew there was no point in pursuing it. One thing he couldn't resist. "Why are you telling me all this, Ms. Choknok? I had heard—" He hesitated.

She stood up and brushed off the seat of her pants. "You had heard that Kelly McCormick was my blue ticket out of Newenham."

"Well, yes."

She offered him a chilly smile. "He was. My parents are so scared I'm going to marry him that they offered to send me away to the University of Washington."

Out of curiosity, Liam asked, "Where were they going to send you?"

"At first, nowhere—they didn't want me leaving home. Then, when I insisted on going to college, they decided on the University of Alaska." The chilly smile broadened, just a little. "Kelly McCormick's alma mater, or would have been, if he hadn't dropped out last year. He told my folks he still had friends there, that they'd look after me."

Not just intelligent, Liam thought, positively Machiavellian. "Well, I wish you the very best of luck, Ms. Choknok." Not that it looked like she needed any, being the kind to make her own. On impulse, he said, "What are you planning on studying?"

Her expression didn't change. "Psychology."

"Of course you are," Liam agreed cordially. "I understand they have an excellent psychology program at U-Dub."

"That is my understanding as well."

Liam folded up his notebook. "Oh, I almost forgot. One more thing, Ms. Choknok. Can you tell me the name of Kelly's boat?"

"Certainly," she said. "The *Yukon Jack*. She's a—"

"—white thirty-six-footer with a red trim line looks like it should be on a Nike sneaker," Liam said resignedly.

"Why, yes. She's parked right next to—"

"—the *Mary J.*," Liam said. He tucked his notebook into his pocket. "Thank you for all your help, Ms. Choknok. Good-bye, and good luck."

She inclined her head once, with all the graciousness of a queen at home on her own court.

THIRTEEN

He went back to the office and called Tatiana Anayuk's number. A breathless, girlish voice with a permanent giggle implanted in it answered. "Yes, this is Tatiana Anayuk. Who is this?"

"This is Liam Campbell, Ms. Anayuk. I'm—"

"Tasha."

"I beg your pardon?"

"Tasha. Everybody calls me Tasha."

"Oh. Ah. Well, uh, Tasha, then. This is—"

"You have a wonderful voice—has anybody ever told you that? Deep, and low, and kind of growly. I like it."

"Thank you," Liam said. "My name is Liam Campbell. I'm with the state troopers, and I'm—"

"Oh, I love your uniforms!"

"Pardon me?"

"Especially the hats. They make you all look like Mounties." Giggle. "And Smokey the Bear."

"Thank you," Liam said dryly, "you're not the first person to say so. Ms. Anayuk, I've just come from talking to Candy Choknok."

"Oh, Candy, sure. She's my very best friend." A momentary pause. "She's not in trouble, is she?"

"No, I just wanted to ask her a few questions about a friend of hers. She said the last time she saw him was at your house last night."

"Oh gosh, I guess you mean Kelly?"

"Kelly McCormick," Liam confirmed.

"Poor Kelly," Tasha said. Another giggle. "That boy sure tied himself one on, and when he does that—look out!"

"How late did he stay last night?"

"Golly, Lee—"

"Liam," Liam said before he could stop himself.

"Liam—isn't that a nice name; is that like Liam Neeson? I just think he's the absolute most. I cried and cried when I saw *Schindler's List*, and wow does he look good in a kilt! Only I don't think he wore a kilt in *Schindler's List*, did he?"

"Tasha, do you remember how late Kelly McCormick was at your party last night?"

"Gosh, I don't know. Mickey Boyd was over, and, well, you know." Tasha's giggle was kittenish and appealing, but Liam was growing tired of hearing it. "We're throwing another party tonight, Liam. You guys have to go off duty sometime, right?"

There were days on the job when Liam thought the larger part of his salary subsidized his patience during witness interviews. Other days he couldn't decide which was worse: a lying witness, or a flirtatious one. "When was the last time you remember seeing him?"

"Gosh, I don't know. After eleven, anyway."

"Why after eleven?"

Again with the giggle. Liam gritted his teeth. "That's when the flatfoot contest was."

"Flatfoot contest?"

"You know, flatfooting pints. Kelly flatfooted a pint of Everclear. Candy said he was going to go blind, but then she's always been such a party pooper."

"A shame," Liam agreed gravely, and made a mental note to offer Ms. Choknok a ride to the airport to catch her university-bound plane when the time came. "And Mr. McCormick left following the, er, flatfooting contest."

"Yeah," Tasha said regretfully. "Larry Jacobson started puking his guts out right after; it was so gross. We would have made Kelly take him back to the boat."

"Larry Jacobson?"

"Yes, him and Kelly are friends. I think they fish together or something, too," she added vaguely.

Liam remembered the lump in the starboard bunk of the *Mary J.*, the lump named Mac. Son of a bitch. He said, "But you couldn't send Mr. Jacobson home with Mr. McCormick because Mr. McCormick was already gone, is that the deal?"

"That's it! Gosh, you're smart, aren't you?"

"And that was the last time you saw him?"

"Who, Kelly? Sure." The giggle was back. "Of course, we all heard about the shoot-out at the U.S. corral."

"Tasha, do you know why Mr. McCormick would want to shoot up the U.S. Post Office?"

"Well, sure, doesn't everybody?" she said in surprise.

"I don't," Liam said hopefully.

"That's right, you haven't been around here long, have you?" she said in a kind voice. "I remember, I heard there was a new trooper coming." She paused, and said uncertainly, "There was some story about some trouble—but that can't be you, you're too nice. And anyway I can't remember it all."

Good, Liam thought. "So why would Kelly McCormick shoot up the post office, Tasha?"

"Because he doesn't want to be a born-again," she replied promptly.

Liam blinked. "What?"

He heard another voice in the background. Tasha squealed with delight. "Benny, hi! I'm so glad you could come over! What's that you got? Oly? Great! No, I'll be right there, I'm just talking with a friend." She returned her attention to Liam. "I'm sorry, Liam, I have to go."

"No, wait, Tasha, I need to know about Kelly McCormick—"

"I told you," she said, impatient with his slowness. "He shot up the post office because he didn't want to go to church."

Liam said stupidly, "Which church?"

"The Trinity Born Again Unto Christ Chapel, of course," she replied promptly. "None of us want to go, but it makes it hell on getting your mail if we don't." Liam heard a door slam and another voice. "Hey, Belle! Listen, Liam, this party's just getting started, you come on over later, you hear? I've always got house room for another good-looking man." She giggled, and then dropped her voice to a confidential murmur. "But don't wear your uniform, okay? That kinda puts people off sometimes, you know?"

There was a click and Liam was left holding a dead receiver. He replaced it carefully in the cradle.

So far, his encounters with Bush villagers were running against type. Generally speaking, you couldn't find an Alaska Native woman who would say boo to a goose. In the space of two hours Liam had interviewed two who had plenty to say and no fear whatever of speaking their minds. True, one was an airhead, the other eighteen going on eighty, but the difference between these two young women and the village women he had been briefed on in trooper school was vast.

Which only went to show that even the mighty Alaska State Troopers were prone to error on occasion. A sobering thought, which reminded Liam that while interesting, this kind of speculation wasn't getting him any forrader. Kelly McCormick had shot up the post office because he didn't want to go to church. Taking a gun to a federal building seemed to Liam an extreme reaction to an aversion to organized religion, not to mention unproductive. Why not just shoot up the church?

Liam caught himself. He'd been in Newenham for three days, and apparently the location was beginning to rub off on him. The obvious course for Mr. McCormick, if he didn't want to go to church, was simply not to go to church, rather than to get out a gun and—

He paused. What had Tasha Anayuk said? Something about not going to church making it hell to get your mail?

What was the name of that church again? Trinity something? Liam got out the phone book and looked in the yellow pages. For a city of only two thousand permanent residents, there seemed to be a large per capita percentage of religious establishments. There were churches Roman Catholic and Baptist, Mormon and Moravian, Seventh-Day Adventist and Jehovah's Witness, Russian Orthodox and Assembly of God.

And there was the Trinity Born Again Unto Christ Chapel, Pastor the Right Reverend Richard Gilbert, presiding, a large

boxed entry touting two separate Sunday services, Sunday
school, Bible study on Tuesday and Thursday evenings, family
services on Wednesday and Friday evenings, and ladies' min-
istry (whatever that was) on Saturday evenings.

He paged back. Newenham had nine churches, and only two
bars, an interesting ratio. Most Bush towns he'd been in, it
would have been eleven bars, one nondenominational chapel,
and the Catholic priest would have flown in from Kodiak to
conduct Mass in somebody's basement before flying on to the
next town to do it all over again that afternoon. Maybe Newenham served as the religious center for the district, and people
flew or boated or snow-machined in for services.

He put the book to one side and drew out the sheet of paper
covered with neatly penciled boxes, each enclosing its own name.

The man with the limp he'd seen talking to Wy at the airport
when he returned from Bill's that first day was Darrell Jacobson. Darrell was Larry's father, who was a friend and possibly
a business partner of Kelly McCormick's. He drew another
box, and added Kelly McCormick's name.

Kelly McCormick had shot up the post office, where the
Right Reverend Richard Gilbert moonlighted as the postmaster.

The Right Reverend Richard Gilbert was married to
Rebecca Gilbert, who had demonstrated great grief at the news
of Bob DeCreft's passing, and whom Liam had last seen bolt-
ing through the front door of Bob DeCreft's house.

Bob DeCreft was Wy's observer.

Full circle.

His sheet of paper now looked like a circuit diagram for the
control panel of a 747. Doing the box thing, as John Barton so
elegantly put it, was not helping him on this case, as everything
and everyone seemed connected to everything and everyone
else, a curse of life in a small town.

He looked at the calendar. It was still Sunday. He opened the
phone book again. The ad in the yellow pages had thoughtfully
provided a map, showing the location of the church, so as to
guide poor sinners unerringly to redemption and reclamation of
the soul.

And it was right on the way to the small boat harbor.

❈   ❈   ❈

The church was a large, traditional building, white clapboard with a steeple, a bell, a wide porch leading up to a pair of handsome double doors, and two lines of rectangular stained glass windows marching down each side. Liam pulled up across the street and parked discreetly behind a stand of alders now coming into bud.

He was just in time; Sunday evening services were letting out. The family of five Liam had seen on the plane led the way, the baby still wailing at its mother's breast. A dozen others emerged and scattered in various directions. Religion in Newenham seemed to be in good shape, as witnessed by the fond farewells the congregation took of its pastor and the warmth with which those farewells were received.

Religion didn't interest Liam; he'd neither felt that leap of faith nor envied it in others. As far as he was concerned, faith was just a euphemism for confidence, as in confidence game, an attitude he'd inherited from his father, who had told him early on, "Never mind praying; make your own luck and don't go whining to some invisible creator when you don't work hard enough to get it."

This opinion was manifestly not shared by Newenham's mayor, the Honorable Jim Earl, the last one out of the church. He paused at the top of the stairs and his voice came clearly through the open window of the Blazer. "I don't know that I ever looked at Leviticus that way before, Reverend. It's always so hard to get through, all them damn, uh, darn laws. Doggone it, and we were just talking about chapter five, verse one, too. Shoot. I'm sorry."

Pastor Gilbert patted Mayor Jim Earl's shoulder consolingly. "It takes time, Jim Earl."

"I guess." Jim Earl paused at the foot of the stairs to grin up at Gilbert. "At least we don't have to go round cleansing no lepers no more!"

Well now, Liam thought. Jim Earl's excessive interest in the post office shooting could not have been made more plain. Liam, who liked to understand the people he was working with and for, was grateful for this illumination of the mayor's motives.

"Where's Rebecca?" Jim Earl said, looking around as if just missing her for the first time.

"She wasn't feeling well." Even from across the block, Liam noticed the wooden quality to Pastor Gilbert's voice.

It missed Jim Earl by a mile. "Say, that's a shame. Tell her I was asking after her, will you? Good night."

Jim Earl clattered briskly down the steps and was off.

Liam checked his watch. Nine o'clock. The sun, two hours away from setting, was casting long shadows across the street. His stomach growled, reminding him he hadn't eaten anything but salami and cheese and candy bars all day. Well, he knew where there was a burger with his name on it. He could stop by the boat harbor afterward.

Halfway there the radio crackled into life. It was Molly, the dispatcher, reporting an assault. "Why are you telling me?" Liam said.

"Officer Berg thought you might be interested," she said, and when she told him the name of the victim, he was.

Make that two stops before hitting the harbor: Bill's and the hospital.

Bill's place was packed to the rafters and Bill herself was a fast-moving blur behind the bar. A party of herring fishermen who had either done very well or very poorly that day were either celebrating their hard work and good fortune or drowning their sorrows, and pounded the table in a demand for more beer.

When he caught her, Liam told Bill, "I'll have a cheeseburger, fries, and a Coke to go."

She scowled at him. "You bring your own take-out bag?"

"On second thought, I'll eat in this evening," he said, and grinned.

"Yeah, Campbell, bite me." She bellowed his order into the pass-through and went back to opening bottles and filling glasses.

Cecil Wolfe was present, in the same booth he had been the day before, a booth overflowing with the crews of all three fishing vessels under his command. Kirk Mulder sat at Wolfe's right hand.

Bill was right—the crew looked as if Wolfe hired by the pound: a group of big, beefy bruisers with pugnacious attitudes and scarred knuckles, some of the scarring fresh. Like Liam's head wound, the swelling beneath the scratch down Mulder's face had subsided. Liam was sorry to see it. Mulder lifted a bottle of beer in one fist, and Liam saw fresh blood on his knuckles. One of the other men noticed and said something, and stoic as ever, Mulder dabbed at the bleeding with a bar napkin.

Wy was there was well, sitting in a chair a little to one side. She was nursing what looked like a very warm beer, and she looked sober and more than a little tense, by which Liam deduced that Wolfe had yet to pass out the paychecks.

Oh so casually, Wolfe stuck out a foot, hooked it around one of the legs of her chair, and pulled her next to him. Over her head he met Liam's eyes, and smiled.

Wy turned her head and saw Liam at the bar. She set her beer down and got up to greet him. Over her head, Liam smiled back at Wolfe, who scowled darkly until Laura Nanalook appeared with a loaded tray. He put the same hand on the same hip he had the day before. She ignored him, unloading her tray with quick, deft movements. When she turned to go his grip tightened.

The other men at the table watched avidly, waiting to pounce on the first trace of embarrassment or fear. She displayed neither, meeting Wolfe's eyes with the same flashing smile she served every other patron in the bar. Wolfe didn't like it much, but when Bill yelled at Laura to pick up her order, he said only a few words, inaudible to Liam over the noise of the bar. The men in the booth laughed with an edge of excitement and anticipation, and when Laura turned to walk back to the bar Liam thought her face was paler than it had been before.

"Son of a bitch," Wy said, standing next to Liam. "Wolfe just can't believe there's a woman around who can resist him. Poor little Laura. She was okay as long as Bob was alive. I don't know what's going to happen to her now."

Laura had been less than okay under Bob DeCreft's dubious protection, but Liam wasn't in the habit of betraying confidences and he said nothing. Laura returned to the bar and began loading her tray. Gary Gruber sidled up, and under the noise of the bar Liam heard him say awkwardly, "Hi, Laura."

"Hello, Gary," she replied, hands not pausing in her task.

He fiddled with the zipper pull on his jacket. "Uh, I was sure sorry to see—I mean, hear—I mean, it's awful about Bob."

She flashed another of her patented smiles. "Thanks, Gary. I appreciate that." She picked up her tray.

"Uh, Laura?"

She paused and said, a little impatiently, "What, Gary? I'm kind of busy here."

"Of course," he mumbled. "I was just wondering if you'd like—if sometime you'd want to—" Beneath her patient stare his words died away. "I'm sorry, Laura, excuse me. It was nothing." He gave a vague flap of his hand and turned back to the bar to bury his nose in his glass.

Not for the first time Liam marveled at how opportunistic his own sex could be. Bob DeCreft wasn't cold and the sharks were already circling.

His eyes traveled beyond Gruber to Wolfe. Some weren't bothering to circle. "You stay away from Wolfe, do you hear?" Liam said harshly.

Wy looked at him in surprise. "I'm hanging until he forks over my paycheck, and then I'm outta here," she said, adding incredulously, "Are you jealous or something?"

He closed one hand around her arm, pulled her around to face him, and said with all the conviction he could muster, "Stay away from him, Wy. Stay as far away from Cecil Wolfe as you can get. The man's dangerous. Don't ever be alone with him."

She pulled free. "You are jealous," she said, but she wasn't certain.

"He's dangerous," he repeated. "Don't be alone with him, not ever."

She stared. "What aren't you telling me?"

Bill appeared with a loaded plate and a glass of Coke. Liam turned back to the counter and waded in. "Sit down," he said, kicking out the stool next to him. "Have a fry."

She cast a look over her shoulder, and then took the stool.

He picked up the salt shaker. Bill rematerialized. "Fries aren't salty enough for you?" she inquired frostily.

Liam put the shaker back down. "The fries are perfect."

"I thought so," Bill said, and disappeared again.

"Jesus, that woman," Liam muttered.

Wy laughed. "I like her."

Liam looked Wy straight in the eye. "If I'd seen her first, I'd be in love with her."

Wy flushed and didn't reply.

Liam finished off his fatburger in half a dozen big bites, mopped up the last of the juice with the last of the fries, and licked his fingers. "I mean it, Wy. Get your check from Wolfe and get out of here." He stood up and pulled out his wallet. "I've got to go; I've got a couple of stops I have to make."

"Where?"

"One's the harbor, the other's the hospital. See you later."

He left her staring after him as he went out the door.

Outside, the raven croaked at him. He ignored it, heading for the Blazer when he caught sight of a white Ford station wagon. He walked over to look inside, but it was empty. He looked around the parking lot and didn't see anyone, other than a couple steaming up the windows of a bright green Toyota Tercel. And he would surely have noticed her if she had been inside Bill's, as would have everyone else, something devoutly to be avoided by a minister's wife—especially, from what Liam had seen and heard, this minister.

The hospital was a three-story building painted a soft white with dark green trim. It had wings leading from either side, and as instructed Liam entered through the emergency door into the right wing. A nurse in a white two-piece pantsuit sat behind a counter. She was short and dark, with a round face and almond-shaped eyes. She spoke English slowly, with a heavy Yupik accent, but she was perfectly understandable. He followed her directions down a hall and into a treatment room, where behind a curtain he found the prone figure of Kelly McCormick.

McCormick had been beaten severely about the face and

head. His eyes were swollen shut, his nose broken and bleeding, his lips split over his teeth. His clothes had been cut from his body to display defensive wounds up the undersides of both arms and great purple and yellow bruises on his chest and belly. One hand looked as if it had been stamped on by a heavy boot, the index finger sticking up at an odd angle.

He was conscious, however. He peered up uncomprehendingly at Liam through slitted eyelids. He grunted something, his mouth too damaged to articulate his words.

"I'll be damned," Liam said. Recognition came hard but it did come. "You're the guy at Bill's. The one who helped to get the rifle away from Teddy Engebretsen."

Larry Jacobson was standing on the other side of the bed. "Don't try to talk, Mac." He stared at Liam, hostility warring with fear in his face. Hostility won. "What do you want?"

"I heard Mr. McCormick had been brought in to the hospital," Liam said. "Thought I'd stop by." Yes, there was one of the dimples sported by Mac honey. He'd have ditched the barfly, too, if he had someone like Candy Choknok waiting on him. And Candy had said that Kelly had started out at Bill's on Friday, before going on to Tasha's party and first prize in the flat-footing contest.

Liam gave an inward sigh. All unknowing he had encountered Kelly McCormick twice in the past three days, the first time on Friday at Bill's, the second time on Saturday, on board the *Mary J.* He wasn't sure what that said for his powers of observation. He wasn't sure he wanted to know.

"We've already talked to Cliff Berg," Larry Jacobson said belligerently. "He took our statement."

"That'd be the local police?" Larry nodded and Liam wondered if he was ever going to meet the mythical local police. He stepped up to the bed and leaned over so McCormick wouldn't have to strain to see him. "Mr. McCormick, I'm Liam Campbell. I'm the new state trooper assigned to these parts. Do you know who beat you up?"

It was hard to read any expression on that battered face, but the head turned away and one maimed hand clawed at Jacobson's arm. "He doesn't want to talk to you," Jacobson said.

"He's too hurt, anyway. I told you, we already talked to the police."

"Mr. McCormick, do you know who beat you up?" Liam repeated. "Tell me."

The maimed hand stilled, the slit in the eye closed, but Liam didn't think McCormick had gone to sleep or passed out on him. "Mr. McCormick? Whoever did this to you, he shouldn't be allowed to get away with it. I won't let him. Tell me who did it."

Nothing. "Did it have anything to do with your shooting up the post office yesterday?"

The slit opened again and a fragment of blue eye looked up at him in alarm. Liam smiled. "Yes, I know about that. I've been looking for you to ask you some questions."

"You got any witnesses?" Jacobson demanded hotly.

"About ten, all together," Liam said dryly.

The blunt answer squelched Jacobson for the moment. "Oh."

Neither McCormick nor Jacobson would be missed by the gene pool if either disappeared off the face of the earth, Liam reflected. "Why'd he do it?"

"Shoot up the P.O.?"

Liam nodded.

Jacobson glanced at McCormick. They seemed to commune telepathically for a moment or two, and then Jacobson looked back up at Liam. "I'm not saying he did do any such thing," he said.

"Uh-huh," Liam said.

"But if somebody," Jacobson said, stressing the last word, "if somebody took a gun and shot up the post office, then somebody might have had a really good reason."

Liam maintained an expression of polite interest. "And that really good reason might be—what?"

Again there was an exchange of looks. "That Gilbert guy, he's the postmaster."

"Yes."

"He's also the minister for the Trinity Church."

"Yes."

Jacobson shuffled his feet, then blurted out, "He won't give you your mail if you quit going to his church."

"Ah." It was about what Liam had expected, and it was yet another instance of how far out of his jurisdiction he was wandering in his new posting. My kingdom for a United States postal inspector, he thought. There's never a federal cop around when you need one. "So Kelly here thought he'd get the Right Reverend Mr. Gilbert to hand over his mail at gunpoint."

"Hell," Jacobson said, suddenly irritated, "the only reason we ever went to that damn church in the first place was because those babe daughters of Walter Sifsof's started going. Couple of stuck-up broads they turned out to be," he added in disgust. "So we quit, and then Gilbert starts holding our mail back."

The slit of one imploring blue eye looked up at Jacobson, reminding him to be cautious. "Anyway, I'm not saying Kelly did or he didn't. But if somebody did, that might may be how it went down."

Liam sighed. "I don't suppose it occurred to either of you to file a complaint with Gilbert's boss? Tampering with the United States mail is a federal offense. You can go to jail for it."

Jacobson stared at him. "But his boss is in Anchorage!"

"Of course he is," Liam murmured. "Okay. We'll come back to this, but right now I've got another question for you."

"Oh yeah?" Jacobson's relief at getting away from the incendiary topic of shooting up federal buildings was almost palpable. "What's that?"

"Did you fish the opener this afternoon?"

Jacobson glanced down at McCormick. "Yeah."

"Your dad with you?"

"Yeah."

Liam nodded at the figure on the bed. "Your friend, too?"

"Yeah, we were on our boat and he was on his." Jacobson was wary but as yet unsuspicious. "Why?"

"Where were you fishing? What area?"

Liam noticed that the figure in the bed had become very still.

"Dutch Girl Island," Jacobson said readily enough.

"Where Cecil Wolfe and his bunch were fishing."

Jacobson shrugged. "There were a lot of boats in a lot of places."

"I was up in the air today, observing for the *Sea Wolfe*. Flying with Wy Chouinard."

McCormick clawed again for Jacobson's arm, but Jacobson had already stiffened. "So?"

"So I spotted the *Mary J.* from the air. Cecil ran over your skiff, didn't he?" A sullen look settled in on Jacobson's young face. "You always fish where Wolfe fishes?"

"A lot of people do," Larry said defensively. "He's high boat, he's got a reputation for finding fish. Sure, we follow him around. Us and fifty other boats."

"Uh-huh. Anybody spotting for you?"

Jacobson and McCormick exchanged a quick look. "We don't need no spotter," Jacobson said, thrusting out a pugnacious jaw. "We got sonar, we got crow's nests, and today was clear, you could see the herring balling up from miles away."

"Of course you could," Liam agreed cordially. "That's why you followed Cecil Wolfe around, because it was so easy to spot the herring on your own."

Jacobson flushed a dull red.

"How about the last opener? Anybody spotting for you then?"

"No," McCormick said loudly, making both his friend and Liam start. "Nobody spotting for us."

Liam sighed. "Figured you'd say that." He went to the edge of the curtain and paused, looking back. "Nice to meet you finally, Mr. McCormick. We'll be talking again, about that business at the post office." He pulled his cap on. "Right now I've got to go down to the small boat harbor. I got a call from the dispatcher on the way to the hospital. Seems that a boat has sunk at its moorage. Little gillnetter by the name of *Yukon Jack*." He settled the cap just so. "Looks like somebody opened her sea cocks and left her to sink."

He couldn't have sworn to it, but he thought McCormick's eyes filled with tears. "Since the harbormaster says the local police are busy, I'm going to go down and take a look."

"That son of a bitch!" Jacobson's face was now as red as it had been white. "That motherfucking son of a bitch!"

He was trying to shake McCormick's grip loose. "No," McCormick said in a harsh whisper. "No, Larry, don't. He'll kill you. He'll kill you." He managed to haul himself up into a sitting position, groaning with pain at the effort. "No, Larry. No."

"The hell with that!" Jacobson raged. "Look what he did to you, and now he's sunk the *Jack*! How far does he get to take this? Who's next? What's next? Does he blow up the *Mary J.* with Dad passed out in his bunk? Does he burn down the house with Mom in it?"

McCormick wouldn't turn him loose. "They would have killed me if he'd told them to. There's too many of them, and they're too big. We can't go up against them. He'll sic them on all of us if we talk, if we say or do anything. Your dad wouldn't survive this kind of beating. Don't, Larry. Don't." McCormick was almost weeping with the last word.

Liam waited as the red faded from Jacobson's face, leaving a drained and despairing expression behind. "Goddamn him. Goddamn him to hell."

Liam met the harbormaster on the slip next to the little gill-netter. Liam remembered catching a brief glimpse of her when he'd helped Darrell down to the boat harbor; she'd been a tidy little craft, neat and clean. Today she was awash up to her jaunty red trim line and then some, listing up against the slip, her crow's nest tilted at a drunken angle. Sort of made her look like her skipper after a rough night, Liam thought. She was stern-heavy and one of her hatch covers had floated away. Some kind soul had fed a hose attached to a pump into her hold, and water gushed forth from the other end in fits and starts. A rainbow sheen covered the water from leaking oil and fuel stores.

There is no more pathetic sight than a once proud vessel reduced to hanging on to the slip of a small boat harbor to keep her bow above water.

From the proximity of the *Yukon Jack* to the *Mary J.* he could make a pretty good guess as to what had happened the day before. Fresh from his armed assault on the might and power of the United States government, as exemplified by its postal system, Kelly McCormick hadn't had enough oomph to get himself all the way home, and had passed out in the nearest friendly bunk. He had been the comatose lump opposite Darrell Jacobson that afternoon. Fishing partner to Jacobson pere et fils, and boon companion to Larry Jacobson, he probably saw the *Mary J.* as a second home.

The harbormaster, a rotund little man with rosy cheeks and a bouncy step, didn't have much to tell him. "Somebody opened up the cocks and walked away," he said sadly, or as sadly as his cherubic little Father Christmas face would allow.

"Did you notice when the *Yukon Jack* got back into the harbor?"

Jimmy Barnes shook his head. "It was a steady stream after the closing. Herring's so quick anymore, the whole second part of the season only lasted twenty minutes. They deliver, they get their fish tickets and checks, and then they pick up their girls — or their girls pick them up; wives in particular like to intercept the paycheck at the dock — and head back into town to drink up their profits."

"Anybody see anything suspicious around this boat during that time?"

"If so, nobody's saying."

With real curiosity Liam asked, "Would you say, if you'd seen anything?"

Jimmy laid a finger alongside his nose and regarded Liam out of wise eyes. "Well, now, Trooper Campbell, it would all depend on what I was seeing, and who was doing what I was seeing, and how many other people were around while I was seeing it. If you catch my meaning."

Liam caught his meaning. He closed his notebook. "What now?"

The harbormaster sighed. "Now we pump her out enough to tow her around to dry dock. We'll leave the sea cocks open, get a lot of the water out of her that way at low tide, close the sea cocks, and pump out the rest. The engine'll probably have to be replaced — saltwater, you know. It's to be hoped that young Kelly is up to date with his insurance. So many of the younger fishermen can't afford it, and the ones who fish alone usually figure they can't be sued, so they don't bother." He shook his head. "Sometimes I think it's a real shame that keelhauling has gone out of style, you know?"

He wasn't referring to the uninsured mariners.

At that moment, their conversation was interrupted by a scream.

FOURTEEN

The scream was followed by the slamming of a hatch and a woman's voice yelling, "Help! Somebody, help, help, HELP!"

Liam knew that voice. His heart in his mouth, he ran toward it, pounding down the slip, past boat after boat after boat, the vessels increasing in size as he came to the end of the floats and the mouth of the harbor. It was barely nine o'clock, and there was still enough light to reveal an occasional lone fisherman climbing out here and there to the deck of his gillnetter or drifter or seiner gape at Liam as he pounded past.

She was standing on the deck of the *Sea Wolfe*, and Liam put one hand on the gunnel and vaulted on board. "Wy! Wy! It's all right, I'm here. I'm here now. What's wrong?"

Her face was white. Mutely, she pointed, a piece of paper crumpled in her pointing hand.

Liam followed her gesture to the door of the *Sea Wolfe*'s cabin and looked in.

This was no little gillnetter with a one-room cabin that served as living room, bedroom, and bathroom combined. This seiner had a separate head with a flush toilet, staterooms with two bunks each, and a galley that resembled the kitchen of a luxury hotel.

The galley, reached through a passageway that ran down the center of the cabin, took up the forward part of the cabin, with side-by-side rectangular windows set into the bulkhead that took in a 180-degree view.

It was the interior view that held Liam's fascinated and

appalled attention. Cecil Wolfe was sprawled backward on the deck, arms outstretched, eyes open and staring at the ceiling. Blood was everywhere—smeared on one of the two doors into the galley, on the table, all over the floor—as if Cecil Wolfe in his dying convulsions had waged an unceasing struggle to retain his grip on the life pouring so rapidly out of him.

Because he was most definitely dead. Liam stooped and put two fingers against Wolfe's throat. The carotid artery was silent and still, and Wolfe's flesh was already cooling.

Liam stood up again. "Shit. Shit, shit, shit."

A gasp made him swing his head around. The harbormaster stood in the passageway, turning an interesting shade of green.

"Jimmy?" It took a minute for the harbormaster's eyes to tear themselves away from Wolfe's body and refocus on Liam. "I need you to phone for the ambulance. And then I need you to go to the trooper vehicle. It's the white Blazer parked on the dock. Here's the keys." Liam dug them out of his pocket. "There's a briefcase in the backseat, and a big roll of yellow plastic tape. I need you to bring them both back down here. Okay?"

Jimmy didn't answer at once, and Liam repeated with more emphasis, "Okay?"

Jimmy Barnes swallowed and said in a weak voice, "Okay." He took the keys from Liam's outstretched hand and tottered back down the passageway, nearly blundering into a pale-faced Wy.

"What happened here, Wy?" Liam said.

"I don't know," she said numbly. "I found him like this."

"What was he doing down here? What were you doing down here?" Liam could hear his voice rising, and he didn't even try to keep it down. "Last I saw of you, you were settled in at Bill's for the duration. What the hell are you doing down here!"

"I was getting tired of waiting around the bar to get paid," she said, still in that numb voice. Either she didn't notice his anger or didn't care. "So I asked Cecil for my check, and he said he'd left them on the boat. He suggested we come down here to get the checks and bring them back to Bill's for the crew."

Liam was unable to contain himself. "And you said you

would? After I warned you how dangerous this asshole was? Jesus, Wy, I thought you were smarter than that!"

Her eyes fell. "I didn't take what you said seriously. I thought you were jealous."

"Oh yeah, right," he said, throwing up a hand in disgust, "like you've been encouraging this jerk all along." He pulled off his cap and rubbed a hand over his hair.

"I'm not a complete idiot," she said, her strained manner robbing her words of indignation. "I didn't come down to the boat with him, I waited for him in the truck."

Liam took a deep breath and let it out, slowly. "All right, you're waiting for him in the truck—what happened next?"

"I got tired of waiting."

"How long did you sit there?" he demanded.

"I don't know. Twenty minutes or so, I guess."

"And then you came down to the boat?" She nodded. "What happened?"

She gestured at Wolfe. "I found him like this."

"When?"

"What? When I came on board. He was—" She gestured. "He was lying right there."

"Just like that?"

"Just like that."

"And you screamed right away?"

She nodded.

"Bullshit," Liam said.

"What?"

"First of all, you're not a screamer. Secondly." He leaned forward and snatched the piece of paper still crumpled in her fist. "Secondly, you looked for this before you screamed."

A faint flush warmed her pale cheeks. "It was in his hand."

"There's no blood on it, Wy," Liam said tightly. "There's blood on pretty much every other goddamn thing in this room, including all over Cecil Wolfe, including both of his hands, but there's no blood on this check."

She said nothing.

"Let's see," he said, "if I were a check, where would I be? In a desk, maybe? Let's look for one, shall we?" He stepped into the passageway and opened a door. "A couple of bunks, a port-hole, no desk." He opened another door. "Shower, toilet—this must be the head. No desks in the head—first law of the sea, I'm sure." He opened a third door, and paused. "Aha. Two bunks, one of them not made up—tsk, bad housekeeping—and one desk. Let's just see what's in it, shall we?" He stepped to the desk and scanned the surface. There was a laptop computer, turned off and folded down. A wire basket suction-cupped to the top of the desk held a small stack of envelopes. Liam took a pen from his pocket and lifted the envelopes up one at a time to read the names scrawled on the outside of each. "Kirk Mulder, Ralph Gianetti, Elmer Ollestad, Angel Fejes, Ben Savo, Joe English, Mike Lenaghan, Tom Howes." He looked back at Wy, framed in the doorway. "Nope, no envelope for Wyanet Chouinard, and she was instrumental in all these guys' getting their paychecks today." He let the envelopes fall back in the basket and stood up. "I ought to know, I was there."

"All right," she flared, "so I looked for the check before I screamed. So what? What's it matter anyway—I didn't kill him!"

"I never said you did," he yelled, "but you're not making it any easier for me to find out who did by screwing with the crime scene! How the hell am I supposed to find who did do it if you're in here stumbling around destroying evidence!"

They glared at each other.

From the passageway behind Wy there was an apologetic clearing of throat. "I'm sorry," Jimmy Barnes said, head down in a conscious effort not to meet anyone's eyes and thereby pre-cipitate an inclusion into the ongoing debate. "Here's the tape and your briefcase, Liam. The ambulance is on its way."

Liam pulled himself together. "Thanks, Jimmy."

"Think nothing of it."

"Mind if I ask you for another favor?"

The harbormaster looked wary. "What?"

"I imagine there are a few people standing around on the slip outside."

"A few," Jimmy agreed cautiously.

"Could you kind of stand guard, keep them off the boat, while I gather evidence?"

Jimmy looked relieved. "Sure. I can do that."

"Thanks. And flag down the ambulance driver when he gets here."

"Sure."

Liam ordered—there was no other word—he ordered Wy to wait for him on deck. When she had gone, he found the crumpled envelope with her name on it in the wastebasket next to the desk, and smoothed it flat. Before returning the check to the envelope, he paused to read it. It had been drawn on Wolfe's business account, imprinted with the business name, Sea Wolfe Enterprises, Inc., with an address in Seattle. Today's date, "Pay to the order of Wyanet Chouinard, twenty thousand dollars," and then the big black scrawl of a signature that took up most of the bottom right of the check.

His heart jarred with a thickening thud, and he read the check again.

He stood in the middle of Wolfe's stateroom for a long moment, thinking hard. In the end, he heard the sound of wheels on wood and read it rightly as an approaching gurney.

With a decisive movement that was nevertheless a little furtive, he stuffed the check back inside the envelope and the envelope inside his shirt and went out to meet Joe Gould, who surveyed the carnage with the same detached expression Liam had noticed at the airport on Friday, his Lucifer-before-the-fall face tonight looking more sinned against than sinning. He squatted beside the body. "Stabbed, huh?"

"What was your first clue?" Liam said.

"No need to be sarcastic, trooper," Joe said tranquilly, "just a passing comment. Help me with the bag?"

Liam helped unroll the body bag and slide Wolfe into it. The blood had dried enough to be sticky, and for the first time since landing in Newenham Liam was glad he wasn't wearing his uniform.

They carried the body out through the crowd clustered on the slip next to the boat, causing a ripple of shocked comment, as well as a few smothered mutters of satisfaction—Cecil Wolfe had not been running a popularity contest from the bridge of the *Sea Wolfe*—and set it on the stretcher. Together, they rolled the stretcher to the ramp and up into the ambulance.

Joe Gould closed the doors and said, "We've only got so much room down at the morgue, trooper."

"Thanks for the information," Liam said. "I wouldn't want to cause overcrowding. Next time I stumble over a body I'll just toss it in the Nushagak."

"Works for me," Joe Gould said without expression, and climbed into the cab and drove away with the remains of a man no one was going to mourn for very long, if at all.

Liam's headache was back. Standard operating procedure in any murder investigation where the murderer is not obvious is to inquire as to the existence of any enemies of the deceased. Given Cecil Wolfe's personality and professional conduct, Liam figured he could put all of Newenham and most of Bristol Bay at the head of the line.

But none of them came before Wyanet Chouinard.

Liam pulled up at the post and, escorting Wy, was just going in the door when Bill Billington pulled into the parking lot in a bright '57 Chevy convertible. Liam felt like knuckling his eyes, but it was a bona fide '57 Chevy all right, painted a bright shiny yellow and complete with fins.

"Hey, Liam," she called, getting out of the car.

"Bill," he said, still staring.

She gave the fender a fond pat. "Nice, isn't she? I bought her new. Only reason I bought a house, so I could park her in the garage over the winter. First time I've had her out this spring."

"Right." Newenham wasn't the Twilight Zone after all. It wasn't even a three-ring circus. It was a doorway into the Fourth Dimension. Where was Mr. Myxlpltz? He said, trying to be civil, "I'm kind of busy, Bill, I—"

"I know you're busy," she interrupted him, "but this won't wait."

"What won't wait?"

She waved a thick manila envelope at him. "This."

He took it, noticing it had been opened and closed again by tucking the flap inside. "What is it?"

"It's the last will and testament of Bob DeCreft," she said.

"How did you come by it?"

"I'm the magistrate, and the district judge only comes around once every three, four months," she said. "Most people file their wills with me. Hell, I help most people write 'em. I hadn't had a chance to read Bob's until this evening."

"What's so interesting about this particular will?"

"Read it and see." She folded her arms and waited.

Liam mumbled something ungracious beneath his breath.

"Just read it," Bill ordered in her most magisterial voice. "Or I'll hold you in contempt of court."

"We aren't in court, Bill."

"Court is wherever I say it is, buddy. Read the goddamn will."

Liam opened the envelope and pulled out the document.

It was short and simple. He read it through twice, to make sure it said what he thought it said the first time.

He let his hand fall, and raised his head to stare at Bill. "What the hell?"

"Yeah," Bill said smugly. "That's what I thought."

"Did you know?"

Bill shook her head. "Didn't have a clue. Neither did anyone else."

A slight smile creased Liam's face. "Even Moses?"

Bill waved a hand as if to say Moses knew everything and so didn't count. She had a point. "Does it help?"

"I don't know," Liam said curtly, the thoughts in his head writhing around like a nest of snakes. No sooner did he have hold of the tail end of one than another raised its head and hissed at him. "Maybe."

Wy was unable to contain herself any longer and demanded, "What's going on?"

Bill looked at her and said, "Bob left everything he owned to Laura Nanalook."

Wy, puzzled, said, "So? She was his roomie."

"She was more than his roomie," Bill said, obviously relishing the prospective effect her news was about to impart. "She was his daughter."

"What?"

Bill pointed at the will. "That's what he calls her in his will: his 'natural daughter.' Oh yeah, and this was in with the will."

Liam fairly snatched it out of her hand.

It was a copy of a birth certificate, issued twenty years before on September 23 at the Alaska Native Medical Center in Anchorage, for a girl child, six pounds, eight ounces. The mother was listed as being one Elizabeth Rebecca Ilutsik, unmarried, of the village of Ik'ikika. The father was listed as unknown. The girl child's name was listed as Laura Elizabeth Ilutsik.

Liam sat down on the top step and stared at the birth certificate. Bill folded her arms and leaned against the railing, watching him. Wy, who had been existing in momentary expectation of being arrested for murder, was simply glad to have the attention shifted away from her.

Liam looked at Bill. "Did you show this to Laura?"

Bill shook her head. "Haven't talked to her at all."

"Good. Don't."

"Why, what are you going to do?"

Liam got to his feet. "I don't know yet." He went into the post and closed the door behind him, leaving the two women to stare at each other, puzzled.

"What are we supposed to do now?" Wy said.

"Beats the hell out of me," Bill said. "I've got to head back to the bar. Buy you a beer?"

"Can you drop me off at the harbor first? We left my truck there."

"Sure."

Wy looked again at the door. "Hang on a minute, okay?"

"Sure. I'll wait for you in the car."

Liam was seated at his desk, frowning down at a large piece of paper with a lot of boxes on it drawn in pencil, when Wy stuck her head in. "Bill's going to give me a lift to my truck," she said. "If you didn't need me for anything else?"

"Like what?"

"Oh, I don't know. Charging me with first-degree murder, any little thing like that."

He flapped a hand without looking up. "No, go on home. I'll talk to you later."

She stood there for a moment, mystified at his abstract tone. He'd been in a blind rage just moments before, which she was smart enough to know was due in large part to his fear for her. Now, he seemed oblivious, to her and to the events of the evening.

Behind her, the '57 Chevy's horn gave an impatient honk. Liam didn't look up. Wy stepped back and closed the door gently behind her.

Liam didn't look up at the sound of the door. He knew Wy was leaving, and he knew what John Barton or any other competent law enforcement officer would have said about turning her loose: Wyanet Chouinard had done everything but shove the knife into Cecil Wolfe's back to get herself arrested for murder.

Everything, but not that. Liam knew it for fact, but that was about all he knew, and the only reason he knew that much was because he knew Wy intimately. It wasn't a reason he wanted to have to swear to in court.

She'd had means—anyone involved in the fishing industry, anyone living in the Alaskan Bush for that matter, could lay hands on a knife. The wounds were big ones. Liam would bet that the weapon, when it was found, would prove to be a hunting knife, or perhaps a sliming knife of the kind cannery workers used to head and gut fish, a wide blade fixed into a plastic handle. Processors bought them by the case, and over the years sliming knives had found their way into the lives and homes of most Alaskans who lived on a coast.

Or a river.

And Wy had had all the opportunity in the world—he cursed her, without heat, for not staying at Bill's, for actually accompanying that asshole to the docks against his explicit instructions, and then for having the colossal stupidity to follow him down to his boat. He thought again of coming upon Laura

Nanalook too late, of how shaken and forlorn and hopeless she had seemed. He didn't ever want to see that look on Wy's face. If he had his choice he'd never see that look on the face of any woman ever again, but given his profession the choice was not his to make.

At least Cecil Wolfe wouldn't be responsible for putting that look on a woman's face ever again. He knew a sudden, visceral pleasure at the thought.

As for motive—he pulled the envelope from inside his shirt. He didn't need to take the check out and look at it—it was burned into his memory. Pay to the order of Wyanet Chouinard, twenty thousand dollars and no cents.

If it looked like a motive, and walked like a motive, and sounded like a motive, it probably was a motive. Wy had had motive, all right—twenty thousand motives.

He swore once, tiredly, and put the envelope in a drawer, then stared at the paper with the boxes on it. He pushed it aside and began to draw a new one.

Bob DeCreft, with a dotted line down to Laura Nanalook. Probably born Laura Elizabeth Ilutsik—why the change of name? He made a note on a pad.

Bob DeCreft, who flew observer with Wyanet Chouinard, both of them working for Cecil Wolfe.

Cecil Wolfe, whose first act upon hearing of the death of Laura Nanalook's roommate—and so far as anyone knew, her lover—had been to stake a physical claim.

Who wanted both Bob DeCreft and Cecil Wolfe dead?

At the side of the page he began a time line.

In 1977, Laura (Ilutsik) Nanalook was born in Icky.

In 1992, Bob DeCreft moved to Newenham, and he and his daughter moved in together.

He remembered the two bedrooms in the DeCreft house, the feminine clutter of the first, the spartan maleness of the second. "I must be slowing down or something," he said out loud. "Of course they were sleeping in separate bedrooms. How the hell could I have missed it?"

Bob DeCreft and Laura Nanalook, father and daughter.

"Wait a minute," he said. *I've known him since I was a kid,* Wy had said. Wy had been a kid in Newenham, when her adopted parents had been teachers for the Bureau of Indian Affairs, back before the state had started building rural schools. Bob DeCreft had been flying in and out of Newenham about the time Laura was conceived. He looked back at the time line he'd drawn. Laura's mother could have been from Newenham. Laura's mother could still live here.

He thought about the cars he had seen in Bill's parking lot that evening, and what was that story Charlene Taylor had told him—six years ago on the river, Bob with some woman? He stared hard at the unrevealing countenance of a fire extinguisher mounted on the opposite wall.

He reached for a phone book and looked up a number. A sleepy voice answered, and belatedly he realized it was almost midnight. "It's Liam Campbell," he said. "I'm sorry; I didn't realize it was so late."

There was a yawn. "It's all right, Liam, we just hit the sack." There was a murmur in the background. "It's okay, honey, go back to sleep, it's that new trooper I told you about."

There was another murmur, and the mouthpiece was covered, but not before Liam heard a male voice say, "Oh, the one with the wife?" He set his teeth and waited.

The voice came back. "Okay, Liam, what did you need?"

"Charlene, you told me you'd seen Bob DeCreft up the river with a woman."

The Fish and Wildlife Protection officer was amused. "What is this, *Cherchez la Femme* Day? God, Liam, that was five years ago. Six."

"I know, and I know you said you didn't recognize her. But you did say she was dark."

There was a pause. Taylor said finally, "Yeah, I remember that much."

"Was she Yupik?"

"Yes," Charlene said immediately.

Liam was taken aback by her immediate certainty; he'd thought he'd have to coax it from her. "How can you be sure?"

He could hear Taylor's shrug over the phone. "She was short and very dark and kind of thick through the middle. She looked the same general shape as most every Yupik woman I've ever met. Some of them are skinnier, some of them are taller, but the skin and the hair and the eyes and the general stockiness pretty much stays the same all up and down the river; you don't need to be an anthropologist to see that. Kind of like most Scandinavians are tall and blond and blue-eyed. She was Yupik, Liam. Or at the very least Alaska Native."

"Okay, Charlene, thanks."

"Sure, but what's this all about?"

"I'll tell you later. Thanks again."

He hung up.

He had to talk to Laura Nanalook.

He found her at Bill's. Wolfe's crew had vanished, and for all that it was a Sunday night the place was subdued. People were clustered in small groups, talking in low tones. Gary Gruber wasn't holding down his usual place, either, gazing upon Laura with the hopeless adoration of a pet dog, a pet dog one wanted frequently to kick.

Nobody seemed to be drinking much, because Laura Nanalook was taking a break at the bar.

Moses looked at Liam from his usual stool and said, "All history is personal."

"What?" Liam said.

"One American congressman kept the war going in Afghanistan because he was still pissed over Vietnam. Hitler killed twelve million people, not counting soldiers, trying to prove he wasn't the Austrian version of poor white trash. Closer to home, Red Calhoun spearheaded the fight for d-2 because it created a national park around his homestead in Prince William Sound. All history is personal." Moses leveled a finger at him. "All of it, and don't you forget it."

"I won't," Liam promised.

"Good," Moses said, satisfied, and turned back to his beer.

"Could I talk to you for a minute?" Liam asked Laura.

She shrugged indifferently. "Sure."

"Let's grab a booth."

"Okay."

She was listless, unalarmed. On the way over Liam had been thinking about the best way to approach this subject, and had at last decided to send out the shock troops. "I wanted to talk to you about your father."

She was startled, at least momentarily, out of her apathy. "My father?" she said warily.

He said gently, "Bob DeCreft was your father, wasn't he, Laura." He nodded at Bill. "The magistrate went through your father's papers and found this." He pulled out the birth certificate.

She studied it for a moment.

"It's yours, isn't it?"

Her mouth trembled. "Yes. I guess so."

"Why the change of name? Ilutsik to Nanalook?"

"I was adopted."

"Oh. I see."

"No you don't," she said wearily. "My mom got knocked up, and had me, and gave me away, like a puppy she was too lazy to raise herself." Her lovely mouth twisted into an ugly line. "To the Nanalooks. She didn't even care what kind of people she gave me to. She didn't care what they did to me, she didn't care if they—"

"Who is she, Laura?" Liam said. "Who is your mother?"

She dropped her head. "I'm not supposed to tell."

"Why not?"

"Because her husband's a preacher, and he can't have his wife acknowledging any bastards she might have had before she met and married him."

"I see." Liam was careful to keep any sense of satisfaction from his voice. "When did you meet her?"

She raised her head, and there was a kind of sick triumph in her eyes. "She came looking for me. She couldn't have any children with her husband, so she came looking for me."

"When?"

"When I was sixteen. I moved out from the Nanalooks' as soon as I was old enough. Bill gave me a job in the kitchen until I was twenty-one and could serve booze."

"What did your mother want?"

Laura snorted. "She wanted to get to know me. Wanted me to get to know her. Wanted me to be her daughter."

"What did you say?"

"I told her it was a little late for her to start playing mother," she spat. "Where was she when Sally treated me like a maid, keeping me home from class to cook and clean and baby-sit her kids so that I couldn't even graduate from high school? Where was she when Harvey started coming down the hall to my room? Where was she when he turned me into his little gussuk whore?" Her voice broke.

After a moment she began speaking again, her voice filled with pain and hatred. "She wouldn't go away though. The only problem was, she said we had to keep it a secret that I was her daughter. Her husband wouldn't like it. His sacred holiness couldn't stand the thought that his congregation would look at his wife and know that she'd had carnal knowledge of another man. No, no, Becky has to be the perfect preacher's wife."

"Becky?"

She stared at him. "Becky Gilbert." She pointed at the birth certificate. "Born to Elizabeth Rebecca Ilutsik, of Ik'ikika."

"You're named for her."

She sneered, an expression that did not sit well on her angel face. "My middle name. Big deal. It's not like she gave me a home now, is it?"

"I suppose not." He leaned back in the booth. "When did you meet your father?"

"When he came here."

"Why did he come here?"

She scratched at the tabletop with one fingernail. "I made her tell me who he was. I found out he was living in Anchorage. I wrote him a letter." She looked up, her eyes full of tears. "He didn't even know about me. She hadn't even told him she was pregnant."

"That was six years ago?" She nodded. "So he moved out here to be with you?"

A tear rolled down her cheek. "He bought a house, and we moved in together. Becky begged us not to say we were father and daughter, she was afraid everybody would find out. So we promised." She wiped away another tear. "I didn't care, and Bob didn't, either." She raised wondering eyes to Liam. "It was so nice, you know? I'd never had a room all to myself before. He would have done everything if I'd let him—the cooking, the cleaning. He wouldn't let me help with the house payments or buy gas for the truck or anything. He wanted me to save my money so I could go back to school, get my GED, maybe go to vocational school or college someday."

Her shoulders began to shake. "He bought me presents. Whenever he went somewhere, he bought me presents. The last time he went to Anchorage, he brought me these." She fingered her earrings, exquisite little drops of green jade and black hematite and ivory. "I told him he was spoiling me, and he said I was beautiful, and that I deserved beautiful things. He was my f-father, and he could spoil me if he w-wanted to."

She began to sob. "Nobody ever called me beautiful before. They just took whatever they wanted, made me do whatever they wanted me to do. Nobody ever called me beautiful before, and nobody ever, ever gave me presents. At least not without expecting me to pay for them."

Bill arrived at the booth with a handful of Kleenex and a glass of water. "You okay, Laura?" she asked, with a hard glance at Liam.

Laura fought back a sob and nodded, used three Kleenexes to mop her eyes and blow her nose, and drank the glass of water down. She looked drained. "I guess I better get back to work."

"Just a couple more questions," Liam said. He hesitated. "Look, Laura, there's no nice way to ask this. That day, the day I came out to your house."

"The day my father died," she said, and fresh tears welled up.

"Yes. Did you call your mother that day?"

"No, she just came over," she said dully. "She'd heard about Bob." She looked up, surprised. "How did you know she was there?"

"She drove up as I was leaving," he said, and hesitated again. This woman had been through enough in her young life, but he had to ask the question, there was no way around it. "Laura, did you tell her about Wolfe?"

Her face shut down. "What about him?"

Liam gave up and went for the jugular. "Did you tell her that he raped you?"

"I don't know what you're talking about. I have to get back to work now."

He caught her hand as she stood. "Cecil Wolfe is dead, Laura."

She stared down at him. "What?"

"Wolfe is dead. Somebody murdered him on his boat a couple of hours ago."

"Cecil is dead?" she repeated.

"Yes, Cecil is dead."

Liam hadn't exactly expected a cartwheel, which was good because he didn't get one. She stood in front of him, staring blankly into space, mute, uncomprehending. He squeezed her hand for emphasis. "He'll never bother you again."

She looked at him then, and he was saddened by the dead expression he saw in her eyes. "It doesn't matter. There's always another one just like him a little farther down the road."

He watched her walk back to the bar, saw her dismiss Bill's concern with a shrug. She picked up her tray and walked over to bus a table and take an order for refills with the bright, flashing smile he had seen her use before, the smile that was so full of warmth, and meant less than nothing.

FIFTEEN

The Gilberts lived in a small white house a few feet from the church. Richard Gilbert opened the door. "Oh." He cast a nervous look over his shoulder. "Trooper Campbell."

"Hello, Mr. Gilbert. I'd like to talk to your wife. Is she in?"

"Well, I, uh, no, she isn't, she's—"

Liam took a not very big chance and said, "I think she is here, sir. I have to talk to her. May I come in?"

"Let him in, Richard," a voice called from the back of the house.

Liam pushed on the door. Richard Gilbert fell back.

"In here, Mr. Campbell." Liam followed the voice into a back bedroom, where he found Becky Gilbert calmly folding clothes into a small suitcase. "I expect you'll want these," she said, and handed him a brown paper grocery bag.

He opened it and looked inside to see a shirt and slacks, both stained with blood. "I was wearing them when I killed him," she said. "Richard insisted on washing the knife. It's in the dish drainer next to the kitchen sink." She went to the dresser and collected some underwear.

Liam judged that the flight risk presented by Becky Gilbert was minimal and went into the kitchen. Sure enough, the dish drainer held a large skinning knife with a yellowing bone handle, still wet from washing. He wrapped it in a paper towel and placed it in the brown paper bag along with the clothes.

Becky met him in the living room, suitcase in hand. He got a good look at her face for the first time.

She had been transformed. He'd seen her at work with her husband, toadying and subservient. He'd seen her submerged in grief at the death of a man he now knew was greatly loved. He'd glimpsed the urgency of a woman on a mission on the way into her daughter's house.

This was a different person altogether from the previous three. She held herself erect, her chin high with pride, and looked Liam straight in the eye in a manner that most women raised in Bush villages did not do. "Let's go."

"All right," Liam said, and opened the door.

"What are you doing?" Richard Gilbert said in a panic.

"Telling the truth," she said.

"But you can't!" Richard Gilbert said in anguish. "What will people say?"

His wife looked at him and replied, "I guess they'll say a mother killed the son of a bitch who hurt her daughter." She paused, and added with a smile, "And they'll be right."

She sat across the desk from Liam, perfectly composed, hair neatly combed, gray knit pantsuit freshly pressed (Liam knew a wistful thought for her obvious ironing skills), her words calm and precise.

"When I was very young I had a daughter. The circumstances don't matter, but I gather you have already guessed who her father is, or was."

"Bob DeCreft."

She inclined her head. "Yes. I was traveling with the Ilutuqaq Native Association Board, as a board member." Her chin raised. "I was the youngest person ever elected to the association board. I wanted to keep my seat after I married, but Richard said . . . well, it doesn't matter what he said. This all happened long before I met him. The board had chartered a plane. Bob was our pilot." She smiled, a wide smile rich with memories. "I was the youngest, so I always got to ride shotgun. My auntie Sada was supposed to be looking out for me, but she would get airsick and take pills to go to sleep." She closed her eyes and shook her head. "We had some fine times in the front of that plane. I'll never forget them."

Liam remembered the first few months he'd flown out to crime scenes with Wy as his pilot. Sometimes her Cub; sometimes, when there was a body to bring back for autopsy, a chartered Cessna. Sometimes four seats, sometimes only two, him sitting behind her as he had today, or yesterday, now. The smell of Ivory soap on her skin, the quick crinkle of flesh at the corners of her eyes when she laughed, the rub of her shoulder against his. It was a long way between places in the Bush, and they'd talked, nonstop it seemed in hindsight, about everything: his cases, her flights, books, music, movies, politics, religion.

It was a hothouse environment, forcing relationships to rapid fruition, with no time-outs to cool down or reconsider. He'd never understood anyone so well or so quickly, and just the memory of it now was so powerful that it took a serious effort to draw himself back to the present, to Newenham and the woman looking over his shoulder with a dreamy smile on her face.

She sighed. "We, well, we were together constantly over a period of three months, flying around the state, talking to legislators and businesspeople and shareholders and boards from other Native regions, finding out how they were managing their ANCSA funds, how they were administering their land grants. We were coming into our share of the ANCSA settlement, and we wanted to do a good job for all the shareholders, not waste the money or give away the lands."

"Like the Anipa Subdivision?"

She bestowed an approving smile on him. "Yes, exactly like that. Native investors funding Native projects with federal backing, built by Native workers for Natives to live in. We were all so charged up and full of purpose. We were like the Blues Brothers."

"I beg your pardon?"

She smiled faintly. "On a mission from God."

"Oh." It had been a long time since Liam had seen the movie, but eventually he got the joke, and returned her smile. "I see."

"And then there was Bob. I saw him almost every day, sat

next to him everywhere we flew. He was funny, and nice, and smart—he was a pilot, after all—and the color of my skin and the shape of my eyes weren't the only things he saw about me. I liked him right away. He was twenty years older than I was, but I didn't care." Her smile was rich and warmly reminiscent. "And then I loved him, and he loved me, and for a month we were happy. So very happy." She paused.

"What happened?"

Her smile faded. "Auntie Sada saw what was happening and called my parents. My parents came and took me home."

"And you went?" Liam said involuntarily. It was almost impossible to reconcile this strong, composed woman with the subservient, submissive wife he had seen at the post office, or for that matter with the picture she drew of the idealistic young board member of twenty-two years before.

"Yes," she said soberly. "I went. They were my elders. It wasn't that easy, Mr. Campbell, not in the seventies; it isn't that easy even today to disobey your elders in the village. And Bob was white. That didn't help. They were horrified that I would consider marrying a gussuk, let alone sleep with him. So I went home, hoping that I could change their minds."

"And when you found out about the baby?"

All the life drained from her face, leaving it a mask with nothing alive behind it. "They sent me to Anchorage to have her, and then they took her from me. They wouldn't allow a half-white child to be raised in the Ilutsik home. They took her from me and gave her to the Nanalooks in Newenham, or so I found out later."

Her fists clenched on the arms of the chair. Liam had not cuffed her. It wasn't necessary. Elizabeth Rebecca Ilutsik Gilbert had already committed her murder. She would not kill again.

"I take my commandments seriously, Mr. Campbell, but if I'd known where Laura was and what the Nanalooks were doing to her, you'd have had to arrest me for murder a long time before this."

Liam didn't doubt it for a minute. "Off the record?" he said. She was curious. "Off the record," she agreed.

"I'd have held your coat."

She smiled at him then, the same wide, warm, transforming smile of before, with an extra dollop of approval added. Liam would have wagged his tail if he'd had one, and for the first time saw the woman Bob DeCreft had been attracted to so many years before. "Thank you."

"How did you come to marry Richard Gilbert?"

The smile faded. "My parents wanted me off their hands and out of their house, and they figured I was already tainted anyway. He was a missionary who needed a link to the community he was trying to convert. They arranged it between them. I didn't much care one way or another, so I went along with it. I thought I could have more children, that that would help. But I didn't."

"I'm sorry," Liam said inadequately.

"Thank you," she said softly. "I am too."

Liam, who had lost his own child, cleared his throat and said, "Why didn't you try to call Bob? When you found out you were pregnant?"

"My parents wouldn't allow it." She added in a lower voice, "And when I was back in the village, I was ashamed."

The words were so simple, and encompassed so much. "When did Bob get in touch with you again? When he moved here in 1992? You went up the river with him, didn't you?"

Enough of the minister's helpmate remained that she looked alarmed. "How did you know that?"

"You were seen. Don't worry, they didn't recognize you, they only recognized him."

"Oh. Good. I guess." The alarmed expression faded, as if it had only been habit in the first place. "It doesn't matter now. We got away by ourselves, and we talked and talked and talked, and he told me that he figured I was never coming back, so he didn't bother leaving a trail for me to follow. I thought he'd moved on to another woman, but he hadn't." Pride showed through again. "He wanted me to leave Richard and move in with him, and have Laura move in with us."

"Why didn't you?"

She paused, thinking it over. "I don't know," she said finally, a puzzled crease appearing between her brows. "I should have. I suppose I was—afraid."

"Afraid of what? Your husband?"

She shook her head. "No. No one who truly knows Richard is afraid of him. No, I suppose I was afraid of what God would think of me if I did." She saw Liam's expression and smiled again, this time without humor. "Yes, I know what you're thinking. Nowadays people sling His name around like they're on a first-name basis with Him. It's true that my parents arranged my marriage to Richard—even if he was a gussuk, they figured that at least he was a holy one—but I said the words. For richer or poorer, in sickness and in health, so long as you both shall live. Those are truly terrible words, Mr. Campbell, if you think about them. Very few people do. But I did, and when I said them I meant them."

Liam had meant them himself, once upon a time. The difference was that Becky Gilbert had kept her vows.

"And," Becky Gilbert added, confirming Liam's previous thoughts, "at that time there was still enough of the preacher's wife in me to shudder at the thought of all the talk."

"You were afraid," he said, repeating her words.

"Yes." She said it without shame.

So was I, he thought. Afraid to leave, afraid to love, afraid to rock the boat.

"So I stayed with Richard."

And I with Jenny and Charlie. "And asked Bob and Laura not to give away your secret."

"Yes. She despises me for it," she added, sighing. "But Richard ordered me to keep it a secret. He said a pastor has to set an example, that we couldn't be seen to be condoning children born out of wedlock, it would send all the wrong messages to the young people in the church."

She folded her hands in her lap. "So I agreed to keep it a secret. She moved in with Bob, and everyone thought they were lovers. Bob wasn't interested in anyone but me"—again that flash of pride—"and Laura . . . well, I don't know if Laura is ever going to have a normal relationship with a man. She has been hurt so much. So that's the way we left it."

"Which was where things were when Bob died."

She nodded.

"Why did you kill Cecil Wolfe, Becky?"

She looked surprised. "Why, I've just told you. Laura Nanalook is my child. She is the child of my body, and of my heart. She is my only child. Mothers are supposed to look out for their children, protect them, keep them safe."

"You killed Cecil Wolfe to protect your daughter?"

"Yes. He raped her. He came into her home on the day her father died and he held her down on her own couch in her own living room and he raped her, he raped my baby girl." Her breast was heaving, her voice was rising, her hands had clenched into fists. "He hurt her, and he had hurt her before and he would have hurt her again. That's what he was. A hurter. A taker. A—a spoiler."

She closed her eyes and took one long, deep breath. "So I waited, and I watched. I've been following him off and on for the last two days. He was so big and so strong, and I—" An eloquent sweep of one hand indicated her small form. "I knew I had to be careful, that if I had any chance to do it successfully I had to take him by surprise, I had to catch him off guard." Her chin came up again. "I was real good at skinning when I was a kid, Mr. Campbell. I could strip a caribou of its hide faster than any other girl in the village, and faster than most of the boys. My father was real proud of me. He took me hunting a couple of times, even when the other elders said it wasn't right for girls to hunt. He even gave me my own knife."

"This knife?" Liam said, pointing at the bone-handled skinning knife, properly bagged in plastic by now.

She nodded. "Yes. That is the same knife. It's a good one; it holds an edge for a long time. My father gave it to me because I was so good at skinning."

"I don't doubt it, Becky," Liam said. "Tell me how you killed Cecil Wolfe."

"Oh, of course. I'm sorry; I know you need all this for my statement, don't you? And it is awfully late. What is it, one o'clock? My goodness, it's almost two o'clock in the morning—

the sun will be coming up any minute." She smiled, and he couldn't help smiling back. "All right," she said briskly, "let's finish this story. Then you can put me in my cell and we can both get some sleep."

"Thank you," he said meekly.

"You're welcome," she said, waving a dismissing hand. "Like I said, ever since I learned what he did to my daughter, I've been watching Wolfe. I kept my knife with me all the time, and I was just waiting for the right opportunity." She spread her hands. "I was looking for him tonight, to see if he was back from herring fishing."

"Yeah," Liam said. "I didn't put it together at first, but I saw your station wagon parked in the lot when I came out of Bill's."

She nodded. "Yes, I was there. I went around the back and went into the kitchen. Bill's cook is a cousin of mine."

"I wondered where you were."

"When Wolfe left with that pilot—I can never remember her name; it sounds like it should have a question mark after it—I followed them down to the boat harbor. When I saw she didn't go down to his boat with him, I parked and went down the west gangway so she wouldn't see me."

Liam remembered getting lost on the way back from the *Mary J.* Two different entrances that doubled as two different exits. It was so easy when you knew your way around.

Becky ended her story with devastating simplicity. "And then I killed him." She pursed her lips a little. "I was horribly angry, and at the same time so completely without fear. His back was to me, and I slipped the knife in up under his ribs, straight for his heart. I must have missed it, though—humans and caribou are built different, I guess—because he turned around as he fell and saw me, and when I saw his face I just had to stab him again. And again. I just had to." She paused. "His blood was everywhere. All over the knife, all over me, all over the galley. I didn't care. It was what I had wanted—his blood on my hands. It was what I had come for."

Liam waited.

She looked up. "I bet I sound like a raving lunatic, don't I?" She smiled a little, an expression made up half of humor, half of resignation, containing neither regret nor bitterness. "Oh well. I don't imagine sanity matters much where I'm going."

Liam typed the statement on the post computer, printed it out, and had her read it and sign it. "Do you know any attorneys, Becky?" he said as he rose to his feet.

"I don't believe so. Unless you count the attorney the association board has on retainer."

"No. He—"

"She," she broke in.

"She, then; she'll be a corporate attorney and she most definitely won't do." He looked up a name in his personal address book, and scribbled it and a phone number down on a piece of paper. "Here. Call him in the morning."

She looked askance at the name and number. "Why? It's not like I need a lawyer to prove my innocence—I've already confessed." She added sternly, "I'm not fighting this, Mr. Campbell. You made me aware of my rights, and I confessed anyway. I did it. I'm glad I did it. I have no regrets and I will pretend to no remorse. My girl needed help, and for the first time in her life I came through for her. If I had it to do all over again, I wouldn't change a thing."

It hadn't occurred to her that she might have been of more use to Laura out of jail, and so held her hand, but she was so filled with righteous triumph that he knew pointing this out to her now would mean nothing.

Wife, mother, murderer. She was positively glowing with righteous wrath. If Patrick Fox could put that same glow on display to a jury, Becky Gilbert had a fighting chance at a reduced sentence, possibly even an acquittal. He had to admit, the prospect did not fill him with dismay.

He nodded at the scrap of paper. "You call him, and you tell him I gave you his number. You tell him every single thing you told me, and you let him decide what's best for you to do."

She fingered the paper uncertainly. "I don't have any money to pay a lawyer."

"Let him worry about that, too," he advised her. When she still looked hesitant he said, "Look, Becky, the judge will appoint you a lawyer anyway. This guy is going to be better than anyone you'll draw from the pro bono pool or the public defender's office, believe me."

Her face softened. "Don't look so worried," she chided him. "I'll call him. And I'll be fine."

She was comforting him, this woman who, not four hours before, had willfully, deliberately, and with malice aforethought taken a knife to a man in one of the most calculated and brutal murders Liam had ever seen. "I know you will," he said. "Let's head on over to the jail, shall we?" He opened the door for her and paused. "Becky?"

"What?"

"I suppose you don't know who killed Bob?"

Her face creased with remembered sadness. "No. No, I don't. I wish I did." She looked up at Liam. "He came here for me and Laura, and he stayed for Laura. It was all for Laura."

All for Laura, Liam thought as he helped Becky into the Blazer. So many Newenham lives had been bound up in Laura's, one way or another. Bob DeCreft had wanted to provide for her, Becky Gilbert had wanted to protect her, Cecil Wolfe had wanted to lay her. Richard Gilbert had wanted to ignore her. Bill Billington wanted to give her a hand up out of her adopted gutter.

Liam Campbell, now, what did he want for Laura?

He just wanted to find her father's murderer.

SIXTEEN

Early the next morning, a Monday, the phone rang. Liam sat up from his sleeping bag nest on the post floor and groped for the receiver. "Hello? I mean, Alaska State Troopers, Newenham post, Trooper Campbell speaking."

A vaguely familiar voice, raspy and irascible, said, "You got a pencil I got those buyers for you."

Liam blinked. "I beg your pardon?"

"This Campbell or what?"

"This is Campbell, who's this?"

"Sparky, and I've got those buyers for you." The voice began reciting names, spelling out the last names as if it didn't trust Liam to get them right.

"Whoa, hold it, slow down, let me find a paper and pencil."

"Hurry it up, I haven't got all day."

Liam got to his knees and scrabbled around his desktop, shivering in the early morning chill. "Okay, go."

Again, the voice read out the names. "That's Wolfe with an *e* on the end of it."

"Got it." Two six-hundred-dollar Icom handheld radios had been purchased by Cecil Wolfe, along with four Kings, in February of this year. "Because we only had two Icoms in stock," Sparky growled in answer to Liam's question. "Wolfe didn't care about the brand, he just wanted 'em tuned to the same frequency, so that's how I sent 'em to him. I got the notes on the order form right here."

Six handhelds all together. That fit: one each for two planes and three boats, plus a spare for the plane. If a radio on one of the boats went out, they could signal to each other from deck to deck. Hell, Liam thought, as close as they were traveling the day before, they could shout from deck to deck.

But the spotter was on his, or her, own. Hence the set bolted to the dash, plus the handheld backup, plus the backup for the backup. Wolfe wasn't a guy willing to miss out on an opener due to problems with electronics. And a man who paid a million bucks for a boat wasn't going to boggle at an extra six hundred for another radio. "What about the two Sonys?"

"The cheapies? Got them, too, but it was three of them. They were one order, sold over the phone to a Larry Jacobson, that's *J-a-c*—"

"Jacobson; I've got it," Liam said. Three radios: one for the *Mary J.*, one for the *Yukon Jack*, one for Wy and Bob.

"His address is—"

"I've got that, too."

"Want his phone number or you got that, too?"

"No, I've got that, too. Uh, sir, what is your name?"

"Sparky—why do you think we call it Sparky's Pilot Shop?"

"Okay, Sparky, thanks a—"

Click.

"—lot," Liam said to the dead line. "You've been a big help. I really appreciate it." He put the receiver down and stared at the opposite wall with a meditative expression. Outwardly calm, he was experiencing a slow, steady interior burn. He picked up the phone and dialed a number he had already memorized. "Hi, it's Liam. Can you come down to the post? Yes, right now. No, it can't wait; find someone else to take them to Manokotak."

Fifteen minutes later she walked in the door, apprehension combined with belligerence in her eyes.

Liam was dressed by then, and sitting at his desk with the contents of the inventory of her Cub spread out neatly in front of him. "Hello, Wy. Have a seat."

She perched on the edge of a chair. "I haven't got much time, Liam, I—"

"You'll make time for this."

Her eyes widened a little as she took in his expression, one she had not seen on his face before today. His gaze was hard, his mouth held in a stern line, and suddenly she saw what had frightened many a perpetrator into surrender and a blurted confession over the years. "What?"

He waved his hand at the inventory before him. "Recognize this stuff? I took it out of your plane the last day you flew it. The day Bob DeCreft died."

She nodded, wary now. "So?"

"So, does anything seem to be missing?"

A slight flush rose into her cheeks. "Not that I can see."

He beckoned her forward. "Take a closer look; be sure." His eyes met hers. "Be very sure."

Slowly, she rose to her feet and stretched out a hand to pick through the items.

The wrappings from the Pop-Tart, the Snickers bar, the M&M's, the Bazooka bubble gum, the Reese's peanut butter cup. "Regular junk food junkies," she said, trying to smile. He didn't smile back, and her eyes dropped to the desk. "The new map's mine, the old map was Bob's. You know where and how we got the floats. Same with the walrus tusk. Not a very good one—it's broken off near the root—but it's ivory, so . . . Okay, my survival kit: two firestarter logs, Bob's parka, my parka, my Sorels, Bob's Sorels." She pointed at the plastic Pepsi bottle. "Bob's pee. Ick, I can't believe you've still got that. That's my clam gun and bucket; I always carry them with me when I know I'm making a beach landing. You never know when you'll hit the tide just right." She picked up the gloves one at a time. One was a cotton painter's glove, the second a woman's Isotoner, and the third a man's worn leather work glove. None of them fit Wy's hand. "I don't know where these came from. Probably passengers dropped them." She paused. "And those are the two radios."

"The radios you used for backup in case the big radio you have bolted to the dash fails." She nodded. "What about the third handheld?"

She went very still. "What third handheld?"

He shot to his feet so abruptly that his chair shot backward and crashed into the wall. She flinched. "The third handheld I found shoved beneath the backseat. The Sony. The cheapie, as Sparky of Sparky's Pilot Shop refers so affectionately to it. The cheapie Sony bought by Larry Jacobson in March of last year, along with another one exactly like it that I saw sitting on the control panel of the *Mary J.*! The handheld I found tucked away in your bedroom dresser night before last! Wrapped in a blue silk scarf that I vividly remember being used for something other than concealing material evidence in a murder investigation, by the way!"

He was shouting by the time he finished. He paused, glaring at her. She stared back at him, stricken.

"You were spotting for the Jacobsons and McCormick on the side, weren't you? I've been up there with you, Wy, I know what it's like now. Bob sat in the backseat and talked to Larry, you sat in the front and talked to Wolfe. Didn't you? Didn't you!"

She was white-faced and trembling, and mute.

"Jacobson bought the radios before last year's herring season, and you said Bob DeCreft observed for you last year, too, so I figure you tried it out last year and worked all the bugs out of it and tried it on again this year. Wolfe figured it out, didn't he? And he didn't waste time getting mad—he got even. First he had your Cub trashed, then he sank the Jacobsons' boat, beating up Kelly McCormick in the process, who I figured caught Wolfe's man in the act and got the shit kicked out of him for it, and then—" Liam reached in the drawer and slammed the envelope containing her check down on the desk. "And then Wolfe stiffed you for over half of what he owed you. Right?"

"He was dead when I got down to the boat," she said steadily.

"And aren't you lucky he was!"

"What?"

"Jesus, Wy, you're a walking, talking motive for murder! You contracted to Wolfe to spot herring for him and his boats, and only for him and his boats, and then your very first year on the job you double-cross him with one of his rivals. He finds out about it and wrecks your plane and takes half this year's paycheck in retaliation. Nice of him not to take it all, but then he probably wanted to keep you on the leash for next year, and what better way to do that than to keep you just broke enough to stay in business but to still need his to get by?"

She said nothing. "And," he said, his voice rising again, "and he hits on you. You had three good reasons to kill the guy, Wy, and those are only three that I know of. How many more are there?"

She still had no answer for him. He could feel his temper bite into him, and battled it back. "Also lucky for you, at two a.m. this morning Becky Gilbert confessed to the murder of Cecil Wolfe."

She looked up then, shocked. "What?"

"Becky Gilbert killed Cecil Wolfe," he repeated.

She was having difficulty taking it in. "Becky Gilbert? The minister's wife? You've got to be kidding!"

"She's Laura Nanalook's mother," Liam said curtly. "Wolfe raped Laura the day her father died. He'd done it before. He would have done it again. Becky found out, and killed him. Tell me why you did it, Wy." Their eyes met. "Tell me why, goddammit!"

"I needed the money," she said simply.

He watched her with angry eyes, arms folded, waiting.

She sighed. Her eyes closed and her head fell back. "The business took every dime I had. You know, I told you back then that I wanted to run my own air taxi someday." She opened her eyes and looked at him.

He gave a curt nod.

She sighed again. "This was it. I knew it as soon as I met Jeff Webster and he showed me around, as soon as I saw the office and the hangar and the house, and the planes. And met the people. And got to know the place." She paused. "And I had to have something. I had to be busy. I had to not think of you."

"Save that," he said shortly.

"All right," she said, submissive. "But it's true." She blinked back what might have been a tear. He'd seen Wy cry only twice, that last day in Anchorage and yesterday when she heard how much she was going to make on her herring check, but the hard knot of anger burning in his gut wouldn't let him acknowledge the emotion he thought he saw now. "And then there was Tim. I found him, I—I guess you could say I rescued him." She tried to smile. "You know that old saying, about how if you save someone's life, you're responsible for it forever after? It's true." She added urgently, "It is true, Liam. Tim is mine now, and I would do anything, I will do anything to keep him safe."

The same way Bob DeCreft would have done anything to provide for Laura. He said, "Anything, including double-crossing your employer."

"Yes," she said simply.

"Anything, including lying to me."

"Liam—"

"You should have trusted me," he said implacably. "After all we had together, you should have trusted me."

She lost her own temper then, shoving her chair back in turn. She leaned forward, hands flat on his desk. "After all we had together? You smug, selfish, self-righteous jerk! I'll tell you what we had together, Liam! We had a thousand dollars in phone bills, most of which I paid because I had to call you so it wouldn't show up on your phone bill, and a four-night stand in Anchorage! That's all we had together!"

He was struck to the heart, and stung into retaliation. "So what are you doing hanging around me now? You figure having a state trooper on a string is going to make you look better to the judge when it comes time for the adoption to go to court? Just a little something to make up for nearly being charged with murder?"

"And afterward you didn't call, you didn't try to come after me, nothing, it was like I didn't exist!"

"I was honoring your decision! You said it was over!"

"And you searched my house! I invite you in for dinner and you search my house! Where the hell do you get off turning a social invitation into an opportunity to invade my privacy!"

"Gee, forgive me for doing what I'm required to do when I'm trying to find a murderer!"

She wasn't listening. "You know what I hate? Not the lies,

and the deception, and the sneaking around, although all that was bad enough. What I really hate is that I fell for a coward."

He was outraged. "What!"

"I fell for a coward," she said, as implacable as he'd been. "You came after me like a freight train, there was no stopping you—and if there is any truth in you at all, you'll admit that I tried to, more than once." Her furious brown eyes bored into his blue ones. "You roared into my life and flattened everything in it and roared out again. You're just pure hell at roaring through, Campbell."

"What was I supposed to do, I—"

"You were supposed to leave me alone in the first place!" she shouted. "And if you were too weak to do that much, then the instant you realized what was happening between us you should have marched right home to Jenny and said, I'm sorry, I've met someone else, I want a divorce!"

Liam opened his mouth, and closed it again.

"Instead, you arranged that little getaway in Anchorage. 'To see if it's real,' you said." She curled her lip. "Like we needed proof. You were just hedging your bets. Admit it, you wanted me, but you were afraid of what would happen if you asked for a divorce, afraid of what your friends would say, of what your boss would say." She paused, readying herself for the cruelest cut of all. "You were afraid of what your father would say. You were afraid he would say that you were just like your mother."

He was so angry that he feared he would hit her. "Get out," he said in a rusty voice.

"Don't worry, I'm gone," she said. "You stick with what's safe, Liam. That's what you're good at."

The door closed silently behind her on its hydraulic hinge.

Liam stood there, impotent with rage. It boiled over. "Goddammit!" he bellowed, and swept everything from the top of his desk to the floor.

The cap on the Pepsi bottle came loose and Bob DeCreft's piss spilled all over Wy's sleeping bag.

It turned out that Bill Billington had an industrial-sized washing machine and dryer in the back of her bar. She was pleased to offer Liam their use. When he saw the ironing board and the iron, he went back to the post and fetched his uniform. It took two refills for the iron to generate enough steam to smooth the wrinkles from the dark blue slacks and the blue jacket.

The shirt was easier. When he finished, he held it up, admiring it. After Liam's mother had left, his father, the compleat air force officer to whom an unpressed uniform was an act of sacrilege against God and country, had taught himself how to iron a uniform shirt so that the creases down the arms were sharp enough to draw blood. He had passed this skill on to Liam as soon as the boy was tall enough to stand over the ironing board. Jenny, a child of wealth and privilege, hadn't known an ironing board from a lawn mower, and the knowledge had come in handy before and after his marriage.

The washing machine cycle ended and he loaded the sleeping bag into the dryer.

And then he put on his uniform—light blue shirt, dark blue slacks with a gold stripe down the outside of each leg, dark blue tie—adjusting badge and nameplate, buckling on his belt and holster, shrugging into the shiny dark blue jacket, getting the round crown of the flat-brimmed hat just so.

For the first time since landing in Newenham, he felt dressed.

When he stepped out of the back room into the bar, Bill was arguing politics with a patron. "I don't care what those goddamn Europeans are doing to each other. We've already saved their asses twice—three times if you count the Marshall Plan. Enough! As far as I'm concerned the only thing worth going to war over in recent memory was Jamaica shooting down Jimmy Buffett's plane. We should have invaded the sonsabitches over that."

She gave the bar a swipe with the bar rag for emphasis and caught sight of Liam in all his glory. She paused, subjected him to a comprehensive study from head to toe and back again, and pursed her lips in a long, low whistle that managed to be admiring and salacious at the same time. "Damn, Liam. I don't know whether to salute or just genuflect and get it over with."

"I'm starving, how about making me a burger and fries instead?"

"Anything for Alaska's finest," she said, and bustled into the kitchen. "Is it true what I hear: Becky Gilbert's hired Patrick Fox to defend her?"

"Is that what you hear?"

Her head popped into the pass-through, and bright blue eyes regarded him shrewdly. "That's what she's done. Where'd she get his name, I wonder."

"Beats me," Liam said unhelpfully.

"Uh-huh," she said. "She sure had plenty to say for herself when I arraigned her."

"That's okay, Pat'll put the lid on her pronto."

" 'Pat,' is it?" Bill said, and Liam tried not to look self-conscious. "Yeah, I figured," she said with satisfaction. "Well, what the hell. Wolfe's no loss; it couldn't have happened to a nicer guy. Not going to hurt my feelings if all Becky Gilbert gets is a slap on the wrist."

Her head vanished again. Soon thereafter followed the tantalizing sizzle of deep fat frying and the arousing aroma of charred beef.

He was going to get tired of burgers and fries if he didn't start cooking his own meals soon, but it hadn't happened yet. He sniffed the air with gusto, and the smell went partway toward easing the ache around his heart that'd been there since Wy had left his office that morning.

"Did you hear?" Bill yelled into the pass-through. "Laura Nanalook's moving to Anchorage."

"Oh yeah?" Reluctantly, Liam removed his hat, smoothing the nap of the crown with an affectionate hand. He set it on the stool next to him. "Her father leave her enough so she could go to school?"

"She tells me that with what she can get for the house and the plane and what she has saved up, she can afford a little condo in Anchorage. She just wants gone. Can't say I blame her. When I get to New Orleans, I might never return."

She bustled back into the bar, plate in hand, and set it in front of Liam. He looked at the juicy fatburger and attendant fries spilling over the side of the plate and said, "Bill, I want you. Marry me now."

She laughed and tossed her long gray mane over her shoulders. Then she said, eyes twinkling, "You could have me today, trooper, so long as you stay in that uniform."

"I thought the whole idea was to get me out of it," he retorted.

She laughed again, a full-throated joyous sound, her breasts shaking beneath her denim blue shirt. The woman was a walking, talking incitement to riot. He remembered the various and sundry ways Moses Alakuyak could hurt him, and reached for his burger.

Serious now, she said, "I don't suppose you're any closer to learning how Bob DeCreft died. Laura's not interested now, but she might be someday. And I'd like to know myself."

He chewed and swallowed. "I'm starting to think it was Cecil Wolfe."

She stared. "What? How do you figure?"

He took another bite, organizing his thoughts. "Sub rosa, Bill, okay? I can't prove hardly any of this, mostly because none of the people involved will ever testify to any of the facts."

She nodded, curious. "Okay. I can keep a secret."

"Here it is, then. Bob and Wy were spotting herring for the Jacobsons and Kelly McCormick at the same time they were spotting for Wolfe. This year for sure, maybe last year, too."

She looked at him in disbelief. "They were double-crossing Cecil Wolfe? Please tell me you're joking."

"I wish. The way I figure it is, Wolfe caught on early this season, right after the first opener." Liam used the same words he had with Wy. "He skipped getting mad and went straight to getting even. He got his crew to trash Wy's Cub and to sink Kelly McCormick's boat in the harbor. I think Kelly caught him at it, and that's why he's lying up at the hospital with about eleven broken bones. And he stiffed Wy on half her herring settlement, probably what he figured was adequate recompense for how much she'd helped cheat him out of."

She listened, a rapt expression on her face. "So you think

Wolfe sabotaged Wy's plane, too? Was he trying to kill her?" She added dryly, "That'd be getting even, all right."

"Maybe he wasn't trying to kill anyone, maybe he was just sending a message. Maybe he figured all that would happen was that someone would lose a finger."

"Still," Bill said. "Seems a bit excessive, even for Cecil Wolfe."

"Well, then, you tell me, Bill. What else is there? Who else is there? Look at the pattern. Wolfe left big tracks. He wanted Wy and Bob and Larry and Darrell and Mac to know that he knew they were double-crossing him, and that he was after them. Kelly knew who beat him up, all right—they didn't even try to hide themselves, and you bet he knew why. Poor little bastard," Liam added. "You should see him up there in that hospital bed, sweating with fear." That was another score to settle with Kirk Mulder, when the time came.

Bill was still dissatisfied. "It's just so, I don't know. So neat," she said.

"Nothing wrong with neat," Liam said, and rubbed a french fry into the salt on the bottom of the plate. "Neat's what wins in court."

"Yes, but in this case there is no one left alive to try."

"Save the taxpayers some money," Liam agreed.

"Well," Bill said. "At least Laura doesn't have to worry about Cecil Wolfe coming around anymore. Which reminds me— poor little Gary Gruber, he was in here when Laura told me she was leaving, I thought he was going to grab for one of my steak knives and hurt himself."

Liam paused, french fry in hand. "What?"

"Gary Gruber—you know, the young fella who manages the airport. Don't tell me you haven't noticed. He's been in love with Laura Nanalook from the first time he walked into my bar and saw her waiting tables." She reflected. "Of course, you could say that about most of the men who walk into this place."

Liam sat very still.

Gary Gruber had been the second person he had seen at the airport. First Wy, standing over Bob DeCreft's body, and then

Gary Gruber, wiping his nose on his sleeve. Chewing that fat pink wad of gum like a cow whose cud was on her third stomach.

And then nearly every time he came into the bar, there was Gary Gruber, perched on a stool and watching Laura Nanalook.

But Laura was Bob's lover.

But Laura was really Bob's daughter.

But no one except Bob and Laura and Richard and Becky Gilbert knew that.

So Gary Gruber might think that if Bob DeCreft were out of the way . . .

All about Laura, Becky Gilbert had said.

It was all about Laura.

He put the french fry down. "What do you know about Gary Gruber?" he said.

"Gary Gruber?" Bill was confused but willing. "Well, hell, the same as everybody, I guess. He moved here from Homer in 1993. He's a pilot; he was spotting herring."

"He was a pilot?" Liam said quickly.

"I just said so, didn't I? He came here on a herring spotting job, and he came into the bar after the season opener, took one look at Laura, and moved here, lock, stock, and barrel. Got the job of managing the airport."

"She like him?"

Bill gave him a look. "Laura Nanalook doesn't like any man. The only one who ever got close to her was Bob, and I'm not sure how close they were, to tell you the truth, no matter what their relationship was. To get close to someone, you have to be able to trust, and given her upbringing I don't know that she's ever going to trust anybody."

"The Nanalooks?" Liam said.

"You know about them?"

"I was told."

Bill gave a grim nod. "Yeah, the Nanalooks. Laura was placed with them as a baby. They didn't have the kind of screening for foster parents then that they do now. They might as well have placed Laura with Hannibal the Cannibal and been done with it."

"So she never had anything going with Gary Gruber?"

Bill shook her head. "She never had anything going with anybody."

But that didn't mean Gary didn't have hopes.

And wouldn't act on those hopes.

All about Laura.

Liam stood up and reached for his hat.

"Hey, where you going, what about the rest of your food?" He threw down a ten. "That's not what I meant and you know it!" she said indignantly.

"Sorry. I've got to run."

In the doorway, inevitably, he ran into Moses, who looked him over sardonically. "You sure are slow."

"I'm a good student," Liam retorted. "Slow, smooth, unbroken, flowing, that's how I'm supposed to be moving, right?"

Moses stopped to stare. A smile crept across his face. "You're learning, boy. You're learning."

From overhead a raven croaked agreement. Liam tossed him a salute before getting into the Blazer and heading for the road to the airport.

There was a crowd of people at the check-in counter. Heads turned, one, two, five, until they were all staring at him, startled and a little apprehensive. He walked forward and the crowd parted naturally, as if before an undeniable force of nature. The office at the back of the airport terminal was unlocked and, when Liam knocked and went in, empty but for a desk, some filing cabinets, and a couple of chairs. He didn't have a shred of a legal right to do so but he tossed the desk on general principles anyway. The bottom-right-hand drawer held a half-empty plastic bag of Bazooka bubble gum.

He thought of the omnipresent pink wad in Gruber's mouth, and the pink wrapper scooped from the floor of 78 Zulu during the inventory.

It wasn't proof, but it wasn't bad. Gary Gruber was on the scene, he worked there every day, so he had opportunity. He was in love with Laura Nanalook, and Bob DeCreft lived with Laura Nanalook, so he had motive. He was a pilot, and could be presumed to be familiar with the innards of a Super Cub and to have tools to go along with that knowledge, so he had means.

If it looks like a motive, if it acts like means, if it quacks like opportunity . . .

Liam strode back through the terminal like a ship under full sail, and reached the double glass doors at the same time Gary Gruber did, only from the other side. They both grasped the handle. The door wouldn't budge. They looked up and their eyes met.

Liam's appearance in uniform had been noticed before. "The man's a walking recruitment poster," John Barton had told a colleague privately, and it was true. Liam didn't just put on his uniform, he merged with it. When the last snap was fastened and the hat set just so, Liam Drusus Campbell became an Alaska state trooper from the bone marrow out. The uniform was sword and buckler, an outward manifestation of the full power and majesty of the law, with Liam as its tool. In uniform Liam looked capable, incorruptible, and virtually invincible.

To Gary Gruber, he looked like the wrath of God.

Gruber ran.

Liam, a heartbeat behind, wrenched the door open and ran after him. "Gruber, stop! Stop!"

It had rained again that morning and the pavement was slick beneath their feet. People stopped, turned, stared as first Gruber ran past and then the trooper in full regalia followed in hot pursuit. Gruber had the advantage—he knew the airport—and he almost lost Liam when he dodged between two buildings and slipped behind a pile of white plastic totes.

Liam skidded to a halt and looked in both directions. He almost missed it, the top of Gruber's head bobbing just above the line of totes. He began to run again.

Gruber ran out onto the apron and crossed the taxiway. A large single-engine craft taxiing for takeoff skidded around in a circle to avoid him. Liam looped around the back of the plane, heart in his mouth. The prop wash blew his hat off and he cursed briefly. The pilot was gesturing and yelling but his voice couldn't be heard above the sound of the engine.

Ahead of him Gruber ran across the runway, casting a white-faced, desperate glance over his shoulder as he did so. Liam was gaining on him, and they both knew it.

A Fairchild Metroliner, possibly the same one that had brought Liam to Newenham the previous Friday, had just landed and was rolling down the runway, gradually decreasing speed. Panicked, Gary Gruber ran out in front of it. The pilot kicked the rudder, too late, and Gary Gruber ran face-first into the portside propeller.

The plane kept turning from the kicked rudder, and Liam, running full tilt too close behind to avoid it, caught the full extent of the prop wash and everything with it—bone, brain, hair, skin, but especially and most copiously blood. It sprayed him from head to toe. There was blood in his eyes, his nostrils, his mouth, and all down the front of his uniform.

He managed to slow down enough to avoid running into the prop himself, barely. He came to a halt next to Gruber's body, heart pounding, gasping for breath, trying not to vomit.

The pilot cut the engines of the Metroliner. The hatch popped and the pilot stumbled down the stairs of the plane, his face white. "He ran out onto the runway," he said numbly. "There was nothing I could do."

His copilot, another fresh-faced, square-jawed young man, was standing just behind him. He leaned over the railing and threw up.

At Liam's feet, Gary Gruber lay like a broken toy, without a head, missing most of his right shoulder, his right arm lying ten feet away.

Liam was back in his office, washing Gruber's blood and brains out of his hair in the rest room sink, when the phone rang. It was John Barton. "Brace yourself, Liam," John said.

His tone was enough to tell Liam what was coming.

"Jenny's dead."

SEVENTEEN

They buried her next to Charlie, a tiny plot of land and an etched marble stone all that was left on earth of their son. The funeral was small and quiet, with Jenny's parents, a few of her closest friends, and Liam attending. John Barton came, too, with his wife.

"Don't blame yourself, Liam," John said afterward. "You didn't put her here. Rick Dyson did."

"I can't help it," Rose, his mother-in-law, whispered, her head hanging. "I'm relieved."

He hugged her. "So am I, Rose. So am I."

Alfred, not a hugger, stuck out a hand and said in his bluff way, "I'm glad you could make it, Liam."

"I wish I'd been here, Alfred. I'm sorry as hell."

Alfred Horner shook his head. "Wasn't nothing you could have done. We weren't here, either—we'd gone out to dinner. The nurse said she was breathing one moment, next moment she wasn't. Doctor said it might happen that way."

"I know. I still wish I'd been here."

"You were here," Alfred said firmly. "You were wherever Jenny was. She knew." He flushed slightly at this unaccustomed detour into fancy, and his grip around Liam's hand tightened painfully. "Don't be a stranger, you hear? You're part of the family. You stay part of the family."

Liam couldn't speak, could only nod, but it wasn't for the reasons that Alfred might have expected.

When you betrayed someone, you didn't just betray them,

you betrayed your families, your community, an entire way of life. He thought of Becky Gilbert, of how her relationship with Bob DeCreft had begun a chain of events that ended twenty-two years later with three deaths. Begun in fire, ending in ice. The poet was wrong; ice was a better destroyer than fire, particularly if you were in the mood for vengeance. Fire was quick and clean, a leap of flame, a wave of heat and then nothing but a pile of soft and formless ash, dispersed with the first breeze. Ice was slow, heavy, corrosive, relentless, grating. It took a long time to get where it was going, and when it got there, it left behind a towering confusion of rubble to be sorted and identified and disposed of. Ice left baggage.

Liam knew he would never be able to look at Alfred and Rose Horner again without remembering that during the last year their daughter had lived whole and conscious and happy upon the earth, her husband had been in love with another woman.

Enough of what Wy had said to him that Monday afternoon was true, but it was not all of the truth. Liam had known Jenny all his life, had gone to grade school and high school in Anchorage with her, and when they had met again after being separated by their college years and her brief sojourn Outside, it was the coming together of old friends. There was a bond of common history, a common language; it had been so easy for them to slip into marriage, especially since it seemed so suitable to his father, her parents, his department, her family having had political connections from statehood on and the money to go with them. Jenny was attractive and amusing and rich, and Liam was deeply envied by his coworkers, which didn't hurt his ego any. Without any false modesty, he knew he had a lot to offer, too, with the promise of better to come.

All this, and they were comfortable together and didn't know any better, and so they married. His father had raised him to prize his word, had utterly condemned Liam's mother for breaking hers when she had run off with the nightclub owner from Bonn. Liam couldn't remember her, or Germany, for that matter; he'd been barely a year old and his father had requested an immediate reassignment. But his father had neither forgotten nor forgiven, and any child of his raising would take his marriage vows seriously. Liam had. Something of a rounder before his engagement, in the time between then and meeting Wy he had not strayed, had not even been seriously tempted to. He was pretty sure he never would have. Not positive, but pretty sure.

But he had met Wy, and he had learned better the levels of communication, of empathy, of desire that were possible between two human beings, and his life had forever changed from that moment. For the first time he saw his relationship with Jenny for what it was. There was nothing of either fire or ice in it; only a tepid warmth, like lukewarm water that when you first stepped in felt comfortable to the skin, but if you stayed in too long would slowly sap the life from mind and body, leaving you numb, spent, incapable even of the few strokes necessary to keep your head above water.

He thought of his father's probable reaction to his son's behavior. Liam Drusus Campbell was thirty-six years old and had been laying down the law to the citizens of the state of Alaska for the last ten years, but he was deeply grateful that Colonel Charles Campbell was safely assigned to flight training in Pensacola, as far as you can get from Alaska and still be in the same nation. Wy had been right about that much, at least.

Besides, he was enough of a disgrace to his father as it was, given his fear of flying.

There was absolutely no doubt that Fate was a woman, he thought that night, lying sleepless in the Horners' spare room. Men weren't smart enough to be this mean. No, no, you're walking the straight and narrow, coping, productive, content, maybe even happy, and Fate comes along and says, "My, don't you look smug," and gives you a big shove and the next thing you know you're wandering around in the wilderness with no idea of where you are or where you're going. You can try to figure out where you've been and how you got there but that's pushing it. All you can really do is feel your way through the brambles and pray you see daylight before you get cut to shreds.

It doesn't help your forward progress any that during all this time you can hear Fate laughing at you.

He'd like to meet up with Fate in a dark alley sometime, he

thought, rolling over and thumping his pillow. With a club in one hand.

He'd like that a lot.

He returned to Newenham three days later, and drove to the trooper post to find Moses Alakuyak sitting on the steps, waiting for him. "You practice while you were away?"

"As a matter of fact I did," Liam said, shutting the door of the Blazer behind him. "I practiced out on my in-laws' deck. They think I've lost my mind."

Moses grunted. "You call her?"

Liam gave the shaman a sharp look. "Haven't had time."

"Make time."

Liam was annoyed. "Mind your own business, old man."

"You are my business, boy," Moses retorted, "and so is she. Let's stand some post."

They stood some post.

After ten minutes his thighs began a fine trembling sensation. He checked out his feet to make sure he was maintaining his three-point connection with the earth—right ball, left ball, heel. Root from below, suspend from above.

"So, your wife's dead," Moses said.

"Yes," Liam said. His stance was solid, but the tremble was still there.

"It wasn't your fault."

Liam said nothing.

"You can carry around the guilt for the rest of your life, that's what you want," Moses observed. "It'll wreck you for sure if you do."

The trembling increased.

"Or you can honor her memory by living your life the best you can."

His whole body was trembling now.

"You got a shot at a new life. Take it."

According to Bill, half the residents of Newenham were there to start over. "I don't deserve it," Liam said.

"Who says?" Moses demanded. "You God, you know all, you see all? If life hands you a lemon, make lemonade. If it hands you a Rolls-Royce, climb in and break out the champagne. Take your preparatory breath."

It took Liam a moment to realize that Moses was going into the form. "Ward Off Left."

He caught up with his teacher at right Push Upward. They did Pull Back, Press Forward and Push, and then Moses taught him Fist Under Elbow. It took Liam thirty minutes to train his body to finish up facing the right direction, but at least it was the right direction, no matter how he got there.

Finally, Moses said, "Enough for today. Practice, practice, practice."

"How'd you take up tai chi in the first place, sifu?" Liam said, managing not to groan as he came upright.

Moses busied himself changing into street clothes. "I was in the navy, stationed at Subic Bay. Took my first liberty in Hong Kong. I got up early the first morning, started wandering around, found a bunch of people in a park doing it. Looked interesting, so I went up and talked to the leader afterward. Turns out he'd escaped from mainland China with some American missionaries. He told me what he was doing, the Yang style, and he ran me through the form a couple of times. When I got back to base I looked for a teacher, found one in Manila." He shrugged.

"What do you like about it so much?"

Moses buttoned his shirt, considering. "I like the control it gives me, and the connection it makes between me and the elements. And," he added casually, "the voices don't hassle me so much when I'm doing form. Sometimes it's the only thing that gets me through the night. What'd you find out about Gary Gruber?"

"How did you—"

"I know pretty much everything there is worth knowing, boy, how many times do I have to tell you? He didn't kill Bob for Laura, did he?"

"No. Or at least, not entirely."

"Big wad of cash in his account?"

Liam, who had been trained to talk trooper business only with troopers, and sometimes not even with them, said to this strange old man, "Yeah. Paid in the week before herring. Drawn on Cecil Wolfe's business account."

Moses grinned. "Trust Cecil to figure out a way to claim murder as a business expense."

"Yeah. Nice to know I wasn't completely off base when I fingered Wolfe for killing Bob DeCreft."

"Even you have to get something right once in a while," Moses agreed.

"I took too long to get there, though. I was so afraid Wy was guilty I couldn't see my way clear to who was. And I should have known Wolfe would never have done it himself. Didn't fit the pattern. He sent Mulder to wreck Wy's plane, the rest of his crew to sink McCormick's boat and beat him up. The only time he took direct action was when he shorted Wy on her check, and he knew he was safe enough there because she wouldn't be able to complain without explaining why she'd been shorted. If she did that, she'd never get hired by another herring fisherman ever again."

Moses finished changing clothes and in the process from sifu back into shaman. "He might not even have meant to kill DeCreft. He might have just wanted to scare him. Maybe let DeCreft know that Wolfe knew DeCreft was spotting for two."

"I suppose that's possible," Liam said, reluctant to concede Wolfe even a negative virtue.

"Doesn't matter what he meant." Moses cocked an eyebrow. "Could have killed Wy as easy as Bob." He stared hard at the horizon before delivering judgment. "In a way, you could say Cecil killed himself. He set the process in motion—he bribed Gruber to sabotage the plane, DeCreft gets killed, Cecil takes advantage of his death to rape Laura, Becky finds out and kills him. Yeah, you could say he killed himself."

You could, Liam thought, if you ignored the fact that Wy and DeCreft had been double-crossing Wolfe to begin with. "Anyway, Gruber had been on Wolfe's payroll for a long time. I had them pull Gruber's account for the last couple of years. When he first came to Newenham to spot herring, he was spotting for Cecil."

Moses nodded. "Figures." They sat in silence for a moment. "So the way it looks, Gruber being in love with Laura

Nanalook and all, Wolfe paid Gruber to do what he wanted to do anyway."

"It looks like it. They're both dead, so we'll never know the whole story."

"We won't miss 'em, either one of them."

From the tall white spruce across the road, a big black raven croaked agreement. Looking up at him, Liam thought he looked like the angel of death, shiny and black and so very well fed. "Three deaths the first week I'm in town," he said. "People are going to think I'm a blight on the community."

Moses grinned. "Sorry, boy, you just ain't that powerful. Or that important," he added with a bark of laughter.

Again the raven echoed him, with a sound eerily similar to Moses' rusty laugh: caw, caw, caw.

"That damn raven—what is he, your familiar or something?" Liam said irritably. "I see him everywhere you go."

"No you don't," Moses said testily, "you see him everywhere you go. He's not mine, he's yours."

"What?"

Moses got to his feet and dusted off the seat of his pants. "He's yours. He looks to you. Poor bastard."

Liam didn't know who Moses was referring to, him or the raven.

Moses leveled an admonitory finger. "You watch out for him—he's a trickster, like all of his kind. He'll bring you the sun and the stars, but you give him a chance and he'll steal your woman away, too. Why didn't you kill him?"

"What?" Liam said, off balance. "Who? The raven?"

"The man who killed your wife. Why didn't you kill him?"

The shaman's eyes were bright and penetrating. Liam felt pinned to a board, with no means of escape but the truth.

Well, what was the truth? He wasn't sure he knew anymore, and he'd been there. "I suppose you mean when I arrested him, after he got out."

"Six months he did," Moses said. "For driving drunk and killing your son and putting your wife in the coma that eventually killed her. You must have been mad."

"Mad?" Liam turned the word over in his mind. "Mad? I

don't know. I couldn't believe it when I pulled him over and ran his plates. I couldn't believe it was him. And then when I walked up to the car, and saw him. He knew it was me; he recognized me from the courtroom." He paused. "He started to cry, and beg." He looked at Moses. "He opened his door and fell out onto the road and crouched down on his knees, shivering and sobbing, snot running from his nose."

"And drunk," Moses said.

"And drunk," Liam said. "I wasn't mad, I was disgusted. I wanted to kill him, all right. I wanted to pull out my gun and put him out of his misery."

"He probably did, too," Moses said. "Better you didn't, though."

Liam looked at him. "Thanks, Moses," he said with real gratitude. "You're the first person to say that to me. Everybody else seems to think Dyson should have been shot while resisting arrest. You should see what it's like when I go into headquarters. There isn't a trooper I know who can look at me without contempt."

"Bullshit," Moses said bluntly. "You did what was right, for you, for Dyson. Even for Jenny and Charlie. Don't matter what anyone else thinks, boy, only you. And your shoulders are big enough to carry the load. So carry it."

The old man stamped off to his truck. The engine turned over and the window rolled down. "Remember," the old man shouted. "Raven'll steal your woman and everything else that matters along with her, but only if you let him."

He slammed the truck into first. "Don't let him!"

The truck lunged off down the road, leaving Liam sitting on the steps, staring up at the raven, eyes bright with malicious knowlege, beak sharp and polished, ebony feathers smooth and gleaming.

"So?" he said. "Mind telling me what I do now?"

It croaked at him.